Patricia Grey was born in Highgate, went to school in Barnet and college in London, and now lives in South Hertfordshire. She became a secretary and worked in all manner of companies from plastic mouldings and Japanese banking through to film production and BBC radio, eventually ending up as a Contracts Manager for a computer company. Her earlier novels, JUNCTION CUT, BALACLAVA ROW and GOOD HOPE STATION, are all available from Headline.

CUTTER'S WHARF

Patricia Grey

KNIGHT

First published in 1998 by
HEADLINE BOOK PUBLISHING

First published in paperback 1999 by
HEADLINE BOOK PUBLISHING

This edition published 2002 by
Knight an imprint of The Caxton Publishing Group

10 9 8 7 6 5 4 3 2 1

ISBN 1 84067 512 8

Printed and bound in Great Britain by
Mackays of Chatham plc, Chatham, Kent

Caxton Publishing Group
20 Bloomsbury Street
London WC1B 3JH

To my father, and everyone who remembers pre-war Kentish and Camden Town (in the hope that you'll forgive the mistakes!) and to everyone who doesn't (since you won't spot them anyway!)

Chapter 1

'What you thinking, Panse?'

'That I wished I'd been born a boy,' Pansy Cutter admitted.

It was hard to see Maury's face in the gloomy February evening, but she could guess that wasn't the answer he'd been expecting. Anxious to make amends, she drew him into the wharf entrance, snuggling invitingly into his chest. Maury promptly responded by clasping her tightly and smacking kisses over her mouth, cheeks and nose.

Pansy steered him back to her lips while removing the hand that was straying inside her coat with practised ease. The last two hours had been spent in a breathless tussle in the back row of the cinema, interrupted by occasional intrusions from the usherette's torch and pointed throat-clearing if she considered the courting was getting out of hand.

That was what Pansy had meant by her remark. Recently she'd become aware that she rather liked what Maury was trying to do and wouldn't have minded him going on doing it. Except of course she couldn't tell him that. Good girls, her mother and Aunt Ursula were always telling her, didn't let boys take liberties.

Boys, though, she thought indignantly, clinging to Maury's neck and mumbling appreciative noises, could do what they liked. And it wasn't *fair*.

She'd said as much to her mother once, when her cousin Ernest had been seen up Hampstead Heath with Carla Rosetti, who everyone knew was fast: 'It's just not fair.

1

Ernest's always been allowed to do things that me and Iris can't.'

With a smile, her mum had smoothed the eiderdown and dropped a goodnight kiss on her forehead. 'That's the way of the world, my lamb. It's always the women who get the blame. So if you're intending to go against what the world considers proper, then you'd better be certain sure that he's the right man for you.'

'Do you think Ernest is the right man for Carla Rosetti?' Pansy had asked, watching her mother turn off the soft glow of the night light.

'Even if I did, I'm certain sure Carla doesn't.'

'She's walking out with him.'

'She's walking out with his eighteenth birthday present. Once the cash Nana Cutter gave him has gone, I'll think you'll find Carla won't be far behind.'

Her mum had been right. Within a week, Ernest was slinking round the wharf with a swollen lip and a sulky expression, and Carla was seen on the arm of an ex-prize-fighter from Somers Town.

That had all been two years ago, and now Ernest was a soldier somewhere in Libya and Carla was engaged to a coster up the Queen's Market – or waiting on the release of her boyfriend who'd just been jailed for stealing a lorryload of whisky, depending on which rumour you chose to believe about her.

Memories of that whisky robbery niggled uneasily at the back of Pansy's mind, while Maury nibbled with considerably more enthusiasm at her ear. The police had suspected Maury of being involved in the crime. Not that anything had come of it. In fact, the man they'd arrested for it had made a statement clearing Maury completely. But she couldn't help worrying. What if her family got to hear about his arrest? Her mum would stand by them, she was sure of that. But what about Aunt Ursula's 'standards'?

Well, Pansy didn't care. There was no way she was giving up Maury, no matter what anyone said. She loved him with all her heart. Had done since they first started going out together, soon after her fifteenth birthday. And in April she'd

2

be sixteen. Old enough to marry if she wanted. She knew Maury wanted it. And she trusted him to look after her.

Spurred on by this thought, she hugged him harder. Taking this for encouragement, Maury attempted to get inside her coat again. His hands fumbled at her breasts. She was starting to feel funny inside – sort of melting and yet wanting as well.

Taking a deep breath, she pushed him away and put on her sternest voice. 'That's enough of that thank you, Maury O'Day. I've told you before, I'm not that sort, and if that's what you want you can just go find yourself another girlfriend.'

'Sorry, Pansy. But it's your own fault for being so beautiful. What's a man to do?'

'Show a bit of respect, that's what, if you want me to come out with you again.'

She tried to keep her voice stern, but they both knew she was bluffing. She'd have walked to the ends of the earth with him if he'd asked.

She adjusted her clothes, smoothed back her hair and straightened up. 'Come on. Let's go in.'

'You sure you want to? We could go up another house. The Court's got Tarzan on.'

'No ta, Maury. I haven't got no money. And it's not fair you having to treat me twice. Anyway, me mum said I was to come round the office after we come out of the pictures. She wants me to take some shopping back home.'

The possibilities that might arise if he was alone in the house with Pansy put an eager spring in Maury's step as he followed her towards the yard.

A lorry turned into the wharf gates a second later, its shaded headlights catching them both in its narrowed beam. They flattened themselves to let it pass and then followed it down on the small wharf.

The weather had been bleak recently, in a way that only a British winter could be. Days of raw winds, sleety flurries, and rain so cold that it stung like fire where it touched the skin, had been made doubly depressing by the lack of any comforting lighting from streets or houses now the blackout regulations were in force.

Eyes screwed up and fixed on the floor in an effort to avoid the half-frozen puddles and lumps of debris, they made their way to a small one-room cottage that stood to the right of the larger storage sheds. They reached it just as the front door opened and closed even faster when the latch was ripped from the opener's fingers by a fierce gust.

'Hello, Mum.'

Muffled in a headscarf and heavy coat, with her feet thrust into a serviceable pair of wellingtons, Kate Cutter shouted at them to get inside. 'There's another ten minutes of fire left in those coals if you poker them up, Maury.' She waved a clipboard at them, moving easily across the dark yard with the confidence of someone who did the same trip several dozen times a day.

Gratefully the other two pushed open the wooden door and slipped inside the blacked-out room. Hands extended, Pansy felt her way across the room towards the light switch. She somehow became entangled with Maury, who took full advantage of the situation.

'Stop that,' she giggled after another couple of breathless minutes. 'Just you go find that switch before Mum comes back.'

Maury stepped across the room, clicked down the brass lever and jabbed vigorously at the apparently dead pile of greying ashes in the little grate. As Kate had promised, the addition of a little oxygen coaxed a red glow deep within them. Peeling off her woollen gloves, Pansy sat on the uneven tiled floor by the hearth and gratefully held her palms to the warmth.

This cottage pre-dated the canal that now flowed past it, and had been old when Pansy's great-grandfather, Samson Cutter, had moved into the area in the 1870s. A lease on the near-derelict building was all he could afford, after a series of ruinous quarrels among his six brothers had left the family farm near destitute and Samson a homeless widower with a young son to support.

Starting out as a jobbing builder, he'd soon realised he could make a tidier profit if he bought his building materials in bulk and sold on the rest at a profit to fellow tradesmen.

4

The money had been used to buy the freehold of the land that stretched along the canal bank, and within ten years it had become known to both the locals and the boat people as 'Cutter's Wharf'.

As the business had expanded, Samson had erected other buildings to hold the stocks of lime, slates, bricks, drainpipes etc., and stables to house the horses that drew the carts which carried the legends: 'Cutter & Son – Builders of Distinction' and 'Cutter & Son – Builder's Merchants – Finest Material Guaranteed'.

Since Samson wasn't one to spend good money on rent when he had the freehold of a substantial area of land, the Cutters had moved into a new set of rooms over the brick store, and the original cottage had been converted to form the office for the business.

By the time Samson died he was able to pass on a thriving business to the son who now had a young family of his own. He'd gone with a final plea to his son on his lips. With the memory of his fighting brothers still as fresh as yesterday, he'd made his son promise not to divide up the business. 'Leave it to one boy. You canna have more than one master in a business. It'll tear it to pieces . . . to pieces . . .' And on this heartening thought he'd died.

His portrait had pride of place between two disused gas mantles on the back wall of the cottage. Maury wandered over to stare into the bewhiskered face, its expression caught in a permanent frown as Samson waited for the photographer's powder to ignite. It was hard to detect any resemblance between the white-haired, beak-nosed old boy and Pansy's round, wide-eyed innocence. Maury strolled on, moving down the generations to Pansy's grandfather, and then her father and uncles. His interest was apparently casual, his attention fixed on the array of photos, but any interesting pieces of paper received a quick sweep of his black eyes as he passed. Maury had always been a great believer in the value of information. You never knew when some obscure fact might become valuable currency. On this occasion he was disappointed. There was nothing lying on Kate's desk except invoices, despatch notices and works orders.

Undeterred he mooched on, peering at the framed photographs scattered over the brick walls, stopping before one of three young men grinning at some private joke as they posed for the camera. Each was slimly muscular, dark-haired and firm jawed, with narrow moustaches under sharp noses. They could have been triplets, but they weren't. Fred Cutter was the oldest of the trio. Peter on the left had been born a year later, and Bernard on the right a year after that. Most of the prints were Bernard's handiwork – a tribute to his passion for photography that had led to him selling pictures to a news agency on a freelance basis and angry rows with his brothers, who saw him wasting precious time and money on his hobby when the family business was struggling to survive.

Maury regarded the face, imprinting it on his memory, and then swung back to look at Bernard's daughter. Clasping her hunched legs, Pansy rested her chin on her knees and stared back at him.

'You don't look much like yer dad, Pansy. Don't look much like your mum neither, come to that.'

'I know.' Sighing, Pansy twisted a brown curl round her finger. 'I wish I had blonde hair like me mum.'

'I don't. I like yer hair just like it is, Pansy. It's real pretty, I think.'

Pansy blushed with pleasure and stared back at him. She liked the way he looked too. Some of the men on the wharf might laugh and call him 'Short-stop' under their breath, but she didn't care. She was only five foot two herself, and Maury's extra two inches made him the perfect height for her as far as she was concerned.

They were lost in the happy contemplation of how lucky they both were to have found the perfect partner when the door banged open, snatched out of Kate's frozen fingers by another spiteful gust.

'Oh, darn the stupid thing . . . Maury, put the light out quick – we'll be in trouble with the ARP warden.'

Maury obligingly leapt at the switch, and just as efficiently reclosed the door and flicked the blackout curtain across it before returning to the roundel.

'Did you two have a good time?'

'Lovely thanks, Mum. Maury took me up the Bedford. And they had real ice creams on sale. First time since Christmas, the usherettes said. Maury bought me a tub.'

'In this weather?' Kate gave a theatrical shiver and hurried over to join her daughter by the glowing ashes for a few minutes' warming, before going across to the cupboard behind her desk and drawing out a full bag. 'Here's the shopping. Your Uncle Pete let me have a couple of hours off so I could queue for all the rationed goods.'

'I could have done that, Mum.'

'No. It's only right you have some fun. You're at work all week.'

'So are you. It's not fair Uncle Pete making you work Saturday as well.'

'It's only the odd weekend, and I don't mind. The business doesn't run itself.'

'Yeah, dead right, Mrs C. You've got to look after your investments. I always do.' Maury leant back in his chair, hooking his thumbs inside his waistcoat and sprawling with the casual nonchalance of an investor in two hot food vans.

'I'd not call this job an investment, Maury.'

'I meant Cutter's. It's a third yours, ain't it?'

'Is that what Pansy told you?'

'No. I just sort of thought . . . I mean, Pansy's dad was a partner, weren't he? It says up there . . .'

As proof, Maury pointed to the trio of brothers. Behind them the wooden name-board proclaimed: '*Under new management. Proprietors: Messrs Frederick, Peter and Bernard Cutter*'.

'Only while he was alive, Maury.'

'Oh?' Maury mulled this over. 'You mean he did the dirty on yer, Mrs C? Left it to someone else?'

'He didn't have any choice.'

The promise old Samson had blackmailed from his son on his deathbed had seen to that. It was all right for Samson – he'd only had the one child to pass the business on to. But his son had had three boys; and when they'd all been spared from the horrors of the Flanders trenches, he'd decided it was a sign he should treat them all equally. In the end he'd solved the

7

dilemma by leaving the company in trust; they could have a say when it came to running the place, but any profits were to be divided into three equal shares each month. One third was placed in a fund that could only be used to improve or replace the yard's assets. 'A new horse, mebbe. Or tiles for the roof,' he had explained to the lawyer drawing up the unbreakable Trust Document. Another third went into a savings fund. 'Then they'll not have to worry about putting a bit by. And the last one will have a tidy little sum to fall back on in old age.' The remaining third was intended to cover the brothers' weekly living expenses. As each brother died, his share would be divided equally between the remaining sons, until one was left as the sole owner of the property.

The lawyers had argued over the inflexible wording at the time, but their client had been adamant. One third of the profits was easily enough to keep three families at that time: 'And if times change, I'll be down here to change things as I see fit, sirs.' It was a reasonable assumption. His own father had lived into his seventies; there was no way he could have foreseen that he'd be dead within the year. Although, given the way things had worsened directly after the 1918 Armistice, perhaps he should have anticipated the building slump of the twenties and early thirties.

The brothers had found themselves in possession of a business they couldn't sell, and taking home a wage that was sometimes less than they paid their own labourers. When Bernard had died of blood poisoning following a ruptured appendix eight years ago, his young widow had found herself with a small child and an even smaller savings account in the Post Office at a time when millions of working men, let alone women, were out of work.

Fred and Pete would have provided an allowance for their brother's family, but Kate would have none of it. She'd work for herself, not take charity. In the end, a compromise had been reached: Kate would learn to type and take over the day-to-day running of all the clerical tasks at the yard. Within a year of her rolling her first invoice into the typewriter's platen, neither brother could imagine how they'd ever managed without her.

'So, I'm afraid if you were thinking you were courting an heiress, Maury, you're in for a bitter disappointment.'

'It ain't that. I don't expect my woman to provide for me. I'm gonna do that for *her*. I don't care if Pansy ain't got two farthings to rub together.'

'Just as well . . . because she probably hasn't, if I know my daughter. Isn't that right, my lamb?'

Still hunched by the now cooling fire, Pansy admitted that she had spent *some* of the spends her mum had given her back from her wage packet yesterday evening. 'But I've got my lunch money. And I kept back what you said I had to, to pay for me shoes to be heeled.'

'Good. You'd best be getting home then. There's some sausages in the bottom of that bag. Put them on. And peel the potatoes. Maury can stay for his tea if he likes.'

'Ta, Mrs C. You coming back soon?'

'I shan't be more than twenty minutes behind you.'

If Maury caught the warning note in her voice, he accepted it with good grace. Taking the shopping with one hand and his beloved with the other, he jiggled the door curtain back with his elbow while Kate turned off the light.

It was one of those moments when the world had stilled. There was no traffic passing along the nearby roads; the invasive rumble of the trains that criss-crossed this entire area had stopped briefly, and the sky was free of the drone of planes.

Kate squinted up into the low clouds dotted with pale stars. 'Not a bomber's sky. With any luck we'll have a peaceful night.'

The words were scarcely out of her mouth when a loud shout followed by a grinding crash reverberated across the yard.

Chapter 2

'What on earth . . . Can you see anything, Maury?' Kate leant across his shoulder. 'I was certain sure it came from our yard.'

They waited. Nothing moved.

'Must have been over in the railway yards. Anyhow, it's all gone quiet again.'

Another angry yell ripped through the air. This time it was accompanied by a selection of curses that would have brought a pink tinge to a docker's ears. It had the effect of galvanising Kate. Flicking her coat round her shoulders, she pushed her way outside. 'It's coming from the canal.'

'Maury. It's awful dark down there.' Pansy fixed her large purple eyes on her beloved.

He went after Kate, thankful that she wasn't a brunette like her daughter. The fair hair was easier to keep in sight as she walked swiftly down to the canalside.

The little starlight that was being reflected slid over the black surface of the canal waters like soap slicks. It wasn't much illumination, but it was enough to define the danger area. And at present it was being aided by the shielded lights on two pairs of canal boats that were wedged side by side against the wharf.

A throaty engine roar burst from the leading boat that had the outside passage. Water boiled under its blades, causing a series of waves that lifted the inner boat up and slammed it against the wharf steps again.

'Leave off, Geoghan, or I'll do for you.'

'Come on then, Dixon. Let's be 'aving you. I'm ready and willin'.'

11

The other man ignored the invitation. Instead he grabbed a long wooden pole, jammed it against the quay and threw his weight on it. The boat rocked and bobbed away from the stone wall.

'What's up, Dixon? Yeller streak?' Another burst of the engine churned the canal waters. The two boats being towed behind rose with the wave and banged together.

The boy on the tiller behind Geoghan's boat shouted a warning. 'Watch it, Blackie! That one nearly stemmed us in.'

'Shaft us off then, you useless lump!'

'Here, have another useless lump,' Dixon's boy yelled. Something left his hand and flew through the air. It caught the man called Blackie on his forehead.

His head jerked back and a trickle of blood ran down his cheek. 'Oi, yer little . . . Wait until I get my hands on yer!'

Thumb waggling against his nose, the boy took a flying leap on to the wharf. He cast around on the ground, snatched up the crumbling remains of a house-brick, and started pitching fragments high-speed at Blackie's mate. Most missed; they heard the splashes as they hit the water. None the less the other boy ducked and scuttled into the cabin.

'Stop that!' Kate called sharply. 'Do you hear me? Get off this wharf right now!'

The boy ignored her. Bending over slightly, he quartered the ground for new missiles like an excited puppy looking for a bone.

Maury measured him cautiously. The two of them were roughly the same height, but the newcomer was of a slighter build, his over-long trousers being held off his boots by a thick leather belt, and his old waistcoat flapping over a man's shirt that couldn't hide the narrow shoulders and thin chest.

Close up, Maury could see that the face under the tweed cap had a downy look to it. This kid hadn't even started shaving yet. With the sang-froid of one who took a blade to his chin at least three times a week, Maury jerked a thumb in the direction of the wildly rocking boat.

'Get lost.'

'Get lost yerself, Shorty.' Hands on hips, the boy faced him down.

12

Kate stepped to the edge of the wharf and shouted above the noise of the engines and cursing boaters. 'Mr Geoghan, if you damage the stonework on this wharf you can be certain sure Mr Cutter will see to it you pay for the repairs. And if that means he has to have the boat seized to do it . . .' She let the sentence hang.

Black Jack Geoghan weighed bravado against expediency. He wasn't going to be ordered around by no woman. On the other hand, he knew from experience the law was always on the side of those with the biggest bank account. Sticking two fingers in his thick lips, he let rip with a shrill whistle.

The boy's head bobbed up from the second boat's cabin. 'What?'

'Get on the tiller . . . Think the boat's gonna steer itself?'

The boy took the wooden bar again. And was promptly hit by another volley of stones.

'*Get back on the butty!*' Dixon's roar sent his own boy leaping back on to his boat in an untidy tangle of legs and arms.

The other boats started to pull away. The Dixons leant against their tillers, trying to keep their craft steady and minimise the number of cracks they were taking against the stone bank. With their attention on their own boats, they didn't notice Blackie draw back his arm. The half-brick caught Dixon's boy full in the chest and carried him backwards out of the boat. He disappeared into the canal in a fountain of spray, which spattered over Maury's shoes and down the front of Kate's coat.

'Oh mercy. The water must be freezing. Maury, do something.'

Maury hesitated. He wasn't a very strong swimmer, and the canal was a muddy tip at the best of times. To his relief, the boy broke the surface spluttering and thrashing vigorously.

'Hang on!' Dixon sprang from the lead boat to the second and ran along the narrow gunwale. Leaning over the stern, he extended the pole. 'Grab it, Addie.'

Addie was staying afloat with vigorous dog-paddles. The effort dislodged the cap, letting a circle of hair float out like stringy seaweed.

'Blimey, Mrs C. It's a girl!'

13

'I know that, Maury. Bring her over to the steps, Taz, it'll be easier to climb out there.'

Braced on the stern, Dixon swung the pole in a slow arc over the water, while the swimmer clung on with both hands and kicked her way to the bottom of the short flight of stone steps. The recent wet weather had left them slippery, and Kate's attempt to pull the girl upwards resulted in her own feet skidding.

'Hang on, Mrs C . . .' Maury crouched beside her. Between the two of them, they dragged the waterlogged Addie on to relatively dry land.

Kneeling on all fours, she hawked, spat out a stream of canal water and announced she'd swing for them bleedin' Geoghans one of these days.

'Addie! We've got to tie up.'

As proof of Taz's warning, the lead boat rocked to a tardy wash from the departing Geoghan's and slammed into the wharf again.

Swishing back the drenched curtain of hair, Addie struggled to her feet and fielded the rope thrown from the stern of the leading boat. Racing to the other end, Taz seized up another line and flicked it on to the wharf.

'Well grab it then, Shorty . . .'

The line had picked up a liberal coating of puddle and dirt. A great deal of it went down Maury's coat, which had been bought at considerable expense from Mr Levy's Secondhand Clothes Emporium with the assurance that its previous owner had been a titled gentleman. Maury chalked it up as another grievance to add to that 'Shorty'.

'Mum, are you all right? I've got Josh.' Pansy flew up to them in a breathless rush. Behind her a large bulky figure lumbered.

'I went to get Uncle Pete but he's not back yet . . . but then Josh came . . . and I thought he's big . . . and it sounded like burglars or something . . . and I hope Maury's not going to fight them . . .'

'I don't think there was much chance of that, was there, Maury?' her mother said, watching with amusement his attempts to swing the bow of the boat in while doing as

14

little damage as possible to his clothes. 'Joshua, can you help tie the boats up please?'

'Joshua can. Joshua knows how, Auntie Kate.'

Taking the rope from Maury, Joshua heaved. The fore-end came round and nudged the wharf. Joshua swiftly whipped the line round the cleat with neat efficiency. Crossing from the stern of the motor boat to the bow of the other, Dixon flicked other lines out. Joshua moved along the wharfside with him until both boats were tied up alongside Cutter's Wharf.

'Right . . . I'm going to take a look at the damage. You'd best get out of those wet togs, Addie.'

'I'll h-h-help yer f-f-first Taz.'

'You'll certain sure catch your death in this weather,' Kate exclaimed.

'Nah. I've 'ad w-w-worse. I'm OK.'

'Don't be silly.' Kate's voice took on the *I don't want any more of this nonsense* tone she reserved for controlling Pansy in her more headstrong moments. 'Come up to the office. There's a fire in there. Maury, run back and put some more coal on it. Joshua, pick her up and follow me. Taz, we'll be in the office when you're finished here.'

'I can walk . . . Gerroff . . .' Addie thrashed and kicked, fending off Joshua's attempts to obey his aunt.

'Quit your moaning, Addie, and go along . . . I'll sort you out some dry togs soon as I've seen to the boats.'

Muttering rebelliously, Addie squelched after Kate and Pansy. Joshua hovered at her elbow, afraid he'd get into trouble for not doing as he was told and carrying the lady.

They found Maury squatting before the grate. He'd added a few lumps of fresh coal to the warm ashes and was trying to get the fire to draw through them.

Addie's thin frame rocked with another series of violent shivers.

'You're going to catch your death for certain. Joshua, can you go home and get me a big blanket and some towels, please? Pansy,' she added in a lower voice when her eager nephew had set off at a trot, 'you'd best go with him, otherwise we're likely to end up with the dog blanket.'

15

Drawing up her coat collar, Pansy picked her way out into the black yard after her cousin. It wasn't far, since Pete Cutter lived in the rooms above the brick store that Samson Cutter had moved into once he'd abandoned the cottage.

Joshua was already in his bedroom by the time she'd climbed the outside staircase and slipped through the front door and into what served as a sitting room. He came to an inner door, a blanket spread wide across his extended arms and chest. 'Blanket.'

'Yours?'

He beamed and nodded.

'Find a clean one, Josh. One that's not on the beds,' she elaborated.

Joshua frowned. His eyes strayed to the dog.

'Not that one neither. She don't want fleas . . . well, no more than she's got,' Pansy muttered, reiterating one of the land-dwellers prejudices against the boaters. Marching to a cupboard, she pulled it open and ran an eye down the stacked shelves. The grey blanket and towels she selected were clean but worn to within an inch of their useful lives. With no woman around to deal with such things, the idea of replacing household linen simply never occurred to either Pete or Joshua.

'Here y'are . . .'

Joshua accepted the armful dumped on him, and Pansy would have turned the light out but before she could reach the switch she heard footsteps climbing the last few treads of the outside stairs, then a sharp rapping, and the door opened.

'Iris! Watch the blackout.'

'Sorry . . . I didn't think . . .' Stepping quickly inside, Iris shut off the solid square of gold that was falling into the yard.

For a moment, all three cousins faced each other across the slightly chilly room. Despite their wildly different appearances, it was easy to see the family connection. They'd all inherited the 'Cutter colouring' of dark hair, creamy skin and striking mauve-toned eyes. In Pansy it had followed the flower she'd been named after, giving her a round face, a halo of soft dark curls and huge purple eyes touched with a sooty smudge.

The finished package was prettily vulnerable, but it would fade as it lost its freshness. On Joshua the same combination was disconcerting. Six foot of solid muscles was intimidating enough. But the light lavender eyes peering out from under a thatch of brown waves and thick eyebrows made him look, in the words of one crone down the Mother Redcap, 'like something you'd as soon not meet up the boneyard unless you'd a crucifix to hand'. It was in Iris that nature had got the mix exactly right. With long brown hair, amethyst eyes, a perfect oval face set on a long neck and a naturally elegant figure, she should have been beautiful. But a pattern of silver scarring spread out like tributary streams from under her fringe and over one cheek, marred the picture.

Ducking her head now, and flicking her hair forward in an unconscious habit, Iris said, 'Mummy sent me to see if Daddy and Uncle Peter were back yet. They're later than they said they'd be.'

'You should have phoned.'

'We tried, but there was no answer from the office.'

''Spect it was when Mum was down the canal. Couple of them boaters was having a fight. Got one in the office, went in the drink. Come on, Josh, else she'll freeze to death.'

'Which boaters?' Iris said, allowing herself to be nudged back on to the stairs as the other two came out.

'The ones that are always causing trouble. Used to be loads of them on the boats before they started calling 'em up.'

'The Geoghans?'

'That's them. And a bloke called Dixon. It's his girl fell in.'

'Are they . . . Is she . . . hurt?'

'Just wet. Boats have taken a bit of a bashing. He's having a look now. *She's* puddling all over the office. Come on, Josh, before she gets pneumonia or something.'

They were opposite the yard entrance by now. Iris turned towards it. 'I'd best get back to Mummy. If Daddy telephones, will you call the house?'

'OK,' Pansy agreed. 'But I'm sure they ain't fallen down a bomb crater. See you later.'

Her mother greeted the blankets and towels with a doubtful

raised eyebrow, and promptly ordered Maury and Joshua to wait outside. Grumbling, both men were forced to huddle, sheltered by a storage shed from the increasingly nippy winds, until a soft whistle from Pansy let them run gratefully back to the office.

Addie was now swathed in the blanket with only her head and feet peeping from opposite ends.

'How are you feeling?' Pansy asked politely.

'Bloody brilliant, ta. 'Ow d'ya think? Them Geoghans is finished when I gets me hands on 'em.'

'Why are you travelling up so late?' Kate asked, lighting the solitary gas ring that she sometimes used to brew up for the men.

'Closed off Sammons Lane lock, didn' they? Reckoned there was an unexploded bomb by the gates. Made us late comin' up.' Addie gave a loud sniff and scratched the blanket. 'This don' 'arf itch . . . Where's Taz got to?'

'Shall I go see if your . . .' Pansy paused, unsure of the relationship.

'Brother,' her mother supplied, ladling cocoa powder and sugar into two mugs. 'Taz is Addie's brother. And I'm certain sure he'll be along soon.'

As if on cue there was a sharp rap on the door. The lights-off-lights-on ritual was followed again.

Addie glared at her brother's empty arms. 'Where's me togs then?'

'Sorry, kid, I forgot. *Rainbow*'s engine's had it. Said it packed up just before Blackie rammed us, didn' I?'

'Again?'

'Been running since Grandad had the boats; got to expect a bit of wear. Reckon we can patch it until we can get her up to Brentford. There's a bloke up there can fix her up proper,' he explained for the rest of the room's benefit. 'Cargo's the problem.'

'Will it spoil?' Kate asked, handing him a mug of cocoa.

'*Rainbow*'s full of steel piping, so that can wait a day. It's the butty. I've flour sacks on board. Gotta be at Camden Wharf by morning. That's why I come up in the dark. And it's gonna take me the best part of tomorrow to get *Rainbow* fixed up.'

18

'That's only a step along the tow-path,' Maury pointed out. 'Won't take you five minutes to drive this butty up there.'

'The butty don't have no engine, Shorty.' Addie adjusted her scratchy blanket, hauling it tighter around her thin body before she took the cocoa. 'Reckon we could bow-haul her up? That's pull it on the towing line to you, Shorty.'

Taz shook his head. 'It's too heavy. Unless we can find a dozen strong blokes. Or a horse. Don't suppose Cutters have got . . . ?'

Kate shrugged regretfully. 'Cutters went over to motor lorries three years ago. More's the pity. We could certain do with the horses back . . . Petrol rationing wouldn't affect them.'

'I can lay my hands on a horse.'

As soon as the words were out of his mouth, Maury regretted them. He didn't want to help this loud-mouthed girl and her grease-covered brother, but that 'Shorty' had touched him. Even if he generally hid the fact, his lack of height was his weakest spot. Having it continually drawn to Pansy's attention bothered him. He felt the need to re-establish himself in her estimation. And as soon as he saw her eyes glow at his resourcefulness, he knew he'd done it. Even if it did mean he was now going to have to borrow a flaming horse for this unattractive pair.

'Ten o'clock suit yer?'

'If yer gotta have yer lay-in.'

'Stow it, kid. Ten suits fine, thanks, mister. We'll be ready for you.'

Maury nodded, thrusting his shoulders back and stretching his spine. He was in charge of the situation again.

'Why don't you walk Pansy and my shopping home, Maury, get the dinner started. I'll stop on here until Addie's fixed up.'

'Right-o, Mrs C.'

They were nearly out of the wharf gates before Pansy remembered she hadn't delivered her cousin's message. She turned back, undecided if she should run back to the office or not, and surprised a dark figure treading stealthily in their footsteps.

19

Chapter 3

'Iris! I thought you'd gone. What you creeping up on us for?'

'I'm not. I was just being careful where I trod. I can't see a thing in this blackout.'

Pansy waited until her cousin had fallen into step with them up College Street before demanding again what she was doing in the yard.

'I went down to the canal. You said there'd been an accident . . . I thought I should offer to help. But there was no one there.'

'They're up the office. I told yer . . . the girl's had a right soaking. Mum's sorting her out. Maury's going to get them the lend of a horse.' The saga of the holed motor boat and the flour laden butty was explained to Iris.

'But what about the damaged boat? It's his livelihood. Where would they be without it?'

'Well, he'd be called up,' Maury shouted, raising his voice above the train rolling across the Camden Road bridge above them. 'No boat . . . no cosy reserved job. I dunno about fish face. Maybe she could get a job as a scarecrow.'

'Oooh, Maury, that's horrible! She's not *that* plain.'

Pansy's voice was scolding, but a smidgen of satisfaction larded the words. She was a good-natured girl, but any female of her own age was a potential rival, and she was pleased Maury hadn't cared for this one.

'Anyway, he . . . Mr Dixon . . . is going to fix it tomorrow.'

'Oh, I see. I'd best run on, Pansy. Mummy didn't expect me to be out this long.'

'It's only a step . . . Walk on with . . .' But Pansy found herself talking to an empty street. Her cousin's dark coat and hat had already been swallowed up by the blackness.

'Honestly, I reckon Aunt Ursula's got her on a big piece of elastic. Get too far away and *whoosh* . . . back she comes. I'm glad my mum ain't like that.'

'Me too, doll.' Maury slid a hopeful arm round her waist.

Pansy gave a shiver to show she was feeling the cold, then snuggled in a little closer to him . . . just to keep warm, of course.

'She ain't allowed to have a job you know,' Pansy said, returning to the subject of her cousin. ''Cept if Mum's off sick; she minds the office sometimes. Aunt Ursula couldn't manage at home without Iris.'

'What's up with your auntie? She looked OK to me that time we went up their house for our teas.'

'Dinner,' Pansy corrected. 'We aren't allowed to call it tea. Aunt Ursula says it's dinner. And she were making an effort. She always makes an effort for guests. It was having the twins hurt her heart, 'cording to the doctor. She gets these terrible spells . . . really scary, they are. Her eyes go all funny and her face gets all grey and sweaty and you can sort of see her heart banging up and down.'

'Sounds like she ought to be in one of them horror films. *Whooo* . . .' With a leering grimace, Maury loomed over her, arms raised and teeth bared.

With a shriek of mock terror, Pansy whacked him with her handbag and fled across the dark road. Maury gave her a couple of seconds' start and then flew after her, howling and moaning with enthusiasm. Breathless and laughing, they reached the front gate of the little terraced house in Kelly Street at the same time.

'Stop it this minute,' Pansy giggled as Maury tried to grab her. 'I've got to find me key.'

After several more attempts by Maury to take advantage of the blackout, she managed to get them both inside the house.

'Now,' she announced, emptying out the bags on the kitchen table. 'You can prick out the sausages while I peel

22

the potatoes. And if you don't behave yourself from this *very minute*, Maury O'Day, you can just go home and have your tea at your mum's house.'

'Dinner,' Maury corrected. 'We better start talking posh too if we're gonna have a big house up Hampstead one day.'

'With a car, and a chauffeur . . .' Pansy said, promptly falling into one of their favourite games. She loved it when Maury talked about the businesses he was going to own, the house they'd have, the cars, the servants . . .

'There's no profit working for someone else,' Maury announced, settling back in one chair and crossing his feet on the opposite one as he warmed to his favourite theme. 'Work for someone else and you just gotta take what they think yer worth.'

Pansy lifted his feet and put a sheet of newspaper on the chair seat before lowering them again. 'I know. But it ain't like that any more, Maury. Not with all the blokes going into the forces. Girls too – two more of the girls up the bakery joined up last month. And Bert Foley the maintenance man has been called up too, even though he's nearly forty. I heard Mr Griswald on the phone shouting at this government bloke about how was he supposed to feed the nation if the dough machines kept breaking down?'

'He's got a point, doll. Food's vital, I reckon. Anything that's on ration's a good line to be in. Supply and demand, see? Customers demand and you supply . . . at the right price.'

Pansy efficiently quartered potatoes into a saucepan of cold water and pointed out that bread and cakes weren't on ration. But Maury wasn't really listening. Half talking to himself, he debated the merits of being in food or weapons. 'Course, later . . . when the war's over, it's gonna be homes people will want. Your game will be the one to be in then, Panse.'

With a loud sigh, Pansy pricked the sausages herself and started slicing off the links. 'It's not my game . . . if you mean Cutter's. Mum told you, the business belongs to Uncle Fred and Uncle Pete.'

'Yeah . . . bit of a facer, that. You sure it's legal, not leaving your dad anything?'

'It must be, Maury. My uncles wouldn't cheat Mum. They're family.'

Personally Maury felt that was a good enough reason to be suspicious. Given half a chance he'd have been happy to put one over on his own five brothers. Not that he was likely to get the chance: four of them were not only older and larger than him, but they had nothing worth taking anyway. And as for Sammy – the only thing he was likely to get was a dose of head lice from sharing a bed with the pest.

'Here's Mum,' Pansy said, hearing the door swinging open.

Standing quickly, Maury flicked his lighter under the grill, took up the pan of pricked sausages and slid it under the softly popping gas jets. He earned a quick smile of approval from Kate and a dirty look from his beloved.

She forgave him enough later to join in a noisy game of Monopoly while Kate sorted out numerous dusty boxes of photos.

'You're not going to get rid of any of Dad's pictures, are you, Mum?'

'No, my lamb. I'd not do that. I just thought I'd change over the ones in the office.'

She tipped out another box, spreading the prints over the carpet. Maury picked up a couple at random. 'Got enough, ain't you, Mrs C? Must be hundreds here.'

'Yes. Bernie was always out with those cameras. Every spare minute he had. It's how we met. He asked to take my portrait. Said I was the prettiest thing he'd ever seen . . .' Her thoughts momentarily flew far away, back to the seventeen-year-old girl who'd been walking in Regents Park all those years ago. With a visible shake she brought herself back to the present. 'Anyway, what shall we have this time? Pansy at six months?' She displayed a print of a fat, naked baby lying on its front on a rag rug.

'Mum! Don't you dare. I'd just die of shame if any of them up the yard saw it.'

'I reckon that ought to have pride of place, Mrs C.'

'You beast, Maury . . . Throw the dice, it's your turn.'

Ignoring Pansy's attempts to divert him from even more embarrassing discoveries, Maury scooped up another handful of photos. 'Tell you what, Mrs C – you still got his cameras? They'd be worth a bob or two, I reckon. I could ask round for yer.'

'Thanks, Maury, but I wouldn't part with them. They were Bernie's pride and joy. He'd not let anyone else lay a finger on his precious lenses.'

'Must have let someone.' Maury twisted round the picture he was examining. It was a formal group, standing in Cutters Yard under a hanging banner proclaiming: 'Cutter & Son – 50th Anniversary – Founded 18th March 1876'. The small work-force was flanked by trestle tables holding a spread of sandwiches, cakes and a beer barrel. Maury pointed to three men standing slightly behind the crowd. 'Ain't that your dad, with yer uncles? He must have let someone else take this one.'

'No, he never.' Reclaiming the picture, Kate traced a nail over the sepia. 'See that? You'd be certain sure it was a hair on the picture, wouldn't you? Well, it was a line . . . Bernie had it rigged up to the camera – it let him trip it from in front. There's a better one here . . .' She picked out another photograph. It was the same scene, except this time four chairs had been lined up in front to provide seating for a dough-faced matriarch, starchily formal in black silk, and three younger women in the shapeless dresses of the mid-twenties. The brothers had moved forward to stand behind their respective wives, and three small children had been placed cross-legged on the dusty floor at the grown-ups' feet.

Maury pointed to the youngest and prettiest of the women who was cuddling a shawl-wrapped bundle protectively. 'That's you, Mrs C. Pick you out anywhere. Reckon your hubby was right about your being a wizard looker.'

'Butter-tongue!' Kate tweaked his ear with affection. 'Me and Pansy. She must have been eleven months old then.' She tapped along from the other end of the row of chairs. 'Nana Cutter. Ursula and Fred with the twins. Ellie and Pete. And Joshua, of course.'

'Always been a size, ain't he?' Maury remarked.

It was true enough. There was only a year between Joshua and the twins, yet the big-boned, awkward child was a good head and shoulders taller than the delicately featured Iris and Ernest.

'And clumsy with it, I'm afraid.' Kate pointed to the boy's father, whose plaster cast from wrist to elbow was visible above his wife's cloche hat. 'He swung a piece of scaffolding at poor Pete's arm. Broke it in two places. He didn't mean any harm, poor boy, it's just he doesn't know his own strength. And sometimes, if he loses his temper . . . Well, it's best not to get into a fight with him.'

Maury assured her he had no intention of ever doing anything so daft. 'Sure you don't want to play, Mrs C?'

'I'm sure. I'll stick to my photos . . . Now, there's a lovely one . . . and you've clothes on in this one, my lamb.' She traced the features of her husband, cradling a toddler Pansy, and a small, secret smile played over her lips.

Feeling embarrassed, as if they were intruding on a private moment, Maury and Pansy threw themselves into the dice-rattling with even more lively accusations of cheating.

At ten thirty Kate glanced at her watch and remarked that it looked as though they were going to be lucky tonight. 'No raid, thank God. Isn't it time you were getting yourself home, Maury?'

She tactfully disappeared into the kitchen while they said their goodbyes in the hall.

'Will I see you tomorrow, doll?'

'Course. I'll come down the wharf. Ten o'clock.' Pansy pressed her lips against his.

'What for?' Maury asked when he surfaced for air again.

'The horse – for the boat. You forgotten already, Maury?'

'What, me? No chance. If Maury O'Day says he'll get something, he gets it.'

Unfortunately Felonious, the horse's minder, had different ideas.

'You can't 'ave him. She'd 'ave me strung up if anything

26

happens to Kitchener. God knows why – he's only fit for the glue-pot if yer wants *my* opinion.'

Maury didn't. He wanted Felonious's horse. Or to be more exact he wanted the horse Fel drove when he was delivering the milk for Ivy Thomas. He'd come round early to Ivy's private dairy behind Willingham Terrace, ready to charm the old bat – only to find the old bat had already flitted to another belfry.

'Sister-in-law in Eltham's got bombed out,' Felonious had explained, gloomily jabbing at a pile of clean straw. 'She's gone over with bits and pieces. I've to see to that four-hoofed devil's spawn.'

Maury regarded the skewbald that was watching the world over the stable door. 'He looks quiet enough to me, Fel. Daresay I could handle him. It just takes a firm hand. Animals sense fear.'

'It's Mr Monk to you. And if you're such an expert you'll not mind walking him out of there so's I can muck out. Tie him over by the cart.'

It looked easy enough. Maury approached boldly.

Kitchener rolled one eye downwards.

'Here yer are, boy . . . Hold still . . .' Maury stretched out for the bridle. The horse's soft pink muzzle nuzzled at his palm. Nothing to it.

He lifted the tether, feeling for the small metal ring he assumed was meant to take the end of the rope, and in a flash Kitchener's jaws opened, revealing a set of yellow slabs that looked large enough to repave the High Street. Startled, Maury leapt upwards and backwards, saving his fingers but sending him straight into the bucket of water Felonious had just drawn from the tap.

With a crow of laughter, Fel watched the two becoming untangled. 'Yer don't wanna do that, Maury – the beast might start thinking you're scared of him. Come to that, so might I!'

Remembering that he still needed the loan of the brute, Maury forced something like a smile. 'I'd have thought you'd be glad to be rid of him for a few hours, Fel . . . Mr Monk.'

27

'I'd be tickled to be rid of him for good,' Felonious admitted. 'But like as not she'd expect *me* to pull the blooming cart. I don't mind telling yer, this going straight is a terrible strain on the back . . . You wanna bear that in mind if yer ever decides to try it.'

Maury bristled. 'That's slander, that is. I'm a respectable businessman.'

'And I'm the Empoora of China, son. Listen, when you've 'ad yer collar felt often as I have, yer knows yer own kind.'

'I ain't your kind. I ain't nothing like you – got that?' How dare this shabby little ex-burglar try to tie them together?

'Well, that's true enough,' Felonious conceded, opening a metal bin and scooping oats into the horse's nosebag. 'I was never stupid enough to hitch meself to a partner who led the coppers straight to the spoils. And as for writing out a full confession . . . Well, it makes me fair glad I was born ignorant.' He shook his head sadly.

Maury drew in a sharp breath. Was it a bluff? Was Felonious trying to get him to confirm what he'd only guessed? After all, the bloke was out of the business and trying to tread the straight and narrow . . . How could he possibly have known about Maury's confession?

Nobody was supposed to know except himself and Eddie Hooper. It had been Eddie's price for lying to the coppers and naming a recently dead mate as his accomplice on the whisky robbery. As Eddie had explained at the time, since he'd been caught red-handed with crates of the stuff, it stood to reason he was going down, but there was no reason an up-and-coming young man like Maury should – providing he was prepared to offer Eddie a guarantee that could be called in later, when Maury was in a better position to honour his debts. Now the signed confession – in Maury's own handwriting – was being minded by one of Eddie's friends until such time as Eddie got out and called in the favour. He'd known at the time it wasn't a smart choice – but it had been the only move open to him if he wanted to stay out of Wandsworth Prison.

Trying for casual nonchalance, Maury leant against the

stable wall and bent one leg so he could pick stray lumps of straw from his trousers. 'Dunno what you're talking about, Mr Monk. You gonna lend me the horse? I'll have it back long before she gets back from Eltham.'

Felonious fixed the horse's nosebag in place and slid the tether in place at the same time. Kitchener stood placidly throughout the operation; he wasn't stupid enough to scare away a meal.

'What's it worth?'

'You mean you want paying? I'd have thought you'd be glad to see the back of him.'

'I see the back of him every day. And it stinks. How much?'

'Two bob.'

'Make it half a crown. And me dinner up your house.'

'You what?'

'I could fancy a home-cooked meal. Lodgings can get awful lonesome. And your mum turns out some tidy grub by all accounts.'

She could turn out the most obsessively neat grub this side of Timbuktu as far as Maury was concerned. But he was quite certain his mum wasn't going to want to serve it up to an old lag.

'Done,' he said promptly.

Fel extended a grubby palm. 'Let's see the colour of yer moolah then.'

Kitchener had become bored with the stable yard. Recognising the harness as a passport to explore, he stood placidly while Fel buckled it into place and only protested briefly when he was led away from the milk cart. Once beyond the gates, however, he plodded beside Maury with a cautious interest. It was a new route for him and if he liked what lay at the end of it, all well and good. If he didn't . . . Kitchener bared his teeth just behind Maury's left ear.

'Pack it in!' Maury snapped as a stream of dribble dripped on his shoulder. Lulled into a false sense of security by the ease of his trip so far, he slapped Kitchener hard on the nose.

With a squeal of protest, the horse reared up on his hind quarters and pawed the air with his forelegs. Open-mouthed, Maury stared at two iron-shod hooves the size of meat plates descending towards his head.

Chapter 4

Something seized the back of Maury's neck. The high street swirled round, his shoes hit the pavement with a thud, the constriction across his throat eased – and he found himself facing the broad grins of a couple of blokes on the steps of the Abbey Tavern. Drawing in a grateful gasp of air, he turned unsteadily and found his saviour beaming at the enraged horse.

'Hello, horse. Joshua likes big horses.' Joshua Cutter's eerie lavender eyes fastened on Maury. 'Nearly squashed yer flat, he did.'

Thrusting a finger between his tie knot and his aching Adam's apple, Maury croaked out his thanks. 'You're a mate, Joshua.'

'Am I?' The idea seemed to please him. 'Mates . . . That's good.' He placed a large hand either side of the horse's bit and drew the muzzle towards him. Very gently he blew a stream of air into the animal's distended nostrils. 'What's his name?'

'Kitchener.'

'He were a soldier. We had a picture of him at school. Used to put ribbons round it on Empire Day.' Joshua patted the large neck, slapping the flesh with a gentle firmness. 'I been up Maitland Park to watch the balloon. They always winch the balloon up Sunday morning. Sometimes they let Joshua have a go on the handle.'

Maury could well imagine the Home Guard manning the barrage balloon being grateful for Joshua's muscles. He intended to exploit them himself to get this flaming nag down to the canal.

The suggestion was happily accepted by Pansy's cousin.

31

Positioning himself at the horse's head, he thrust his hands into his pockets, whistled softly and set off towards the canal. Dropping his head and pricking his ears, Kitchener ambled after his new friend with all the placidity of a geriatric donkey.

The sight of Pansy's admiring smile as she ran from the edge of the canal to meet them cheered Maury up considerably.

'See – I knew you'd not let us down,' she said in a tone which told him that others hadn't had her faith. Glancing beyond her, Maury saw her mother standing on the wharf talking to Pete Cutter and that boater bloke. Which of them hadn't expected him to show up? All of them probably, he decided, following Kitchener's swishing tail. He knew most people thought he was all talk.

People around here couldn't see beyond their noses, that was the problem. They left school at fourteen and it was down the Labour Exchange and take anything going. Well, that wasn't for him. If he had to graft hard it would be for himself. By the time he was thirty, Maury intended to be rich, respected and rid of this dump. Somewhere posh where the nobs lived – that was where he and Pansy were going.

He watched her now, offering Kitchener a lump of carrot. If anyone had pressed him, he couldn't have said why he felt the way he did about her. It was just something about her round, wide-eyed face, with its halo of dark curls, that appealed to his protective instincts.

Kitchener lifted his head and shook it vigorously, sending his mane slapping in alternate waves. His descending muzzle caught on Pansy's beret and with a squeal she stepped back and took it off. Replacing it and tucking her hair up, she said, 'I wish you hadn't got rid of Cutter's horses, Uncle Pete. They were much better than the lorries.'

'You wouldn't say that if you'd the choice between riding in a dry cab or up the front of an open cart after a day's work. Although I'd not deny it would be handy to have some transport that didn't need petrol coupons.'

'We could get a horse, Dad. Joshua could look after it.'

'Aye, I'm sure you could, son. Still . . . best be getting this

32

one hitched up now, eh? Get this boat under way again. Can we lend a hand, Taz?'

'We can manage, ta, Mr Cutter. Addie!'

A shrill whistle brought the girl's head popping out of the butty's hatch. Seen together like this, there was very little resemblance between brother and sister. Taz was tall enough to make the five-foot-seven height of the boat's cabin at least four inches too short for comfort. His lean, tanned face, with its slightly hooded brown eyes under a mop of dark hair, was enough to make him quite a catch among the boater women, and several hopeful girls made a point of looking their best if there was a chance their boat might pass the *Rainbow* somewhere on the canals.

About the only thing Addie had in common with him was a slimness of build. Now it was no longer dripping in rats' tails, her hair proved to be a shade somewhere between light brown and ginger. Despite the constant exposure to the weather, her skin remained stubbornly pale, with a liberal sprinkling of freckles that would darken from straw-coloured in the winter to a treacle toffee shade under the summer sun. If she had had her brother's brown eyes it might have helped her looks; but Addie's were a pale grey, set in a face that was wide at the forehead and narrow at the chin.

Between them, Taz and Addie ran a thick coconut-fibre rope through running blocks on top of the covered cargo area, secured it with a twist round a T-stud near the cabin, and contrived to attach the other end to Kitchener's harness.

'Right, kid, let's get started.'

'Ain't no need for you to come, Taz. Best get the engine fixed; we're losing time.'

'Don't talk daft, Addie. You can't manage by yourself. What you gonna do up the warehouse if they want you to unload?'

'Josh will give you a hand,' Pete Cutter interrupted. 'He always gives the blokes a hand to unload at the wharf. Isn't that right, son?'

Joshua beamed and nodded happily. It was a good plan. He liked helping.

33

'Me and Maury will walk round with you too,' Pansy said.

Maury would have argued with that one; the idea of spending Sunday morning in the company of this foul-mouthed girl, Pansy's half-witted cousin and a homicidal horse, was about as appealing as being called up. But Addie jumped in before he could say anything.

'What's Shorty going to do? Bet I'm stronger than him.'

'I've got to watch the horse,' Maury said promptly. If she didn't want him along, then that settled it for him. He'd go with them.

'Why? Does tricks, does he?'

'Stow it, kid.' Taz turned to Maury. 'We'd be grateful for the help. Now get this lot under way and I'll see if I can find somewhere to do a bit of welding.'

'What's the problem?' Pete asked, his professional instincts aroused.

In answer, Taz reached down to the motor deck and retrieved two halves of a greasy metal rod. It meant very little to most of his audience, but they gathered it needed to be fixed before the engine could be restarted. 'I can get a new one turned and fitted up in Brentford. If I could just get this one patched up for now . . .' He scanned the watching faces hopefully.

'It's Sunday . . .' Kate said doubtfully. 'It's certain sure a lot of places work through now . . . for war orders. But, well . . . perhaps the bus depot up Chalk Farm . . .'

'No need to bother them,' her brother-in-law interrupted. 'Tell you who'll be there. Bloke up Whitcher Place. Got the lock-up, strips down scrap. If the door's locked son, just give a knock. He's there from cock-crow to the last owl hoot. Mention my name.'

'Thanks, Mister Cutter. You sure you'll be OK kid?'

'Nothing to it.'

Addie flung back her hair in a gesture that was presumably meant to convey competence, and it spun away from her head in a spreading curtain. At that moment a weak shaft of sunlight fought its way through the low, graphite-coloured clouds and illuminated the ginger within the mousy locks, giving her a brief illusion of prettiness. Joshua's eyes widened with admiration. It reminded him of the thick, warm manes on the cart horses he'd groomed as a child.

Addie glared at him. 'What you gawping at?'

'Nothing.' Dropping his head, Joshua retreated to the other side of Kitchener.

'Right. Best get this lot along then.' Addie took a hitch on her thick leather belt which held up another pair of cut-down man's trousers. Her shirt was a hand-me-down from Taz, and the sleeveless waistcoat had been sewn from an oilskin. She seemed oblivious to the wind that was nipping at the others' coats, pullovers and jackets.

'What have you done with your wet clothes?' Kate asked. 'If the engine isn't working you've nowhere to dry them.'

'Got 'em in a bucket, miss.'

'Give them to me then – I'll put them through the tub for you. You can pick them up when you come down again.'

'No need, miss – I can manage. But wait there, you've put me in mind of something I gotta give yer.' Scrambling back on to the *Rainbow*, Addie disappeared into the cabin and re-emerged clutching a rotting sandbag sack. 'Here yer are.' She held the knobbly package out to Kate. 'Best take care. Dust comes through the weave. It cleans off easy, though.' As proof, she turned over a couple of grey palms and slapped them vigorously against her bottom.

Kate took the heavy sack. 'What's this?'

'Coal. On account of yer having to light the fire up again last night to dry us off after them bastard Geoghans knocked me in the canal.'

Kate tried to pass the parcel back. 'I'm certain sure you're welcome to a few pearls. You'd have done the same.'

Addie backed away. 'Dixons always pay their debts, miss. You've got to keep it.'

'Don't be silly . . .' Kate advanced.

With a stubborn pout Addie retreated, insisting that the Dixons didn't take what wasn't theirs. 'We pay our way, miss, always have.'

Seeing that this could easily go on all morning, Kate dropped her arms. 'All right. I'll take your coal and thank you for it . . .'

Addie's narrow shoulders relaxed.

'. . . but only if you let me take your wet clothes home.'

'Give her your togs, kid, and let's get moving. That load's got to be up the interchange. And fetch me some cash from the tin. Ten bob be enough, do you reckon, Mister Cutter?' He lifted the broken rod.

'If he charges you more than five, you come see me, son. Half a crown would be fairer, I reckon.'

Addie re-emerged once more with a basket of sodden clothes, a ten bob note, and a sullen expression. Ignoring the last, Kate accepted the basket and told her to pick them up from the office next time the *Rainbow* was on the down trip to the London Docks. 'If I'm not there, knock on Mr Cutter's door.'

Pete nodded his acquiescence. 'That's right. I'm up over the brick store. Any of the men'll point you in the right direction. Josh or me's usually there.'

The name brought the person to mind. They both looked towards the patiently waiting horse. His nose pressed into the offside mane, Josh peered at Addie across the animal's neck. As soon as he realised he'd been spotted, he turned away and ground his boot into the tow-path.

'Right . . . gidd-him-up then, son.'

Joshua thrust his hands into his pockets, whistled softly and started walking. With a snort, Kitchener shifted his huge shaggy feet, obtained a better grip and leant into the collar. The tow rope strained but the craft stayed stationary.

With a grunt of determination, Kitchener heaved his weight forward again. They saw his muscles and sinews bulge as he rose on the front of his shoes. This time the boat slid forward. With what could have been a sigh of satisfaction, Kitchener relaxed and started his slow amble round to Camden Wharf.

Addie leapt aboard and seized the tiller. With a nod of thanks, Taz returned to the motor, placed the water can inside the cabin and started to slide the flap across and lock up.

Another weak ray of sun struggled down and picked out the brilliant splashes of colour that swirled in the patterns of cabbage roses, castles and entwined vines that decorated the sides of both vessels and illuminated the gilt lettering on the prow of the butty: *Crock of Gold.*

'Oooh, aren't they pretty, Maury?' Pansy breathed.

'Yeah, great. Come on.' Since they had to walk somewhere, he supposed it might as well be along the tow-path.

Pansy glanced back to wave goodbye to her mother. 'There's Iris again.'

Since she'd stopped, Maury paused to watch Pansy's cousin picking her way across the yard. He hoped she wasn't planning to join the excursion.

Apparently not. 'I came to ask if you'd like to eat your dinner with us today, Uncle Pete,' she called, skipping over the final few feet in a set of inappropriate high heels.

'And you've dressed yourself up special to do it, eh, my pet?'

'What? Oh, this . . .' Iris touched the black velvet hat perched over one eye. 'I've been to church. We had a talk afterwards by a lady from the Red Cross. About packing parcels for prisoners of war. I thought I might volunteer. It's only a few hours. Mummy wouldn't mind, I'm sure.'

'No reason why she should,' Pete agreed. 'But I daresay she will.' He took the sting out of his words with a grin.

Iris gave him a tight smile and turned to Kate. 'You too, Auntie Kate. And Pansy. I was coming round to your house next. You've saved me the trip.'

'Well, erm . . .'

'Do *please* come . . .'

The hint of pleading in Iris's voice was hard to resist. Kate accepted the invitation. 'If you're sure you can spare the rations . . .'

'Oh yes. We can, thank you. Are you coming too, Pansy?'

Maury understood the message being conveyed by his beloved's fingers, which were digging like cat's claws into the flesh of his forearm. 'Me mum's expecting Pansy up our house for her dinner, Mrs C.'

'I see . . .' Kate saw very well. But aloud she supposed it would be just her and Pete. 'That'll be it,' he agreed. 'You're not expecting Josh too, are you?'

37

Iris paled and then flushed. 'I'm sure, I mean . . .'

'It's all right. He'll be happier here than round your mum's, Iris. He's used to fending for himself.'

Swinging round, Pete inserted two fingers in his mouth, preparatory to letting rip with a whistle. And then let them drop again. The *Crock of Gold*, with its horse and handler, had already rounded the bend in the canal at the end of Cutter's Wharf and was out of sight.

'It's all right, Uncle Pete. Maury and me will tell him. Come on, quick, let's catch them up.' Pansy hurried after the butty before anyone could change their minds and decide she must eat round her aunt and uncle's.

'See yer then, Mrs C.' Pushing back the brown trilby he habitually wore and thrusting his hands into his pockets, Maury set off after her.

'I'll walk round Kelly Street with you, Kate. Take a look at that blocked pipe.' Pete thrust a wrench into his jacket pocket. 'Walk you out at the same time, eh, Iris? I've got to rechain the gates now the horse is in.'

'How will he get out again?'

'Josh has a key. He'll see to 'em. What about you, son?' he called across to Taz, who'd been tactfully standing out of earshot from the family discussion. 'Be all right to shin over the gates if Josh's not back before you? I'll leave the dog locked up.'

'No problem, Mr Cutter,' Taz agreed. 'Thing is . . . this – what you call it – Whitcher Place. I don't know it.'

'Walk up with us. We'll set you on the right path.'

The first part of the journey was straightforward. With the two men leading and Kate and Iris walking behind, they made their way out into Camden Street, under the railway bridge and up into Kentish Town High Street. Once there, Pete stopped. 'Kate and me's heading for Kelly Street up there on the left, and you're wanting to go right here. Tell you what . . . Iris, could you set him right for Whitcher Place? It's just a step round from your house . . .'

'I'm a bit late . . . Doris will be expecting me to help with the . . . Oh, all right, if we're quick, Mr Dixon . . .'

'Quick as you like, miss.'

With a small nod to the other two, Iris swung quickly away down Rochester Road. She didn't bother to look behind her and see if Taz was following. Head up, she clicked quickly past the houses with their sandbagged basements and brown-paper-covered windows.

Taz's long legs carried him easily abreast of her. She kept her eyes fixed ahead.

'Missed me, Iris?'

'No.'

'Don't believe you.'

'Believe what you like, Mr Dixon.'

'Taz.'

'Mr Dixon.'

'Are you coming out with me again?'

'No.'

'Why not?'

'I told you why not, Mr Dixon – my parents wouldn't approve.'

'You mean they would have the other times?'

'No. I daresay they wouldn't, but . . .' Stopping abruptly, Iris swung to face him, her mauve eyes pleading. 'You promised you'd never tell them.'

'I won't. About time *you* did though, isn't it? Aren't you old enough to choose your own friends?'

'My mother—'

'Is sick. Lots of mothers get sick. Mine did. Died when I was twelve. Don't mean she stopped me having friends.'

'My mother doesn't prevent me . . . It just worries her that I haven't . . . I really don't want to discuss this. Whitcher's round there. I'm not sure which lock-up you want—'

'Third one along,' Taz said promptly. 'Only place does a bit of welding around here Sundays. Local knowledge.' He grinned and tossed the two broken sections of bar in the air, catching them one-handed like a juggler.

Doubt flickered across Iris's eyes. 'Did you deliberately . . . How could you know I'd come . . . ?'

Taz's smile became broader. 'Did, didn't you? Twice, by all accounts. Heard you came down last night as well.'

'That was to deliver a message for my mother. How could I possibly have known you would break down at our wharf?'

'Fate, I reckon. Something whispered in your ear, get yourself down to that wharf Iris my girl and he'll be waiting for you.'

Iris swung round and blocked his path. Indignation made her forget to duck her head or hold her hand to her cheek for once. 'You've a very high opinion of yourself, Taz Dixon.'

'I have indeed, Miss Cutter.' He dropped one hooded eyelid in a slow wink. 'And well deserved, I'm told. Fancy coming up the Mother Redcap with me tonight?'

'Of course I don't.'

'You're quite right. Not the sort of place you take a decent girl at all. Where's me manners? It'll have to be the Forum then. See you in the one-and-threepenny queue, second house. Bye, miss . . . for now.'

Chapter 5

'Can't you get a move on? That horse is only borrowed, yer know. I've not hired it for the duration.'

'Be a lot quicker if yer lent a hand, Shorty, 'stead of worrying about getting yer fancy togs mussed up.' Clambering across the flour sacks that were tightly packed into the cargo area of the *Crock of Gold*, Addie twisted both hands round a canvas neck and heaved, levering the sack free and ready to be slung up on to the wharf.

Joshua edged closer, peering earnestly at her. 'Shall Joshua throw it?'

'No, ta. Best wait for the lorry to turn up.'

'Where is it then?' Maury asked. 'I thought you was expected.'

'We are. Taz gave 'em a ring from the phone box last night. They said they'd be here. Here yer are – this'll be the bakery lot now.' She waved down a covered lorry bumping towards them along the wharf.

'Oh, Maury, look, it's going to the ABC! I work there,' Pansy explained to Addie. 'In the wages office.'

'Yeah? Must be deadly dull. Hey Josh – you gonna show us how far you can throw one of these sacks?'

Addie discovered that the large-muscled young man took conversations very literally. Seizing the first sack, he swung it like a shot-put and let go. The canvas missile hurtled across the width of the wharf, slammed into a warehouse wall, and burst open to release a cloud of white dust in all directions. The freshening wind caught the flour and rolled it over the startled group on the dock.

'Bloody hell!' Maury gasped, choking in the dust.

Addie laughed and clapped. 'Nice shot, Joshua.'

'Oh yuck.' Pansy snatched off her beret, bending forward and shaking out her hair before banging the hat against her hip. She straightened up, flicking the curtain of locks from her face, and smiled at the two men descending from the lorry. 'Hello, Mr Griswald . . . bet you didn't expect to see me today.'

'Oh . . . er, no. Young Pansy, isn't it? Wages office? Just out for a walk?'

'We came round with the boat. Fancy it being for the ABC. I thought all our flour came down on the train.'

'War on, Pansy. Take what you can get. Best to keep it to yourself, there's a good girl. Don't want others finding out about our suppliers. It's every baker for himself these days. Right, Jed. Let's get this lot loaded, shall we?'

'He wasn't very friendly,' Pansy murmured to Maury, watching Mr Griswald help stacking the lorry. 'Normally we get on really well. He said I added up the time-cards better than any other clerk they ever had. I can even do one-and-a-quarter overtime and piece rates in my head.'

'I reckon your Mr Griswald can add up the difference in profit between flour bought regular and flour that fell off a ship in the docks.'

Pansy wrinkled her nose in puzzlement.

'He's bought it cheap,' Maury explained patiently. 'But I bet he'll charge the company the regular price.'

'Maury!' Pansy looked at her boss with wide-eyed surprise. 'That's stealing.'

'No, Panse. That's business.'

It was too rawly miserable to stand still. Putting his free arm through hers, Maury walked her a little way along the quayside. Behind the walls of the goods yard there was a constant rattle of LMS carts and lorries over the cobblestones, and the usual pall of gritty smoke and dust was drifting across from the rail tracks and engine sheds further down the line. They paused for a while to watch a barge on the far side of the basin unloading petroleum at the depot, and wandered back just as another tied up at Dingwall's Wharf with a full load of timber.

42

'Drinks local, does he? Your Mr Griswald?'

'I don't know. At least, I think he goes to the Golden Cross sometimes. Why?'

'Contacts, doll. You got to make contacts in business.'

Eventually the wooden base of the *Crock of Gold* was bare – except for the inevitable drift of white dust in all the crevices – and the canvas flaps of the truck were laced back into position. Addie twisted the mooring ropes free with fast, competent movements. 'Let's be getting along back. Shift yourself, Shorty.'

Maury snapped, 'Watch your mouth. You ain't exactly no oil-painting yourself, Skinny.'

'Yeah, but there's still a chance I'll grow into me looks – and me curves. But I reckon you've got no chance of getting any taller. That why you ain't in uniform? Didn't want no midgets in khaki?'

Maury found himself torn between anger and a small glow of pleasure that she'd taken him to be over eighteen.

Pansy promptly spoilt the moment by telling everyone he was only seventeen.

'Cor! Shorty, you ain't no older than me.'

'*You're* seventeen?'

'Will be,' Addie said, 'come April fourteenth.'

'That's the same as me!' Pansy cried. 'At least – I'll be sixteen. Fancy that, Maury, we've got the same birthday.'

'Yeah, terrific. Can we get going? I gotta get that horse back.'

The journey back was only slightly faster. Despite the lighter load, Kitchener insisted on a plodding pace. Seething with impatience, his head full of plans as to how he could exploit what he'd just found out about the manager at the ABC, Maury tramped back along the tow-path.

'You ever seen a fish in the canal, Maury?'

'Never. Why?'

'We used to fish off Cutter's Wharf – me and Iris and Joshua and Ernest. The men laughed at us. They never said why, though. 'Spect it's cause they knew there wasn't any, don't you?'

''Spect so. Still, ain't important now. You're all grown up

now. Leastways, you will be come the fourteenth of April. I got you a special present.'

'What?'

'It's a surprise.'

'Tell me.'

'Wouldn't be a surprise then.'

'*Please*.' Pouting, Pansy twisted her fingers into his and fluttered her lashes.

'Nope.'

'Oh . . . you!' His hand was thrown away.

Maury bounced along, apparently without a care in the world.

Pansy's nature was too straightforward for sulking. Hurrying to catch up, she seized his arm again. 'Will I like it?'

'Course you will. I chose it, didn' I?' He relented slightly and explained that she couldn't see it because he hadn't picked it up yet.

Pansy held him a little closer. 'Is it expensive?'

'Wouldn' get you nothing cheap, would I, doll?' Maury said, relapsing into the American accent he occasionally borrowed from Hollywood films.

They were rounding the bend of the canal that brought them in sight of Cutter's Wharf again. With an excited skip, Pansy gave him one last hug before they arrived.

'Taz ain't back yet,' Addie shouted, steering the butty against the wharf behind the motor. 'Well . . . ta for the help. Best get Taz's dinner on.' Without another word, she disappeared into the boat's cabin.

'We better get a move on too, Pansy. Couldn't be a mate and bring the horse up for us, could yer, Josh?'

Felonious was wearing a groove in the pavement by the time the quartet wandered into sight of Willingham.

'Where you bin, for Gawd's sake? What if she'd come back an' found that blessed nag weren't here?'

'You could have said he'd been nicked, Fel. Tell 'er one of your mates was short of a Sunday roast.'

'I told yer, young Maury. It's Mr Monk to you.'

Not now he'd got what he wanted it wasn't. 'Well, here's

the nag. Josh'll stick him back in his stable for you. We got to go. Mum's expecting us for our dinner.' Tucking his beloved's hand in his arm, Maury set off back the way they'd come.

It was a quiet lunchtime. The weather didn't encourage anyone to linger. An ARP warden wished them good afternoon, confirming that it was well past noon and Eileen O'Day would be fretting over burnt potatoes and an overdone meat course.

An unspoken message passed between them. Holding hands, they ran across the high street, flew up the Prince of Wales Road, and arrived in a breathless rush at Maury's front gate.

'It smells lovely . . .' Pansy sniffed the air appreciatively.

It was true enough. War or no war, most local housewives still made an effort to put a decent Sunday dinner on the table, even if the weekday offerings were scratch and make-dos depending on the state of their ration cards and the deliveries received at the local shops that week.

Maury ushered Pansy into the front hall, turned to shut the door and discovered Joshua fumbling open the gate catch.

'What you doing here then? Fact, how'd yer know where I lived?'

'The man told me. Kitchener's man.' Joshua stepped on to the doormat, his large feet obliterating the 'welcome' message.

'So, what d'yer want?'

'Joshua's come for his dinner. Your mum's expecting him.'

'Me mum? Who said she was?'

'You did, Maury,' Pansy whispered. 'Up at the dairy.'

'Yeah . . . but I never meant him—'

'Maury, is that you? Get yourself washed and sat at this table before it spoils!'

Eileen bustled out of the kitchen, tucking back stray wisps of hair that had escaped and curled in the steamy kitchen. And stopped, biting back the scolding she was about to administer when she saw that Maury wasn't alone.

'Hello, Mum. I invited Pansy round fer dinner.'

'You're very welcome, love,' Eileen said faintly, her eyes

45

fixed on Joshua's large bulk which was obscuring the light from the street. 'And who's he?'

Josh answered before Maury could explain. 'Hello, Maury's mum.' He held out a large hand and took Eileen's slim fingers. 'We're mates. Joshua's come for his dinner.'

Eileen rescued her arm, which was being jerked up and down like a pump handle. The look she shot at her second-youngest could have stripped paint. 'Well, you'd best come through, hadn't you.' She led the way down the three steps to the back kitchen and scullery. A cold draught from the open window skittered through the clouds of vegetable-scented steam. Sammy and Annie's voices could be heard yelling and shouting in the back garden. Judging by the indignant squawks, one of Eileen's hens had escaped from its coop and was taking exception to the children's attempts to recapture it. The wooden table had already been covered with a cloth and set for five. Obviously not brother Pat, Maury reasoned. His mother wouldn't have bothered with the cloth for immediate family. 'Mr Stamford coming over for his dinner, is he?'

'No. He ain't. Jack's gone away on a course. Special duties for Scotland Yard or something.'

This was good news as far as Maury was concerned. Annie's father was a Chief Inspector in the CID. Maury had always felt uncomfortable in the man's presence, and since that business with the stolen whisky, when Mr Stamford had actually taken him in for questioning, things had become well nigh impossible. You'd think the man would have a bit more gratitude, given all that cooking and cleaning Maury's mum did for him. Not to mention raising his kid for him, now her mother was dead or interned somewhere in occupied Europe . . .

'Thought Mr Stamford was up Agar Street Station permanent, now he's a cripple.'

'A touch of arthritis in his arm ain't exactly like losing a leg,' Eileen said shortly, lifting a sizzling, spitting meat dish from the oven and banging it on the draining board. 'Put a couple of stools up to the table for the children, Maury. And lay up two more places.'

'I'll do it,' Pansy said quickly. 'That looks real tasty, Mrs O'Day. What is it?'

'Spiced brisket.'

'It's ever so big. You must have ever such a nice butcher.'

'He's very obliging.' Eileen lifted the meat to a dish with two forks. 'And we've five ration books . . . six if you count Annie's dad's. A week's ration can be stretched if you've a fair few coupons to juggle with.'

The look Maury received over his girlfriend's bent head told him very clearly that this *was* the whole week's ration and his mum had intended it to stretch for the next few days.

Joshua's pale lavender eyes were fixed on the feast in front of him with the expression of Dracula after spotting a fat neckful of virgin's blood. Eileen shivered slightly and commented on the nasty draught coming through the window. 'Shut it for us, Maury – and tell those children to leave the hen be and come in. She'll not go far from the coop. That'll be Sarah . . .' She added as the sound of the door knocker reverberated in the hall. 'Let her in.'

'I'll go.' Pansy whisked away.

That solved the mystery of the fifth place setting. A woman police sergeant was nearly as bad for giving Maury indigestion, but at least Sarah McNeill might have a smaller appetite than Annie's dad. With luck there might be a morsel of that spiced beef left over, and they wouldn't be eating vegetable and oatmeal pudding for the rest of the week.

Sarah was muffled in a black coat against the cold, but her brown-gold hair was hatless and for once hung loose over her shoulders: a sure sign she wasn't on duty, as she normally wore it in a twist to comply with police regulations for neat and appropriate dress for female officers.

'Good afternoon, Eileen. Not late, am I?'

'No. We're about to sit down.' Eileen forced a smile through gritted teeth. 'We've a couple of extra guests.'

'You've three.' Sarah stepped down and to one side, revealing the small figure who'd been hovering behind her. 'I found him on the doorstep. He says Maury invited him for dinner.'

Felonious Monk – newly shaven, hair greased in honour of

47

the occasion, and in his best and only suit – smiled at them from the frame of the kitchen door.

Maury looked wildly between the former burglar and his mum . . . and suddenly wished that Joshua hadn't been so quick in dragging him from under Kitchener's hooves.

Chapter 6

'I can't go. I *shan't* go.'

Why couldn't he leave her alone? He'd disappear for weeks, leaving her jangled emotions to settle, and then, just when she thought her life was under control, he'd turn up, demanding her . . . her what? She couldn't even put a name to it. What did Taz Dixon want? Love? An affair? Or just the thrill of chasing what he couldn't have?

Iris stared at her wide-eyed reflection in the dressing-table mirror. As usual when she was agitated, the silver snakes of the scar seemed to leap out from her creamy skin. Most people ignored it – or at least pretended to – although she could see their eyes being drawn back to it whenever they thought she wasn't looking. No one had actually commented straight out on their first meeting.

Until Taz Dixon, three months ago.

'Haa d'yer do that then?' he'd asked, folding the cargo receipt she'd just typed up for him and pushing it into his trouser pocket.

'Do what?' She'd been so used to the tactful pretences, it hadn't occurred to her he might be talking about the scar.

'Your face.'

Hitching himself on to the desk in the yard office, Taz had leant across and taken her chin in his fingers, gently turning her face to the dull November light coming through the small windows. The contact had unnerved her. Apart from her father and uncles, he was the first man ever to touch her.

A callused forefinger traced the wavering line from forehead to cheek and then slid on down to her lips. She'd sat, mesmerised, like a fighter caught in a searchlight's beam and unable to climb to safety.

Leaning nearer, he'd kissed her. The warm taste of his lips on hers had been frightening and exhilarating at the same time. She'd wanted him to stop, but at the same time she had wanted it to go on for ever.

A lump of coal, spitting and cracking as it crumbled in the grate, had finally jerked her out of limbo and back to reality. With a gasp of indignation she'd drawn back her hand and slapped his face.

'Well now, what did you do that for? Just when we were getting along so well.'

'We were doing nothing of the sort, Mr . . .' She'd glanced down at the delivery docket he'd handed over. 'Mr Dixon. Please leave immediately.'

'Mrs Kate usually brews tea while the boat's being unloaded.'

'Mrs Cutter isn't here.' She had known the blood was flooding into her face, could feel the pulse thudding wildly below her jaw and the heat exuding from her cheeks. It must have made the scar stand out. Nothing else, not even the embarrassment of kissing a man she didn't even know, was as awful as knowing that her disfigurement was growing more prominent by the second.

She'd put her hand to her face in an automatic gesture and Taz had taken it away. 'It's you, isn't it? Same as yer eyes and nose and hair. It's what *makes* you you.'

'It undoubtedly does that.' Iris had tried to reclaim her hand but he'd kept hold, rubbing his thumb over the back of it. She knew she ought to have slapped him again. Instead she found herself hoping he might try to claim another kiss.

He had grinned at her from the desk where he was still perched, rubbing her hand between his as if it might be cold. 'Name's Taz. What's yours then?'

So he didn't know who she was. Well, no doubt finding out she was the owner's daughter would put him in his place. 'Iris Cutter. Fred Cutter is my father.'

Taz had shown no sign of being abashed by this revelation.

'Where's Mrs Kate today then? Not gone and joined up, has she?'

'Auntie Kate has the influenza. I'm minding the office for now, Mr Dixon.'

'And doing it real well, I'm sure. Except you've maybe not got your auntie's talent with a teapot . . .'

It was an excuse to move. Twisting free, Iris had crossed to the gas ring. Her hands had shaken and the match wavered over the hissing holes before they ignited. The kettle was empty.

'Here. Fill this from the yard tap, if you please.'

'Yes, miss. Certainly, miss.' He'd pulled a lock of his curling brown hair in a gentle mockery of her imperious tone.

She'd watched him from the window, seeing him raise the kettle and wave it in the direction of the boats. A boy in baggy trousers and a flat cap had been balancing on the cabin top watching two of Cutter's men unloading roofing tiles. He raised a thumb in acknowledgement.

The gesture had restored Iris's confidence. It was just a game with this man. He probably flirted with all the girls along the canal; that kiss was no more than a way of cadging a drink . . .

By the time he had returned with the full kettle she was ready to face him calmly. Setting the water to boil, she'd remarked that he had once travelled with an old man.

'Noticed me, did you? Well I'm flattered.'

'I noticed the old man,' she had reminded him. 'Where is he? Retired?'

'You could say that. Grandad went to a better mooring, you might say.'

It had taken a second for her to understand what he was trying to tell her. 'Oh? I'm sorry.'

'He died on the water. It's what he wanted. He couldn't have stood being marooned ashore. Now it's just me and Ad.'

'Your boy?'

The description had seemed to amuse him, although she hadn't understood why until he'd gone to the door and whistled loudly. The 'boy' had run over, obeying Taz's

51

jerked thumb to come past him into the office. As he'd passed, Taz had whipped off the tweed cap allowing the long hair to tumble out.

Grinning at Iris's surprise, Taz had made the introductions. 'This is me sister, Adelaide Mary. But she answers to Addie. Or kid if you like. This is Miss Iris Cutter . . . old man Cutter's her dad.'

'Which one? You ain't that gormless lump's sister, are yer?'

'No. I'm his cousin. How do you do, Miss Dixon?'

Iris hadn't intended to sound so distant and, well, condescending, but she knew she had done just that when Addie wrinkled her nose, extended a limp hand as if she expected it to be kissed, and informed her she was 'just bloody la-di-da, ta very much'.

'Stow it, kid, or you won't get no tea or biscuits.'

Iris had hurriedly filled two of the metal mugs used by the yard men and pushed them over. 'There's sugar in the tin.'

'Ta. But we'll not be using all your rations, miss.' Delving into her pocket, Addie had taken out a tobacco tin, removed two lumps of sugar from it and added one each to hers and Taz's drinks. Before Iris could offer a spoon, Addie had taken a pencil, casually swirled the liquid, licked the wet end and returned it to the desk.

'Go keep an eye on the cargo, kid.'

'It ain't going to run away.'

'Scarper. I want a word with the lady. Go on.'

Helping herself to a biscuit, Addie had wandered out again. Iris had immediately moved to put the desk between herself and Taz.

'Hope you don't mind, miss,' he'd said, taking a chair and moving it away from her rather than towards. 'Thing is, I need a bit of advice. From a woman.' Spinning the seat with one hand, he'd straddled it and leant his arms across the top, regarding her with a seriously respectful expression. 'I want to get Addie something a bit special for Christmas this year. It's our first without Grandad, see?'

Iris had nodded cautiously.

'Only, I ain't sure where to go. We just get our supplies

from the shops along the canal normally. Don't go up fancy stores. No call, you see?'

'Yes. I understand. Well, there's some lovely shops in Camden, if you just walk out—'

'No. I want to go up to the West End. Got shops big enough to lose this lot in, they say. Would that be right?'

Feeling on safer ground, Iris had agreed that they had indeed. 'Oxford Street is what you want, Mr Dixon. Some of the stores have been hit in the air raids, I'm afraid, but I'm sure you'd find something pretty . . . What was it you were looking for exactly?'

Taz had admitted he wasn't sure. 'But I'll know it when I see it. Now, how would I be getting to this street Miss?'

She had launched into directions that had become more and more tangled as, first of all, he wanted to walk, then to go by bus, and finally he'd decided he might try to take a tube train.

'I've never done that before. Gone under the ground. Gone through canal tunnels, of course. Would it be like that?'

Iris didn't know. She'd never been on a canal boat.

'What – you living by the canal and never taken a ride along? I'll take you if you like.'

'No, thank you, Mr Dixon. Do you intend to shop for your sister today?'

'I don't have that much choice. Have to take a day when I can. Trips schedules have to be stuck to. But as it happens I reckon I can spare a few hours this afternoon and still make my next pick-up on time. If it's all right to leave the *Rainbow* moored up at the wharf . . .?'

Iris had assured him it would be. 'There's bound to be someone around. Uncle Pete, probably – he lives in the yard. If you shout he'll let you back if the gates are locked.'

'No need, miss. I can always hike round the tow-path.'

It was true enough. In order to allow clear passage for the horse-drawn boats, the yard's fences didn't meet the canalside. There had been several moves to make the wharf more secure, but they'd never come to anything. With Pete and Joshua acting as almost permanent nightwatchmen and the dog tied up outside, the most any opportunist thief could hope to remove was less than the cost of employing a man to stand by on any gate and open it for the passing canal traffic.

'What about your sister? Will she stay on board?' Iris had been pleased to discover how calmly she was handling this conversation.

'I'll give her a few bob. She can go up the pictures.'

'Does she enjoy the films?'

'Couldn't say. She's never been. Know a place she can go, do you, miss?'

'The Palace has a good programme at the moment. I'm taking my grandmother this afternoon, as a matter of fact. Perhaps Addie would like to sit with us . . .' She'd half regretted the invitation as soon as it had left her mouth. Addie Dixon hadn't looked too clean. But he'd accepted the suggestion with pleasure, and it had been such an easy way of getting his disturbing presence out of the office that she'd heard herself arranging to meet the girl outside the cinema at two o'clock.

Nana Cutter took the addition to her weekly treat philosophically. 'No harm meeting a few new faces. Are these your friends?'

Iris turned. It was easy to see how Nana had recognised the Dixons with such ease. Even though trousers were acceptable for women in public now, not many chose to walk out in cut-down men's corduroys held up by an enormous belt and topped off with a man's jacket that dangled over the knuckles. At least she'd left the cap off.

Taz removed his own as they came closer. 'Haa d'yer do?' He urged his sister forward with a firm grip on her shoulder. 'Here she is then.'

Addie scowled and announced she didn't see why she couldn't go with him. 'Dunno that I want to see the pictures.'

'I should, m'dear,' Nana Cutter said, untwisting a sticky paper bag and offering a peardrop. 'It's a double programme, with cartoons and news. Might even get a bit of a turn if we're lucky. They had a juggler last month.'

Pouting, Addie stuck a sweet in her mouth. Her mouth

54

stayed boredly downturned, but her eyes glinted as they greedily took in the brightly coloured posters outside the cinema.

Iris formally wished the girl's brother a successful afternoon. 'The underground station is just—' She got no further.

'Thing is . . . I was hoping you'd come along with me. I'll treat you to your tea.' He patted the breast pocket of a decent-looking tweed jacket he'd changed into.

'No thank you.'

'Why not?'

'Because I don't want to go anywhere with you, Mr Dixon.'

'Yes you do. And it's Taz.' He stood before her, casually exuding self-confidence.

Iris had been conscious of Nana Cutter, Addie, and half a dozen others in the one-and-threepenny queue who were within earshot. 'I assure you I don't, *Mister* Dixon. And even if I did, I've arranged to take my grandmother to the pictures this afternoon.'

Taz promptly turned that lazily charming smile on Nana. 'You'd not mind me stealing her for a few hours, would you, ma'am?'

'Well now, that would be up to Iris, young man. Would you oblige me by keeping my place in this queue while I have a word with my granddaughter?'

'It would be my pleasure, ma'am.'

'And less of the honey, young man. The only things you catch with that are flies.'

With a grin and a wink, Taz had stepped into the queue.

Iris was drawn out of earshot. 'Go with him,' Nana said firmly.

'Pardon?' She'd been expecting a lecture on the dangers of encouraging unknown young men.

'I said go. I'll watch the little girl. She can come back to my place after the pictures. Have a bit of tea. Listen to the radio.'

'But . . . but . . . Nana . . . I don't want to go. I mean, I hardly know him. He's a boater.'

'You said.' The old woman took Iris's hands in hers and

55

looked up into the pale face. 'Listen, my dear, I know it feels like you'll be young for ever now, but it don't last. One day . . . soon . . . you'll wake up and wonder where all those years went. Where all those opportunities went. Now a good looking young man is offering to take you out for a few hours. It's not like he's wanting you to go off on a dark bomb-site with him, is it? You'll be in the busiest area of London. Now go along and relax and enjoy yourself.'

'But mother . . .' Iris said faintly. 'A boater . . . She'd never approve.'

'Then don't tell her. She thinks you're with me up the picture palace.'

'What if there's an air raid? They've been over every night for weeks.'

'Go down a shelter – that's what me and the girl will be doing. Your mother's not going to be expecting you to run home through the bombs, is she?'

Iris looked between the wrinkled, earnest face under the feather-edged hat, and the queue that was beginning to shuffle forward as the next house started to file in. 'I can't . . .' She twisted her hands free. 'Really, I'd much rather stay with you, Nana.'

'Well of course you would. There's no effort being with your old Nana. But it's time you got out into the world. You're old enough now.'

'Old enough for what?'

'To have an adventure, my girl. Every woman should have at least one adventure in her life. Now you go on and have yours.'

Chapter 7

Taz had raised no objection to her buying her own tube ticket, although she'd been half braced for an argument if he wanted to 'treat' her to that too. During the journey to Tottenham Court Road she found she didn't have to make conversation because his attention was caught by the novelty of the trip. Everything interested him: the escalators, the brightly lit platforms, the wooden bunks and canvas-screen lavatories they'd started putting in for the shelterers at some stations, and the rattling, dimly lit carriages.

London born-and-bred, Iris found his reactions almost as entertaining as he plainly found the train.

'Can't imagine living down here. Can't imagine living in a town if it comes to that.'

'I can't conceive of living in a tiny cabin. How do you manage with so little space?'

'It ain't that hard. Everything's got its place. Come aboard and I'll show you.'

She was spared the necessity of inventing a plausible excuse by the changing note of the train's rattle that said it was leaving the tunnel and coming into Tottenham Court Road station. Rather than change to the Central Line, she decided they'd walk the length of Oxford Street. The sober evidence of the air raids was more intrusive here than in the Camden and Kentish Town areas, where there were pockets of destruction among the relatively intact streets; the West End had been blitzed intermittently for the past few weeks, and the repair squads were still struggling to clear debris, fill in holed roads and demolish unsafe buildings.

'Is there much bombing on the canals?' Iris asked, turning away with a shiver.

'Hardly none. Leastways, I never heard of none. Not along the paths neither. Not much to bomb, see, 'cept down along the docks.'

Iris felt him looking sideways at her. She'd automatically positioned herself so that the scarred cheek was away from him. But if he wasn't looking at that . . . then what? Finally she couldn't stand it any longer. She'd faced him full on. 'Is there something the matter?'

'I was wondering if it upset you . . . me being in a cushy, reserved job when there's your brother abroad fighting the Germans.'

'How do you know he is?'

'Mrs Kate said.'

'Oh.' Iris moved on again. 'Why do you call her Mrs Kate? Why not Mrs Cutter?'

'T'other one . . . the la . . . the lady . . . your mum. *She's* Mrs Cutter. It's a sort of way of telling them apart when we're talking.'

It was getting dark and the stores would soon be shutting. Few places stayed open late any more. It simply wasn't practical given the blackout regulations. 'I think we should go to Selfridges. It's a big store and you're bound to find something you like there.'

'Whatever you say. You going to answer my question? About reserved occupations?'

'I never thought about it,' she admitted. 'It's just the way things are. All the men have to do what they can for the war effort, I suppose. And if you're more use delivering essential supplies, then that's what you should do. Ernest – my brother – wanted to enlist. If he had had the choice to stay home, I don't believe he would have taken it. Ernest sees the war as a great adventure.'

Her words were an uncomfortable echo of her grand-mother's instructions. What would her parents say if they knew she was spending the afternoon with a man from the boats? The canal people were a closed society. It was generally held that they couldn't read or write much beyond their trip

58

tickets and cargo receipts. And they were dirty. It stood to reason – they must be, what with all the family packed on those tiny boats and only a bucket and a water can for personal business.

She looked at Taz again. His brown hair was curling softly in the light rain that was starting to fall, rather than lying flat in the brylcreemed neatness favoured by most of the young men they passed. His skin had the tan of outdoor living, but the chin was newly shaved and his clothes seemed well kept. She glanced down to see if his shoes were polished . . . looked up to find him regarding her with a slightly quizzical gaze . . . and felt her whole stomach turn over and her heart beat wildly. Had he grabbed her and kissed her again at that moment, she'd have responded with her whole being.

Instead he stopped walking, plainly expecting her to say something.

She blurted out the first thing that came into her head. 'Taz is a funny name.'

'Not half as funny as Theodosius.'

'Really?'

'I'm afraid so. Some priest told me mum it meant "God's gift".' His face split into that oddly lop-sided grin, causing Iris's stomach to do another loop-the-loop. 'And she said that's what we better call him then – cause he's the dead spit of his dad, and the Lord knows *he's* always thought he was God's gift.'

'Where are they? Your parents, I mean. Have they got another boat?'

'*Rainbow* and *Crock of Gold*, were theirs. Proper theirs, I mean. Owned legal, not just registered in me dad's name.'

She caught the note of pride in his voice at this statement and asked if all the boaters owned their boats.

'No. Canal carrying companies own most. Haven't you seen their names painted on the side?'

She supposed she must have. She just hadn't taken much notice. 'Is it better then? To own your own?'

'Means you don't have to call nobody master, don't it?'

'I see.' Iris glanced at him again, wondering whether he'd

deliberately changed the subject. 'You didn't answer my question . . . about your parents.'

'Me dad got pleurisy. Died when I was nine. Grandad came to help Mum run our pair. Then she upped and died when I was twelve. Me and Grandad did our best by Addie, but it's not easy, her being a girl . . .'

'Wasn't there some other relative . . . aunt, grandmother?'

'No. A lady from the orphanage came once when we was moored up Berkhamsted way. Said she could get Addie a place. Grandad knocked her in the canal. Is this the place?'

They'd reached the store without her even noticing. She led the way inside the porticoed entrance. 'What would you like to look at first? There's a children's department, I think.'

'Kids?' Taz laughed. 'Addie'd not thank you for that. She's sixteen. I know she's a bit on the skinny side, but see, thing is . . . I reckon it's time she had some proper woman's clothes. A dress. And maybe . . . well, you know . . . stuff that goes underneath. She can't keep sewing up my hand-downs.'

Iris saw. She also saw why he'd wanted her to come this afternoon. It was almost a relief. He had no personal interest in her; he simply hadn't wanted to be seen buying women's knickers!

'Come along then, Mr Dixon.'

'Taz – please. Otherwise I can't call you Iris, and it suits you that well.'

She'd given in. Taz he was as she led him around the departments, her senses drinking in the scents of perfume and make-up and revelling in the rich colours and textures of the handbags, gloves and hats. The small, discreet notices regretting that some products were not for sale but for display purposes only, and trusting their patrons would understand in these difficult times, really didn't matter. It was fun to look.

'We'd best go upstairs to the ladies' modes,' she finally said, regretfully abandoning a display of gauze and silks. 'It's nearly dusk. They'll be closing around us.'

He hung back as an assistant approached, wondering if they required some help. Iris took charge, laying out their requirements. A selection of dresses suitable for a younger lady were held up for inspection. After one look at Taz's helpless expression, Iris threw herself into the choice with enthusiasm.

She finally selected two. 'This one,' she spread a long-sleeved dress in a rich rust-coloured wool against herself, 'would be lovely in the winter. Or this . . .' She held up a button-through crêpe rayon with short sleeves and square shoulders in a pattern of coffee and cream shades. '. . . would be suitable for warmer weather.'

Taz looked doubtful. 'Addie likes a bit of colour. Like the painting on the boats.'

Iris thought of the riot of brilliant pinks, greens and reds that decorated most of the narrow boats. She shuddered mentally at the idea of Addie's freckled face and strange gingery-brown locks poking through the collar of a creation in that combination. But it wasn't up to her, was it? She made to hand the dresses back to the assistant.

'No. I'll take them. Both of them. How much please, miss?'

'Three guineas for the long-sleeved frock, sir. And the other is two pound and ten shillings.'

Taz took out a grubby roll of pound notes. Pulling off the elastic band, he peeled off six. 'Thanks very much for your help.' He smiled at the middle-aged assistant. She responded with an almost flirtatious toss of her head and an envious look in Iris's direction.

This was a new experience for Iris. She was used to pity or revulsion. Nobody had ever wanted to change places with her before. Her hand slid to the familiar contours of the scar as they made their way to the lingerie department. Taz captured her fingers before they could complete their journey from forehead to cheek.

'You never did tell me how yer did that.'

'I didn't.'

He kept hold of her hand. She left it resting in his, enjoying the sensation of strong fingers linked through hers. 'Joshua did it.'

'The big ox? Your cousin?'

'Yes.' It had been a game, that was all. They'd frequently

61

played among the stacks of materials in the yard, which had variously been an African jungle, an Indian fort, a pirate's camp. On this occasion, Joshua had been a captured cowboy. Ernest had insisted on tying him to a stake and whooping around like a red Indian. Then he'd decided to scalp his cousin. With a blunt knife he'd started hacking off hunks of Joshua's hair. It had hurt, but Ernest had ignored the crying.

Finally the enraged Joshua had kicked and lashed his way free. Seeing that he'd gone too far, Ernest had fled. Shrieking with rage, Joshua had seized a roofing tile and thrown it like a discus. One side was already chipped off to expose a razor-sharp edge. Travelling at speed, the ragged clay had sliced Iris's skin as surely as a scalpel, but not nearly as cleanly.

'Daddy took me to the best surgeon, but he said it could never go away completely.'

'How old were you?'

'Eight.'

Too young to understand the difference it would make to her life. At first she'd expected the ugly blemish to fade away like the scabs and scars from the measles and chicken-pox had done. 'Mummy did her best. She did my hair so it fell over my face and told the teachers they had to leave it like that, but . . .'

Iris glimpsed her reflection in a gilt mirror standing on one of the counters. Her hand automatically drew a skein of hair down the scarred side of her face. Taz reached round and flicked it back. His hand stayed lightly on her shoulder as they entered the thickly carpeted lingerie department.

They managed to buy a set of cami-knickers in artificial peach silk, and three pairs of plain white cotton panties.

'What about . . .' Taz nodded in the direction of a brassière displayed on a metal stand.

Iris advised him to picture his sister.

'Well, I know it ain't wanted yet . . . but in a year or so, maybe . . .'

'How would you know what size to buy?'

'Well, I don't know. Can't we get a small one? Let her grow into it?'

'No. At least,' Iris corrected herself – since it was, after all, his money, 'you could, but it would probably make her feel self-conscious. If there was nothing to . . . if she couldn't fill . . . Oh, you know what I mean. Shall we buy some stockings?' She turned to an assistant, 'Do you have any in stock?'

There was nothing in silk, but the drawers under the glass counters yielded some fully-fashioned rayon and a small suspender belt that would fit snugly over Addie's bony hips.

Clutching the packages to his chest, Taz left the department with obvious relief. 'Now let's see about getting our tea. Is there a place near?'

'There's a Lyon's Corner House just a step up the road. But we can go Dutch.'

'I'm not sure I like Dutch food. What do they eat?'

'No, I meant . . .' She saw the twinkle in his eye, realised she was being teased and blushed.

'No reason for you to pay. I can treat a girl to tea.'

'All right. And thank you. Shall I take some of those parcels?'

He gave her the two lighter ones.

'You know, I've been thinking . . . There's nowhere on the boats I can keep this that Addie won't find. I was wondering . . . maybe you've a spare corner at Cutter's? I could pick them up on a trip nearer Christmas?'

There were lots of spare corners, but nowhere that wouldn't involve her in explanations.

Taz saw her expression and said it didn't matter. 'Maybe one of the lock keepers will hang on to them for me.'

But it did matter. An ingrained habit of trying to please made Iris say, 'Nana Cutter wouldn't mind.'

'The old lady? You think she'd stow them?'

'I'm sure she will. Just let me carry them in when we get back and Addie won't even suspect.'

They joined a knot of customers filing into the lift. Iris examined the seamed stockings as they rode down. 'This is a very attractive shade. I wish I'd bought myself a pair now.'

'We could go back again.'

The lift had already reached the ground and the attendant was holding the doors open as the passengers flowed out and headed across the largely empty departments. The assistants were spreading dust cloths over the counters. There was already an uneasy crackling expectation in the air. The raiders had come every night for the past couple of weeks.

'No. You wait by the main doors. I'll slip back.'

Her ride upwards was in solitary apart from the attendant, although more last-minute customers were waiting to come down as the store closed around them. Iris hurried across to the lingerie section, hoping she wasn't too late. The assistant who'd served them was already wrapping sheets around the display garments. Another woman was serving the only two customers left. Stepping back from the counter, the woman shook out a pale blue set of cami-knickers.

Iris paused for a moment to watch. She and Taz had looked at that set, but the real French silk trimmed with Belgium lace had been well beyond his roll of notes. Addie had had to settle for the artificial peach silk.

And this one should have done the same, Iris, who had a fair eye for colour decided. The artificially red curls under the woman's green hat would look dreadful with that particular shade of blue.

The woman reached out to run her fingers over the soft material before the assistant packed it away. She said something to the man with her; her voice was low and too indistinct for the words to travel across the width of the room. Reaching up, she adjusted his tie and brushed a speck from his coat lapel.

He'd had his back to Iris until that moment, but as he half turned to accept the gesture, she saw his profile just before his stronger, deeper pitched tones carried easily to her.

'It's a pleasure, my dear. I promised you something a little special this time, didn't I?' Iris's father said.

Chapter 8

Iris had been surprised at her ability to detach herself from the knowledge that her father was having an affair. At first she'd imagined she would have to avoid him or she'd give herself away. But it had proved amazingly easy to meet his eye, to talk in a normal voice about everyday topics. It was almost as if that brief encounter in Selfridges – unnoticed by him – had never happened.

In fact, after a few weeks, she'd more or less convinced herself she must have misread the situation. The woman with him hadn't been young. And she was plain as well, with a lumpy body and sturdy legs. Not a patch on Iris's own mother. She was probably a secretary or something in one of their supplier's offices. These days you didn't just ring up and place an order; you practically had to beg some of the companies to deliver your materials, according to her Uncle Pete.

Or perhaps she was something to do with the local councils. Iris knew her father sometimes sent along whisky and cigars to various clerks of the works. 'A little bonus,' he called it. No doubt that was all the expensive silk underwear was – a bribe to put Cutter's name at the top of whatever list that plain redhead typed up.

After Iris had run the scenario through her head several times, it had proved easy to accept it as the truth.

The memories of Taz had proven harder to shake off. Mainly because he didn't intend to be shaken.

He had returned as promised just before Christmas to collect the presents; arriving at Nana's house one Saturday just as they were about to leave for the pictures. That time he'd left the *Rainbow* moored at the Regent's Canal dock at Limehouse and taken the underground to Kentish Town – absurdly pleased with himself for tackling the tube system on his own.

Nana had invited him to accompany them to the Forum cinema. But as they reached the head of the queue, she'd announced she didn't fancy this picture after all and skipped off, leaving the pair of them to enjoy several hours in the warm intimacy of the back row.

On his second visit, shortly after Christmas, he'd walked up to them from the Hampstead Road lock.

'Canals will be frozen solid higher up,' he'd said, holding his hands gratefully to the blaze in Nana's grate. 'They'll have to send the ice-breakers in.'

'Will you lose money?'

'A bit, maybe. But rest of the boats are locked in too.'

He gratefully took the drink Nana had brewed and winked his thanks when she tipped in the 'medicinal' brandy. 'I just come up to say thanks. Addie liked the presents.'

'Rubbish. I'll wager she did nothing of the sort.'

'Fair enough. I lied. *I'm not wearing this stupid girl's stuff* . . .' He mimicked his sister's higher tones. 'Except she didn't say stupid.'

'She'll change. Once she finds a young man she's sweet on.' Nana stood up again, grunting at the pressure on her knees. 'Well, I'm off upstairs to beat Ludovic at chess. There's some bread in the kitchen. Put that blaze to use and toast it.'

'But . . . but . . . we're going to the pictures, Nana,' Iris had protested.

'No we're not. That young man didn't come all this way for the pleasure of *my* company. There's a tin of sardines somewhere. Throw that cat out before you open them.'

She'd gone, leaving Iris and Taz alone in the warmly lit flat, its blacked-out windows shutting out the world, and the soft glow of the fire flickering over Taz's cinnamon-shaded skin and dancing in his deep brown eyes.

Disconcerted, she'd said, 'How is business, Mr Dixon?'

'Not too bad, thank you, Miss Cutter,' he'd grinned.

'Oh. Good.' Iris sat down on the sofa, her backbone stiff with tension.

'Tell you the truth,' Taz said, sitting next to her. 'It ain't too good. Thought I'd pick up more loads with all the war transport, but carrying companies are putting on more boats themselves.'

'I'm sorry.' Now that the conversation was on a commonplace track, Iris relaxed slightly. 'What will you do?'

'Carrying company wants me to turn over *Rainbow* and *Crock* to them. They'd guarantee me loads and they'd do all the maintenance. And they'd pay a regular wage.'

'But you'd have to call them master.'

'Yep. That's it. If it wasn't for Addie I'd loan them the boats for the war and join up. Get myself on a battleship and maybe go see the world.'

Images had flashed through Iris's mind. Shots of convoys braving heaving seas that lashed the cinema screen in the Pathé newsreels. She wasn't stupid, and could easily imagine how it really was behind the flag-waving propaganda that the Ministry of Information allowed into the news reports. They didn't tell you about the depth charges and the drownings and the men slowly dying in icy cold waters.

'But you'd have officers. Lots of them. Captains, admirals, petty officers . . .' She'd racked her brains trying to dredge up naval ranks. Her awkwardness at finding herself alone with Taz had evaporated in her agitation. She'd twisted to face him and looked earnestly into his eyes.

A glint of amusement twinkled in them, and the suspicion that she was being teased suddenly took root. 'You're not really going to join up at all, are you?'

'I doubt they'd let me. Occupation being reserved like. Let's go get that supper, shall we?'

They'd ended up slicing crumbling doorsteps of bread and crouching on the rug to hold them on a toasting fork. Margarine and the oil from the sardines had run down their chins. Taz had reached over to wipe Iris's face clean, using first her handkerchief, then his thumb, and finally his lips.

After an initial murmur of resistance, Iris had responded. When Taz had started to push her gently back on to the rug, she'd been conscious only of a desire for this to go on for ever and ever.

The cat had saved her that time. Scenting the fish oil on their faces it had tried to lick them clean with its pink sandpapery tongue. Its determined head, with its ticklish whiskers and plaintive meows, had kept intruding between their lips. Iris had started to giggle at Taz's exasperated expression . . .

'Iris? Darling, are you all right?'

With a gasp, Iris jerked her thoughts back to the present. She'd been daydreaming in front of the dressing-table mirror. Now, as usual, the scar, followed by her face, leapt into focus.

Her mother came into the room, anxiety creasing her round face. Ursula was forty-five, the same age as her husband, but time had been kind to her – there was no grey in the waved brown hair, few lines in the pale skin, and all her muscles were winning the battle against gravity. She sat down beside her daughter now, a white and manicured hand clasping a bracelet to the opposite wrist. 'Fasten this catch for me, please. They make the wretched things so small these days.'

Iris looked more closely at her mother. Under the drift of face powder, she seemed rather pale. 'Are you feeling bad? Would you rather have a tray in your room?'

'Of course not. We have guests. I shall make an effort.' Ursula patted her daughter's hand. 'Were you worrying about the scar? You mustn't, darling. We hardly notice it any more. Now come on downstairs. I think your uncle and aunt have already arrived.'

Arms linked, they made their way downstairs. A lot of the neighbouring three-storey houses with their capacious basements were shared by several families. But Ursula had always insisted on keeping their home to themselves. Even in the lean years, when they'd only been able to afford to heat a couple of rooms, she'd refused to allow lodgers into the home.

So the Cutters had shivered in draughty rooms, and had

locked the doors when the girl came twice a week to whiten the step, black-lead the grates and help out with the laundry, so that she couldn't see how little furniture they had.

As business had improved the rooms had been opened up and the coal cellars filled, until finally they had achieved the three things Ursula had set her heart on: a full-time maid, a small car and a fur jacket.

If Ursula had had her way they would have moved to a more prestigious address in Highgate or Hampstead as well, but Fred liked to be near the business, and saw nothing wrong with living among working folk. He even saw it as an asset when it came to getting on the council.

'Let them see I'm like them,' he'd say. 'Not one of these blokes who's never got his hands dirty. Pete and me can still lay a brick wall faster than any man in the yard, you know.'

Ursula did know. Mainly because he told her once a week. So the Fred Cutters had stayed in Bartholomew Road and Ursula had comforted herself with the fact that the motor car that stood against the kerb outside plainly marked them out as being a class above their neighbours.

As they descended the staircase, the slap of flat lace-up shoes along the hall tiles announced the passage of the maid from the basement stairs to the front parlour.

'Doris. Have our guests arrived?'

Doris stopped and peered upwards. 'They're all 'ere.'

'Madam,' Ursula prompted.

'The old madam come first,' Doris agreed blithely.

Iris felt her mother's gentle sigh of exasperation. Doris was hard-working and obliging, but she'd never lived up to Ursula's ideals for the perfect servant. However, they could hardly get rid of her now. Not with so many women going into war work that no doubt paid a great deal more than a general maid's wage.

'We'll take luncheon in five minutes then,' Ursula said.

'Luncheon be blowed,' her husband snorted, coming down the stairs behind them. 'We'll have our dinner same as usual, Doris.'

Doris giggled. 'Yes, sir. I'm just laying out them horses doovrays like the missus said.'

'Horse? Good heavens, Urse, meat rationing's not got that tight, has it?'

'She means *hors d'oeuvres*. I thought they would make an elegant change from soup.' Ursula blocked her husband's path. Standing one step below him, she took the tie he was struggling with and jiggled the knot into place under the starched collar points.

The gesture was uncomfortably similar to the one Iris had witnessed in Selfridges. She bit her lip. Her parents seemed as easy with each other as they'd ever been. Over his wife's shoulder, Fred caught Iris's eye and raised his eyebrows, inviting her to share the gentle fun they'd always enjoyed at his wife's pretensions. With a tight smile, Iris preceded her parents downstairs and into the dining room.

The *horses doovrays* proved to be cold potatoes, cold leeks, beetroot and sardines neatly arranged on huge willow pattern dinner plates. They were followed by an enormous Yorkshire pudding and a very much smaller sliver of beef.

'May I pass you some roast potatoes, Nana?' Ursula asked. 'At least they aren't in short supply.'

'How would you know? You've not started doing your own queuing, have you?'

Ursula smiled serenely at her husband's mother. She was used to Nana Cutter's acerbic tongue. 'Doris and Iris promise me that I can be extravagant with the vegetables. They're such godsends – I really can't think how I'd manage without either of them . . .'

'You'd have to do a bit of work, I daresay.'

Kate hurriedly diverted the conversation. 'I hear the trek to the East End was worthwhile, Fred.'

'Certainly was, my dear. Plenty of work out there. What Hitler has knocked down, Cutters shall rebuild. At a very tidy profit, I have to say.'

Yesterday's meeting had been called in response to a necessity to start repairing some of the damage caused by the three-month blitz at the end of last year, before the housing problem became too acute.

The brothers exchanged a look of complacent satisfaction. They'd retained the close physical resemblance that had been so obvious in the photographs of their earlier years, although a settled family life and regular meals had put more flesh on Fred. Age had faded the Cutter colouring in their irises, so the mauve no longer had the startling intensity of their children's, and the black hair was now lightly frosted with grey.

'Skilled labour is not going to be that easy to come by. There's not that many left over conscription age, anyway,' Kate said.

'Government's releasing 'em. Temporary discharge from service until this lot's straightened. And Sir Warren Fisher, God bless him, is giving what's left a deferment on their call-ups.' Fred happily smeared horseradish on his meagre portion of the meat. 'Best contact the labour exchange. Let 'em know we're taking on.'

'I'll do it tomorrow. First thing.'

'Don't know how we'd manage without you. Do you, Pete?'

'No.'

It was a simple response, but the way he said it brought a faint flush to Kate's cheeks. Rather too brightly she said, 'Did I tell you I'm a member of the Street Fire Party?'

'Same here,' Nana said, nodding enthusiastically. 'Ludovic and I do it together. Although he always insists on wearing the helmet.'

'Mother!' Pete stared at her. 'You're too old. And how old's Ludovic, for heaven's sake?'

'He's seventy-two. And we can yell "Fire" as loud as the next man, I'll have you know. Even if Ludo's teeth do tend to shoot across the road when he does it.'

Fred blew a breath – half exasperation, half admiration – through his own teeth. 'If you won't move to the country . . .'

'I won't,' his mother snapped instantly. 'What would I do in some hotel in the middle of a load of fields?'

'Then I wish you'd come and live with us, Mum. There's plenty of room – isn't there, Urse?'

'Certainly. If that's what Nana would like.'

Ursula's expression stayed serene. She knew perfectly well it wasn't what her mother-in-law would like. They'd had the same conversation several times a month since the year her father-in-law had died and Nana had packed up, moved into a flat off Maitland Park, and declared her intention of not being a burden to any of her family.

Of course, she'd been a relatively young widow then; as she became more infirm it might be necessary to make other arrangements. Helping herself to more Brussels sprouts, Ursula wondered whether it would be best to persuade Pete or Kate to move to more suitable accommodation. She was well aware that Nana would never choose to live with her and Fred. The mutual antipathy that had always festered in their relationship was only bearable if they could keep their contact to family occasions such as this. It was surprising that Fred had never noticed. But then, being a man he had a facility for only seeing what it was comfortable to see. There seemed to be another crisis brewing right under his nose that he plainly hadn't noticed. She'd have to find the right moment to point it out to him.

Indicating to Doris to clear the dinner plates, Ursula apologised for the strange look of the rice pudding.

'We had to make it with condensed milk,' Iris explained. 'I had to save the fresh for Mummy's bedtime drink.'

'Never mind,' Pete said. 'Khaki – very patriotic. We'll be showing a bit of solidarity with young Ernest. Any news from that front?'

From Ernest's latest letter, the conversation drifted to the call-up, reserved occupations and the boaters.

'Get that one tied to the wharf sorted out, did you?' Fred asked, scraping his pudding dish noisily despite his wife's small frown of correction.

'More or less,' his brother answered. 'The bloke's gone round the Whitcher scrap merchant to get a bit of welding done. Iris not tell you?'

'I pointed out the road to him,' Iris said quickly. 'He was grateful. He said he'd be able to get his boat fixed this afternoon, and be away again by the morning.'

Her voice was casual, but the eyes on her grandmother held a message. The old lady gave no sign whether she understood or not.

'Pansy's boyfriend found a horse for them,' Kate said,

daintily laying down her spoon. 'They hauled the butty round to Camden Wharf.'

'Is it still young Maurice?' Ursula asked.

'Of course. I don't think Pansy would look at another boy. They're much too young, of course. But the call-up will sort the problem out. Either she'll grow tired of waiting for him, or she *will* wait and they'll both be old enough by the time this war ends.'

No one contradicted her. The early hopes and promises that this war would all be over by last Christmas had dissolved with Dunkirk and the recent bombing blitz. It was now tacitly accepted that there was a long fight ahead.

'He seems a pleasant young man,' Ursula said. 'Rather an odd taste in clothes, but apart from that . . . Something to do with the retail business, isn't he? Comestibles, I believe he said. Whatever they are.'

She looked round the table. The only person who could have told her that they were meat pies and mugs of tea from a couple of mobile food vans chose not to do so. 'What does the father do?' Ursula asked.

'He's dead,' Kate replied. 'But I think he was a bus driver.'

'Nothing wrong with that,' Fred said, leaning back in his chair and hooking his thumbs under his waistcoat to ease a certain pleasant tightness. 'Good, honest working man's job. Sort of people who keep this country running smoothly.'

'Come down off the platform, dear,' his wife advised. 'You have our votes already. We'll take coffee now, Doris.'

Nana Cutter suddenly broke into noisy hacking coughs.

'Has something stuck?' Fred struggled to thrust his chair back. 'Hit her on the back quick, Iris.'

'No need.' Gasping for air, Nana waved the girl away and fumbled for an edge of lace to dab at her watering eyes. 'Touch of bronchitis. Don't you worry about it.' She exploded in another series of dry rasping coughs.

'Well, that settles it. You're not going home tonight. Iris, put a hot water bottle in the spare room.'

'Don't you tell me what I can and can't do, Fred Cutter. I'm still your mother, and I prefer to sleep in my own bed.'

73

'But, Mum, you shouldn't be on your own. What if you were taken ill during the night?'

'Ludo and I have a system. I'll bang on the ceiling with the broom.'

'Mum, I won't hear of it . . . You *must* stay. Tell her, Urse.'

'Possibly just for the one night . . . We wouldn't force you to stay longer if you didn't wish to, Nana.'

'I won't. I'm not in my dotage yet . . . oh dear . . .' Seizing her water glass, Nana drowned another paroxysm.

'Mother, I insist—'.

'I want my own bed.' Nana's lips set in a stubborn line. Then relaxed. 'I've an idea, though. Maybe Iris wouldn't mind sleeping up her old gran's place tonight?' She turned a feeble and pleading look on her granddaughter, who was probably the only person at the table who detected the mischievous gleam in the black eyes.

'I suppose . . .' Iris looked to her parents for her cue.

'Go on,' her father said promptly. 'I'll stop here until Doris comes in the morning. Your mum won't be on her own. And see you call out the doctor if he's needed, understand?'

'Well that's settled,' Nana murmured in an even more feeble tone. 'You can spend a cosy evening with just your old gran for company.' She directed a look of languid helplessness across the table.

Iris bit the inside of her cheek. Once more, anticipation and dread at the idea of an evening in Taz Dixon's company churned her insides.

Hours later, once the blacked-out house was quiet and deserted except for the two of them, Ursula sat in bed watching her husband set out the Thermos, dressing gowns and torches handily, in case they needed to go down to the Anderson shelter during the night.

'Did you notice how . . . friendly Peter and Kate were?' she asked.

'Always have been, haven't they?'

'Yes. But I meant . . . *particularly* friendly.'

'How do you mean?' Lifting up the eiderdown, Fred slid in beside her.

'For heaven's sake, don't be so obtuse! You know perfectly well what I mean.'

'Oh?' Fred turned this idea over in his head, then gave his opinion that nothing would come of it. 'Can't, can it? I mean, I know there's not much chance of Ellie marching back home . . . Well, must be how long?'

'Fifteen years at least.'

'Must be. But Pete's never divorced her. Although I daresay he could for desertion. But there wouldn't be no point if it's Kate he's got his eye on making the second Mrs Pete Cutter. You can't marry your brother's widow.'

'I know that. But it doesn't have to be a *formal* marriage, does it?'

'What – you mean . . . live over the brush?' Fred considered this novel view of two people he'd known intimately for years. The idea made him chuckle. 'Well, well . . . that would be a turn up, wouldn't it? Mind, I wouldn't have thought Kate would . . . Not the sort.'

'How do we know what sort she is? We never knew much about her *before* Bernie married her. And we've found out precious little since.'

'She's an orphan. Parents kept a shop up Birmingham way.'

'So she said. But that isn't the point.'

'What is, then?'

Ursula drew in a sharp breath at his obtuseness. 'Your father's wretched will is.' She turned, resting her weight on one arm on the pillow. The movement caused her nightdress to open a little at the front, revealing a glimpse of surprisingly large breasts. 'At the moment, if Pete dies first, Cutter's will pass in its entirety to you. And you can pass it on to Ernest. If, heaven forbid, *you* die first, the business will go to Pete. But he's hardly likely to leave it to that idiot son of his, is he? So it will still come to Ernest in the end. But if he and Kate—'

'You're thinking of young Pansy? No, he'd not do that – any more than I'd leave it to Iris. This business needs a man at the helm.'

'For heaven's sake, Fred, I'm not thinking anything of the sort! Kate is still a young woman. She can't be more than – what? Thirty-five? Easily enough time to produce another son.'

Her husband grappled with this even more bizarre idea. 'Yes . . . But he'd not be a Cutter.'

'Why not? It's Kate's surname, isn't it?'

'I suppose it is . . . Well, well, well . . .'

'Is that all you can say? We're discussing Ernest's inheritance. He's been brought up to expect to take over Cutter's.' Ursula placed a palm on her husband's chest and her voice softened. 'Promise me you'll take care of our son's future.'

Fred patted her hand reassuringly. 'Course I will. Don't you worry, Urse.'

'Thank you. Could we have the light out now?'

Grunting Fred fiddled with the cord on the bedside lamp. By the time he'd rolled back, Ursula had moved over to her own side of the bed. But his body had reacted to the sight of those partially exposed breasts and the touch of soft fingers on his skin. 'Urse?' He located the top of her thigh, massaging it under the silky material of her nightdress.

Ursula turned away from him, wriggling to the very edge of the mattress. After a brief moment of struggling with an impulse to demand his rights, Fred turned his back and moved back to his side of the mattress. They slept as they had done every night since her pregnancy with the twins had been confirmed – in the same bed, but quite alone.

Chapter 9

'Hello, Maury's mum.'

Eileen jumped and took several deep breaths to steady her heart which had leapt into her throat. Her hearing had been fully occupied by the water in the copper coming to the boil, a stream of cold tap-water rinsing out the pile of laundry sitting in the scullery sink, and the kettle and several saucepans rattling on the gas cooker. Now she'd turned back from peering out of the steam-covered window and assessing the likelihood of getting anything dry outside, to find the kitchen door blocked by that huge ox Maury had brought round for his dinner yesterday.

'How did you get in?'

'Joshua came in the front door. Came along that passage.'

He turned to point out the hall passage as if Eileen, who'd lived in this house for most of her married life, might have somehow missed this structural feature.

'Didn't your mother teach you to knock?'

'Joshua can't remember.' He shuffled the large feet again, his startling eyes fixed intently on her.

'Well? What do you want?'

'See Maury.' Joshua beamed proudly. 'We're mates.'

'He's not here. But he'll be back very soon,' Eileen added quickly.

'Good.' Joshua nodded his satisfaction. Taking one hand from behind his back he extended half a dozen wilting daffodils, their stems already crushed by his fierce grip. 'For you.'

'Me?' Eileen was temporarily flummoxed. She couldn't remember when anyone had ever given her flowers.

'Ladies like flowers. Joshua's Auntie Kate likes them. My dad bought her flowers. She was pleased. She put them in a vase.'

There was a vase on the mantelpiece in the best room, but Eileen preferred to stay where she was: with the door to the back garden comfortingly near her back. She found a milk bottle and arranged the blooms in that.

'There. Now I can see them while I do me washing. You get along and I'll tell Maury you were looking for him.'

'Joshua can wait here. Maury will be back very soon.'

Joshua was regarding the boiling copper with fascination. The rolling bubbles were popping in clouds of steam. He reached out and touched the scalding water.

'Don't do that!' With an instinct honed by keeping six sets of tiny fingers from doing just the same thing, Eileen snatched the hand out, pulled Joshua to the sink and thrust it under the stream of cold water still cascading over the rinsing sheets.

'Let me see,' she instructed when she finally released it.

Joshua obediently spread the huge fingers.

'I've no butter to spare to put on them,' Eileen said briskly. 'You'll have to suck them. For mercy's sake, didn't your mum teach you not to touch scalding water?'

He took out the saliva-covered digits to mumble that he couldn't remember. 'She used to sing to Joshua. And play games. And make cakes like . . .' His wet forefingers and thumbs formed a triangular shape.

'Pyramids. She made you coconut pyramids did she, love?' Now he'd been reduced to the level of one of her sillier sons, Eileen found him less intimidating.

'Pyramids,' Joshua agreed.

'But not any more?'

'Went away when Joshua was little. To be an angel.'

'Ange . . . Oh, I see. Well, I'm very sorry to hear that. I expect you miss her.'

'Yes. Joshua would like to have a proper mum. Not like Ernest and Iris's mum. She's not like a real mum. Not like Pansy's mum because Auntie Kate is nice but works in my dad's office. Joshua wants one like you. Doing washing and cooking. You're a proper mum.'

Touched at the picture of the little boy, motherless and unloved, coming home to an empty house, Eileen patted his cheek in a gesture of comfort.

Before she knew what was happening, Joshua had swept her up in both arms and was gripping her in a fierce bear-hug, crushing all the air from her lungs.

Panicking, she beat her fists on his shoulders and kicked.

Another voice snapped sharply from behind them: 'Let her go this instant!'

Joshua could recognise authority when he heard it. But instead of lowering Eileen, he simply spread his arms out to the side and she dropped to the linoleum, putting out a hand to steady herself against the mangle.

Eileen extended the other one to prevent Sarah McNeill from using the rolling pin she'd snatched up from the kitchen and was now holding over her shoulder like a truncheon. 'It's all right, Sarah,' she managed to gasp. 'He didn't mean no harm. He just don't know his own strength.'

'I can see that. You're not to do that again. Understand?'

Joshua, bewildered but ever willing to obey orders – especially if issued by police officers in uniform – nodded and shuffled.

'Not cuddle Maury's mum any more. Right. Joshua won't.' He dared to raise his eyes and look Sarah full in the face. His own expression brightened. 'You're that lady who had dinner with Joshua yesterday.'

'But not much of it, Joshua.'

The ironic tone was lost on Joshua, who'd eaten his way through everything on the table yesterday like a starving hog.

'I brought my meat ration round, Eileen.' Sarah passed over a small package. 'Not much I'm afraid, but it might help out this week.'

'Don't be daft, love. I don't want your rations.'

But Sarah insisted. 'I can eat up the police canteen.' She pushed the package at Eileen. 'I must go. I'm on duty – I shouldn't really be here. Shall I see Joshua out?'

Eileen looked at the crestfallen young man. She was no longer scared; he was just like a large, untrained puppy that didn't know how to behave. 'No. He can stop here and wait for Maury. He can give me a hand with the washing. You'll not mind doing that, will you, Joshua?'

No, he didn't mind at all. It was one of the things he liked best, helping.

Under Eileen's direction, he lifted the heavy, soaking laundry, wrung, folded, mangled and pegged out.

'Well, love,' Eileen said finally, rolling her sleeves back down. 'That's the easiest wash day I've ever had. I could use you again. And just in time too. Here's the children home for their dinner.'

The crash of the front door being thrust back on its hinges followed by the thunder of feet announced the arrival of her youngest, Sammy, and Annie Stamford, the little girl she minded. They both skidded to a halt at the sight of Eileen's assistant.

'Oh, blimey. He ain't gonna eat all our dinner today too, is he?'

'Watch your manners, Sammy O'Day, or all you'll be getting for your dinner is my hand across the back of your legs.'

'But *Mum* . . .'

'Wash your hands and sit down now. Have you seen Maury?'

'He's coming now.'

The news that his mate had been waiting for him most of the morning didn't seem to fill Maury with unalloyed joy. 'Why?' he said baldly.

'Joshua wants to ask you something.'

'Go on then.' Maury drew out a chair and sat himself at the kitchen table, which his mother was laying up.

Eileen glared at him. 'What are you waiting for?'

'Me din . . . You never meant it, Mum?'

'I did,' Eileen informed him.

As soon as Joshua and Felonious Monk had left on Sunday, she'd read the riot act to Maury about inviting people round without giving her any warning – particularly those who'd spent the best years of their lives as guests of His Majesty, or looked like they ought to be. And she'd finished with the warning that he wouldn't be eating at home for the next week, so he'd better make other arrangements.

She folded her arms now and continued to stare down at him.

Maury shrugged and stood up again. 'I was going to check on me investments anyway.'

He sauntered out again, flicking his hat off the peg stand as he passed through the hall.

Joshua hung eagerly on his shoulder. 'Where we going, Maury?'

'I told you – I'm going to check on me investments. What did yer want to ask me? If you want the borrow of another horse for the boats, you can go ask yourself.'

'Boat's gone. Dad wants to buy another horse. Joshua is going to look after it. Not what Joshua wanted to ask.'

'Well spit it out then.'

'Joshua wants to get a girl.'

'What?' Maury stopped and gaped up at his huge shadow.

'A girl, Maury. The girl from the boat. The one with the hair like a horse's mane. Joshua wants her to be his girl. What should Joshua do?'

'Well, don't tell her her hair's like a horse's mane for a start. Say it's like silk or something. They like to hear daft things like that.'

'Silk,' Joshua repeated obediently. 'What else?'

Maury considered. He couldn't think of anything more ridiculous than the idea of any girl wanting to go out with Joshua Cutter. On the other hand, the experience of somebody actually asking for his advice was quite novel. With all those older brothers he was more used to being given it – whether he wanted it or not. 'Well, you could ask her out somewhere. Take her for a walk up the heath. If it ain't cold enough to freeze your . . . well, never mind. Otherwise you'll have to ask her up the pictures. Sit in the back row.'

'Why?'

'Because . . . Well, just watch what everyone else is doing, OK?'

'OK.'

Satisfied that he'd done his bit for romance, Maury strode

down Marsden Street. Shoulders back and with the slightest swagger in his walk, he imitated the American gangsters in the films. No one pushed those blokes around. Just see them coming and people stepped back into doorways to clear the pavement for them. That was the sort of respect Maury wanted. But so far it was proving difficult to come by.

Take 'Busted' Johnson, who ran the hot food van up Queen's Crescent market. Hadn't Maury bailed him out when he'd run into temporary financial difficulties – on account of his inability to believe that, just because the first dozen hands he'd been dealt in a card game were lousy, there was absolutely no reason why the next dozen shouldn't be totally ruinous?

Maury had covered his losses in return for a third share in the future profits from the van. But did he get it?

'Is that it?' Maury demanded, examining the sparse pile of silver and a ten-bob note in his left hand while he munched on a hot meat pie.

'Business is chronic, Maury. It's all these voluntary do-gooders. It's wicked the way they take business from ordinary folk. Everywhere you looks it's canteen vans from the Women's Voluntary Service, the Auxiliary Fire Service, the YMCA, the Salvation Army and heaven knows who. There just ain't the customers to go round. Look for yourself.'

It was true enough, customers were sparser than bananas in the market at present. But what else did you expect on a Monday morning? There had been plenty of trade on Friday and Saturday. Maury knew, because he'd made a point of slipping up to check.

He scowled. 'You're holding out on me, Busted.'

Busted shrugged. 'Matter of opinion, ain't it, Maury? I'm telling you that's a fair share.'

Despite being six inches shorter than Busted, Maury thrust his face into the older man's, and said threateningly, 'Hand over the rest, or I'll have to take it orf yer.'

'You can try if you like, son.' Busted was unimpressed. He lit a Woodbine and blew an untroubled cloud of blue smoke over Maury's head.

Snatching the burning cigarette from the man's lips, Maury ground it under his heel.

'Hey! The old girl had to queue for those . . .'

Busted took hold of Maury's lapels, lifted him on to his toes and shook him.

The next minute, Maury was standing back on his own feet, looking down at Busted, who was sprawled the length of his van, vaguely fending off the mugs and utensils that were raining down on him from the serving counter. Several costers looked over at the noise, decided it was none of their business, and went back to calling their wares.

'Joshua didn't hit him too hard, did he, Maury?'

A perplexed frown screwed Joshua's heavy eyebrows down over his eerie, lavender eyes. He was puzzled by the effects of a little tap from his huge right hand.

Staggering upright, Busted found himself confronted by over six foot of muscles wearing an apparently vicious scowl and limbering up his right fist before smashing it into Busted's face again.

'You met my mate Joshua?' Maury enquired lightly.

'Maury's mate . . .' Joshua smiled, baring all his teeth. To the already rattled Busted he looked like a cannibal preparing for the next meal.

He stepped back. 'Pleased to meet you, I'm sure.'

'You'll be meeting him again very soon . . . If you're certain these takings are right . . . ?' Maury rattled the cash in his pocket significantly.

Busted drew the back of his arm over his nose, turning the wiry hairs from grey to rust. 'Maybe I did miscount a bit . . . Just 'ang on there a minute.' He reached under the counter for an old tin cash box, inserted the key hanging from a string on his belt, and scrabbled out two pound notes. 'That it?'

Maury was prepared to argue, but a warning whistle from a neighbouring market stall followed by a hissed 'Rozzer' sent the cash into his pocket and Busted back into the van. By the time the uniformed copper passed on his routine beat, Busted was swabbing down the back counters with a disinfectant-soaked dishcloth, and Maury and his shadow were casually browsing their way out of the market and towards Maury's other 'investment'.

The van by St Pancras station was run by the last owner's widow. She had little sense of managing money, but none the less her eyes widened in disbelief when she was informed that Maury was collecting near enough four pounds a week from his other van.

'Oh, I can't manage that, Mr O'Day. It's such a muddle . . . I don't know where the money goes . . .'

Maury informed her that he didn't expect her to pay out four pounds a week. 'But I'll expect three minimum from now on. Understand?'

'Three! But I'm not sure. I'll never—'

'Have you met my mate Joshua?'

Maisie had. He was currently munching his way through a currant bun filled with margarine and jam that Maury had given him without asking her.

'He's ever so strong. Show the lady how you can pick up that end.'

The van was a four-wheel trailer. Joshua bent his knees at the tow-bar end, flexed his arms, put his huge hands underneath and heaved upward. He only succeeded in tilting it a fraction, but it was enough to send food, crockery and utensils crashing to the floor. Maisie swayed, grabbing at the swinging cupboard. The gas pipe that ran through the back wall to power the urns and burners creaked warningly.

'Put me down! All right, Mr O'Day – three pounds it is.'

'Stop messing up the lady's van, Joshua. Stick it back down.'

Joshua did as his mate told him.

'Where we going now, Maury?' he asked eagerly, following him back into the Euston Road.

'Well, I'm going home. You'd best do the same.'

'Joshua could come home and help Maury's mum some more.'

'No. I don't think me mum wants any more help today, Josh. Tell you what, though . . . You know the Golden Cross?'

'It's a pub.'

'Yeah, I know that, Josh. I'll meet you there at . . .'

Maury made a few calculations. Hanging around in pubs was always a problem since he was under age and his lack of height made it virtually impossible to get away with pretending otherwise. But Joshua was turning out to be a lucky charm . . . and with his 'mate's' help, Griswald might put Maury in touch with those who dealt in the serious black market.

'Meet me at seven. I've a feeling we're going to have a good night, Josh, you and me.'

Chapter 10

The bar was packed already. That suited Maury; crowds meant anonymity.

He'd never been in the Golden Cross before, but it had looked classy enough from what you could see in the blackout. A three-storey Victorian building standing on a corner site in a square of big terraced houses, sandwiched between the Hampstead Road and Eversholt Street.

The promised clearance of the day had continued into the night, resulting in a virtually cloudless sky sprinkled with early stars and an icy nip to the air. It had provided enough light for Maury to make out the sandbagged searchlight battery and see the surreptitious glints of shielded fags wreathed in small clouds of frosted breath as he'd walked across the wide street listening to the almost inevitable crash and rumble of trains being shunted through Euston Station. Taking a deep breath, he had pushed open the pub door, slipped between the double curtaining system that prevented light spilling into the street, and stepped into the public bar.

Joshua was sitting on a stool at the end of a bench seat. As soon as he spotted Maury he rose and lumbered forward eagerly. 'Joshua came at seven o'clock like you said.'

'Good man.' Maury looked over to the big clock on the wall. It was a quarter past and there was no sign of Griswald. But then you wouldn't expect to find a white-collared manager in this area. The outside of the Golden Cross was deceptive. The public bar was uncompromisingly a working man's pub, with its scrubbed floors still covered in sawdust, solid wooden furniture and walls permeated with the thick fug of cheap tobacco that hung in a heavy cloud under a plastered ceiling stained brown with age and nicotine. It was doubtful if this room had changed much in the past fifty years.

Despite – or perhaps because of – the decor, the Golden Cross was plainly popular with the staff from the nearby railway stations and goods depots. Most of the men in here seemed to be connected in some way or other to either the rail companies or the engineering sheds.

All except the group of soldiers lined up along the polished bar bantering with the barmaid as she drew pints of bitter. From what Maury could make out they were due to relieve the crew on the searchlight battery. But to a man they preferred to stay inside in the warm and flirt with the pert piece on the pumps.

She didn't seem to object to the arrangement. Her hand brushed a wrist and slid down fingers as she took a ten shilling note for the round. A ribald remark as she stood ringing up the change brought a sharp response that was softened by a slow provocative look over one shoulder. Handing over the man's change, she tossed back thick black hair, a gesture which caused her breasts to push against her white blouse.

It was a polished performance in teasing. Even Maury, his mind still full of Pansy's parting cuddle half an hour ago, was momentarily attracted.

You couldn't call her pretty; her narrow face, with its green, cat-like eyes, was almost sly. And her figure wasn't any more than average. But she had a way of using them both that sort of promised that things could be very different if she took fancy to you.

Maury nudged Joshua forward, pushing a two shillings into his palm. 'Ask for a pint of bitter and half of lemonade.'

The woman nodded and pushed a pot under one of the pumps. ''Ello, Maury. I'm goin' up the clink Thursday – d'yer want me to give Eddie your love?'

Already calculating his best approach to Griswald, it took Maury a second to drag his mind back to the present, and then send it a few weeks back into the past to that damned bungled whisky robbery. He focused on the barmaid again.

'Carla Rosetti,' she prompted.

'Oh? Yeah.' He'd seen her with Eddie a couple of times, but

the change of surroundings had thrown him for a moment. 'How are yer, Carla?'

'Fair to damned, ta. Yourself?'

'Not bad thanks.' He watched her put the full pint on the counter and unscrew a bottle of lemonade. Any contact – however tenuous – with Eddie Hooper was to be avoided. But Eddie had that signed confession he'd extracted from Maury as a promise for keeping his mouth shut. And Maury definitely needed to keep in touch with that incriminating sheet of paper. Because while it existed Eddie was always going to have a hold on him – no matter how high he and Pansy went in the future.

'Who's the big boy then, Maury? Ain't I gonna get an introduction?'

'Joshua Cutter. A mate.'

'Maury's mate.' Joshua reached forward to shake hands. Carla took the big paw. 'Pleased to meet you.'

Maury asked, 'You still seeing Eddie then? Even though he's . . . yer know . . .'

'On remand? Yeah, seemed the least I could do. He was always good to me, Eddie.'

Maury forced a laugh. 'Glad to hear you're being true, Carla. I heard this rumour you was going with a coster up Queen's Crescent market.'

'Yeah. I step out with one some nights.'

'But you're engaged to him, I heard.'

Carla shrugged. 'If he wants to think so. That's one and a penny please, love.'

She put money in the till and handed over Joshua's change in pennies. He laboriously started to count each separate coin, sliding it down his palm as he did so.

'Any of Eddie's other mates going up the prison?' Maury asked casually.

'I ain't never seen none. You want to come?'

He certainly didn't. In fact he never wanted to see Eddie Hooper again if he could help it. 'Best not. Might give the coppers ideas. You know, what with Eddie swearing blind I had nothing to do with his . . .' 'Thieving' seemed a bit tactless. '. . . With his business dealings,' Maury finished.

'Fair enough. I'll tell him yer were asking after 'im.'

'Yeah. You do that. Fact is, Carla, I'm here on a bit of business meself. You know a bloke called Griswald?'

'The landlord?' She indicated a plaque Maury hadn't noticed, stuck to the wall by the till. It indicated that Terence Cecil Griswald was licensed to sell intoxicating beverages on these premises.

'One I want works up the ABC bakery.'

'That's Verne, Terry's brother. 'Ang on.' Going to the end of the bar, Carla rose on tiptoe and craned her neck, scanning the lounge bar at the rear of the premises. 'He ain't in yet. Comes in most evenings, though.'

Maury looked round and selected a corner seat farthest from the bar. 'Be over there. Give us a call when he arrives?'

'Hokey-doke.'

Maury picked up the lemonade and indicated to Joshua to follow him. Once they were seated out of sight, he put his lemonade glass in front of the big man and took the pint. 'Best not have that, Josh. Beer can do funny things to those that ain't used to it. Where's me change?'

Joshua handed over the pile of coins. 'There's eleven, Maury. Joshua counted them.'

Maury dropped them into his waistcoat and took a sip of beer, trying not to make a face as the sour-tasting liquid slid down. He'd have preferred the lemonade but sharp dealers didn't drink kids' pop. He settled back to wait for Verne.

It was a long wait. Joshua gulped his way through four glasses of lemonade and – despite nursing the warm liquid carefully – Maury had to buy another pint. Carla served it with a wink that indicated she knew whose throat it was intended for.

'You sure he's coming?'

'Ain't no guarantees in life, Maury. But he's in here most nights.'

He spent another hour playing Joshua at shove ha'penny and darts. Surprisingly the large, ungainly frame hid a delicate touch and a sure eye, and Joshua beat him every time. Once he'd got over his initial resentment at suddenly finding their relationship turned on its head, Maury used the situation to his advantage by challenging a couple of railway workers to a doubles match and taking five bob off them.

'Thanks, gents,' he said confidently, pocketing the two half crowns.

'What about yer mate's 'alf?' one asked.

'We're partners. What's his is mine and what's mine's mine. Ain't that right, Josh?'

'Partners.' Josh nodded happy confirmation. 'There's Uncle Fred.' He pointed. Peering through the fug that now hung like a tangible blanket over the bar, Maury made out one of the Pansy's uncles threading his way from the lounge bar towards the front door. He called his farewell across to the room. To Joshua, Maury assumed. But it was Carla who lifted her head from the pump and purred a throaty 'Goodnight, Mr Cutter.'

'Know him, do you?' Maury asked, pushing his way to the counter.

'He comes in sometimes. Yer'd be surprised at the people I know. There's someone you want ter know just come in . . .' She jerked a thumb over her shoulder at the lounge bar.

'Is he on his own?'

'Is now. He'll talk to the boss after he closes up. They got a private bottle.'

Maury flexed his shoulders. This was it. 'What's he drink?'

'Scotch.'

'Give me a large one.'

Verne Griswald greeted the drink with pleasure and Maury with blank indifference.

'We met, son?'

'Up the wharf Sunday. Maurice O'Day. My girl works for yer – Pansy Cutter. Family owns Cutter's Contractors and Building Merchants,' he added hurriedly, just in case Griswald thought he was dealing with a nobody.

'Oh yes, young Pansy. Well, cheers . . . much appreciated.' He tipped the Scotch in one quick movement. 'Not having one yourself?'

Maury hadn't liked to bring the beer through in case the landlord, who was serving over this side, started asking to check his identity card. And there was no way he was

91

sitting here nursing a lemonade. 'Got one keeping warm next door.'

'Right. Well . . .' Verne Griswald wasn't sure what more was expected of him.

When Maury told him, it didn't have the expected result. He'd rather hoped for a men-of-the-world exchange of information. What he got was a sharp jab in the chest that nearly knocked him off the bar stool and an angry face thrust in his while he was informed that Vernon Griswald didn't deal in stolen goods and if he started repeating talk like that he'd be very sorry. 'Understand, son?'

Another rigid forefinger hit the centre of his waistcoat. He wished he hadn't told Joshua to wait in the other bar; the idea of this smug little bully being dumped on the threadbare carpets was very appealing. Taking a deep breath, Maury made himself speak calmly.

'I never meant to suggest yer did, Mr Griswald. It's just . . . us both being businessmen, I thought you might be able to put me in the way of a suitable supplier. I'm by way of being a bit of a general trader . . .' He was pleased with that description. It sounded almost exotic. 'So if you was to be hearing of any *particular* opportunities, I'd be very appreciative . . .' He took out his wallet, which he'd taken care to fill before he set out. Much of the space was taken up with torn newspaper, but it looked impressive.

'What sort of *opportunities* had you in mind?'

That was better. Maury relaxed a little. 'My distribution is pretty flexible. I was thinking of food . . .'

'Got a licence to sell from the Food Control Committee have you?'

'No. Course I ain't.'

'Won't be needing any *opportunities* then, will you? Thanks for the drink.'

It was a clear dismissal. Maury might have argued if Carla hadn't appeared in the bar. Stooping, she took a bottle of blackcurrant cordial from a lower shelf. As she turned to go, she caught Maury's eye and indicated that he should follow.

She stepped through the flap that separated the two bars,

but Maury had to go round. By the time he regained the public room she was serving cordial and stout. He had to wait for the sickly mixture to be paid for before Carla came back down the bar, vigorously wiping up spills along the counter.

'All that beer you've sunk, Maury, you must be busting by now . . .'

'No. I ain't.'

Carla's cat's eyes narrowed.

'Yeah, well, now yer mention it . . . Where's the, er . . .'

'Straight through the back.'

The small lavatory block was younger than the public house. Leaning against the back wall it was cold, unwelcoming and designed to discourage lingering. Bolting himself in a cubicle, Maury relieved himself of the two pints, pulled the chain loudly and then sat on the seat and waited.

The outside door opened and closed. Footsteps walked up and down the row, pausing at each cubicle. He heard the wooden doors creak slightly on their hinges as they were pushed wide. Finally the feet stopped.

'You the geezer looking to buy?'

Maury slid the bolt back and sauntered out. It was one of the dart players Joshua had taken for five bob.

'Might be. What you offering?'

'Beef. Wannit?'

'If the price is right.'

'Tenpence a pound.'

It was a good deal. They were paying double that at the butcher's for a decent cut.

'Eight.'

'That a joke?'

'No.' Trying to stop his hands shaking with excitement, Maury held them under the single tap, deliberately keeping his back to the man.

'Nine.'

'Eight. Take it or leave it.' Flicking water from his cuffs, Maury dried himself on the grubby slip of towel.

'Eight, then. But you'll need to collect it by Saturday.'

Maury nodded. He offered a newly washed hand. His new partner's was ingrained with coal-dust. 'Stoker,' he said, rubbing it off on the seat of his trousers. 'Twenty odd years.'

'So, where'd I collect this meat from?'

'Goods yards. There's a gate. I'll let yer through. Make it eleven o'clock. And bring the cash. All of it.'

'How much you got?'

'Hundred and twenty pounds a carcass. Thirty carcasses.'

Maury just managed to keep his jaw from hitting his chest. 'Where the hell did you get that much meat?'

The stoker licked his lips nervously. Even his spittle had the greyish tinge of coal-dust. 'It's condemned.' Seeing the alarm in Maury's eyes he added hurriedly, 'It's OK. Nothing wrong wiv it, honest to God.'

'What's it been condemned for then? Woodworm?'

'Ya what? Nah. It were a raid, weren't it? All the wagons got plastered by Jerry. Anyhow, they haul them down here, stick 'em in a siding 'til the salvage squad from the Ministry of Food can give the OK for them to destroy the stuff. They have to say, see . . . for the insurance. So me and my mate decides to 'ave a look inside.'

'So what you find?'

The grey worm emerged from the porthole of his mouth again. It flicked nervously over the dried lips. 'There was this one wagon – hadn't 'ardly a scratch. So we moved it. Puts it somewhere nice and snug and sticks a different one in its place.'

'Empty?'

The man shrugged. 'Who's to say it wasn't before? They do hitch empty wagons on sometimes.'

'What about this salvage squad?'

'They looks at the food, don' they? If there ain't no food in the wagon they ain't going to bother with it.'

'Someone must have a record.'

''Spect they do. But by the time they miss that load, it's gonna be long gone and you and me's gonna be that much richer. Ain't we, mate?'

Maury hesitated. The truth was he hadn't the money. His total capital at present amounted to just over sixty quid. And he was going to have to get a lorry from somewhere. To give himself time to think, he asked how long the meat had been standing around.

'Three, four days tops. It ain't gone, I swear. It's been brass monkey weather, ain't it?'

It wasn't quite that bad. But the temperature had certainly been low enough to keep meat in outside meat safes fresh. Maury made up his mind. 'Where'd I fetch this van to?'

The man dipped a finger in the sooty spittle and drew a map on the cracked washroom mirror, using the back of his sleeve to wipe it off as soon as he was sure Maury had got it.

'Bring all the dibs.' The stoker rubbed his fingers together. 'No rhino, no beef.'

He left, chuckling at his own joke.

Carla was leaning against the wall in the darkened passage when Maury stepped through the back door into the pub. 'OK, Maury?' she asked.

'Yeah. Fine. Ta, Carla.'

She raised her cigarette. 'Got a light?'

He didn't actually smoke himself. Like the beer, he disliked the taste. But a case and lighter were part of his image. He'd picked them up in a pawnshop. In dim lighting the worn patches in the rolled gold overlay hardly showed at all.

He would have liked to return to the bar, but the way she was leaning, with one leg stretched and the other bent against the wall behind her, made it difficult to get past.

'How old are you, Maury?'

He was tempted to lie, but recalling that artful glance as she'd served the beer, he guessed she already knew he was under eighteen. 'Seventeen . . . going on eighteen.' Going on for the next ten months if he was being honest. 'How old are you?'

'Ain't polite to ask a lady's age.'

'Maybe I ain't a polite sort of bloke.'

'Thanks, Maury.'

'What for?'

'Most blokes would've said I weren't no lady.'

'So, how old are you then?'

'Twenty-three.'

She brought her cat's eyes down from her contemplation

of the ceiling and looked directly at him. 'We're alike you and me, Maury.'

'Are we?'

'Yeah. We both know what we want out of life. And we both intend to get it.' Pushing herself from the wall, she put down the bent leg and drew back the other, leaving him enough room to get past. Her eyes returned to the wreaths of blue smoke curling upwards from her open mouth.

The implied dismissal annoyed Maury, but at the same time he found himself secretly rather flattered that she saw something akin to herself in him. Returning to the bar, he collected Joshua and set off for Eversholt Street. It was early enough for the buses to be still running – with any luck he'd be able to jump on one going up to Kentish Town.

They'd scarcely gone half a dozen steps in the darkness when the rising wail of the air-raid warning filled the night. Maury glanced down to the south-east and saw the questing searchlight beams lancing into the blackness. South of the river, he guessed – maybe they were going for the docks again.

But the silver patterns came closer, criss-crossing over the West End, and then up across Bloomsbury. The searchlight in the square behind them burst into illumination at the same time as the air to the south was filled with exploding ack-ack shells and the deeper, throaty roar of the bombers vibrated in the distance. The air above the square was suddenly filled with light, and an incendiary hit the road with a crash ahead of Maury, followed by several others in quick succession. He contemptuously kicked a fizzling cylinder into the gutter, looked round for something to dump on top of it but was unable to find anything.

Best to get away, he thought. If they'd dropped incendiaries, the high explosives could follow next. He started running.

Suddenly a screaming roar, like a massive sheet of silk being ripped in two, filled the air, and behind them a building exploded in a roar of shattering brick and crashing glass. It was far enough away for them to feel no more than the blast of hot air on the backs of their neck, but Maury's hat flew off and bowled along the pavement ahead of them.

'Bloody hell!'

A figure was striding towards them. The striped wristband and white-painted P on his tin helmet stood out even in the blackout. Overcoming his innate distrust of coppers, Maury yelled, 'Where's the nearest shelter?'

'Follow your nose. Harrington Square. Street shelter.'

Maury sprinted forward, hearing Joshua's heavy feet and easy breathing lumbering behind him. The guns ahead of them in Regent's Park were already sending up streams of exploding shells.

There was a succession of explosions behind them, a second between each, as the bombs reached their targets.

The street shelter was easily spotted, its squat brick shape further strengthened by a barricade of sandbags. Maury flung himself at the dark doorway.

It seemed to illuminate as he reached it. A roaring filled his ears and he appeared to be flying, his feet a few inches above the pavement. Then the floor came up to meet him and a tremendous weight crushed the air from his lungs.

Chapter 11

'You all right, Maury?'

Joshua's large face loomed over him as it had done a dozen times during the past night. He seemed to take his part in Maury's recent injuries very seriously. Which he damn well should, Maury thought resentfully, sitting up cautiously and wincing as his ribs protested again.

The blast last night, which had sent him face-first into the shelter floor, had also picked up Joshua and dumped him on top of Maury's sprawling figure. Maury had ended up winded, bruised and minus a chip of his front tooth.

The only good thing had been the fact they'd had the shelter to themselves, apart from an ARP warden who'd been assigned as shelter marshal.

'No one to organise most nights,' she had said regretfully. 'I don't know why. I suppose they go down their cellars or the underground stations. Still, it lets me get on with my knitting. You two sort yourselves out?'

Since there hadn't been much to do but curl up uncomfortably on the rudimentary bench seats, they had both nodded.

The warden had seemed to feel the need to provide a running commentary. Each roar of sound was greeted by 'S'gun', or 'S'bomb'. In between, she knitted. The end of each row had been marked by a squishing click, as she'd sucked down the top set of her dentures. Occasionally she had wondered aloud why more of the locals didn't use the shelter.

The all-clear had been sounded at three o'clock, when the warden had left, clanking into the darkness with her knitting, her Thermos flask, her stirrup pump and her ill-fitting false teeth.

'Are we going home too, Maury?'

'Suppose.' Rolling off the bench, Maury groaned. His unconventional bed had added a stiff neck to his other aches. Outside there had been the inevitable stink of cordite and burning in the air, but at least the clear skies had provided a little starlight. They'd started northwards.

'There's a fire, Maury.' Joshua pointed. 'Something's burning.'

'Brilliant. Just bloody brilliant . . .' Maury muttered. His left knee was hurting too. Maybe he'd slept with it twisted under him. He limped onwards. The ghostly white armbands and painted Ws of the wardens seemed to be thicker in Camden High Street. He remembered now. This was where their headquarters was located. His mum had tried to persuade him to come down here and volunteer to be a messenger.

'It's bloody miles up to me house,' he moaned to Joshua. 'And there's no buses this time of night.'

'You could come stop at our home. Joshua's and Joshua's dad's.'

Maury hesitated. The wharf was nearer. And he'd probably get offered some breakfast – which he certainly wouldn't at home.

'Thanks, mate.'

They had been getting nearer the source of the flames they'd seen glowing in the sky earlier. The crackle and spit of burning wood was unmistakable, together with the rush and gurgle of falling water from the firemen's hoses. The more ominous rumbles were followed by warning shouts and the sounds of masonry or stone hitting the ground.

'Look, Maury. It's King Street.'

'It's Plender Street.'

'No, Maury. Joshua remembers his mum bringing him here. Lemonade and crisps. Sit on stairs. Be a good boy. Don't tell. More lemonade next time. King Street.'

'Yeah, well, it *used* to be King Street . . . but now it's . . .' Maury had broken off. What did the name change matter anyway to a bloke who could hardly tell whether it was half past three or Tuesday?

There had been two fire engines standing down the far end

100

of the street. A cloud of dust from a recently collapsed wall had been still rolling over the firemen and heavy rescue workers. It looked like several shops at the end of the row had been hit. The glitter of their smashed glass windows had mingled with the oily glint of spreading hose-water and caused the road surface to sparkle with reflected fireglow. Still, Maury had thought, it might be worth investigating . . .

He'd moved confidently, trying not to think about what all the dirty water and shattered brick was doing to his shoes and trouser bottoms. His eyes had darted eagerly over the piles of twisted wood, brick and metal. There were biscuits spilling from a large barrel, but already reduced to a mush by the firemen's hoses, and . . . Maury had peered closer . . . they were dog biscuits anyway. The place must have been some kind of animal feed store.

The next one had been a paint and paraffin shop. The remains of the foam that had been smothered over it were dripping down the mounds of debris. He'd moved to the end of the row. A shattered board advertising Gold Flake tobacco was twisted in the wreckage. Maury had edged closer. There was always a ready market for cigarettes and rolling shag – especially these days.

A quick look back had confirmed that the emergency services were all busy with the burning shop and the casualties. Technically speaking you could get life for looting . . . not that anyone took much notice. Mostly it was just a case of finders keepers. Even Pat, Maury's irritatingly honest eldest brother, had been known to come home from a fire with a few tins in his uniform pocket.

But it looked like he was out of luck. The emergency services had had first pickings if there had been anything going. He'd started up Camden Street when his foot had jarred painfully against something, nearly tripping him over for the second time that night. With a gasp of pain, he'd hopped on one foot.

Joshua leant down and picked up the obstacle. 'Look, Maury. It's a saucepan. Why did someone leave a saucepan in the street?'

'Probably got blown out of one of the flats over them

bombed shops.' He'd tried to massage his toes through his leather shoes. 'Let's have a look.'

It was solid steel and seemed to have survived its flight without damage. And better still, there were three tins of golden syrup wedged inside. It could be the way back to his mum's dinner table. 'Bring it along, Josh. I just remembered someone was gonna leave it out for me.'

Joshua had carried the heavy weight happily, handing it over when he'd had to take a heavy key from round his neck to unlock the padlocked yard gates. A challenging woof and a threatening snarl had been hushed with a quiet whistle.

'You sure your dad won't mind me staying?' Maury asked, following the large feet up the creaking stairs.

'I don't think so, Maury. Joshua's mate.' Joshua had crept into the darkened room with a clumsy heaviness, panting loudly as he'd reclosed the door, repositioned the blackout curtain and turned on the light. Maury looked round the room. It was better than he'd expected, although still not his idea of how a businessman should live. If he had a half-share in the profits of Cutter's he certainly wouldn't have been living over the shop – so to speak.

'Where do I sleep?'

Joshua pointed to a sofa.

'Ain't you got a bed?'

'Joshua's bed is in there.'

'Let's have a look.'

The plainly furnished bedroom looked reasonably clean. Maury sniffed the bedclothes on the single bed. Not too bad. 'I'll stop here.'

'That's Joshua's bed.'

'But we're mates, aren't we? If you was to stay up our house, I'd let you have my bed.'

Joshua had frowned, thinking this over. Finally he'd arrived at the correct conclusion. 'Joshua will sleep on the sofa.'

'That's the idea.' Dumping the saucepan, Maury stripped off one pillow and a blanket and bundled them into Josh's arms. 'Here yer are. Make yourself comfortable.'

Josh opened the wardrobe and removed a wooden hanger. 'Get undressed first.' He looked behind him as a sleepy Pete

102

Cutter had suddenly appeared in the bedroom door. 'Hello, Dad. I've been to the pub with Maury. He's Joshua's mate. We played darts. Joshua won.'

Pete thrust a hand through his hair, causing it to stand on end. 'I didn't think you'd be back tonight.' He looked at Maury. 'Spending the night at your place, son. That's what he told me.'

He looked at Maury. Who shrugged. Who knew what went on in Joshua's head? If his dad didn't what chance had the rest of them?

'Spend a good night with Maury, that's what he said. I thought you were having some sort of do up your place.'

Maury couldn't see what the bloke was so aggrieved about. He'd taken his pride and joy off his hands for most of the night, hadn't he?

'Sleeping in here are you, son?'

'Joshua wouldn't have it any other way. Reckoned he'd be up good and early to cook me breakfast.'

'Breakfast? Breakfast . . . of course.' An odd look slid over Pete Cutter's face. He nodded as if making up his mind. 'Well goodnight then son. What's left of it.'

He shut the bedroom door as he left. A little too casually for Maury's liking. Sliding off the bed, he crept across the room and applied his ear to the crack.

The conversation was disappointingly ordinary. It seemed the Cutters were out of milk. 'Take the jug . . . the big white one . . . first thing. Go up your Uncle Fred's house . . . back door mind . . . wait for that girl of theirs to come. Ask if she can spare us a drop for our breakfasts. Got that?'

Joshua had repeated his orders, and then added that he'd rather go round his Auntie Kate's.

'No! Don't you go bothering your Auntie Kate. Uncle Fred's, understand? And take the dog with you – give him a bit of a walk.'

Waiting until he heard Pete's door reclose, Maury walked quietly back to the bed and lay on top. He couldn't be bothered to undress for the sake of a couple of hours sleep at most. Burying his cheek into the pillow, he'd closed his eyes and fallen into an uneasy doze.

*　　*　　*

He woke up feeling stiff and sore. And cold. He should have got under the blankets after all. Lying in the dark, he tried to detect a sign of life in the flat. All was quiet. It must be too early for Josh's errand.

He looked round for something to do until breakfast. There were no books in the room, not even an old newspaper. It was hardly surprising. He wondered idly if Joshua could actually read. Probably not – they usually sat you at the back of the class and told you to weave raffia mats if you were soft in the head. Maury had had a daft lump like that in his class up Riley Street. They'd sent him off to the loony bin when he got too big to manage. Why hadn't the Cutters done that with Joshua? Perhaps they would eventually. He must already be costing them a blooming fortune in food, judging by the way he'd eaten most of the O'Days' rations in a single sitting last Sunday.

Recalling the way that roast had disappeared into Joshua's steadily champing jaws brought his mind back to his mum's withdrawal of her catering services. And from there it jumped to the 'present' he'd just acquired for her.

He dragged the heavy saucepan from under the bed and examined it more closely in the daylight. It looked fairly new, and the outside didn't appear to have been scratched. If the inside was OK too he could give it a quick wash and polish and give it to her for her birthday. He'd use the syrup to bargain his way back to the dinner table.

The Tate & Lyle tins were wedged firmly inside. Twisting and jiggling, Maury managed to lever one free. Its weight told him something was wrong. It was too light. 'Don't tell me I've got someone's bloody button collection,' he muttered under his breath, trying to lever off the lid with his nails.

He shook it against his ear. Nothing rattled. At least that was hopeful. Maybe it was tea. Or dried fruit. Anything on ration or scarce would be very acceptable. Taking a pocket-knife from his jacket, he inserted the thin blade under the lip and twisted. This time the tin released its grip with a soft 'plop'.

There was a roll of folded paper curved around the circular

enclosure. The thin, creased, grubby edges of banknotes were unmistakable.

Maury's mouth dried with excitement. Inserting one finger, he scooped the money out on to the blanket. The fat sausage unravelled into a pile of one-pound notes. There must be a hundred there at least! His heart thudding noisily, Maury grabbed the next tin, jammed the knife under the lid's lip and ripped it off. Scrabbling with shaking fingers, he added that pile to the one on the bed and tackled the third tin.

He started to count, dividing the thin paper into piles of ten. In the end he had twenty separate stacks ranged over the grey blanket. Two hundred quid!

It was a miracle. Better than that – it was a sign that fate was on his side. He had his stake – enough to cover the cost of the railway beef and fix up a lorry as well. He, Maurice O'Day, was a step nearer to that posh place up Hampstead.

A creak of floorboards outside followed by the low murmur of voices startled him out of his blissful daydream. He scrabbled to collect up the notes. Some eluded him, falling over the sides of the bed and fluttering over the floor. Panicking, he dived after them. Saucepans and rations were fair game, but someone's life savings was another kettle of trouble. If the owner started asking around and Pete Cutter put two and two together, it could lead to another spell in the coppers' den.

He heard the outer door open and heavy steps descending the outside stairs. Joshua was on his way to fetch the milk. Maury risked padding quickly across to the light switch and flicking it off. Had they noticed the gleam under the bedroom door? Even if they had, there was no reason for Pete to come in.

He stood quietly, holding his breath, his hands full of the precious stake money. Soft footsteps crossed the outside room. He sensed Pete Cutter on the other side of the bedroom door, listening as intently as he was.

What was the bloke doing out there? He willed Pete to move away.

Chapter 12

'He's asleep, I reckon.'

'Are you certain sure?' Kate sat on the bed, slipping her shoes on. She had a way of wriggling her toes inside first and then easing the heels into position that Pete found incredibly erotic. He'd always had a partiality for pretty feet.

Delicate feet had been one of the things that had first attracted him to his wife, Ellie. Kate's were larger and higher-instepped, but none the less when he remembered her lying under him last night, one leg sliding delicately up his own until her toes were gently massaging the back of his knee . . . He reached out for her.

Kate evaded him. 'Don't, please, Pete. I have to go before Joshua gets back – or Maury wakes up.'

'Does it really matter? Let the whole damn world know, I say. We're both free.'

'You aren't.'

'Ellie? You can't be worrying about her. It's been years. I'll go see a solicitor, see if he can fix me up with a divorce if that's what's bothering you, Katie. I reckon fifteen years is long enough to prove desertion.'

'Keep your voice down,' Kate whispered urgently. 'And what good would a divorce do? I can't undo my marriage to Bernie. I'm your brother's widow, Pete. We can't ever marry . . .'

'There's those that live together . . . happily, too. I could make you happy, Katie—'

'I know. But I have to be certain sure . . .' She touched his arm lightly and brushed his cheek. 'Be patient, Pete.'

'I'm trying, but God knows it ain't easy. I want to shout it to the world: I love Kate Cutter. I want to parade you up the High Street on my arm. I want to buy you things . . . decent things, not second-hand rubbish like this . . .'

'There's second-hand and second-hand.' Kate wrapped the fine beige wool around herself and snuggled the thick, dark-brown Astrakhan collar up around her ears. 'This cost fifty guineas new. Imagine anyone paying that for a coat.'

'I'd pay it if it was for you.'

'Then I'm certain sure I shouldn't have you, Pete Cutter. Because you'd plainly be insane.' Kate drew her breath back sharply, wishing she could catch the words back as she realised what she'd said. 'Oh, Pete, I'm sorry, I didn't mean—'

'That it was me responsible for how Joshua is?' He drew her close by the lapels of the coat and kissed her tenderly. 'I know you didn't, Katie.'

'I'm very fond of Joshua, Pete.'

'And he's taken with you. We could be a proper little family, Kate. You and me, Josh and Pansy.'

'I know.' Gently she loosened herself from his grip. 'But I need a bit more time. Wait a little longer – or find someone else if you can't.'

'I don't want anyone else, Katie. I'll wait. Long as it takes.'

'I'd best go before Joshua gets back.'

The coldness of the morning took her by surprise after the warmth of the bed and Pete's body. She hadn't intended to stay the night. She never had before. But the air-raid warning had started when they'd been lying in each other's arms, lazy and sated and not wanting to spoil the moment.

'Do you want to go down the shelter?' Pete had murmured into her neck.

'No. Do you?'

'What do you think?'

They'd woken later to the sound of Joshua crashing around in the living room. And so Kate had been trapped until the morning. The only blessing was that Maury hadn't been sleeping on the sofa, she reflected ruefully. Otherwise she'd probably have been stuck in the bedroom until the men started arriving for work. And that would have been the end of her secret affair.

She knew Pete wouldn't have minded. But, as she'd told Pansy, it was the woman who got the blame – so she was the one who had to be certain sure.

Unlocking the gate chains with her own key, she made her way into the dark streets. Guessing that Joshua would probably take the direct route down College Street, she made her way westwards, using the streets and bridges to follow the route of the canal.

Letting herself into the Kelly Street house quietly, she turned on the lights, lit the gas and filled a bowl with hot water. The house had a bath. One of the few in the road that did. It sat against the kitchen wall, with a levered top they let down to use as a table and a tiny gas heater that took forever to fill. Though Kate had plenty of time to run one now, older habits prevailed and she set the bowl on top of the wooden table and had a strip wash instead.

When she'd finished she put on clean underwear and outer clothes and stored the ones she'd been wearing out of sight in the bottom of her own wardrobe. She'd have to remember to rescue them next washday. It was stupid, but somehow she was always convinced Pansy would smell the sex on her one day and be disappointed . . . or shocked. The effect on her daughter was one more thing that had to be considered if she and Pete decided to live together openly.

She suddenly felt an overwhelming need to talk to someone.

Turning the lights out, she flicked back the curtains and let herself out of the house. It still appeared to be the middle of the night, despite the fact the clocks said seven o'clock. How many more winters, she wondered, before the lights were switched on again? Despite the army's successes in Africa against the Italians there didn't seem much hope of this awful fighting and bombing ever ending. Perhaps Pete was right and they should grab at their chance of happiness now. Who was to say they had a future to plan for?

'Stop it!' She shivered violently and took a deep breath.

109

She wouldn't think like that. You had to believe everything was going to be all right.

Hurrying up to the Prince of Wales Road, Kate turned left, followed it as far as Queen's Crescent, then walked briskly up that road. Several women pushed prams loaded high with bedding, toddlers clinging to their skirts, while older children trailed behind, called cheery good mornings as they trooped home from another night spent in the Hampstead underground station.

Nana Cutter opened the door to Kate and let her in without comment.

'I was passing . . .' Kate explained, making her way into the kitchen.

'I often go for walks on cold dark winter mornings myself,' Nana agreed. 'Take a seat. I'll put the kettle on. Have you had your breakfast?'

'No. But I won't eat your rations, Nana.'

'You'll eat what I see fit to put in front of you. It's one of the joys of old age – you're allowed to turn into a bully and call it eccentricity. Now, sit yourself down.'

Kate settled herself at the big wooden table, drawing pleasure from the room as usual. It was a strange house, this; it appeared to have been designed by an architect with a fixation for the middle ages as portrayed by a Hollywood film studio – with crenellated battlements, polished wood and coloured glass windows. Nana had rented the lower floors when her husband died. At present the upper ones were occupied by a retired music teacher.

'Did the raid disturb you?' Kate asked.

'No. I'm a great believer in the saying "When your time's up the good Lord will call you".'

Disappearing into the larder, Nana bustled back with a china basin half full of cold porridge and started patting it into cakes and covering them with breadcrumbs as they talked. 'Pansy well?'

'Very well. She stayed at her friend Lottie's house last night. I hate it when she's away from home . . . in case anything were to happen. But if it did . . .'

'There'd probably be precious little you could do anyway. Don't you go wrapping Pansy in cotton wool. We've enough of that with Ursula keeping that girl of hers tied so tight to her apron strings the poor thing's near choking to death.'

'She worries about . . .' Kate touched her own cheek. None of the family ever openly referred to Iris's scar.

'Rubbish. What frets Ursula is the idea of losing an unpaid companion. I don't know what gets into men when they go chasing brides. Present company excepted, of course. You were always the best of the bunch.'

'Ursula might not agree with you. Not if she knew where I came from.'

'None of her business. Anyway, what's she got to be high and mighty about? Her father was nothing but a back-street chemist. I always thought she was an artful little thing. But Fred couldn't see it. Mind, the will took her down a peg or two. She was sure Fred was going to get the business outright. I'll never forget the look on her face when the solicitor read out the bit about all three of the boys sharing Cutter's.' Lighting the gas ring, she wiped two greasy rashers of bacon over the bottom of the frying pan and set the porridge cakes to fry before asking Kate if she could keep a secret.

'Why? What have you been up to?'

With a twinkle in her black eyes, Nana told her about Iris and Taz Dixon.

'Nana! You shouldn't have . . . I mean, you must know that Fred and Ursula would never allow anything to come of it. And even if they would . . . it's a hard life . . . Iris hasn't been brought up to it . . .'

With a snort of impatience Nana flipped the sizzling cakes over and added the bacon rashers to the pan. 'There's plenty of girls doing what they've not been raised to these days. Anyway, I'm not match-making. He's a bit of a scamp, that one; not husband material at all. I just wanted Iris to have a bit of an adventure. Knock some backbone into the girl before it's too late.'

'And if her parents find out?'

'Might be for the best. A good juicy row is just what's needed if you ask me.'

111

A plate of fried cakes and bacon was banged down in front of Kate. She added salt and vinegar and cut off a slice before asking, 'Nana . . . what was Ellie like? I mean,' she continued hurriedly, 'I know I knew her . . . but I never really took much notice. She was just . . . Ellie,' she finished lamely.

Luckily Nana seemed to understand. 'You and Bernie were so wrapped up in each other and little Pansy those first couple of years I doubt you'd have noticed if Ellie had had two heads. Not that she had . . . She wasn't what you'd call pretty – well, not what *I'd* have called pretty,' Nana amended.

'I remember what she looked like. I didn't mean . . . I meant what was she *like*? I remember her as being . . . bright.'

'Bright?' Nana considered this description for a moment and agreed that it fitted well enough. 'Shall I tell you who puts me in mind of her? That little red-headed girl from the boats. Dixon's sister.'

'Addie Dixon? How do you know her?'

'Long story . . . Thing is, she's not got Ellie's looks but there's something about her . . . She's a bit of life burning in there – a bit of spark like I wish Iris had.'

'Why did Pete marry her?'

'Lust. Same for her, I reckon.'

Kate blinked. She hadn't meant to blurt out the question like that. But she'd been even less prepared for the answer.

'Oh, don't look at me like that! I've enough with one prim-and-proper daughter-in-law. Do you think my generation don't know what passion is? Put Pete and Ellie in the same room together and it was like sitting in a meadow with a summer storm brewing – there was that much electricity in the air it made all the hairs on your arms stand up. They were a wild pair. Both as hot-tempered as each other. I doubt there was a pot in Ellie's kitchen that hadn't been thrown at Pete's head before they were six months wed.'

'Pete's not hot-tempered. He's one of the most even-tempered men I know.'

'Not as a child. Always the devil of my trio, Pete was. Had a temper on him that was so fierce it scared me sometimes. I think that's where Joshua got it from. I know everyone thinks it's because the boy is addled, but I'd not discount what's bred in the bone myself. Pete changed after Ellie left. It was like they were a pair of flints. Without each other to spark off, there was no blaze.'

'Why did she leave . . . if things were really as you said?'

'Joshua,' Nana said baldly. 'Things were never the same after he was a year or so. At first he looked normal enough, but as he got bigger and didn't pick things up like other babies . . . well, I reckon Ellie started to fret about giving birth to another one that was soft in the head. She wouldn't let Pete near her, although he was keen enough still. Made no sense. There's no other idiots on our side of the family . . . could just as easily have come from bad blood on her side. But you can't argue with what's inside you. Ellie was ripe for someone to sweep her off her feet. And Aloysius Barber had more practice with that particular broom than most.'

'I remember him. Very charming.'

'And very dishonest. Two hundred pounds they say he took from the office safe.'

'Do you think Ellie knew . . . about the money, I mean?'

Nana considered. 'I'd say so. She liked comfort, Ellie. She'd not have run away to starve in an attic.'

'Do you think they'll ever come back?'

'I can't speak for her. But Aloysius would be a fool to show his face around here. The police have long memories. Will you have him?'

'What?'

'I'm not blind. It's plain as the nose on your face that Pete wants you. I'm asking if you'll take him.'

'I can't . . . Bernie . . . the church won't let us.'

'Not official. Not sanctioned by a vicar. But that's never stopped others.'

'That's what Pete said. But it's different for a man. If we'd been able to go away somewhere . . . somewhere we weren't known . . . But we can't leave Cutter's. And it's me that will—'

' . . . have to stand in the ration queues and hear the whispering behind you,' Nana finished. 'Well, I can't deny that. It's your reputation that will be lost, not Pete's. Men can get away with what we can't – it's always been the way.'

They'd finished eating. Nana collected up the plates and poured a weak second cup of tea from the pot. 'Do you love him?'

'I don't know. I think so . . . It's all so *strange*. I've only ever loved Bernie before. And I think I did right from that first day in the park. He just made my stomach turn over and my heart beat so fast I couldn't breathe. And I was certain sure at that moment. But Pete . . . He's been like a brother, I suppose . . . for years. I thought no more or less of him than . . . well, Fred.'

She couldn't even remember the moment when being in Pete's company had stopped being routine and become something to be treasured and gone over in her mind when she was alone. 'Would you mind?' she asked Nana. 'If Pete and I were to live together?'

'Why should I? In fact . . .' she admitted with a twinkle in her eyes. 'I'd quite enjoy breaking the news to Ursula.'

'You're a wicked old woman.'

'I know. Fun isn't it?'

The clock on the kitchen shelf clanged its noisy chimes. Startled, Kate jumped to her feet. 'It's half past eight. I didn't realise . . . I must run.'

'Don't wait too long, Kate. Promise?'

'I promise. Goodbye, Nana.'

The light had started to wash over the houses. It promised a cold, crisp morning. Good working weather for the men. Kate hurried on, aware that the drivers would be waiting to pick up delivery dockets.

And Pete would be there, in the office, waiting for her. Her heart fluttered and a tightness closed over her chest that had nothing to do with her rush through the chilly winter air.

114

Chapter 13

As soon as he'd started making plans to collect the meat from the goods yard, it had occurred to Maury that he didn't actually know how much space a full-sized carcass would take up. Mentally drawing on half-recalled pictures in kids' picture books, he reckoned cows were about the same size as horses.

Mooching along towards Torriano Avenue, he came across Felonious on his milk deliveries and stood in thoughtful contemplation of the bad-tempered skewbald – until Fel reappeared with a crateful of empties and asked him what he thought he was doing.

'Trying to think what he'd look like without his head. And his feet.'

''Orizontal. He'd fall over, wouldn't he?' Fel dumped the crate and climbed up on the cart. 'Not that that ain't how he's likely to end up. She's selling up the dairy, ain't she? Gonna keep a boarding house with her sister. So that's him and me out of a job.'

Maury sensed an opportunity. 'That definite, then? You won't be wanting the horse no more?'

'I *never* wanted him. Stupid four-footed glue pot. Why?'

'Just might take him off your hands. Tell Mrs Thomas I'll be round later to see if we can come to a deal.'

'I'm sure that'll fair make her day, son. Giddup!'

Kitchener shambled on towards his stable and Maury mooched southwards. He was going to need a fair-sized lorry by the looks of it. And somewhere to store the meat afterwards until he could find a buyer. He was almost tempted to pull out of the deal; he wasn't in a position to handle something that

115

size yet. Turning into Camden Road, he was startled back to the present by a sharp whistle and a shouted, 'Whatcha, Maury.'

Maury blinked the face in front of him into focus. One of the Andrews twins – he never could tell them apart. They'd been in his class at Riley Street School.

''Lo, Percy,' he said without enthusiasm. 'How are you?'

'I'm Horace. Can't grumble, thanks.' Horace's round, freckled face broke into a happy beam. 'I'm doing pretty well, matter of fact. You hear I got a job as a pageboy up West after I left Riley Street?'

'No.'

'Davenish Hotel . . . Fancier than the Ritz and the Savoy. There's all sorts stop there. Sirs and ladies every week.'

'That's nice.' Maury tried to step round his old classmate.

Horry shuffled sideways, still keen to catch up on the past three years. 'Yeah, it is. And guess what? I've been promoted. Under-footman. And they've promised to keep me job open when I get called up.'

'I'm very happy for yer, Percy . . .'

'Horace . . . Percy works down Dingwall's . . . makes packing cases. We both fell on our feet, I reckon . . . Good steady jobs to come back to after we've whopped the Germans. How about you, Maury – what you doing?'

Maury straightened his shoulders. Was that what he wanted? Forty years in a dead-end factory job or grovelling to those that thought they was better than him because they had the money and he didn't? If he couldn't handle a big deal now, then when would he be able to?

'Got me own business, matter of fact, Horry . . . Must go. Got to meet a contact.'

He only had one useful contact that he could think of. And he didn't know where she lived.

The Golden Cross was closed. A passer-by seeing him rattling the double doors informed him the boozer only opened evenings nowadays. 'There's a war on, haven't you heard?'

Maury didn't even bother to reply to that well-worn joke. He wasn't giving up that easily. No one shouted or challenged

116

him as he made his way to the back and climbed over the yard wall. He slapped the door with the flat of his hand. 'Hello! Anybody 'ome? Mr Griswald, can I have a word? Oi!' He attacked the wood with more enthusiasm.

'Knock off that bleedin' row, can't yer!'

Maury stepped back and looked up. Carla – one hand holding a dressing gown closed over her breasts – was leaning from a top window.

'Oh. 'Ello, Maury.'

He'd only intended to ask Griswald for her address. It hadn't occurred to him that she actually lived over the pub.

'Hang on. I'll be down in half a mo.'

By the time she slid the bolts on the back door she'd re-tied the robe more securely, but seemed totally unabashed that he'd caught her half-dressed.

'Been 'aving a lie in. No sense getting up if yer don't have to,' she explained, leading him up the winding staircases.

The top corridor was just bare floorboards. Maury caught a glimpse of a claw-footed bathtub in one room. Carla stopped at the door opposite. 'In 'ere.'

The dark, heavy bedroom furniture was old-fashioned, but it gleamed with the soft sheen of regular polishing, and his nose detected the fragrance of lavender and beeswax. Clearing her clothes off a chair, Carla invited him to sit down and disappeared behind a Chinese lacquered screen set across one corner of the room. A second later the robe appeared over the top.

'Didn't know you lived in, Carla.'

'Yeah. It ain't so bad. See I got me own bath over the way? Griswald 'ad it put in years ago. They was gonna take in lodgers. War's done for that. Course he's always sneaking up here 'oping to get an eyeful of me in me birthday suit.'

'Does he?'

'Depends. Sometimes I give him a quick flash. Keeps him sweet. It's all he does do – look. There's plenty who've wanted more.'

She re-emerged, fastening her skirt over a jade green jumper, and extracted two stockings from the jumble of clothes she'd dumped off the chair. Sitting on the bed, she

117

concertinaed the first stocking down to the toe, slipped it on and smoothed it up her calf, over the knee, and attached it to the suspenders dangling against her thigh.

Maury tried to keep his jaw from falling open while she repeated the performance with the other leg. Despite his determined courtship of Pansy, he'd never actually seen anything above her knees.

Standing up, Carla hitched her skirt and turned her back on him. 'Me seams straight?'

'Yeah . . . yeah, they're fine.'

'Good.' She dropped the hemline. 'I know there's a lot saves their stockings for best these days, but I don' feel dressed wivout them. And there's always someone knows how to lay their hands on a pair.'

'Yeah . . . Talking about laying your hands on things, I need a bit of help, Carla.'

'Tusker's meat?'

'That his name – Tusker?'

'One of 'em . . . Probably best you don' know, innit?' Taking a packet of Players from her bag, she put one in her mouth and leant forward.

Maury produced his lighter. 'Fact is . . . I need the loan of a lorry.' Belatedly he remembered her landlord's creeping habits. He jerked his head towards the carpet and lowered his voice. 'Is Griswald . . . ?'

'He's out. I can get you a lorry, I reckon. Cost yer, mind. What you plannin' after you've done the pick-up?'

'Stick it in a shed . . . basement, maybe. Go round the butchers . . .'

Carla shook her head decisively. 'It ain't gonna last for ever, Maury. Longer it stands, more chance of someone nosing it out. Best get yer buyers fixed up first. That's what Tusker should 'ave done, but he ain't used to big deals . . . And I don't reckon you ought to go for butchers . . .'

'Why not?'

'They all suddenly start 'aving a free hand with the steak and chops, someone's gonna notice how they suddenly got the longest queues this side of the river. Best put it somewhere they can sort of slide it on to the plates, no questions asked.'

118

'Like where?'

'Hotels. Restaurants. Posh ones, mind. The more money people 'ave, the less they think they ought to be giving up.'

It made a certain sort of sense. He told her about the Davenish Hotel.

'There yer are, then. There's our first customer.'

'*Our* customer?'

Carla narrowed her eyes in that cat-like fashion of hers. 'I gotcha the deal, didn't I, Maury? Tusker wouldn't 'ave gone near yer if I hadn't put in a good word.'

'Why did you?'

Carla uncrossed her legs and brushed flakes of ash from her skirt. 'Things Eddie said. He reckoned you was on the up. Or would be one day. That's why he wanted that letter. Eddie ain't too bright, but he figures to ride up on yer coat-tails, Maury.'

So she knew about that damn confession too. At this rate Hooper might as well have put an advertisement in the *St Pancras Gazette*.

Carla fixed her gooseberry-coloured eyes on him. 'I ain't greedy, Maury. I know you're putting up the cash . . . You 'ave got it?'

He nodded.

'But I can help you. I'll get you the lorry. And I can find yer other buyers. I know places.'

'And what do you get out of it?'

'Ten per cent this time. And if things work out, maybe we could go equal partners on other deals? I've got a bit put by. I ain't planning to stay one step up from the gutter all me life neither.'

Maury hesitated. It sounded OK. Ten per cent was reasonable if she could really do all she said. And as for the other deals, time would tell.

He stuck out his hand. Carla spat into her palm and slapped it against his. 'Let's go get 'em, partner.'

The Davenish Hotel wasn't as he'd imagined. He'd pictured something big and ritzy with acres of flashy hall. But this one looked like a private house. He thought the bloke in a black

119

frock coat who whipped the door open for them was a guest until he started looking them up and down and asked if 'Sir and Madam' had a reservation.

'We've business with the manager,' Carla said. She didn't bother to try and hide her working-class accent as he might have been tempted to do.

'Have you an appointment?'

'Just tell him it's important. We've something to sell that he'll want to buy.'

'Trade representatives go to the back door.'

'We don't.' She stuck her hands on her hips and shifted her weight to her left leg, allowing the right to bend slightly.

The man looked away first. 'If you'd like to wait here, madam. What name shall I say?'

'Smith.'

With a slight bow, the frock coat made its way to the rear of the hotel.

'Come on.' Carla clicked across the tiled floor and into a room on the left. Selecting a sofa, she sat herself down.

Maury perched beside her, envying her easy self-assurance. The hotel oozed wealth and privilege from its brickwork. He couldn't have said why – some of this furniture wouldn't have raised three farthings in a salvage sale. And his mum wouldn't have been seen dead in the shoes that old biddy at the writing desk was wearing. But it didn't matter. You knew these people were different. This was the sort of world he and Pansy were going to be moving in one day, so he'd better start getting used to it.

He tried to relax, leaning back like Carla was doing and looking round with casual indifference. A kid in a blue uniform with gold buttons and a pill-box hat walked in carrying some kind of notice. He'd got it stuck up over his head like a banner. When he reached them, Carla casually raised her hand and dismissed him with a flick of her wrist. Maury was impressed. It was like she was born to this lark.

Another figure appeared in the doorway. The dark suit and perfect buttonhole plainly said: manager. Maury would have risen if it hadn't been for the warning pressure of Carla's foot against his ankle.

The man came silently over the thick carpet. 'Mrs Smith?'

'Miss.' Carla offered a handshake from her seat. 'And this is my partner, Mr Smith.'

'Should we perhaps adjourn to my office?'

'If you like.'

She preceded them into the hall. Maury saw the man's appreciative glance at her swaying hips and felt better. The bloke was no better than him for all his fancy voice and snooty looks.

The manager's office was a cubby hole at the rear of the building. He settled himself behind his desk, linking his hands on an expensive leather blotter and waited expectantly.

'What about some coffee?' Carla asked.

'Coffee?'

'Still serving it, ain't yer?' Taking out her cigarettes, Carla inserted one between carmine lips. Maury's hand instinctively went to his pocket, but she looked expectantly at the manager.

He slid a table lighter across the desk. 'My time is rather limited, Miss Smith. This is a busy position, as I'm sure you'll appreciate.'

'We can talk as we drink.'

With an audible sigh, the manager went to the door and disappeared back into the hotel.

'Pushing it a bit, ain't yer, Carla?'

'Let 'em see we ain't rubbish, Maury. You start acting like rubbish, that's 'ow they treat yer. We may be the ones selling hooky meat, but he's the one gonna buy it, remember.'

'We hope.'

'He'll buy. See that lot outside? They don't wanna hear "Only two courses allowed, madam", or, "Cellars are empty, sir, no champagne for the duration". They just want *now*.'

The manager reappeared, followed by a geriatric waiter carrying a heavy tray loaded with silver pots and tiny china cups. The waiter was dismissed with an instruction to tell them not to put any calls through for the next ten minutes.

'Now,' the manager relinked his fingers over the virgin sheet of blotting paper. 'You have . . .' He hitched up a crisp shirt cuff to consult his watch. 'Nine minutes and forty-five seconds.'

Carla seemed unimpressed. Taking the smaller silver pot, she added warm milk to her own and Maury's coffee and helped them both to a spoonful of demerera sugar. 'My partner and I are in the meat business. Wholesale.'

'We are quite satisfied with our present suppliers, thank you, Miss Smith.'

'Are yer customers?'

'I beg your pardon?'

'Heard a couple of them talking out there. Reckoned dinner was a bit tough last night.'

'Indeed?' Indecision flitted over the manager's austere features. He didn't believe her, but if there was the possibility . . . ? He was too old for the regular services, but he lived in secret dread of being whisked away from the comfortable position he'd created for himself here and directed into some ghastly factory job making bombs or guns or heaven knows what. If complaints started to reach his employers ears . . . 'If that is so, I shall speak to the chef. Thank you for bringing the matter to my attention.'

'You're welcome, I'm sure. And while yer 'aving a chat with this chef of yours, ask him how he'd fancy cooking a few fat fillet steaks. Or maybe a roast of prime rib?'

'I'm sure he'd be delighted. However, with the present food control restrictions . . .'

'There's restrictions and there's restrictions, ain't there?'

'Are there?'

Stretching out his arm, Maury checked his own watch. 'I reckon we're down to seven minutes. Better stop foxtrotting round each other and get down to business, ain't we?'

Carla's eyes flashed their approval from under the black netting, before she said sharply, 'My partner's right. We ain't got time to waste neither, mister. We've got beef carcasses. Best quality. You won't find nothing better down Smithfield. How many yer want?'

'I'm not sure I require—'

'We're busy people. If you ain't placing an order, we'll be off. But I can tell you this . . . you're gonna be sorry you let this opportunity slip past yer. When it gets round there's other hotels serving prime beef dinners . . . Well, people want a bit of cheering up these days, don't they? Blokes who've got a leave pass deserve a bit of spoiling, don't they, after they been protecting us from invasion and bombing? And they'll be wanting to treat their girls right. Might be the last time for some of them . . .'

Even though most of their clientele was non-military, the manager seized on the suggestion of patriotism as an excellent reason for bypassing the food control regulations. Plus of course making a small personal profit, since the beef was so much more reasonably priced than their usual supplier's stocks.

'When can we expect delivery?'

'Saturday night,' Carla said promptly. 'Maybe early Sunday morning. You live in?'

The manager nodded.

'Tell the porter to fetch yer then. And make sure you got the cash ready . . . We don't drop off until we got the money.' She stood up and thrust out her hand.

After a fractional hesitation, the manager took it. 'Nice doing business with you, Miss Smith.'

'Same here I'm sure, Mr . . . ?'

'Smith.' For the first time the manager's face showed a flash of humour. 'There are a lot of us around these days. Indeed, the wheels of commerce would grind to a halt I fear if our esteemed family weren't assiduously greasing them. Don't you agree, Mr Smith?'

'Too right, mate,' Maury said with heart-felt feeling.

Chapter 14

Joshua was thrilled to hear that his mate wanted him to come out again when Maury ran him to earth at the wharf.

'Go to pub?'

'No. Yes.' It might, Maury realised, be best to pick up Josh down in Euston rather than collect him from the wharf. If he was seen by the Cutters in a strange lorry with Carla Rosetti it could lead to a lot of awkward questions. 'I'll see you in the pub at half past nine. Tell your dad yer definitely going to stay up our house all night this time,' he instructed Joshua, remembering how put out Pete Cutter had been last time by him turning up with Josh at three o'clock in the morning.

Joshua's smile became even broader. 'See Maury's mum.'

'Yeah, well . . . you might do.'

Joshua clasped his knees and leant forward on the stack of cement bags he was using as a seat. 'She's back.'

'Who is?'

'Me girl.'

'You've got a girl?'

'Going to ask her. Like you said.' Joshua stood up and beckoned to Maury to follow him to the edge of one of the storage sheds. Standing half hidden behind it, he peeked round.

Puzzled, Maury strolled over and crouched behind him. The *Rainbow* and the *Crock of Gold* were moored up alongside Cutter's Wharf. Taz and Addie Dixon were clambering over the cargo section of the motor, untying strings and rolling back tarpaulins.

'See? Joshua's girl.'

Maury followed him across to the wharf mainly out of

curiosity to see the cargo. A lot of these boats carried coal, and a couple of sackfuls would come in very useful at home right now.

He was disappointed. The final cloths were peeled back to reveal that the length of the motor was packed with slate roof tiles.

'You made good time,' Pete said, climbing on to the gunwale as Taz and his sister efficiently folded tarpaulins and coiled ropes for storage. 'Get that bit of bother with your engine fixed up, did you?'

'Yes, thanks, Mr Cutter. Bloke had a spare rod going begging. Didn't even have to wait for it to be turned or nothing. Never lost no time at all.'

'That was lucky.'

Addie leapt on to the wharf, setting up a slight rocking in the motor. 'Yeah. Weren't it just? He's a regular marvel, that bloke in Brentford. You could almost kid yerself there weren't nothing wrong with the engine to start with. Where'd you want these tiles, mister?'

Pete organised a chain, passing the load up from the boat and storing them in the handcart Josh had dragged across.

'Not gonna lend us an 'and, Shorty?' Addie grunted, heaving another stack up to one of the labourers, balancing one foot on the quay and the other on the gunwale.

'No. I'm not,' Maury said frankly. He looked at her with dislike. She'd tucked her hair under that old tweed cap again and you could see the sweat forming circles under the arms of the man's shirt she was wearing beneath the battered leather waistcoat. He bet she smelt as well. It was no wonder Joshua fancied her. Only an idiot would.

The idiot in question had already shuffled across to the edge of the wharf several times during the unloading and then lost his nerve as he came close to his dream girl. Now he trotted back with the empty cart once more for the final load.

His resemblance to a cart horse put Maury in mind of something. 'You still looking for a nag, Mr Cutter?'

'Might be, son. Why?'

'Reckon I can put you in the way of a bargain there. I'll get back to you soon as I've got me latest deal sorted.'

A muffled snort of laughter came from under the tweed cap.

'What you sniggering at?'

'Nothing at all, Shorty. We ain't been keeping you from no big deal to sell tanks or somefing, 'ave we? Only we'd hate to think of Mr Churchill struggling along without yer on our account.' Taking off the cap, she shook her hair loose, giving it a rudimentary comb with her fingers.

Joshua shuffled across on large boots again. His lavender eyes lit with admiration. 'Your hair is like silk.'

'Yer what?'

'Silk. Joshua thinks your hair is like silk.'

'You taking the mickey?' Addie demanded.

'No.' A puzzled frown drew Joshua's eyebrows down over his eyelids. She was supposed to be pleased. He turned to Maury for help.

'Oh, I see. Put 'im up to it, did yer, Shorty?'

'That's right. 'Cept he got it wrong. Straw I said, not silk.'

'No you never, Maury. Said Joshua was to say silk. And ask her to the pictures.' He fixed that intense stare on Addie and kneaded his cap between his massive fingers. 'Please, miss, will you come to the pictures with Joshua tonight?'

Unexpectedly, the suspicious scowl melted from Addie's freckled face. In a kinder tone, she thanked Joshua for the invitation but explained they'd be letting go as soon as the last load was off the boat. 'Got to take the butty's cargo down to Mile End. Ain't that right, Taz?' she shouted over to her brother.

'What?'

'Casting off in about ten minutes?'

'No. Matter of fact . . . Be all right if we stayed tied up here tonight, Mr Cutter?'

'It's all right with me. But don't you have to be getting on?'

'Yes,' Addie snapped.

'No,' Taz countered.

An angry flush darkened Addie's pale face. 'We ain't got the time to waste for you to go chasing some girl.'

127

Pete laughed and slapped Taz on the shoulder. 'Doing a bit of courting, are you son? Well good luck to you.'

'He won't need luck,' Addie said angrily. 'He'll need a flamin' miracle if her mum and dad find out.'

'Stow it, Addie. I don't have to answer to you.'

'You'd best come up the office, son. I'll settle up with you for the load now. Got your bill?'

Taz nodded. He disappeared into the cabin and re-emerged a second later with a slip of paper. The look he shot his sister before heading across the yard with Pete very clearly told her to keep her mouth shut.

'Miss?' Joshua shuffled sideways in an agony of hope.

With Pete out of earshot, the labourers didn't bother to hide their amusement. 'Go on, love. Make 'im the happiest man on earth.'

'Belt up or I'll make you the most toothless bloke on earth.' Addie raised the boat pole.

Still laughing, both men clumped back into the interior of the yard. Joshua looked uncertainly between them and Addie. 'Miss? Will you come to the pictures with Joshua? I've got money, see?' He proudly displayed a handful of silver coins.

Addie's eyes spat an angry message at Maury. This was his fault. If he didn't want his mate's feelings hurt he'd best sort things out.

Maury didn't give a damn about Joshua's feelings. But he did have a more pressing reason for vetoing the date. 'You're coming out with me, remember, Josh? Meeting me up the pub half-nine?'

Joshua ground a metal-shod boot into the yard. A slightly mulish expression settled over his features. 'Go out with Joshua another day then?'

Maury had seen her seizing on the fastest way to get rid of her ridiculous but persistent admirer. After all, the boats hardly ever stopped at Cutter's Wharf overnight.

'Yeah, course. Next time, eh, Joshua? See yer then.' Jumping down into the cabin, she hastily banged the doors shut.

A beatific smile spread across Joshua's thick lips, up his tanned cheeks, and lit up those startling eyes with an intensity that nearly qualified for blackout shutters. 'Hear that, Maury? She's going to be Joshua's girl.'

'I'm really happy for yer, mate. See yer nine-thirty. Now I got to go sort out *my* girl.'

Sorting out Pansy didn't prove easy. She was less than happy to discover that he could only come to the first house at the pictures.

'But why?' She huddled closer to him, using his body and the wall of the Gaisford to cut off the wind. The continuance of the clear skies had led to a distinct drop in the temperature.

'Got a bit of business to sort out.'

'But Mum says we can bring fish and chips back. And use the best room. *Please*, Maury.'

'I can't, Panse. Not tonight.'

Pansy straightened up, drawing away from him. 'Well, if you don't want to be with me, maybe you'd better just not bother to come in at all. I can always find someone else to go to the pictures with, I'll have you know.'

'You can come in with us if yer like, Pansy.'

Maury turned to find that Pansy's gormless friend Lottie was just behind them in the queue, with another girl he assumed must be a sister since they were so alike.

'She don't want to come in with you. She's with me.'

'Said she weren't.' Lottie tossed back her plaits and breathed deeply, releasing a cloud of paregoric fumes from the sweet she'd been noisily sucking.

'Well she is. Aren't you, Panse?'

'Suppose so. Hello, Lottie. Hello, Sheila.'

''Lo.'

The four of them were being carried by the queue towards the doors. Pansy tried once more. 'Please come back with me, Maury. Can't you do this business some other night?'

'No can do, doll. She's probably already . . .' He was about to say 'picked up the lorry' but bit it off as it occurred to him that it could lead to questions about what he needed a vehicle for. But the damage had already been done. He felt Pansy stiffen.

'*She*? Who is *she*?'

'No one. Just someone I'm doing a bit of business with.'

'What sort of business?'

'I can't say, doll. Careless talk and all that, you know.'

'Careless talk indeed! You needn't try to kid me you're doing war work, Maury O'Day, because even I know better than that!'

He longed to put his arms round her and reassure her that everything was all right, but instinct told him she wouldn't approve of what he was doing. There was an innate sense of fair play in Pansy; while she might ignore a bit of petty pilfering, Maury knew she'd never agree to outright theft.

'You're seeing someone else, aren't you, Maury?'

'Course I'm not! You know you're the only one I want.'

'Bet he is seeing another girl, Pansy. Our mum says you should never give a man a second chance.'

Maury glared at the two Abbott girls, who were blatantly eavesdropping as they noisily sucked sweets between adenoidal breaths. 'I don't suppose they'd want a first chance with you.'

'Don't you be beastly to my friend, Maury. And if you can't get out of this deal of yours tonight, then I'm coming with you.'

'No!'

'Hah!' Lottie dug an elbow into her sister's side.

The sight of their two smug faces between the identical flaxen plaits was enough to bring tears of vexation to Pansy's eyes. 'If you don't take me, Maury, then . . . then I'll never go out with you again.'

'Don't be daft, Panse . . . It's business. Yer understand, don't yer?'

'I certainly do. *Funny* business is what it is. Well, you can just go off to her . . . and she's very welcome, I'm sure.'

With a toss of her dark curls, Pansy stalked away and darted across the road.

'Pansy!' Maury hurried after her. 'Don't be daft!' He grabbed her sleeve.

'Let me go!' Angrily Pansy brought her foot down hard on his toe-cap.

'Ow!' He hopped in agony and his feet slid out from under

him on the icy paving stones. He sat down with a thump to the ironic cheers of the queue outside the fish and chip shop.

Pansy didn't even look back to see what the laughter was all about. The last Maury saw of her was the pale gleam of her legs flicking out sideways in that awkward way girls had when they ran.

It was lucky, he decided, making his way southwards to Euston, that he loved her so much, otherwise he might really have been tempted to take up with another girl.

He went to the Golden Cross, since it was the warmest place to while away the time. Seeing Carla laughing and joking behind the bar came as a shock. Sidling through the press of drinkers, he hissed across the polished counter: 'What's up? I thought you were gonna get the you-know-what. It's still on, isn't it?'

'Talk proper,' Carla instructed. 'People listen to whisperers. I told Terry I'd give him a couple of hours – before I went off to sit with me sick Auntie, poor old duck. What yer want? Lemonade?'

'Do me a favour!'

'I am. If a copper comes in and nicks you for underage drinking, that's our deal up the spout. You can swap with yer mate if I don't see you.'

Peering through the thickening fug, Maury made out Joshua pushing his way towards him with a huge smile of recognition.

'It ain't half nine yet. Can't you tell the time?'

'Dad sent me. Said not to be late – Joshua should go now.'

Maury supposed he couldn't exactly blame Pete Cutter for wanting to rid himself of his son's sparkling company for a couple of hours, but it meant another period of nursing warm beer and being beaten at skittles and darts before Carla slipped away from the bar at nine-fifteen.

Maury waited until half past, then casually strolled out with Joshua padding behind like a well-trained wolfhound.

She'd said to meet on the far corner of the square. The only vehicle parked there was a lorry marked: *'Morton's*

Industrial Laundry and Pressing Service – We Collect and Deliver – A Prompt and Efficient Service is Guaranteed'. A bloke in workman's overalls and cap was walking diagonally across the square, apparently heading for the lorry. Maybe it was his vehicle.

Maury made a show of looking at his watch and then up and down the road. They were just a couple of blokes out waiting for their dates.

'Give us a chance. I 'ad to change,' the 'workman' murmured.

'Carla?'

'Who'd yer expect?' Crouching, she felt up under the wheel arches, emerged with a key and unlocked the driver's door. ''Op in, then.'

'You driving?'

'Unless you got any objections?'

He hadn't. In fact he was secretly quite relieved. He'd managed to cadge a few lessons – mostly from 'Busted' Johnson, when he'd been on a bigger losing streak than usual and had been desperate to borrow money from Maury – but the hot food van was a quarter of the size of this monster. He couldn't imagine he'd ever have been able to negotiate the tighter bends and narrower alleys in the blackout with only the odd lick of white paint to warn where the kerb started and the road stopped.

Carla didn't seem to have any such problems. She steered competently around the dark streets, deftly avoiding the suicidal pedestrians who seemed determined to step out under their wheels.

'Busy, ain't it?' Maury said.

'Got to 'ave a good time, ain't yer? War or not. Haven't you got a girl?'

'Course I have. Pansy. I saw her earlier.'

'Joshua has a girl too.'

'Have you, muscles? Well that's all of us fixed up, ain't it? You owe me ten quid by the way, Maury. For the lorry.'

'Yeah . . . OK.'

Carla extended a palm. Taking out his wallet, Maury counted out single notes.

'That's nine,' Carla said. She hadn't taken her eyes from the windscreen.

'You're in for ten per cent, remember?'

Unexpectedly Carla laughed. 'I knew you and me would suit, Maury.' She thrust the notes into the top pocket of her overalls, steering them one-handed to a halt before a small barred gate. A shadowy figure stepped into the dim glow of their shaded headlights and swung the gate open, beckoning them forward with short agitated gestures before climbing on to the running board.

'What if we're stopped?' Maury asked.

'Just act like yer supposed to be here,' Tusker instructed. 'It's a goods depot. They're used to pick-ups.' He directed them round behind the biggest shed. A carriage was standing at the end of a single pair of lines. Another man in workshop overalls materialised from behind it, carrying a shaded track-man's lamp.

Tusker's fingers shook so much releasing the padlock that it took him three tries before he finally managed to slide the doors open. The familiar odour of dead flesh rolled into the night, mingling with the smells of coal dust and oil that lay across the yards from King's Cross to Euston like a sticky cobweb.

'Step aboard then . . .'

Taking a torch from his pocket, Maury played the beam over the hanging carcasses. It was an odd sensation, walking among the forest of eviscerated fat and bones. He pushed the heavy bodies out of the way. The skeletons beneath the smooth skins felt almost like human rib-cages. He swallowed hard and concentrated on what he was doing. Tusker had been right. The recent cold weather had helped to keep the meat fresh.

A warning whistle and rap on the wagon side made him flick the light down quickly before it could give them away.

'Tusker . . . rozzers.' The hoarse warning came from Tusker's nervous mate.

They froze as two railway police stepped across the tracks.

'Move,' Carla hissed. 'Don't stand around like a load of waxworks.' She hurriedly replaced her cap and went across to the lorry, clambering up to slide off the bolts and open the back doors.

It made sense. Act as if they were meant to be there.

Maury joined her, and discovered that the interior of the lorry was already full of racks of dirty linen.

'What the hell we gonna do with this lot?' he asked through gritted teeth.

'Show you in a minute.'

The open doors blocked their view, but they heard the unhurried feet cross the tracks further down and walk away in the direction of the canal.

Maury let out his breath in an explosive sigh. Carla leant out and called Joshua over to give her a hand. With his help she slid out a few dowelling rods and revealed that the 'racks' were just eight plywood boxes designed to bolt together and block off the interior of the lorry. Behind them was a large empty space. 'Let's get to work, partner.'

Tusker planted himself in front of the wagon's door. 'Cash first, mate.'

'Half now, half when we're loaded. And it's Mr O'Day to you.'

Maury took out his wallet, extracted a wad of fives and tens and counted them into Tusker's outstretched palm. He kept his thumb on the last one, preventing the hand from closing. 'Well?'

Tusker looked puzzled for a moment. Then he got the message. 'Oh. Yeah. Thanks. Thanks very much . . . Mr O'Day.'

Maury nodded and jerked a thumb at the interior of the wagon. 'Get in, Josh.'

Even with Joshua taking most of the strain, the weight of the carcasses took him by surprise. As the stack got higher, the effort became greater. By the time they were fully loaded, Maury's heart was hammering, his breath coming in short gasps, and sweat was running down his face. It was the hardest he'd ever worked in his life.

None the less he managed to peel off the rest of Tusker's money with a steady hand and to insist on another 'Mr O'Day' before they left.

'Very smoothly done, partner,' Carla grinned, turning back down the Euston Road.

The London deliveries passed off easily enough. No one gave a second glance to a laundry truck collecting and delivering from the back doors of hotels and restaurants. It wasn't until they left the West End behind and headed for their last two deliveries at the road-houses out of town that trouble struck.

They'd gone up by the Whitestone Pond, intending to cut through Hampstead, and noticed too late the stealthy figures darting over the deserted roads and flitting into gardens.

'It's another one of those flamin' Home Guard exercises,' Carla complained.

'They look like regulars to me,' Maury said, straining to make out the uniforms. He exchanged a silent question with his new partner.

'Go on,' Carla said.

'Go on,' Maury agreed. Their luck had held so far. It was a pity not to trust it for those final few miles.

Unfortunately, luck had decided to bail out at the Spaniards Inn. A copper materialised in the headlamps. It was the worse possible spot: the road narrowed to go between the corner of the pub building and the gate-post on the other side of the road. There was nowhere to go.

The policeman paced to the driver's window with the slow-footed stride of one who knows his own importance – and rates it ten times greater than its real value. 'May I ask your destination, sir?'

Carla kept her head tilted so that the cap brim kept her face in shadow. 'Hendon, officer. We have a couple of hotels to pick up from out there. Is there something wrong? All these soldiers . . . We thought perhaps the invasion had started.'

'Just an exercise, my dear. Nothing for you to worry about.' He played his shaded torch further into the cab, illuminating Maury and Joshua. 'Is this your vehicle?'

'My husband's. He's been called up. I'm trying to keep the business going for him.'

'And these two?'

'My employees.'

'It's a funny time to be taking in laundry, isn't it?'

'We had engine trouble.' Carla's voice dropped, acquiring a huskier, pleading note. 'It's happened before. They . . . the hotels say if I don't do better, they're going to give the business to another firm. I just can't afford to lose the money.' Her voice shook on a slight sob.

The constable stepped back. For a moment they started to breathe easily again.

'Can you step out, please?'

'Out? Why?'

'I want to see your identity cards.'

'But surely we don't look like spies, officer . . .' Carla coaxed.

'That's for me to decide. Come on, now. Step down . . . lively like. And open up the back.'

Reluctantly they started to climb out, taking it as slowly as they dared. And praying for a miracle. By unspoken consent Carla and Maury appeared to forget the request for identity cards; there was no sense getting their names in the constable's pocket-book if there was any chance it could be avoided.

With Joshua ambling along behind them, they made their way to the back of the lorry, the keys for the padlocks jangling conspicuously. The greased bolts and door hinges slid back silently, revealing the banks of dirty laundry apparently stacked to the top of the roof.

'You've a tidy little business there, m'dear.' The dim circlet of light slid over the crumpled and stained piles.

'I've several big 'otels, all them sheets and pillowcases. But if I don't get going . . . *please*, officer . . .'

The constable nodded vaguely. But instead of stepping away, he moved closer, gripping the chains of the tailboard preparatory to hauling himself up.

In the starlight, Maury saw the flash of white as Carla's eyes widened. The false wall wouldn't stand a close scrutiny. Even worse, the smell of raw meat to which they'd become inured was suddenly thick on the air. How the copper had missed it

136

was a mystery. He must have no sense of smell. But surely if he got any closer . . .!

The familiar rising banshee wail of the alert screamed into the night. Instantly, half a dozen searchlights on the heath carved silver paths into the black skies. Whistles and orders were shouted from different directions. A group of soldiers clattered up the road behind them. The lorry was blocking the entrance, forcing them to squeeze past in single file. Someone shouted an order to get it out of the way.

'You heard him. Get this thing moving,' the constable barked, backing away.

Slamming the doors closed and bolted with a willing enthusiasm, they leapt back into the cab. Carla crashed her gears and raced down the hill.

'Wow . . .' Maury let out his breath in a gasp. He looked at Carla. She grinned. He smiled. Suddenly they were both laughing so much the lorry started to sway in a rumba over the empty roads. Unsure of the joke, but reasoning there must be one, Joshua chuckled happily.

'We've done it, partner,' Carla said when she got her breath back.

'We sure have.'

Maury patted the bulging wallet. It was more money than anyone else in his family had ever had in their lives. He and Pansy were on their way up.

He wished suddenly that she could have been here to share this, his first big deal. Closing his eyes for a second, he sent out his thoughts to her . . . wanting this night to be as memorable for her as it had been for him.

Which in a way it was: because Pansy would certainly never forget this particular night.

Chapter 15

She'd run the short distance to Kelly Street in a couple of minutes, half expecting Maury to catch up with her, to tell her not to be silly and of course he'd come back home with her.

At the entrance to the street she'd stopped, looking back. Waiting. Couples passed her, heading for the cinemas in Camden or the bus stops where they could catch a ride down to the dance hall in Tottenham Court Road. Single figures hurried along, heads dipped, collars up. She didn't need to see their features; she knew just by their way of moving that none of them was her Maury. He wasn't coming. He'd gone off some other way. Probably to this mysterious 'she' – whoever the scheming cow was.

Pansy sniffed. The cold weather was making her nose and eyes run. She stamped her feet in the thinner leather of her best shoes. It was stupid to stand here. She might just as well go home.

She walked a few paces up the street to keep warm. The pungent scent of hot chips caught her nose. Well, she might as well get her supper, even if Maury wasn't going to share it with her.

She bought sixpence worth of cod and twopence of chips; shaking salt and vinegar on until it rose in a delicious tangy cloud that made her eyes water.

The next queuer pointed to her newspaper bundle. 'I'll 'ave same as her. How much?'

'Eightpence to you, son.'

'Whatcha mean "son"? You trying to take the mickey?'

'No need to take that tone with me, young man. I call all

me young gentlemen "son". There's no offence intended, I'm sure.'

Pansy saw the problem, as did several others in the queue. Addie Dixon had added an over-large navy blue duffel coat to her usual ensemble, but apart from that she was wearing the cut-down men's outfit – including the heavy boots and the tweed cap that covered all her long hair.

A few sniggers and nudges rippled down the waiting customers.

Addie scowled. 'What's so funny?'

'Nothing at all . . . sonny,' someone called from the back.

Addie picked up the vinegar bottle. The heckler was saved from a soaking by the arrival of her order.

'Eightpence . . .'

Diving into her pockets, Addie laid out a threepenny bit, two pennies and four half pennies along the counter.

'You're a penny short . . .'

'I know. I can count, can't I?' Addie scrabbled in the duffel's capacious pockets. A flush spread over her pale face, flowing between the freckles like a tide creeping between the islands in an estuary. 'I 'ad a sixpence . . .' She drove her fingertips even deeper into the seams of the pockets.

With a look to the rest of the waiting queue to solicit their support, the assistant reclaimed the greasy newspaper parcel.

'I'll lend you a penny . . .' Pansy put the coin on the counter before Addie could refuse.

Addie made a point of unwrapping her chips and helping herself to the salt and vinegar before they left. 'I did 'ave sixpence,' she said as they stepped through the double blackout curtaining and back into the cold street.

''Spect it dropped out your pocket,' Pansy offered.

'Yeah, 'spect.' Addie crunched into her fish. 'Walk round the boat with me, I'll give you yer penny.'

'There's no need. You can give it to mum in the office.'

'She ain't there. I asked. She's still got me clothes – ones that got soaked when I went in the canal thanks to them bleedin' Geoghans. She said to get 'em from the office next time we tie up, but it's all locked up.'

140

'She's gone to a meeting tonight. About doing first aid. I could ask her for them . . . When are you leaving?'

'Who knows? When Taz says. Sure you don't wanna come round the boat and get yer penny? I've got it, you know. I wasn't trying to cadge me dinner. The Dixons always pay their way.'

Pansy hesitated. Despite living near the canal all her life, watching the boats and barges tying up and unloading along the wharves, she'd never been aboard one. It just wasn't something you did. The water people and the land folk didn't mix except on a business level. On the other hand, she'd often wondered what lay inside the brightly painted cabins.

'All right then. I don' mind walking round if you like.'

Addie led her down to Hampstead Road lock. 'We can get down the tow-path from there,' she explained. 'Yard gates are locked.'

It was something Pansy hadn't considered. She didn't mind the tow-path in the daylight, but now, when it was silent and deserted, it had an eerie feel to it.

'You all right?' Addie asked. 'What's the matter? You changed yer mind?'

'No. I was just seeing where I was going,' Pansy fibbed. It seemed silly to admit she was scared of the canal. After all, this was more her home than Addie's. And the other girl didn't seem at all bothered at the prospect of wandering down strange footpaths on her own.

They set off again, munching hungrily on the hot chips. At least it was easy enough to stay away from the edge, thanks to the clear skies and reflected stars sliding smudgily over the black water. However, under the bridges that carried the road and rail traffic across the canal, the shadows were denser, which is why they didn't see the two figures standing under the Kentish Town Bridge until a hoarse whisper instructed one to: 'Hurry it up, supposing a copper sees us.'

'What if he does? It's a natural thing, ain't it? Even coppers got to do it.'

If the two girls had had any doubt as to what was going on, it was resolved by the thin tinkle of water meeting water. Pansy would have turned and walked away, her cheeks burning with

141

embarrassment, but Addie continued to wander forward, munching unconcernedly on her chips.

'Evening. All together.'

They heard the brief interruption in the steady descent into the canal as the urinator swore under his breath.

'They got proper lavs in towns, yer know, Blackie. 'Spect one of the townies would show you how to use one if yer asked. Don't 'spect you could work it out for yerself. Evening, Matthus. Want a chip?'

Addie had by now come face to face with the younger Geoghan. Awkwardly he accepted a chunk of potato. 'Ta.'

Blackie swaggered back from the canalside, defiantly rebuttoning his flies. 'I'll have one too.'

'No yer won't. We know where yer fingers have been, don't we, Pansy?'

Blackie planted himself before Pansy, leaning close to make out her features in the heavy gloom. 'Who's yer friend then, Addie? Ain't we getting a chance to say haa d'yer do?'

'This is Miss Cutter. Of Cutter's Wharf.'

'Posh pals you're mixing with these days, Addie. A great pleasure, ma'am.' Blackie whipped off his cap and bowed low. At least, that was his intention. But the bottles of beer he'd been drinking since midday had the effect of convincing his centre of gravity that he was heading for disaster – head first. He grabbed at Pansy's coat to steady himself. Frightened, she dropped her chips and struggled to keep her own balance. Blackie put his other hand on her waist. His only intention was to use her as a support to straighten up again, but the large hands and beery breath panicked Pansy.

'Let me go!' she screamed and tried to pull away.

Blackie tightened his grip.

'You 'eard her. Leave off, Geoghan.'

Taking a flying run at him from behind, Addie aimed one of her metal-shod boots straight between Blackie's legs. He jerked upright with a shout of agony and then doubled over moaning and cursing.

'Get her! Get that little bitch, Matthus!'

142

Matthus pried himself from the brickwork, saw Addie shifting her weight prior to another kick, and shuffled sideways instead.

'Come on . . .' Locking her fingers round Pansy's wrist, Addie dragged her away along the tow-path. Half running, they flew along the gravel track until they arrived in a breathless rush at the narrow gap between the canalside and the fencing that marked the beginning of Cutter's Wharf.

Addie slid back part of the roof, opened the double doors that led down into the cabin and invited Pansy to step aboard the *Rainbow*. 'Sorry I can't show a light until we're shut up again. Here, take me hand.'

Clinging tight to the other girl, Pansy half stepped, half fell into the cabin, and then was forced to sit in total darkness while the doors and slide were reclosed.

Addie lit a paraffin lamp, hanging it from a hook in the centre of the roof. Pansy looked around with interest. The narrow space reminded her of an Anderson shelter, except it was far better fitted out. She was sitting on top of a locker that had been made up as a narrow bed. Facing her was a tiny range, complete with a proper oven, black-leaded so thoroughly it looked like satin and ringed by brass guard-rails that glowed and winked like molten gold as they reflected the lamp's flame. She let her gaze slide further along. The rest of the wall opposite seemed to consist of a bank of drawers and cupboards, all painted brown and decorated with great swirls of pink, red and yellow roses or landscapes of castles, mountains and waterfalls.

'Oooh, isn't it pretty!'

'Whatcha expect?'

'I don't know. I never thought . . . You don't have to sound so angry,' Pansy said, bridling at Addie's aggressive tone.

'Sorry.' Addie, cap and coat discarded, flopped down beside her. 'It's just I'm fed up with landies turning their posh noses up at us, like we ain't good enough for them. I seen inside houses. I wouldn't keep a pig in some of 'em.'

'Well, you would in ours!' Pansy said indignantly. Then she realised what she'd said, caught Addie's eye, and they both burst into giggles.

When they managed to stop Addie said, 'Want some cocoa?'

Pansy accepted, mostly out of curiosity to see where everything was kept in the cabin. The coal, she discovered, came from the box that served as a step down into the cabin. Having added a couple of lumps to the range and blown them into a glow, Addie put the kettle on a hot plate and made her way to the biggest cupboard at the far end.

Fascinated, Pansy watched her undo a couple of latches and then lower the door like a drawbridge until its edge rested on the locker opposite.

'Taz's bed. Normally keeps it made up, 'cept when he ain't sure who's coming calling. Not that she's likely to come courting in here, is she?'

'Is who?'

'Er . . . nobody. Just this landie Taz has his eye on. He ought to 'ave the sense to stick to his own kind. It's not like a landie is gonna be any use on the water. Same as boaters ain't never really happy on land. Boaters should marry boaters.' Addie dragged out the bedding that had been folded inside the cupboard and left it on the bed board. The upper cupboard shelves held crockery and some groceries.

'It's all ever so clever, isn't it?' Pansy said.

'Is it?' Addie looked round blankly. It was the only home she'd ever known. Cleverness didn't come into it. Is was just the way things were.

There was one thing that had always intrigued Pansy. Where did they keep the lavatory?

'Bucket in the engine room. Want to go?'

'No thank you.'

Addie ladled spoonfuls into the mugs until Pansy protested she was being too generous with the rationed sugar.

'It's OK. We've plenty. We draw seaman's rations. It's double what you landies get.'

'Don't you ever wish you could stop in one place?'

'No. You got to keep on the move if yer a real boater. *Goo stiddy, but keep gooing*, that's what Grandad always used to stay. Taz oughta remember that,' she added in a sour voice. She squeezed on to the bunk beside Pansy,

144

where they sat swinging their legs and sipping the chocolatey liquid.

'Do you think you'll marry a boater?'

''Spect so.' Addie's boots swung with more vigour. 'Don't know anybody else, 'cept that soft-headed cousin of yours. He wanted to take me up the pictures tonight.'

'Joshua did?'

'Yeah! I thought first off your bloke put him up to it. Mind, I don't reckon he can have, cause he called him off. Taken him up the pub.'

'Maury took Joshua with him tonight?' Pansy's voice rose hopefully.

'Meeting him up the pub. Half nine – that's what he said.'

An enormous weight lifted off Pansy's chest. There was no way Maury would take Joshua on a date with another girl. He must have been telling the truth: it *was* just business. She'd go round to his house first thing tomorrow and make it up.

Hugging her cocoa mug to her chest so that it formed a little pool of heat between her breasts, she said, 'Maury and me's getting married one day.'

'Yer official? Engaged?'

'Oh . . . we sort of are. 'Spect we'll do it regular, with a ring and everything, after the fourteenth. It's my birthday.'

'I know. Yer said. It's mine too.'

Of course it was. Pansy remembered now. This strange girl was going to be seventeen. It was hard to believe. Covertly she observed the man's shirt, baggy trousers and heavy boots. 'Don't you ever wear girl's clothes?'

'No sense in it. Can't work the locks in a frock.'

'Lots of women do. I've seen them going along. They have dresses and aprons over them.'

'Pinners!' Addie snorted. 'You won't catch *me* wearing no bloomin' pinner!'

Faced with such scorn, Pansy retreated into silence. It went on for so long that she started to become uncomfortable. Draining the last gritty dregs of cocoa, she started to wriggle off the locker.

'Can I show yer something?' Addie said abruptly.

145

'If you like.'

'They're in the butty. I'll go fetch 'em.'

The packages from Selfridges were more or less as Taz and Iris had carried them home that Saturday in November, since the idea of buying special wrapping paper for Christmas presents would never have occurred to her brother.

Pansy examined each item with pleasure. 'But these are really pretty. Bit too nice for dirty work. But you could wear them for best . . .'

'I ain't got no best to wear them to. I only go on the boats. Or up the shops for the groceries.'

'But don't you ever go out? For fun?'

'Went up the pictures once. And I been up some pubs with Taz. But they're all boaters in there. They'd think I'd gone daft if I wore fancy stuff like this.'

Impulsively Pansy said, 'You could wear it to my birthday party.'

'Could I? When is it? On yer birthday proper?'

Pansy had to admit they hadn't set a date yet. Her mother usually managed to put some sort of spread on the table – cold meats and cakes and jellies for her friends and the cousins. But this year it was different. She was sixteen. Officially that made her a woman; you could get married at sixteen. Surely that deserved a grown up party – even if there was a war on?

'You can ask next time you come past the wharf. Or telephone the office. Mum wouldn't mind. Will your brother bring the boat here for the day?'

''Spect so. If we're working this stretch. Don't seem able to stay away from the place.' She balanced on one leg, using the other to fan out the dress skirt. 'You think this will fit me?'

'Haven't you tried it on?'

'Ain't tried any of it. I told you, it feels stupid.'

'For heaven's sake, Addie Dixon, you are a case!' Pansy placed her hands on her hips, taking control of the situation as she found herself on familiar ground. 'Fancy owning all these pretty things and not even putting them on. You take off those boy's clothes right now and try these on.'

Addie did as she was told – revealing darned and sewn-up

men's pants and vest, and pale skin weathered to red in the V of her neck and on her hands.

'Put this on,' Pansy instructed, shaking the creases out of the peach silk teddie. 'And this belt.'

The suspender belt cut into Addie's bony hips and the top of the teddie hung limply over her flat chest. She became entangled with the stockings and took half a dozen tries before she managed to get the seams at the back straight.

'Blimey!' she finally announced, straightening up and sweeping the curtain of hair out of her red face. 'What a palaver. You do this every day?'

'Not exactly. Here, put the dress on. And some shoes.'

The dress was slightly too long but could easily be shortened. The shoes were impossible. Addie only owned a pair of lace-up boots.

'Don't you dare!' Pansy squealed as the other girl went to step into them. 'They'll ladder yer stockings. Can't you buy a proper pair of girl's shoes? There's a Cable's up Kentish Town Road, does ever such nice shoes. Or there's a second-hand shop – Mr Levy's Emporium – in Camden, if you want something a bit cheaper.'

'We *ain't* poor. We can afford proper shoes same as landies!'

'Never said you was, did I? Maury shops at Levy's. He says second-hand posh clothes is better than cheap new.'

'So who wants to look like Shorty?' Addie muttered, flopping down on the side bed and kicking the boots under the table.

'Well, if you're going to be mean about Maury, Addie Dixon, I'm going home.'

'Go on then. I didn't want to go to some stupid party anyway.'

'All right I will.' Pansy ripped the doors open, forgetting the blackout, and stepped back with a squeal as she found herself face to face with Matthus Geoghan.

'Sorry, miss. Didn't mean to cause no scarifying . . .' He whipped off his cap and bobbed his head.

Behind them Addie demanded sharply, 'Whatcha want, Geoghan?'

'Talk.'

'We ain't got nothing to say to yer. Get off our boat. You never asked to step aboard.'

'It ain't you I want to talk to. It's her. Yer showing a big light out 'ere. Can I come inside? It's like this, miss . . .' For the first time Matthus got a good look at Addie. It caused him to draw his breath with a sharp hiss. 'Blimey!'

'Wha's the matter?'

'You look like a proper girl, Addie!' His pointed chin dropped lower as he took in everything from the loose hair to her stocking feet. 'Gawd, you ain't bad at all when yer dressed up! Tell you what, I wouldn't mind walking yer along the tow-path one evening . . . if we're tied up close enough.'

A china plate spun through the air, caught the lamp and ricocheted past Matthus's ear.

'Addie!' Pansy had jerked backwards against the range, which fortunately had lost most of its heat. 'Stop it! What do you want to see me about, Mr Geoghan?'

'Mr . . .' Matthus sniggered at this unfamiliar word. It had the effect of displaying a set of upper teeth a rabbit would have been proud to own. With another nervous snigger, Matthus asked her not to report Blackie to the rozzers. 'Thing is, miss, he never meant no harm. It's just the drink. He's sleeping sweet as a babby now. You can come see if yer want.'

It was the last thing Pansy wanted. And it hadn't occurred to her to report Blackie Geoghan anyway. She'd never have heard the end of it from her mother and Aunt Ursula. They might even stop her going out in the evenings in the future if they thought there was a chance of her being accosted by drunks.

'Tell him not to do it again,' she said grandly. 'And I'll try to forget it this time.'

'Ta, miss.' Matthus bobbed, displaying his coney-like dentistry once more.

'So now get lost!' Addie snapped.

'Yeah. OK . . .' Matthus backed out, his eyes still fixed on Addie. Light spilt from the cabin over the tiller and the figure just climbing aboard.

'Oi! You're showing a light, kid! What the hell . . . What you doing on my boat, Matthus?' Taz demanded.

Before the younger man could answer he was thrust back into the cabin and the doors banged closed again.

'Kid? You okay?'

'Course I am. Take more than the runt of the Geoghan litter to bother me. Anyhow, he come to see her.'

Taz became aware of Pansy. 'Oh. Haa d'yer do, Miss Cutter? Is there something wrong?'

'No. Addie was just showing me her new clothes.'

'She says I can wear them to her birthday party,' Addie explained, the earlier squabble forgotten. 'If we're tied up local.'

'So what's *this* doing on me boat?'

'Nothing . . . honest. I never meant no harm. Ta, miss . . .' Matthus bobbed frantically, trying to shuffle past Taz and to the safety of the deck. He half fell up the coalbox step and ended up crawling outside on all fours.

Taz demanded once more what a Geoghan had been doing aboard.

'Seeing 'er, I told yer. Didn't think you'd be back so soon. Something up?'

'Ir . . . Her mother was taken ill. Can I see you home, Miss Cutter?'

Pansy took the hint and assured him she'd be fine. 'I'll get me Uncle Pete to let me out the front gates. There'll be plenty of people in the streets still. Goodnight.'

''Ang on.' Addie knelt and drew out a drawer. Taking out an old tin decorated with pictures of Edward the Seventh's coronation, she extracted a single penny. 'I ain't forgotten. Dixons always pay their debts.'

Accepting the copper, Pansy allowed Taz to help her over on to the wharf. The sudden coldness took her by surprise after the warm fug of the cabin. She stood still for a minute, allowing her eyes to become accustomed to the dark and watching the small cloud of breath swirling in front of her mouth. Surreptitiously she jigged from one foot to the other. She'd been dying to go to the lavatory for the past hour, but there was just no way she was going to use that bucket.

Gradually the well-known outlines of the yard buildings solidified out of the blackness. Confidently she picked her way across the uneven ground towards the brick store, trod lightly up the outside staircase, opened the door cautiously and slipped round the blackout curtain. The sitting room was in darkness. Since it was too early for her Uncle Pete to be in bed, she assumed he must have gone out. It didn't matter. She knew where the spare keys to the yard were kept.

Clicking on the light, she headed gratefully for the door to the lavatory. Half-way across the carpet, she became aware of a sound from the bedroom. A heavy panting intermingled with low moans and a rhythmic creak of metal and wood.

Perhaps Uncle Pete was ill. She touched the handle and the door slid away from her touch, swinging in on well-oiled hinges.

Her Uncle was lying face down. She could see the beads of sweat rolling down his naked back as he rocked back and forth. His head was back and his eyes were closed, his expression twisted in an expression of agony.

Pansy took all this in in a second before her eyes met those of the woman lying under him.

With a gasp, Kate Cutter tried to still her lover's frantic movements. It was too late. By the time they'd uncoupled, Pansy had fled.

Chapter 16

'I'm sorry. So very sorry . . .'

Iris took one of her mother's cold hands and squeezed it reassuringly. 'Don't be silly, Mummy. It's not your fault.'

'But I've spoilt your lovely evening out.'

'Supper with Nana and Ludo? I can do that any time.' *But not*, a small voice whispered in her head, *with Taz there as well*.

He'd accosted them outside the cinema after Nana's afternoon treat. Still smelling faintly of shaving soap and shoe polish, he'd formally asked whether he might take her dancing tonight.

'No.' The flat statement had come out less graciously than she'd intended, but she'd had no practice in turning down dates with tact. Cornered in the dark street, with the rest of the cinema-goers streaming out around her and the Saturday shoppers jostling past, she'd said the first thing that came into her head.

She didn't want to be alone with him. It was too long since their last date. The ease that had started to creep into their relationship had solidified into a cold, hard lump of shyness in her chest. She felt awkward and uncomfortable in his company again; she wanted the old and the familiar.

But the old familiar had decided not to co-operate. 'Course she'll go dancing with you, young man. Come back to my place while Iris powders her nose and telephones her parents. Tell them you're having supper with your poor, lonely old gran.'

'No. I'm not going. Thank you for the invitation, Mr Dixon, but I'm going home now. My mother needs me.'

151

Nana Cutter's snort of derision had blown a cloud of humbug-flavoured breath into the chilly afternoon air. 'Needs you indeed! *I* need you. These pavements are freezing up . . . see?' She'd scraped a sole over the surface. 'The least you can do is see me safely indoors.'

'Well, yes, of course I will, Nana.' Iris had offered her arm to her grandmother . . . and had been less than pleased when Taz had done the same on the other side. With the old woman tottering between them they made their way slowly along the Prince of Wales Road, past the bath-house and laundry that was exuding a pungent smell of chlorine and soap, and between the students streaming out of the special Saturday classes at the technical college.

Iris hadn't been deceived by her grandmother's achingly slow shuffle. She was well aware that, had she suddenly announced she would go dancing with Taz, Nana would have found the energy to skip up the rest of Queen's Crescent.

Most of the market stalls had gone already. There was little point in staying open when no lights could be displayed after dusk.

'Did I tell you I got a couple of rabbits from a coster up here the other day?' Nana had asked. 'Swapped them for a bottle of Ludo's parsnip wine. He makes it himself, you know.'

'Sounds like a handy bloke to have around,' Taz had remarked.

'Oh he is, he is. I'd have offered you a rabbit, Iris dear, but I know your mother won't eat the meat. Not elegant enough for madam. Do you like rabbit, young man?'

Iris had stiffened, sensing where the conversation was leading.

Taz admitted they often took one for the pot from along the canal banks. 'Or maybe something a bit fancier – pheasant if the gamekeeper's not around.'

'We've nothing like that, I'm afraid. Not many in town have these days. But I can offer you a bite of rabbit and mushroom pudding with me and Ludo.'

Iris had anticipated her own invitation. 'I have to get back to Mummy.'

'Well I'm not stopping you, am I? But I'm not going to

152

pass up the chance of spending me evening with a handsome young man, even if you are.'

Iris had bitten her lip, but said nothing until they were outside Nana's front door and the older woman had disengaged her hand so that she could search in her pocket for her key. 'I must go. Goodnight, Gran. Goodnight, Mr Dixon.'

'Iris, wait!' Taz had followed her a few steps back down the path and snatched her hand. 'Wait . . . please. Stop with us – just for a little while. I won't say nothing about . . . well, you know, about things you don't want to talk about. We can just talk to your gran and the old boy.'

She'd known she ought to say no, that staying was just encouraging him to have hopes – hopes that she had absolutely no intention of fulfilling. The kindest and most honest thing to do would have been to go home right then and let Nana play her silly games on her own.

'All right,' she had said. 'Just for an hour perhaps.'

In the end she'd stayed to eat the savoury pudding Nana had left simmering on the hob before they went out. With some fresh winter greens from the patch Ludo was cultivating on the flat roof and a bottle of the home-brewed parsnip wine, the four of them had eaten in the kitchen – something her mother would never have allowed.

Afterwards, Taz had played cribbage with Ludo while she and Nana washed up. The warm glow fired by the wine, the informal atmosphere and undemanding company had just started to relax her when the phone shrilled in the hall.

'Drat. Whoever's that?' Nana dried her hands roughly and went through into the colder passage.

'Hello? Yes, she's here . . . For heaven's sake stop gabbling, girl. Take a deep breath . . . now hold your nose . . .'

'Doris,' Iris said. It was the tone of voice Nana reserved for the Cutter's well-intentioned but none-too-bright maid. She walked into the hall and held out her hand for the receiver. With raised eyebrows, her grandmother relinquished it.

'She's gorn down again,' Doris trumpeted.

'Let go of your nose,' Iris ordered. 'Where's my father?'

Drawing in a relieved gasp of air, Doris told her that Mr Cutter had gone out. 'Gorn to see a man about business. I'm

153

to stop on . . . I don't mind, miss. You know that. I like to listen to your wireless . . . But she's gorn down. She's asking for you miss.'

'Yes. All right. I'm on the way, Doris. Have you telephoned the doctor?' Apparently that was Doris's next task. Iris replaced the receiver and met her grandmother's impatient expression. 'Mother's having another turn.'

'Your mother has that many turns it's a wonder she's not screwed herself into the floorboards.'

'I'll walk you back,' Taz said.

'There's no need.'

'It's on me way to the wharf. If I don't walk beside you, I'll have to walk behind you. Goodnight, ma'am . . . sir. Thanks for me supper.'

The streets were busy and clearly lit by the stars under the near cloudless skies. Iris held the warm wool of her scarf against her nose and mouth.

'You hoping no one's going to recognise you?' Taz had asked, striding long-legged beside her. 'Or you just hiding the scar?'

The abrupt reference to her disfigurement had thrown her off balance again. 'Neither. The air's cold, that's all.'

'Yep.' He'd craned his neck to examine the constellations twinkling above North London. 'It's a bomber's sky, for sure. Pity we're tied up here. Don't see much of the raiders once we're clear of the towns. Will you be all right with yer mum . . . if they start dropping bombs?'

'We've an Anderson. Doris and I can carry Mummy on a chair-lift if the alert goes.'

'Thought yer maid went home.'

'Not if there's an alert on.'

They were at the entrance to Bartholomew Road. She'd have turned away if he hadn't taken her arm. 'Goodnight, Iris.'

'Goodnight.' She'd tried to pull away, but he kept his grip.

'Can I come see you? Up the house?'

'No. Please don't.' She twisted away. 'Leave me alone, Taz. Whatever it is you want, I can't give it to you. I just *can't*.'

154

She had run the last few steps to the house. The doctor's car was already parked outside. She heard his heavy, stentorian wheezing from the top landing as Doris helped her inside the hall.

'How is she, Doris?'

'Better now the quack's here, miss. She gave me a regular fright. I'd just finished washing up her supper tray and there she was . . . gorn down, right on that very spot you're standing on.'

Iris nodded abstractedly, wriggling out of her coat and outdoor shoes. 'Did you take her upstairs?'

'She insisted, miss. And I had to put her in her best nightie set and brush her hair before I was to call the doctor. You know what she's like.'

Iris did indeed. As she ran lightly up to her mother's bedroom she found herself singing the old playground rhyme under her breath:

> *Siddons, Siddons and his magic bottle,*
> *Did the dirty on Lieutenant Pottle.*

It was unfair, of course. The poor man had been seriously burnt in a mustard gas attack in Flanders and had eventually committed suicide with an overdose of morphine; but the rumour-mongers had whispered of negligence on Siddons's part even after the inquest had completely exonerated him. It had had an effect on Siddons's business, but most of his patients had stayed loyal – and some, like her mother, were devoted to him and flatly refused to be treated by anyone else.

Siddons was the fattest man Iris had ever seen. He'd been enormous when he'd treated them all as children, but with each year since he seemed to have added another inch to his stomach. It was straining now against his pin-striped waistcoat as he fumbled in the pocket for a half-hunter. Taking out the gold watch, he held it in one hand while the other clasped Ursula's wrist.

Ursula smiled weakly at her daughter. 'Darling, I'm so sorry. I didn't want to spoil things. But I just . . .'

'Don't try to talk, Mummy.'

'Quite right too. Listen to this young woman. Lie quiet, my dear lady.' Siddons's wheezing breaths formed a counterpoint to the rhythm of the bedside clock as his wet lips silently counted out Ursula's pulse. Finally he tucked her hand back under the covers with a grunt and repocketed his watch. 'Fast. Too fast. Let's listen to your chest. Same as usual was it? No warning?'

'Just the same. I was in the parlour, listening to a concert on the light programme . . . and just felt these waves of dizziness. I tried to get to the hall to call Doris . . .'

Grunting with the effort, Siddons retrieved his bag from the floor and extracted a stethoscope. Iris sat on the other side of the bed and helped her mother raise her gown at the back. She smelt lavender oil mingling with peppermint cordial and guessed her mother had dabbed on perfume before allowing Doris to call out medical help. Ursula's skin felt cold despite the slight film of sweat on it, and Iris could feel the vibrations of her heart thudding frantically under the rib-cage.

'Banging away like a steam hammer as well, dear lady. Whatever are we going to do with you?'

'I'm so sorry. I feel such a fraud when there are real casualties out there. And to drag you out at this time of night . . .'

'Rubbish.' Siddons took both his patient's hands in his own pudgy grasp and assured her he was at her disposal – day or night. 'You, my dear Mrs Cutter, are one of my favourite . . . no, I tell a lie . . . you *are* my favourite patient. I should be quite devastated if you were to even think of consulting another practitioner.'

'But I feel such a nuisance.'

'Ill-health is not something we can help, dear lady. Have you taken any medication?'

'Just the peppermint.' Ursula nodded wearily at the small bottle of sticky green cordial standing on the bedside table. 'It's the only thing that seems to help. Do you think I could trouble you for some more?'

Siddons tutted, pursing his wet lips doubtfully. 'Another bottle already? Surely it was only last week . . . ?'

'Your prescriptions really are the *only* thing . . . Well, you've seen the evidence yourself . . .'

'Of course, of course . . .' Siddons scribbled out a prescription. 'I'll mix it myself. The boy will bring it round. Now I want you to stay here in bed for as long as you consider necessary, dear lady. And you, Miss Iris, are to call me immediately if you have the slightest concern about your mother's condition. Do you understand . . . the *slightest* concern.'

Iris nodded automatically. She knew the routine.

Ursula reached up and touched her daughter's face. 'Don't you think she's looking better, doctor?'

Siddons took her chin in a firm pinch and tilted her face into the light. Iris tried not to flinch. 'Hmmm . . . not bad. Won't fade any more. Told you that, haven't I?'

'Yes. You did.' She wanted to free herself, but she knew from years of previous examinations that he would simply tighten his grip until it hurt if necessary.

'What's this?' He rubbed a thick thumb over her lips, smearing off the lipstick.

'She doesn't wear anything over the scar, do you, darling?'

'No. But . . . don't you think . . . just a little powder or foundation? I mean, if it's not going to get better, ever . . .'

'It could get worse, young woman.' With a final pinch, Siddons released her. 'Keep all that muck away from it. Plain soap and water – that's all that's required.'

'She'll remember, doctor. And thank you again. I'm so sorry to be a nuisance.'

'You could never be that, dear lady.' Siddons creaked forward gallantly to kiss Ursula's hand.

Once the doctor had been shown out and Doris had been despatched with thanks and assurances that she wasn't needed, Iris had re-climbed the stairs and sat on her mother's bed, warming her hands while she listened to her mother's whispered apologies for spoiling her evening.

'Don't be silly, Mummy. You can't help being ill. Shall I fetch you a hot water bottle? And a milky drink?'

'Thank you darling. That would be lovely. Why don't you bring your own up and sit with me for a while?'

She set the kettle on to boil in the back kitchen before stepping outside into the garden. She needed to clear the cloying scents of mint cordial and lavender essence from her lungs.

The slightly sour smell of London clay rose up to meet her nose instead. She'd done her best to follow the government's instructions to 'Dig for Victory', but the thick glutinous soil had largely defeated her. She just couldn't force a spade through in some areas, and the resulting crops had been spindly from shallow planting or deformed and rotted. Her father had pleaded pressure of work to be excused, and of course she couldn't expect her mother to help.

Leaning back against the house wall, she let her eyes become accustomed to the darkness again. Shapes unmelded easily from the blackout. She knew every corner, every line, every curve of this view. She'd never lived anywhere else and until recently it hadn't occurred to her that she might even want to. But now . . . it was almost unpatriotic to want to stay at home, wasn't it?

She thought of the cuttings she'd stored in the recipe books in the kitchen drawer – advertisements urging women to release a man to fight. Everyone wanted her – the Wrens, the ATS, the Air Force, the Auxiliary Fire Service, the ambulance service. The idea of a job – a real job, somewhere far away from home, perhaps – was both frightening and exciting.

And now Taz had raised another possibility. She'd always believed that no man would ever be interested in her because of her deformity. A future with Taz was impossible, of course, even she could see that. The life of a boater's woman was so far removed from what she'd been used to that it just wasn't sensible even to daydream about it. But if Taz found her attractive . . . then perhaps someone else might, someone able to offer her a different sort of future.

A movement on the earth-buried Anderson shelter caught her eye. One of the neighbouring cats on the prowl, she assumed, until it paused on the roof, silhouetting its bushy tail and pricked ears against the navy blue sky.

The wild fox turned its head in her direction. She saw the glitter of its eyes and held her breath, wondering if it could see hers. It was rare to see one down here. The pickings must be lean up on the heath. It had been forced to leave its own familiar haunts to come exploring in a strange world. Had the idea scared it too?

She was just debating whether to go in and see if there were any scraps that could be spared from the larder, when the kettle announced it had reached boiling point with a shrill whistle. The fox seemed to freeze for a second, then, with a whisk of its white brush, it melted into the night.

With a sigh, Iris stepped back into her own world, bolting the door and drawing the curtains before switching on the lights and making up two drinks and a hot water bottle as she had done for many years.

Her father returned at eleven o'clock.

'What's this then? My two girls having a cosy night in?' Fred said jovially, bringing the rough liveliness of cold street air, tobacco and beer fumes into the warm bedroom.

'Mother had another turn. We had to call Dr Siddons in.'

'That right, Urse?' Fred put his coat away with the slightly clumsy movements of a man who's had a few drinks but not enough to make him drunk. 'How are you now?'

'It was terrible, Fred. Quite frightening. One of the worst attacks I've ever had. For a moment there I really thought I might die. But I'm much better now. Thanks to Iris. She's been reading to me.' She patted her daughter's fingers. 'I don't know what I'd do without my lovely girl.'

Above the alcohol and tobacco, Iris's sensitive nose detected something else. The faintest aroma of . . . not perfume exactly . . . powder – that was it. The delicate scent of face powder. She glanced sharply across at her mother, but Ursula was calmly smoothing out the turned-back sheet and settling herself for the night.

Fred eased off his outdoor shoes with a grunt of relief. 'They're saying outside it's a bomber's moon. Want to get settled in the shelter just in case?'

Ursula turned the idea down flat. 'The cellar was bad enough – but the Anderson . . . ! Can't we go back to the cellar?'

159

Fred removed his collar studs with a satisfied explosion of breath. 'I told you about the places we've cleared.'

One result of Fred and Pete's emergency 'patching up' after the heavy rescue squads had finished was first-hand experience of the aftermath of a bomb incident. And the most striking feature had been the way solid buildings had collapsed inwards like packs of cards, burying anyone in the cellars under tons of masonry and wood. The little tin-roofed Anderson shelters, however, seemed capable of surviving anything short of a direct hit.

The Cutters' was luxurious by most standards, with its wooden floor, white-painted walls bespeckled with cork lumps to absorb the condensation, electric lighting and bunks constructed by a professional carpenter. But it still flooded like all the Andersons in this area that suffered from being criss-crossed by the long-buried tributaries of the River Fleet.

'I'm not going down that dreadful box unless I absolutely have to. And it's so late now, I'm sure they won't come.'

'Please yourself, Urse. What about you, Iris?'

'I'll stay in my room too, unless there's an alert. Goodnight, Mummy. Daddy.'

Sleep wouldn't come. She tossed and turned restlessly, willing herself to be tired. But Taz's face kept getting in her way. She remembered his touch. His smile. The way his lips felt on hers. The way his arms had felt as they pulled her into his chest.

'This is ridiculous,' she told herself, twisting and pounding her pillows. 'When you're with him you practically give him ice burns . . . and if he were to walk in right this minute you'd . . . you'd . . .' What *would* she do if she found herself trapped in a bedroom with Taz Dixon? Or any other man, if it came to that? She really didn't know.

Frustrated and aware that her head was starting to thump painfully, she switched on the light and groped for the alarm clock. The white hands were splayed wide at ten to two. She was just replacing it on the bedside table when the alert that had saved Maury and Carla from their officious policeman on Hampstead Heath wailed into the night.

Already feeling worn out, she padded out on to the landing.

Her father joined her. 'What do you think?' Fred asked. 'Shelter?'

Iris frowned, straining to untangle the sounds outside. 'It's coming nearer.'

Fred made his way to a side window and tweaked back the blackout. 'Barrage is up on the heath . . . lights too. Looks like they're heading this way. I'll get your mother. Urse? Come on, turn out there . . .'

With arms full of folded blankets, Thermos flasks and hot water bottles, they trooped down to the shelter. All along the gardens the low voices, protesting wails of disturbed babies and frantic barking of dogs indicated that their neighbours were doing the same.

Bunks were hurriedly made up and they scrambled inside. The roaring crash outside was getting louder – and closer.

'Leave the light on, Fred.'

'If you like, Urse.'

The single bulb hung from the curved roof on its well-insulated cable. The next explosion sent a vibration through the thick soil piled over the corrugated metal. The light shivered, sending shadows teasing into places they didn't normally explore.

'Fred, it's never done that before.'

'Don't go worrying, Urse. You'll bring another turn on. It's just a bit closer than normal. Take a dose of your peppermint stuff.'

'I left it in the bedroom.'

'I'll get it.' Iris flicked back her blanket.

'No!' The sharpness of her father's tone startled her. He grabbed her wrist.

'You're . . .'

She meant to say 'You're hurting me, Daddy,' but she never got past the first word. The world went black, the floor seemed to rise up under her feet, and a roaring battered against her ears and forced its way inside her skull.

161

Chapter 17

Iris had come off worst. Since she was standing up in the shelter when the blast hit next door, the shockwave had thrown her backwards against the bunk. The back of her skull had collided with the wooden uprights and split open. When Fred had managed to grope his way to the tin that held their supply of matches and candles and strike a Vespa, he'd found her body crumpled on the Anderson floor, her dark hair gleaming wetly with the blood soaking into it.

For once Ursula had been of use. Instead of succumbing to another attack she'd climbed out of her bunk and covered her daughter with blankets while Fred struggled through the debris covering the entrance to the Anderson. Ignoring the rolling explosions and the answering crash of the ack-ack guns, he'd stumbled towards the house. The telephone was dead, but the ARP Warden from the post had run up, and between them they'd managed to organise a rescue squad to dig out survivors from next door, and an auxiliary ambulance and first-aid worker to tend to Iris. It wasn't until her daughter was safely on her way to hospital that Ursula had finally collapsed.

Both women had insisted on being discharged the following day. It was useless Fred pointing out that the electricity, gas and water were all off, or that the interior of the house was covered with dust and glass splinters. Home – even covered in blast damage – was preferable to a public ward . . .

'Well you can't stop here, that's certain sure,' Kate said, huddled in her coat against the winds whistling through the open windows and fluttering the shredded curtains.

She and Pete had arrived on the doorstep just as Fred had

163

drawn up with his wife and daughter. The car windows had gone the same way as every other piece of glass in the street, but at least the vehicle was driveable. And when Joshua had lumbered up behind Pansy and Maury a few minutes later he'd been handed a broom and told to clear up the splinters.

'Fred will arrange things,' Ursula announced. 'You can send some men up from the yard. What's the point in owning one otherwise?'

'The point,' Fred said grimly, 'is to make money. Which we do by working for others. Not ourselves. And we've contracts signed – with penalty clauses.'

'Fred – you're not going to leave us sitting here like this! I refuse. Iris and I will go to a hotel.'

'Don't be daft, Urse. No sense paying out good money on a hotel when you can stop with relatives.'

'You're certain sure welcome to stay with us. Pansy can share a bed with me and you and Iris could have the other room.'

Pansy said quickly, 'I can stay up Maury's. His mum won't mind. Will she, Maury?'

'I was thinking of Nana's,' Fred said.

'Nana's!' Ursula stiffened, colour miraculously returning to her cheeks.

'Well why not? She'll enjoy the company. I can stay here, keep an eye on the place.'

Ursula smiled thinly. 'I don't think it would be fair to expect Nana to cope with the extra work at her age. Iris is hardly in a fit state to help.'

'I'm all right. Really.' Iris touched the bandage around her head. 'It scarcely hurts at all now. And I'd like to stay with Nana.'

'That's settled then.' Fred slapped his hands together with hearty cheerfulness. 'And I'll send Doris up to lend a hand.'

'I'll make a start clearing up here,' Kate offered. 'Pansy can help me.'

'I've my best clothes on, Mum.'

'No sense doing more than sweep up the glass for now,'

164

Fred shrugged. 'You'll just get more dirt blowing in until we can get the windows fixed.'

'I'll do that then. Come give me a hand, Pansy.'

'Josh's got the broom, Mum.'

'I'm certain sure there's more than one. Come on.'

Maury promptly announced he was off.

'Don't, Maury. Please stop.'

'Gotta go, Panse. Business. Glad to see your family's all OK. Tell yer what, I'll come round tonight. Take yer up the pictures proper this time. That OK, Mrs C?'

'Yes,' Pansy said before her mother could answer.

'Good. See yer. Pleasure to see you ain't hurt serious, Mrs Cutter. By the way, sir – might have a bit of good news for you on the nag business. I'll call at a better time and set the price.' Maury tipped his hat in Ursula's direction before setting it in place and swaggering out, one hand thrust inside his breast pocket in a vaguely Napoleonic fashion.

Reluctantly Pansy followed her mother to the back scullery. It was even colder here and it smelt of sour churned earth and stale gas.

Kate shut the door firmly behind them. 'Where did you get to last night?'

Pansy mumbled that she'd stayed up at Maury's. She nudged shards of broken china with her toe, refusing to meet her mother's eye.

'Pansy . . .' Kate tried to take her daughter's hand.

Pansy quickly put them behind her back. She didn't want her mother to touch her ever again. Not after what she'd seen in Uncle Pete's bedroom. Of course she'd always known that grown-ups *did* things to each other – the sort of things that Maury sometimes tried to do to her – but until last night she'd always managed to cloak it in a sort of romantic haze. Now she knew what the sweaty reality looked like, and her mother was still doing it. It was horrible and embarrassing, and it made her feel sick.

'We didn't mean for you to see . . . Your Uncle Pete and me . . . Well, we . . . He loves me.'

'He can't love you. He's still married to his wife, isn't he?'

'Well, yes . . . but I doubt your Aunt Ellie's coming back now. Your Uncle Pete would like us to live together. All four of us.'

'At our house?' Pansy didn't think she could bear that. Just the idea of laying in the next room, knowing her mum was . . .

'We haven't talked about that much. I expect we'll rent another house. A bigger one.'

'You don't have to. I 'spect me and Maury will be getting married soon.'

'I'm certain sure you won't! You're too young.'

'I'm sixteen. Least, I will be come the fourteenth.'

'You still need my permission.'

'Well, I don't see why I can't have it. If you and Uncle Pete are going to live together like you're married, then me and Maury can do it proper.'

'Maury hasn't a regular job.'

'He's a businessman.'

'Yes. And don't think I haven't heard the stories about his "business", young lady.'

'They're lies!' Pansy tossed her curls, eyes flashing. 'Anyway, if you think that, why'd you let me go out with him? Not that I'd stop, even if you told me to, so there!'

'Don't you take that tone with me.' Kate took a deep breath. This wasn't helping. She had to repair the damage that last night had done right now, before it grew into an impossible rift between herself and her daughter. 'Maury will be called up soon, won't he?'

'Next January, I 'spect,' Pansy admitted.

'Then surely he can see it would be best to wait until he's out of the Army, or whatever – when you can make a proper home together.'

The pupils of Pansy's eyes grew until they swallowed up most of the purple irises. 'But, Mum, the war could last ages. Years and years. I'm not waiting until I'm old. I want to be with Maury now.'

Kate found the fact she'd used *I'm* rather than *we're* reassuring. 'Has Maury asked you to marry him?'

'Course. We talk about it all the time. And he's giving

me an extra special present on me birthday. It's gonna be an engagement ring, I just know it is.'

Kate relaxed a little more. Talking was one thing; making a definite promise was quite another. Taking a dustpan and small brush from the scullery cupboard, she started sweeping debris from the table and cupboard tops. 'Why don't you go and ask Uncle Fred if he has a really thick pair of gloves you can borrow? We can at least pick up all the broken glass before it treads into your Aunt Ursula's carpets.'

Pansy accepted this tacit closure of the subject for now. By watching her mother and Uncle Pete and making sure she wasn't left alone with either, she managed to busy herself helping to clear up as best they could, and packing what Ursula and Iris would need for their short stay with Nana Cutter – including a share of the rations Iris had drawn for the next week. The suitcase and shopping bag were loaded into the car's boot and the two walking wounded were tucked into the back seat.

Fred tapped the petrol gauge that was showing near empty and murmured, 'Filter out a gallon from the lorries' cans when you're down the wharf, Pete. I've no more coupons left for the car.'

Pete winked. 'No trouble. Give Mum my love. Tell her . . . tell her me and Kate will be up to see her soon. Got a bit of news for her.'

Fred nodded absently, his attention fixed on the car that needed to be coaxed into life. Ursula, however, stiffened, her eyes flickering between Kate and Pansy, who were standing by the garden gate ready to wave them off on their short journey.

She leant forward. 'Pansy, wouldn't you like to come up with us and say hello to your grandmother?'

'Yes. I would.' Pansy darted forward, pleased to be handed this excuse to get away.

Nana welcomed both her granddaughters with open arms, her son with a cool peck on the cheek, and her daughter-in-law with a malicious smile that let her know she was well aware she didn't want to be here. 'Isn't it lucky I'd aired the sheets for that spare bed only a couple of days ago? You and Iris will have to share, but I daresay you'll not mind that . . . you being so close all the time.'

If Ursula had heard the edge to the words she gave no sign. Instead she offered to peel some vegetables for lunch. 'If that would be helpful.'

'I thought Iris was the one who'd got the knock on the head.'

Ursula's lips tightened but she kept her voice pleasant. 'I assume that means yes. Goodbye, Fred. Don't take too long with the repairs, will you?'

'Isn't he stopping for his *lunch*? Or dinner, as we common folk call it?'

'He's anxious to get back and make a start on the house. We wouldn't wish for looters to get in.'

Fred was dismissed to make his own arrangements for dinner. Iris was taken off by her grandmother to help make up the spare room, and Pansy found herself in the kitchen with her aunt.

'You don't mind helping to scrape these carrots, do you, dear?'

Pansy shook her head. She concentrated on making the peelings as thin as she could. Her aunt had no such scruples: the curl of peel she detached from a potato was almost half an inch thick!

'Maury's mum bakes potato peel for her hens.'

'Does she, dear?' Ursula dropped her potato into cold water and picked up another. 'He seems a very pleasant young man.'

'Oh he is. Maury's ever so nice.'

'His mother's a widow, isn't she?'

'Yes.' The tip of Pansy's tongue protruded from a corner of her mouth as she sliced a carrot into rounds and placed them in an enamel bowl of cold water.

'That must be difficult – raising a child on your own.'

'Mrs O'Day has six. But they're not children. I mean, four of his brothers are already grown up. One's in the fire service and one's in the Army, one's in the RAF and the other one's in the Navy.'

'Plainly the country may sleep a little easier,' Ursula said. She'd selected a second potato but was making no attempt to peel it. 'Personally I don't know how I'd have managed the twins if anything had happened to your Uncle Fred. I do admire the way your mother coped. It must have been hard for her, on her own. And it's the same for your Uncle Peter, of course.'

''Spect so.'

'Which is why it's lucky they get on so well, don't you think?'

''Spect so.' From beneath her long lashes, Pansy could see her aunt twisting the unpeeled potato between her fingers. She had lovely hands, soft and white with buffed nails.

The rotating fingers stopped, and Pansy's stomach tightened.

'It's in the kitchen that most men are so hopeless, aren't they? I don't suppose your Maury could cook a meal to save his life.'

'No.' Pansy felt the tightness in her midriff relaxing again. She didn't mind how much she talked about Maury. 'But his mum cooks all his dinners and things. 'Cept when he comes round our house.'

Ursula split the skin on the King Edward. 'And your Uncle Peter and cousin Joshua. Do they come round for their dinner as well?'

'Sometimes.'

With her thumb behind the blade, Ursula was coaxing brown peel away to expose the tender cream flesh underneath. 'You can't have many rations left after you've fed your cousin.'

'Mum cooks stuff off the ration. Batter puddings and sausages and stuff – when she can get it.'

'Peter always had a partiality for a good Yorkshire pudding. He must enjoy calling.'

''Spect so.'

'I've never understood why he wanted to live in that tiny flat in the yard. He could easily afford to rent a house and employ a woman to come in. Your mother does some of his washing for him, doesn't she?'

'Ironing,' Pansy mumbled, her head bent low as she concentrated on dissecting another carrot into perfect rings.

Ursula gave a light laugh and touched her niece's wrist with her manicured nail tips. 'I don't suppose he invites you round to sample *his* home cooking?'

'No.'

'What about your mother? Does she visit the flat often?'

'Not often.'

'But sometimes.'

''Spect so.' The memory of the twisted bodies in the flat's bedroom flooded back. ''Scuse me. I've got to go to the lav.' Knocking back her chair, Pansy fled.

Ursula set down the naked potato with a thoughtful look. Things were plainly moving faster than she'd anticipated. If her son's inheritance was to be protected, she'd have to do something soon – before Kate produced a little bastard to inherit Cutter's.

Chapter 18

Maury hadn't bought an engagement ring. He didn't even know he was expected to. Instead he'd been laying out a weekly payment for a necklace and earrings he'd spotted in Thomson's window months ago. As soon as he'd seen the delicate cluster of mauve and white-painted enamel pansies held on a gold filigree chain with matching posy earrings, he'd known he had to have them for Panse's sixteenth. Now, finally, he'd paid out the last pound.

'And I'll have that too.' He pointed to a silver bracelet.

The assistant twitched it from the display case and showed the price tag. 'It's silver and turquoise, sir. Three pounds, ten shillings.'

Maury peeled four notes off the roll and flung them down casually. He liked that 'sir'. The man's tone held a definite note of respect now.

'Don't say nothing about what I just bought,' he instructed Joshua as they left the shop.

'Another secret?'

'That's the idea. Birthday presents for Pansy and me mum. Women like all that jewellery stuff. It keeps them sweet-tempered,' he announced grandly.

'Maury's mum's birthday?'

'Saturday.' Maury patted the two packages and allowed himself a small self-satisfied smugness. He'd still give her the saucepan he'd discovered with the syrup tins. But he'd surprise her with the bracelet as well. It would undoubtedly be the most expensive present she'd receive.

'Look, Maury, there's the man with the meat.'

Tusker was strolling along the other side of Chalk Farm

Road, his hands thrust into the pockets of his boiler suit. Maury half expected him to pretend he didn't know him, but Tusker glanced across and touched his cap brim. It was a worker-to-boss sort of gesture. Maury's backbone grew a few more inches.

'Come on.' He nudged Joshua, who'd been standing in slack-mouthed fascination, admiring a couple of large shires hauling a carrier's cart into the entrance to the LMS Yards. 'We got business to do.'

Both hot food vans handed over his cut of the takings without any verbal protest when they saw Joshua looming – although their looks could have melted ice in Antarctica. As he'd expected, neither could manage more than thirty bob.

His next call was at the Golden Cross. He'd deliberately left it until later – partly because Griswald seemed to be out in the afternoons, and partly to let Carla see who was boss.

'Been busy. 'Ad a couple of me other businesses to sort out,' he explained as she let them into the bar.

'I weren't bothered. I told yer – I trust yer. 'Ello, muscles. Want a lemonade?'

She poured Joshua a large glass and added a bag of crisps from under the counter, then drew two halves of bitter for herself and Maury. She didn't bother to put any money in the till.

'Where's Griswald?'

'Out. I told yer. Don't worry, he never gets back 'til opening time.'

'Where's he go?'

'Card game.'

'Every day?'

'Most days.'

'Does he win?'

'Hardly ever. And talking of winnings . . .' She rubbed her fingers. Maury handed over a sheaf of folded notes. Hitching her skirt, Carla tucked them into her stocking-top, giving them an enticing glimpse of white flesh.

Shifting uncomfortably on his bar stool, Maury caught the amused gleam in her cat eyes and knew she was teasing him. Well, let her. She needed him to do business and she knew it. Reaching over, he deliberately ran a finger down her shin. 'Where'd you get your stockings, Carla? It's me girl's birthday next month. Might get her a few pairs as a present.'

'Surplus stock, darlin',' Carla complacently straightened one leg, displaying the sheer silk. 'Fell out the back of a warehouse.'

'Pretty.' Joshua imitated Maury's stroking gesture.

Carla gave a deep throaty laugh. 'Well get you, muscles! Like me legs, do you?'

'Like stockings.' Earnestly Joshua fixed his eyes on her. 'Joshua wants to buy some. For a present too.'

'Well, well . . .' Carla slid off her stool. 'Got a girl, have you?'

'Joshua's girl. Pretty hair. Like silk.'

'She sounds a real smasher. Maury give you any wages for helping out the other night?'

'He don't need wages. He ain't got nothing to spend it on.'

'Then he can stick it under the mattress, can't he? Give him something. Stop here, muscles . . . I'll be back in a tick.'

She wiggled away and they heard her heels clicking up the uncarpeted internal staircase. Maury extracted two pound notes from his wallet and reluctantly handed them over. He didn't have to do as Carla said, of course – he was the boss – but he supposed it might be a good idea to keep Joshua sweet . . .

Carla reappeared and handed a packet to Joshua. 'Black silk, muscles. She'll look like a film star in these, see if she don't. 'Ope they fit. 'Ow tall is she?'

'Small. Like Maury.'

'I *ain't* small.'

'Yes yer are. For a bloke. Don't matter. They're right about size not mattering.' With another teasing wink, Carla let them both out.

His last call was at Ivy Thomas's dairy. The yard gate was already bolted, a chalked notice informing customers: 'Business Closed'.

Maury had already agreed a price of seventy pounds for the

173

bad-tempered nag and its harness, with his present owner, but the Cutters had insisted on examining Kitchener before they parted with the ninety pounds he'd fixed with them.

Only Pete was on the wharf when they arrived.

'Go see Kate – Mrs Cutter – in the office, son,' he said after Kitchener had paraded up and down the wharf to everyone's satisfaction. 'She'll settle up with you.' Raising his voice he shouted to Joshua to hitch up the old cart and start loading the cement and timber he'd find behind the brick store. 'He can start earning his keep right away. We'll take 'em round your Uncle Fred's place.'

Maury made his way to the office, glad of the chance to get into the warm. The early promise of spring had definitely gone now, and a biting wind was whipping round the corners of the storage sheds and ruffling up the canal waters. He found the small cottage surprisingly crowded. At least six men were lined up in front of Kate's desk. She handed the first one an insurance card and told him to report at seven tomorrow.

'Will there be any overtime, miss?'

'I'm certain sure there will be. We've three big repair contracts.'

With a smile the workman bobbed his head, resettled his cap and left. Maury fitted himself in by a filing cabinet and casually read a newspaper while he waited for the other five to be dealt with. They all seemed well within conscription age.

He said as much to Kate once they'd all gone.

'Temporary release from the services for essential war work. We're repairing all this blitz damage.'

'They seem dead pleased about it, Mrs C.'

'They're on union rates. Better money than they can get in the services by far. They're married men, with families to support. It's not easy to manage on Army pay. Not for the women anyway.'

'I suppose not.'

'You'll be called up soon, won't you, Maury?'

'Next year I expect, Mrs C.'

'Soon enough.' Kate leant her elbows on the desk. 'Maury,

174

if I ask you something, will you tell me the God's honest truth?'

'Course I will, Mrs C.' The lie tripped out of his mouth. He'd tell her what he wanted her to know, but he'd do it so it sounded like the truth.

'Are you planning to get engaged to Pansy?'

'Well course I am, Mrs C. I thought yer understood – about me and Panse. I ain't playing fast and loose with 'er, if that's what yer thinking.'

'No. It's not. I'm sure you *do* care for her, Maury. But she's very young . . . I'd not feel happy her thinking about marriage, not for another year at least. Or better two.'

'Two?' Maury tried to imagine two years in the future and couldn't. It was a lifetime. Until that moment he'd never actually thought about *when* he and Pansy would marry . . . now suddenly he wanted it to be soon. He opened his mouth to tell Kate that it was OK, he had plenty of money, enough to look after her daughter better than she'd ever been treated before . . . and was frustrated by the arrival of Ursula.

'That woman is quite impossible,' she announced, sweeping into the office with a total disregard for the blackout regulations.

'Nana Cutter?' Kate asked, coming round her desk to redraw the door curtain.

'Who else? Good evening, Mr O'Day.'

'Evening, Mrs Cutter. Hope you're feeling better.'

'Thank you. I am a little recovered. Although I shall most definitely have a relapse if I am forced to spend another night under that woman's roof. In fact I feel quite peculiar just thinking about what I've had to put up with.' Setting her handbag on the desk she removed a small stopper bottle and asked Kate for a teaspoon. Two doses of the sticky green liquid gave her sufficient breath to demand what had happened to her husband and his promise to make a start on the house repairs.

Kate informed her that Fred had gone down to a site to check out they'd shifted an unexploded bomb before he sent workmen in, but Pete and Joshua were taking the materials round to Bartholomew right now. 'It will only be a few days, Ursula. I heard the survivors from next door got sent down a rest centre. I'm certain sure Nana's is better than that.'

'Are you? Well you, of course, are not privileged to be in the same house.' Carelessly abandoning the sticky spoon and bottle on Kate's desk, Ursula drew her coat round herself and sat down. She crossed her legs, the upper foot tapping against air in a frenetic rhythm.

Kate and Maury exchanged a look. 'Well, I'll be getting on, Mrs C,' Maury said. 'Mr Cutter said you'd see me right for the horse.'

'Of course.' Taking out a locked cash box, Kate counted out the notes.

Tipping his hat to both women, Maury wished them a good evening and headed for the door.

The scrunch of thick boots on the gravel surface coming up from the wharf made him think for a second that Joshua had returned.

'Oi, mate! Anyone left in the office?'

Definitely not Joshua. Although he knew the voice . . . and the large, stocky figure outlined against the dying light could almost have been Joshua's double when seen like this without features. Closer up, he made out the heavy jaw and broader nose of Blackie Geoghan.

'She in, mate?'

'Yeah. She is.'

A more sensitive man might have taken offence at the expression on the occupants' faces as he strolled into the cottage office. Blackie, however, had always been indifferent to others' opinions – particularly female opinions.

'OK to leave the boats tied up, missus?'

'I suppose so. Aren't you going down to the docks?'

'Tomorrow, missus. Got to see a man down the Redcap tonight.'

'You'll have to come back along the tow-path. I'm locking the gates soon.'

Ursula was holding a handkerchief over her mouth and nose to deaden the mixture of stale sweat and beer that was exuding through Blackie's skin. Through this linen gag, she said, 'We shall of course be checking the yard in the morning. If there is anything missing . . .'

'You calling me a thief, missus?'

'I am merely making you aware of the situation. Everyone knows what they say about boaters.'

'And what's that then?'

Ursula wrinkled a fastidious nose. 'That they are among the great unwashed, Mr . . . ?'

'Geoghan. Is that all the landies say about us then?'

Ursula had had a trying day trapped with her mother-in-law's sharp-edged tongue snicking sly taunts at every opportunity. She'd stormed out intending to give her husband a piece of her mind, only to find that he'd managed to dodge before she could pitch it. And now this smelly lout was standing in their office speaking to her with an insolence that simply wouldn't have been tolerated before the war.

'No it isn't, Mr Geoghan. You're also known to be infested with lice and vermin and heaven knows what. Besides being appallingly ignorant.'

'Do they now?' Blackie rasped a thumb stained by engine oil over his chin stubble. 'You'd be the other Mrs Cutter, wouldn't you? Your girl's the one with the cut-up face.'

'I am Mrs Frederick Cutter, yes.'

'I hear your girl's courting. Just goes to show there's a lid for every pot, don't it? If you ain't too fussy about the fit. And I don't suppose her can be, can her?'

'Iris? Courting? I think you've made a mistake. Whom do you imagine my daughter is courting?'

Blackie told her.

Chapter 19

'Happy birthday to you. Happy birthday to you. Happy birthday, dear Mum . . . Happy birthday to you!'

'You shouldn't 'ave,' Eileen O'Day protested for the tenth time since she'd stepped through her front door to find the banner Sammy and Annie had made stretching across the hall and a party tea being laid out in the kitchen.

'Open your presents,' Sammy demanded. 'Mine first. It's bound to be loads better than Maury's. His is a saucepan . . . anyone can see.'

'That's enough, Sammy. Saucepans is always useful. Especially after you took me best aluminium pot without a by your leave.'

'We had to take a saucepan up school to 'elp make a Spitfire. Ain't that right, Mrs Goodwin?' Sammy appealed to his oldest brother's fiancée, who taught the infant class at Riley Street school.

'That's right, Sammy,' Rose agreed. 'Although we did ask you to get your parents' permission first. Not that a lot did, I'm afraid,' she admitted ruefully.

'Oh, well . . . can't grudge the RAF something can you?' Eileen said, tearing off the newspaper wrapping on Maury's present. She weighed the solid pot in one hand with pleasure and smacked a kiss on Maury's cheek. 'Thanks, love.'

Smirking slightly, Maury dropped his hand to his pocket to extract the tissue-wrapped bracelet. Now he'd really show them.

'Mine now!' Sammy thrust a clumsily wrapped brown paper package into his mother's chest. It was a large pot of cold cream, which released a potent scent of violets

179

when Eileen unscrewed the lid and dabbed a smear on her hand.

There was a bottle of scent from Annie that smelt so strongly of cheap violets she'd probably got it from the same market stall as Sammy, a pretty tin of decorated biscuits from Rose with a matching tea canister from Pat, a pair of gloves from Shane and Conn, with a card in Pat's handwriting explaining that they'd both sent postal orders to buy something so he'd put the money together.

'Nothing from Brendan?' Eileen looked to Rose for an answer, since Pat had mysteriously disappeared muttering something about an errand.

'No. Not yet. But it's probably just got delayed in the post.'

'Yes. That'll be it. They'd not have sent him off anywhere without telling us first, would they?'

Since it was quite likely that, if Brendan's Regiment *had* been ordered abroad, the first their families would hear about it would be a letter from some foreign camp, Rose mumbled what might be vague reassurance.

Maury took a deep breath and stepped forward, the bracelet in his hand.

A bustle of arrivals filled the front hall. 'It's only us!'

Frustrated, Maury replaced the package in his pocket once more as Rose's mother walked in, together with some ancient crone of a relative who lived in their basement, her middle-aged daughter, who seemed to have even less wits than Joshua in her ration card, and that damn cockney kid, Nafnel, whom Rose was fostering. More contributions were added to the tea table.

Maury tried to give his mum the bracelet again. 'Mum . . .' He squeezed through the partying room. The talk and the temperature were getting higher.

'Yes, love? Oh, here's Pansy!'

That was one interruption at least he was pleased about – until Joshua loomed behind his petite cousin.

'What the hell are you doing here?'

'Don't use that language in my kitchen, Maury, or you'll go straight out of this house. Understand? I said he could come for his dinner today.'

Joshua's face split into the usual wide beam. Several neighbours who weren't used to him shuffled nervously nearer the back door.

'Hello, Maury's mum. Happy Birthday. Joshua's got you a present.' He held out the stockings Carla had given him.

Eileen's jaw dropped. 'Black silk! Good heaven's, I can't wear them!'

'Don't like?' Joshua's expression melted from happiness to abject misery.

Eileen stood on tiptoe and hugged him. 'Well, of course I *like* them. It's just . . . you shouldn't have gone spending all that money on me.'

Joshua returned the hug and told her it was all right. 'Didn't spend any money on them. They fell out the back of a warehouse.'

Several people laughed. Maury's toe itched with the urge to kick the big stupid lump right where it would hurt most.

'Mum, I got yer—'

'Mind your backs there!' The hall reverberated to rolling wood and metal as Pat reappeared, bowling a small beer keg.

'Oh, Pat, no! Wherever did you get it?'

'Pumped out a pub cellar last week. Landlord sold us one.'

'We'll never drink it all!'

'This lot will!' Pat straightened up and jerked a thumb over his shoulder. Husbands, who'd been uninterested when their wives had headed across the road for a tea and cakes party, had suddenly been struck by an urge to wish Eileen many happy returns. They came clutching glasses, mugs and – in one case – a jam jar. Someone started a sing-song, accompanying himself on a set of spoons.

The moment had gone. Hardly anyone would see him now. Maury shifted the bracelet to an inside breast pocket. Perhaps he'd find a customer for it down the Golden Cross.

The shift and eddies of the guests pushed Pansy up against him. She snuggled an arm inside his. 'I'm sorry I never got your mum a present, Maury. I meant to – but I've got to save my spending money.'

'It's OK, Panse, don't suppose she expected one. Want a lemonade?'

'Please.'

He fetched her a glass. Rose and her mother were handing out plates of cold meat with pickles and cold potatoes.

'Oh, Marge, you really shouldn't have,' Eileen said again. 'All this meat! I've not tasted beef this good since this lot started. It's not off your ration, is it?'

Marge gave her a conspiratorial elbow in the side. 'I wouldn't normally take more than me fair share . . .'

'I know that, Marge.'

'But special occasions, like yer birthday . . . and me daughter's wedding—'

'Everyone does it. Can you get any more?'

'Couldn't say. What do you reckon, Maury?'

'Maury?' Eileen shot a sharp look at her second youngest, who was helping himself and Pansy to pickled cauliflower. 'Oh, I see. Well I hope we ain't about to have no coppers looking under the beds for pinched pork chops.'

'No. We ain't.' Maury reached for the bowl of potatoes and was beaten to it by Joshua, who tipped the entire contents on to his plate.

'Blimey,' Marge muttered under her breath. 'I'm glad I ain't feeding him. Where'd you find him, Eileen?'

'He's a friend of Maury's.'

'Don't mean you have to invite him up here, Mum.'

Eileen admitted that she felt sorry for the poor love. 'His mum dying when he was a little 'un . . .'

'Joshua's mum didn't die, Mrs O'Day.' Panse was thrust into their huddle by the swelling crowd. 'She ran off with the insurance man.'

'Really, love? That's funny. I could have sworn he told me his mum was an angel.'

'I think that's what Uncle Pete told him, make him feel better. Like his mum hadn't gone off without him deliberate.'

Maury stiffened and jabbed a fork towards the doorway. 'Blimey, Mum, you ain't invited him too!'

Felonious Monk craned his neck over the heads and located Eileen. Drawing himself up he dropped down the few steps from the hall and wriggled through to her side. 'Madam.' He took one hand and kissed it. 'I 'ope you'll forgive this 'ere intrusion, but I 'ad to take the opportunity to wish yer the best of felicitations on yer . . . er, felicitous day.'

'Beg pardon?' Eileen reclaimed her fingers.

'He said,' Maury translated. 'Happy Birthday. And he's hoping to scrounge free grub and beer.'

'There's no call for that. I 'appen to find yer mother a fine woman. It's a privilege to be called 'er friend.'

'Pint, Fel?' Pat shouted across.

'Thought yer'd never ask. Ta.' With a sly smirk at Maury's scowling face, Fel headed for the barrel. As he left he remarked that he was glad to hear Maury had got shot of that flaming nag.

'Nag?' Eileen's face went pale apart from a flush along the cheekbones. 'You bought a horse?'

'Yeah. Sort of. What of it, Mum?'

Eileen put her hand over her mouth. Wide-eyed, she looked round at her guests tucking into plates of roasted meat. 'I'll never forgive you for this, Maury . . . never!'

'You what?'

Bewildered, Maury watched his mother thrust her way out of the back door and disappear into the back yard lavatory.

'Maury. Can I talk to you?'

'Course you can, Panse.' Taking out his handkerchief, he soaked a corner under the scullery tap and scrubbed a smear of artificial chocolate icing off her nose. 'What's up? Yer been real quiet this week.'

'Not here. Let's go in another room.'

It was easier said than done – Half the square seemed to be packed into the place.

'I got an idea. Stick yer coat on . . . I'll be back soon . . .' He slid back through the crowded kitchen. The din was incredible and a warm fug of condensation and tobacco smoke was fogging up the windows. Maury headed for the dresser, casually slid one of the drawers open a fraction and slipped his fingers inside. The key was right at the front. He pocketed it quickly and forced his way out of the crush and back to Pansy.

183

'Come on . . .' He tried to push her out of the front door, but she resisted him.

'What's up? Thought you wanted to go.'

'Yes. No. Maury . . .' Tears filmed Pansy's eyes. 'Maury . . . me birthday present. The special one . . . Can I have it now? Today?'

'Today?' He was surprised. The necklace and earrings were in his bedroom and there was no reason why he couldn't go and get them. But he'd been looking forward to making a big fuss of her on the day, perhaps even taking her out to a posh restaurant with flowers on the table, fancy waiters and big silver serving dishes like they'd seen at some of the places that had bought the beef carcasses.

'*Please*, Maury . . .' The tears had started to tremble over her bottom lashes.

'Yeah. OK, Panse. Wait for us in the front. I'll just go get it.'

She was watching a game of knock-about football in the street by the time he struggled back down the crowded stairs. He eyed the players. One of them was a mate of Sammy's.

'Oi, Piggy!'

A plump child with owl-glasses looked up from his crouching stance between the makeshift goalposts.

'There's cake and lemonade left if anyone wants . . .' As he'd hoped, the whole team took this as an invitation and thundered down the path to claim their share of the treats.

'Quick . . .' Grabbing Pansy's hand, he ran her across the briefly deserted street to Chief Inspector Stamford's house. Inserting the spare key his mum used when she came over to clean, he ushered Pansy inside.

'Maury . . . we didn't ought to.' Pansy's fingers twisted in his.

'Don't see why not. He's always over our house. Don't fret, Panse, he's away. Has been for weeks.' He quickly calculated his best tactics. The possibilities of being alone with Pansy in an empty house occurred to him. 'Come and 'ave a look at his bathroom.'

'What for? I've seen plenty of bathrooms.' Pansy tossed her

head but allowed herself to be pulled upstairs nevertheless. 'Can I have my present now, Maury?'

He opened the door to Jack Stamford's double bedroom on the first floor and drew her down to sit beside him before handing over the oblong package.

'Is this it?' Her voice shook.

'Yeah.' He was puzzled by her stillness. 'Aren't you gonna open it?'

She did so – very slowly. The filigree chain and painted enamel fell into her lap.

She let it lie, a pool of gold and mauve against her mulberry coat.

'It's a necklace, Panse. And earrings. French, the bloke said. Cost a packet.'

He'd imagined her flinging herself into his arms, telling him how clever he was, how much she adored him. Instead she was just sitting there with head bent forward so that her dark hair obscured her face.

'What's up? Don't you like 'em?'

'They're very nice.' Her voice shook and caught on a sob. Lifting her head, she twisted to face him. Tears were flowing down her cheeks.

'Panse! What's the matter? If you really hate 'em I'll get yer something else.' To hell with it, he decided. He'd even spend some of his capital if necessary. He couldn't bear to see her like this.

'I thought . . . I thought . . . it would be an engagement ring. I thought you wanted to marry me, Maury.'

'Well I do. Course I do! Yer know that, Panse. We talked about it . . . the big house, remember? Up Hampstead?'

'I don't care about a big house, Maury. I don't care if we have to live in one room, long as we can be together. I won't go and live with Uncle Pete.'

He didn't understand the reference to her uncle, but he did grasp that he'd let her down. 'Panse, don't cry. I'll get yer a ring, I swear. We'll be engaged from right now if you like.'

'Can we?' Pansy raised a hopeful face.

'Don't see why not. We're engaged. That's it. OK?'

Pansy sniffed up her tears and ran the back of her sleeve over her eyes. She managed a watery smile. 'Oh, Maury, I do love you.'

'I love you too, Panse.'

She lifted her lips. Putting his arms round her he kissed her; awkwardly at first, but then with increasing enthusiasm. The bouncing movement of the mattress tipped them backwards on to the bed quilt. Maury found himself on top of her. He tried to undo her coat and was pushed off. Pansy wriggled out and sat up, panting slightly, her face flushed and her eyes sparkling.

Confused, Maury sat up too. 'What's up?'

'Nothing. I mean . . . Maury, do you know what to do? What married people do, I mean – in bed?'

'Course I do, Panse.'

'How?'

'Well . . . er . . . blokes do, Panse.' The truth was that his own knowledge had been picked up from sly sniggers and hints in the playground, the markets and the pubs. 'It will be all right. I won't hurt you or nothing.'

'Let's do it then.'

Maury's jaw dropped. 'What?'

'Let's get it over with right now.'

'I . . . er . . .' It was what he'd hoped for, but he couldn't believe she was actually prepared to do it.

'Don't you want to, Maury?'

'Yeah . . . yeah, of course I do.' He tried to sound eager. But he suddenly wished he'd practised a bit with someone else first.

Pansy sprang up and started unbuttoning her coat.

'Hang on!'

The idea of doing it on Mr Stamford's bed made his stomach turn over. His mum came in here to clean regularly. She'd be bound to notice – in the way mums had of noticing things you thought they'd never ever find out. He took Pansy's hand and led her up to the second landing. The back room was Annie's bedroom, but she invariably slept over at the O'Days' house in Eileen's bedroom. The room felt cold and unused in the dying afternoon light.

Pansy looked down at the small, narrow single bed. 'Wait outside until I call you, Maury.'

Alone on the dark landing, Maury found himself caught between dread that Stamford would return before Pansy called him in and a half hope that he might. He wandered restlessly, sticking his head into the third room that gave off this landing. It was little more than a narrow passage really. Some houses had it fitted up with a cooker and sink if the top floor was let off separately. Maybe he and Panse could do that in his mum's house.

'Maury. You can come in now.'

He pulled up with a gasp, suddenly aware that he'd been pacing round and round the landing. Taking a deep breath, he twisted the door handle.

Pansy was lying under the covers, the sheet drawn up to her chin. Her clothes were neatly folded over a chair. 'You now, Maury. I won't look if you don't want me to.'

He could only make out Pansy's outline in the bed; her features had disappeared in the quarter light. He hoped it was the same for him as he added his own clothes to hers until he was left in just his underpants.

Feeling for the edge of the blankets he lifted them just enough to slide inside. Pansy wriggled away to give him room, but the mattress was an old one that had been used by Stamford himself prior to his marriage; in consequence, there was a slight hollow in the centre. As they turned to each other in the darkness, the natural dip tipped them into each other in a tangle of bare flesh and sudden, confused but irresistible feelings.

Later, much later, lying together, warm and dazed by what had happened to them, Pansy whispered, 'I'm so happy, Maury.' She snuggled closer so that her nose was almost touching his. 'I want everyone to know I love you. Don't you feel like that, Maury?'

'Of course I do, Pansy.' How could he not after the past few hours? He wanted to stay in this room marvelling at the beauty of her body and drowning himself again and again in the incredible intensity of the experience.

'Listen, Panse.' He held her close. She tried to kiss him. 'No, listen. We'd best not tell anyone about the engagement . . . until yer birthday.'

'Why?'

'Well, you'll be sixteen then. I ain't exactly sure it's legal for you to be engaged if you ain't sixteen. You don't want them sending you off to one of them homes for bad girls, do you?'

'They wouldn't, Maury . . . would they?'

He didn't suppose so for a minute. But there was a danger the coppers who had it in for him might get to hear and start asking her questions. An engagement was OK, but what they'd just done . . .

'I don't know, Panse. But it's only a few weeks. It can be our special secret 'til then.'

'Special secret.' She said the words as if she were tasting each one. 'I think that's ever so romantic.' With a small laugh, she pushed her lips into the hollow of his throat.

Reluctantly he suggested they'd better go before the party broke up and they were seen leaving the house.

With a small sigh of pleasure, Pansy wriggled away from him and slipped out of the warm bed. Watching her re-dressing, Maury asked if she was having a party for her own birthday.

'I . . . I don't know. Mum usually . . . but I don't want . . .' Once again Pansy found she couldn't tell him about what she'd seen in her Uncle Pete's bedroom. It didn't seem right to be talking about her mum like that, not even to Maury. 'I don't feel like a party, Maury. I'd rather go out. Tell you what – they're having a big dance at the old piano factory on Easter Saturday. In aid of prisoners of war. We could go to that, couldn't we?'

Her mum couldn't object to that – it was for the war effort. She was being patriotic.

'Suppose.' Maury swung his legs out of the bed. 'How much are the tickets?'

'Six shillings and sixpence,' Pansy admitted. 'And we'd have to take Addie Dixon as well. I sort of promised she could come to me party, so if I don't have one . . . I'll pay

188

for her myself,' she added hurriedly. 'I expect gran will give me some money for me birthday.'

Maury wouldn't hear of it. After the last couple of hours he felt ten feet tall and in love with the world. Even Skinny. 'I'll pay,' he said grandly. 'Just leave it to me, doll.'

Chapter 20

If he'd stopped to think about it for a few minutes, Taz would have seen the sense in changing his clothes and cleaning up before going round to the Cutter house. But the rumours brought up the canals by the boats and barges over the past week had become twisted like Chinese whispers, until it had seemed both the Cutter women were lying in hospital, burnt, blasted and not expected to recover.

The talk hadn't reached the *Rainbow* until they'd tied up for the night near the floating barge that held the boaters' school at Bull's Bridge wharves. At which point a couple of eight-year-olds had described in gruesome and highly imaginative detail what had happened to the 'posh liddies' from Cutter's Wharf.

Even discounting most of the unlikely elements, it was obvious that something had happened. Taz had begged the use of a phone in one of the boating companies offices, but there was no answer from the wharf office, and the plum-voiced operator hadn't been able to connect him to Nana Cutter unless he knew her telephone number.

In the end he'd dashed back to the boats and, ignoring Addie's protests that it was too late, too dark and too bleedin' likely to snow to move any further, he'd put the *Rainbow* ahead at full speed, unleashing a furious barrage of shouts from the vessels that were caught in his wash.

By the time he'd reached Hawley Road he'd more or less convinced himself he was panicking for nothing. Surely if Iris had been hurt real bad the old girl would have found some way to let him know?

He'd known that most of his relationship with Iris was

191

down to Nana Cutter's manipulations. Not that that had come as any surprise; it had always been part of his technique to charm the mothers and grandmothers. What had been a shock had been realising his feelings for Iris were deeper than for any of the other girls he'd flirted with and bedded along the canal banks.

At first she'd been just a challenge. That quiet shyness and reserve had been irresistible. He'd had to see whether he could succeed where others had so obviously failed. The scarred face hadn't bothered him. In fact, he'd hardly noticed it after the first few hours in her company. Instead he'd seen the grave way those amazing mauve eyes regarded him from under thick black lashes; the way her nose wrinkled unconsciously when she was thinking over her answer; the tiny short curls at the nape of her neck that you could only see when she tied the longer hair back, and the figure that swelled in interesting curves under the slightly staid clothes that she always seemed to wear.

He'd found himself thinking about her as he steered unseeingly along the long-learnt canal routes, his arms and body weight moving the heavily laden boat without any conscious thought on his part. No one had ever taught him how to steer. Like all boaters' children, as soon as he was old enough to sit up he'd been tethered to the cabin roof, where his parents could keep an eye on him and he could safely watch as they manoeuvred the boats along the waters and through the locks. By the time he was tall enough to stand on a box with the tiller bar tucked under his arm, he'd known what to do without having to be told.

It had been the same for his mum and dad. And his grandparents. You were born on a boat, grew up on the boats, raised your family on the boats, and likely as not you'd die on the boats unless your family had got themselves a cottage by the canal where the old 'uns could stay once the work got too hard for them.

Addie was right. It was daft to think of taking a woman who wasn't used to the life on the water. Especially one like Iris Cutter. He'd never been to her home, but he could imagine her life. Warm fires in the winter instead of having to break through the ice; a bit of light dusting and sewing rather than struggling with straps frozen solid over the cargo tarpaulins; proper meals at a real dining table instead of standing at the tiller with a plate in one hand and a stoop of water from the can to wash it down.

No matter how much he wanted to, he couldn't see Iris using the bucket latrine in the engine room, or stoving out the cabin with candles and formalin to get rid of the bed bugs. It would be best to get himself fixed up with one of the girls from the boats. There were several who'd indicated they'd be more than willing for him to step across to their boat when they tied up. But at night, lying on the board bed that had been his parents', he'd found himself imagining Iris lying next to him as he explored that intriguing body under the grey blankets.

It was his bad luck that Ursula opened the door to the Bartholomew Road house. She and Iris had moved back from Nana Cutter's that morning only to find that Doris was covered in an unspecified rash and had to be sent home. Faced with the choice of going back to her mother-in-law's or helping to sweep, polish and wash down the re-plastered and re-glazed rooms, Ursula had found a sudden taste for housework.

She'd come downstairs to fetch up a scuttle of coal to help dry out the slightly damp smell coming from the new plaster in her bedroom when the knocker had sounded loudly in the hall.

Her eyes took a few seconds to adjust to the dark street. She only saw the outline of a tallish man on the step. Touching his cap he said, 'I just seen Mr Cutter down the wharf . . .'

A light flurry of snow blew over Ursula's ankles and sprinkled the door mat. Assuming he was a labourer from the yard, she stepped back and told him to come in, 'before we both freeze'.

She heard his light breathing behind her as she locked up again, switched down the light and swung round to face her visitor. Her slightly condescending smile faded.

'You! How dare you come here! Get out now.'

Taz took his cap off and wished her good evening. 'I'm glad to see you're in better health than they're saying on the boats. I've come to see Iris.'

'I can assure you, my daughter has absolutely no wish to see you. Get out of this house *this instant*!'

'Not until I've seen Iris.'

'Taz?'

Iris stood with one hand resting on the landing banister, her eyes large with surprise. He grinned and took the stairs two at a time. Grabbing her shoulders he kissed her long and hard.

Taking a deep breath, Ursula squeezed the bottom newel post until her knuckles gleamed through the white flesh. By the time Iris was released, gasping for air, her mother managed to say in a reasonably steady voice, 'Well, darling, aren't you going to introduce me to the young man?'

'You seemed to know who I was well enough a moment ago.' Twisting his arm through Iris's, Taz led her downstairs until they were facing Ursula. 'You'd best make the introductions, Iris. After all, I can't have my girl's mother not knowing who I am – or pretending not to at any rate.'

'Taz!' Iris's gaze flicked between them. It settled on the scuttle. 'Oh, Mummy you shouldn't have carried that. I'll fetch it.'

She reached down. Taz pulled her upright. 'Never mind the damn fires, Iris. I've been worrying myself into a frizzle since I heard you'd been hit. Now isn't it time you made up your mind? If you want me to go, just say so and I'll be off and I won't bother you again. But if you want us to keep seeing each other, then I reckon it's time we made it regular. I don't know that I want to court a girl who's too ashamed to take me home.'

'I'm not . . .' Iris disentangled her arm from his. 'And it seems to me it's up to me who . . . and if . . . I introduce to my parents, Taz Dixon.'

'Fair enough, I reckon. So – are you going to?'

She stared between Taz's grimly determined eyes and her mother's, which were misting over in a familiar expression of gentle reproach. 'Mother . . .'

'Iris, darling . . . I . . . feel a little . . .' Ursula swayed slightly, her hand going to her chest.

Before Taz or Iris could grab her, a deluge cascaded over Ursula's head, jerking her back upright with a gasp of shock.

'Cold water,' Nana said from the landing. 'Best thing for a faint.'

'You . . . you . . .' Ursula swept back her wet hair. Water was dripping off her nose and chin and dampening the front of her jumper. 'You've soaked me! I shall catch my death of cold!'

'Don't exaggerate. It was only a glassful. And it's worked. You don't look near so faint now. Well, go on, Iris, introduce Taz to your mother. It's time they met.'

Ursula noted the familiar use of Taz's Christian name, but managed to keep her temper, and even to suggest that Iris might care to take her friend into the sitting room?

'No, ta.' For the first time Taz became aware of his boat-stained clothes. 'I reckon I'll mess up your furniture.'

'Take him into the kitchen, Iris,' Nana suggested.

'Yes, do.' Ursula was determined to re-establish her position as mistress of the house. 'I'm sure Mr . . . Taz . . . would like something hot to drink. It must be cold out there on those boats.'

'I'll take a quick cup of tea if you can spare the rations, thanks.'

She let them go ahead of her. Her mother-in-law descended the last stairs, the empty glass tumbler still in her hand. Ursula waited until their faces were on a level and then thrust hers forward. 'You interfering bitch. You did this on purpose to spite me, didn't you? Well don't think you'll get away with it. Fred might be scared of you, but even he isn't going to stand for this! That young man can say goodbye to any future orders from the Cutters, I can tell you that!'

'Hollow threats, Ursula . . . There's a war on, in case you've not noticed. If Fred don't take the loads there's plenty will. And I'd not have had to find a young man for Iris if you'd have let her fly free to find her own, instead of keeping her penned in here making up for Fred's inadequacies as a husband.'

Genuine tears sprang to Ursula's eyes this time. 'You spiteful old witch! It's time we considered a home—'

'I have a home. Maybe it's time Iris had one of her own too instead of being obliged to run yours.'

'I do what I can. I have never asked anything of Iris—'

'No. You've coerced and blackmailed and manipulated – but *asked*? No. That would be too straightforward . . . too honest for you, Ursula.'

'Don't you dare speak to me like that!'

'I'll speak to you how I please. It's time that girl had a life of her own.'

'Iris *has* a life. The one she wants.'

'Well, it seems she's changed her mind, don't it? Now she wants a bit more. And about time too. Of course, if you don't care to have a boater for a son-in-law, there's an easy enough answer: get the girl to join up. She'd look fetching in one of them Wren's uniforms. Might meet a better class of boater too. Wouldn't an admiral suit you, Ursula?'

Ursula could taste the bile at the back of her throat. Swallowing hard, she forced herself to breathe evenly and suggested they join the others in the kitchen. A fight with her mother-in-law wouldn't help her to keep Iris. Getting rid of the young man was the only way to achieve that.

Iris had lain a cloth over the table and was setting out an odd assortment of cups and saucers.

'You'll have to excuse us, Mr . . . erm . . . ?'

'Taz.'

'Taz.' Ursula managed to make the single syllable sound faintly absurd, but she continued to smile as she apologised for the mismatched tea-set and explained that a lot of the crockery had shattered when the bomb went up.

'Bad one, was it?'

'We were fortunate. Next-door took most of the blast. There was some damage to this house – which my husband has repaired – and a few negligible injuries to myself and Iris, which have largely healed. Nothing to make a fuss about.'

'That'll make a rare change . . .' Nana said, sotto voce.

Ursula ignored her. 'Would you care for some cake . . . er . . . Taz? Iris made it. It's her own recipe – isn't it, darling?'

'It's from a magazine,' Iris mumbled to the tablecloth. 'It's probably not very good.'

'It's as good as anyone else's,' her grandmother said. 'Take a slice, young man.'

'Yes, ma'am. Ta . . . I mean, thanks.'

Taz reached for the generous slice Ursula slid on to a plate, and stopped in consternation at the sight of his own grease-stained and blackened hands. 'Sorry. Engine's leaking a bit.' He tried to rub off the dirt on his trouser legs.

'Perhaps you'd care to wash them?'

'Yeah . . . I mean, thanks.' He stood up too quickly and knocked his chair backwards. It fell on the kitchen tiles with a clatter. 'Sorry.' Bending to right it, his head collided with Iris's, who'd leapt up to help. 'Sorry. I'll just . . .' He jerked a thumb in the direction of the scullery.

'Guests use the bathroom. Please, let me show you . . .' Ursula extended an encouraging hand.

Iris thrust her hair back from her flushed face, the scar white against the pink rosiness. 'I'll go . . .'

'There's no need, dear. I'm sure . . . Taz can find it. Top of the stairs and second room on the right.'

They waited in silence until they heard his boots moving along the landing above their heads.

'Well . . .' Ursula laid her hand over her daughter's. 'You have been devious, haven't you, darling? How long has this been going on?'

'Nothing's going on, Mummy. We're just friends. I helped him buy some clothes for his sister. Christmas presents.'

'Christmas?' Ursula was aware of a cold chill running down her back that had nothing to do with the fact that the house had been unheated all week. She'd assumed the relationship was only a few weeks old. Now it seemed it had been going on for months. The slight flash of triumph in her mother-in-law's eyes didn't escape her either. Her free hand curled under the table. One day she'd pay the interfering old bitch back, but for now . . . She forced her lips to curl into a welcome as Taz reappeared, and managed to keep a friendly if stilted

197

conversation going until he'd finished his tea and declared it was time he got back to the boats.

'I'll walk with you.' Iris stood up, automatically asking her mother if she'd be all right.

Her grandmother intervened before Ursula could speak: 'Of course she will. I'll be here. Plenty of water in the pipes if she comes over funny again.'

'Darling, it is rather dark . . .'

'There's a blackout, Ursula. It's always dark outside. Don't tell me this is the first time you've noticed.'

'No. Of course. I simply meant . . . it's up to Iris.'

'I'll be careful, Mummy.'

Muffled in coat, scarf and short boots, Iris stepped out into the night promising she'd only go as far as the wharf gates and not use the tow-paths.

As soon as the door was shut and the lights re-lit, Ursula sat down heavily on a stair tread. 'I feel ill.'

'When don't you?'

Ursula raised a grey face. 'I don't care what you say. I really don't feel at all well, and I shall have to lie down for a moment. You can do whatever you like.'

She did look genuinely ill. Grudgingly Nana said she'd wash up and see what she could find for supper.

Ursula dragged herself up the stairs with effort and lay down on top of the bed quilt. Her bedroom felt cold and slightly damp. She'd left the coal downstairs. Perhaps a cardigan might help. There was one in the chest of drawers.

Rummaging in a pile of folded woollies, she felt the hard edges of her jewellery chest.

The desk sergeant at Agar Street gave his caller an encouraging smile. She looked like the sort who wasn't used to a police station. Lost her ration book, maybe.

'Yes, madam? What can we do for you?'

'I want to report a theft. A necklace . . . a very *valuable* necklace . . . has been stolen from me.'

'I see.' The sergeant opened the ledger and picked up a pen. 'Well, if I can have your name, madam . . .'

'Mrs Frederick Cutter.' Ursula lifted her chin. 'And I know the thief's name too.'

Chapter 21

'Hello *Rainbow*! Anyone aboard? Come on now, show yourselves.'

If the words were muffled in the snug, narrow cabin, the brisk tone and delivery clearly said 'Authority'.

'Oh blimey, what now? Bet Geoghan's told 'em we've been running with lights in the blackout. Told yer we oughta stop up Bull's Bridge 'stead of coming down here to find out Miss Snooty-drawers ain't got no more than a nasty headache.'

'Stow it, kid. And don't ever talk about Iris like that again. You hear?'

Taz's hand had shot across the table and grabbed his sister's wrist so hard that she dropped her knife and fork on to the supper plate. It startled her. Neither Taz nor her grandfather had ever struck her when she was growing up. Now Taz was hurting her. And on account of some landie who probably couldn't even moor up let alone help him work the boats. Addie hated Iris Cutter. And mixed in with the hatred was a miserable fear that her life was about to change. And she didn't want it to.

'Come on, now, let's be seeing you.' Authority had climbed on to the boat and was banging a fist on the cabin side.

'Clear up. I'll see what they want.' Taz extinguished the light and pushed open the end doors, letting a sharp blast of cold air into the fugginess of the cabin.

Addie could make out Pete Cutter's voice outside, and the low rumble of another one she didn't recognise. And then Taz's, raised in protest.

'That's bloody ridiculous! I've not stolen anything.'

'You'll not mind if I search then, will you, sir?'

Standing quite still in the dark, the dirty plates clasped in her hands, Addie found herself holding her breath. Something awful was about to happen.

She must have missed Taz saying he *did* mind, because the next thing was Pete Cutter's voice again: 'Best let him get it over with, son. Prove you've nothing to hide, eh?'

There were two of them. One, a burly uniformed constable, was so tall and broad-shouldered he was forced to stoop and huddle in the tiny space between the coal box and the table. The other was thin, middle-aged and in civilian clothes. He turned a face steeped in deepest misery on Addie and regarded her over a drooping grey moustache. 'Good evening, miss. I trust we haven't disturbed your meal.'

'No. We always have rozzers for puddin'.'

'Stow it, kid. And latch the table up so's we can all move.'

''Old these.' She thrust the dirty plates and cutlery into the miserable one's hands. Heaving on the table, she slammed it up within half an inch of his nose and secured the latches.

'Very snug, miss.' He looked round the cabin with approval. 'Very snug indeed. The lady wife has often expressed a wish to holiday on one of these vessels.'

'We're not bloody weekend sailors. This 'ere's a working boat, mister.'

'I can see that, miss.' He set the dirty dishes on top of the locker. 'And the sooner we are able to search, the sooner you can get back to your work and I can get back to—'

Addie mimicked his old-fashioned voice: 'The lady wife?'

'Unfortunately not, no, miss. The lady wife has taken herself off . . . somewhere . . . for the present. I do, however, have an appointment with a mock Welsh rarebit in the police canteen. So if we might proceed, sir?' He directed an enquiring look at Taz, who was perched on the coal box, his legs hunched to his chest.

He shrugged. 'Look wherever you like. We've nothing here that shouldn't be.'

It was obvious they couldn't all stay inside the cabin. Addie exploded with anger at the suggestion she should be the one to go. 'I ain't! I won't! What's up, Taz?'

202

'They're saying I stole a necklace, kid. It's rubbish. Best let them look and see.'

'Who's saying?' Addie turned, flashing eyes on the CID man, but it was Taz who answered.

'Mrs Cutter. She says I took her necklace when I went up their house today.'

'And they believe the lying bitch?'

'Watch the language, kid.'

Addie sniffed, shrugged and tossed back her rusty-shaded hair. 'It's only cause he went out with her precious daughter and she don't like it. She's lying, mister.'

Under the air of deepest depression, she thought she saw the slightest flicker of sympathy from the plain-clothes bloke. None the less he repeated that he had to search the boats. 'A complaint has been made, miss. I'd be failing in my duty not to investigate. Why don't you step up on to the wharf – keep warm in one of the sheds?'

Pete Cutter echoed the invitation to shelter when she stepped out into the dark. 'Or come over the flat? I've a fire there.'

'Well yer can just go stick the poker up yer—'

'This is not down to me,' Pete interrupted her sharply. 'I'd no choice but to let them in.'

'It's your bleedin' family calling us thieves! We ain't thieves! The Dixons always pay their way.'

'Best let the coppers get on and prove it then. Sure you don't want to come inside? You look half frozen.'

'I'm all right.' Addie hopped from boot to boot, hugging her arms across her chest and wishing she'd picked up her cap and coat. The snow had stopped and what little had settled was now melting and adding to the wet sheen over the yard and shed roofs. The tarpaulins over the cargo areas would be slippery with dirty slush and the securing straps swollen with water. She just hoped the coppers wanted to search under them. She'd make them do their own unsheeting; that would teach them to accuse her brother of theft.

She listened to the sounds of the search filtering from the cabin. Drawers and cupboards were being opened, lockers lifted, the coal box emptied. They'd have gone through all her private things, all the bits and pieces handed down from her mum and grandad. She hated them – all those rotten, stuck-up Cutters – thinking they were better just because they lived in a house.

The miserable-looking one climbed back on to the wharf, touched his hat formally to her, and made his way along to the butty. He rummaged inside that cabin too, turning out all the new clothes Taz had bought for her. She longed to go back and get her coat, but was blowed if she was going to show any weakness in front of the rozzers.

The uniformed constable was searching the engine room. He finished and climbed back on to land just as the other one reclosed the doors to the butty. They exchanged a brief head-shake.

'Satisfied, mister?' Addie snarled. 'Now you gonna go back and tell that lying cow we Dixons don't take what ain't ours?'

The plain-clothes man's face was no more than a pale disc in the darkness. 'Well now, miss, this is a proper puzzle and no mistake. The lady swears her necklace was there before your brother called at the house. Checked it no more than a few minutes before, in fact. And then it's gone after he leaves. What are we to do?'

'Tell her she's a bleedin' liar.'

'Unfortunately that one isn't in the procedure book, miss.'

'Bet it would be if it were some boater tellin' you this pack of rubbish. It's only cause her old man owns this place. Bet if he were just a road-sweeper you wouldn't be licking her boots—'

'Kid!'

Taz's explosive interruption cut short his sister's protest. There was a short silence, broken only by her panting breaths and the slight murmur of disturbed water against the wharf steps.

Taz stepped over from the boat and dropped a hand on his sister's shoulder. Its slight pressure acted as both a reassurance and a warning to keep her mouth shut. 'Is that it, then? You've found nothing that shouldn't be here.'

'That's very true, sir. But I'll still have to be asking you to step up the station.'

'What for?'

'Further enquiries. I've a new sergeant, sir, and he's a stickler for further enquiries. Do you want to get a coat? You too, miss.'

'What do you want Addie for?' Taz asked sharply. 'She never went up Bartholomew Road.'

Apparently it didn't matter. She had to come too. She expected Taz to put up an argument, but he just meekly told her to get her coat and step along with the copper.

As they left, the miserable one raised his hat to Pete Cutter and wished him a good night. 'And thank you for your assistance, sir. Much appreciated. It was very nice to see you again.'

'Have we met before, Mr . . . erm, er . . . Sorry, I forgot what you said your name was.'

'Detective Constable Bell, Mr Cutter. We have met. A good few years ago now. My first case after I joined Agar Street CID, in fact. I took your statement.'

'I've never given a statement . . . Oh, the money Barber made off with. I'd forgotten.'

'Really, sir? Surprising – considering he made off with Mrs Cutter at the same time.'

'Water long gone under the bridge, Constable. You must have taken a thousand statements since then.'

'As you say, sir. I was saying to the lady wife only last month, it's frightening how the years pass. Well, goodnight again, sir. Come on, you two.'

Addie had been half-afraid they'd put handcuffs on them, but the policeman in the suit, who seemed to be the one in charge, was content to let Taz walk ahead with the uniformed copper while he brought up the rear with her.

Once they reached the police station, they separated her from Taz and she was left to kick her heels in a corridor. Uniformed coppers passed back and forth, looking her over curiously. She glared back defiantly. The Dixons didn't take what wasn't theirs. She hung on to that fact.

A policewoman with three sergeant's stripes on her uniform jacket came through – a thin stick, with brown hair and a long face. Addie was just thinking to herself that she'd bang her head regular on the cabin top if she were a boater when the woman stopped in front of her. 'Miss Dixon?'

'Yeah.'

'My name is Sarah McNeill. I've been asked to search you.'

'Who by? The one who looks like his cat just died?'

A slight smile passed over the austere face. 'I'm not sure Ding-Dong has a cat.'

'That his name?' Addie was intrigued despite her situation. 'There's a family on the canal – the bleedin' Geoghans – their mum called them after locks. I thought that was daft enough, but *Ding-Dong* . . . Don't that just take the prize?'

'It's a nickname. His surname is Bell.' While they'd been talking the sergeant had been guiding Addie into a side room. She'd been half expecting a cell or something, but this wasn't too bad at all. It was like a little sitting room, with its armchair before the fire grate.

'Matron's room,' the other woman explained. 'She deals with the female prisoners . . . when she's here.'

'Am I a prisoner then?' Addie said doubtfully. ''Cause it ain't bleedin' fair if I am. It's all lies! The Dixons don't take what ain't theirs. You ask anyone on the canal.'

'I believe you. And no, you're not a prisoner since you've not been arrested. You're just helping out your brother.'

'How?'

'By proving he didn't hand this necklace over to you.'

'Sounds daft to me. If 'e had I could have hidden it down the wharf, couldn't I?'

'Yes. And that's what anyone with a lick of sense – and I'm sure you've a whole tongueful of that, Miss Dixon – would have done. But it's Sergeant Spain's orders. And orders are orders.'

Even though her voice was even, Addie sensed that the policewoman didn't like this Sergeant Spain. Maybe that would be useful. Sitting on the floor, she pulled off her boots and a pair of socks that were more hole than sock. Anticipating the usual landie's reaction, she said defensively, 'The boats is a full-time job. I ain't got time for darning.'

'I have. But I don't do it anyway,' the policewoman said cheerfully, feeling inside the boots.

Addie's coat, shirt, waistcoat and trousers all got the same treatment, although she was allowed to keep her vest and knickers on. As usual they were an old set of Taz's that she'd sewn up. The officer patted lightly over the greying fabric stained with navy-blue dye from something that had leaked in the washing bucket.

For the first time in her life, Addie experienced a niggling embarrassment over her appearance. 'I've proper woman's clothes too. Real posh ones. Taz bought them for me.'

'I expect these are better for working the boats, aren't they? Must be mucky work. You can get dressed again now.'

'Yeah, that's right. Be daft wearing me good stuff to unload the cargo.' Addie wriggled back into her clothes. 'Can we go now?'

'I'll see. Wait here.'

The sergeant left, closing the door behind her. Addie waited a few moments, then crept across the room and eased it open a crack. The dimly lit corridor seemed deserted, but she could hear the murmur of voices. Sergeant McNeill was talking to the miserable cove with the silly name.

'That's ridiculous! He hasn't got any evidence. It's the woman's word against the suspect's.'

'It's Cutter's though, isn't it, Sarge?' Ding-Dong's mournful tones were easier to pick-up than the female Sergeant's. 'It's like the little girl says – they're posh, got a tidy business there too. And Fred Cutter's taken to helping his community on the council.'

'Helping himself more like.'

'Very likely. But it doesn't help us with you-know-who.'

'Boot-licker.'

Addie guessed the policewoman's scornful remark was directed at this Sergeant Spain, who'd got Taz rather than Ding-Dong Bell, and was glad – even if she didn't much care for that 'little girl'. She hastily reshut the door and was sitting on the floor relacing her boots when the woman re-entered and told her she could go.

'What about Taz?'

207

'He has to stay a bit longer.'

'What you done with him?'

'Sergeant Spain has arrested him for theft.'

'He can't do that! You never found no necklace, did yer?'

'No.'

'Then you gotta let him go. You ain't sticking my brother in a cell, you cow!'

'Watch your mouth, Miss Dixon.'

That 'Miss Dixon' warned Addie she'd gone too far. It was common sense not to upset a rozzer who seemed almost on her side. 'Sorry, miss,' she mumbled, 'but Taz ain't never been in prison before. Can't you let him come home?'

'It's not that simple.' Extending a hand, she pulled Addie to her feet and started shepherding her out of the room and towards the front desk. 'Look, if your brother had a proper address – not a boat – he'd probably get police bail.'

'What's that?'

'They let you go while they make further enquiries. Give you a piece of paper giving you a date to come back to the station.'

'Well we could do that, miss. The *Rainbow* goes up and down the canals all the time. We could come back any time you say.'

The sergeant shook her head. 'It's not up to me. And, like I said, a boat won't do. Maybe he could get a room at a men's hostel somewhere.'

'And how's he gonna pay for it if he can't work?'

'I'm sorry. There's not much more I can do.'

'Can I see Taz?'

'No. Sorry, it's against regulations.'

Forgetting herself again, Addie let rip with her opinion of regulations. The female sergeant heard her out calmly, then wished her goodnight on the sand-bagged steps of the police station.

' 'Night.' Addie muttered grudgingly. Thrusting her hands in her pockets and with her head held high, she marched towards the junction with the High Street. Tears stung her eyes. Angrily she brushed them away with the back of her sleeve. At least it was so dark no one could see her blubbing.

'You're not a kid,' she told herself angrily. 'There's girls your age married with babies. You can manage.'

The howling banshee wail of the air-raid sirens suddenly ripped through the night, catching her by surprise. Like most people, she'd grown used to the bad weather keeping the raiders away.

It was harder to keep track of the days on the canal, but she guessed it must be Saturday night again. A fortnight since she and Pansy had walked down here eating chips and the other girl had invited her to her birthday party. Well, she wouldn't go now if they paid her.

She stepped across several side-roads, not caring whether there was any traffic coming or not. Ahead was the canal, the only home she'd ever known. She needed to reach the safety of the tow-path.

The rumbling roar from the south was growing louder. The raiders were definitely coming this way.

She hesitated at the steps. Perhaps she should run back to the street. She'd heard people talking about sheltering down the tube stations. Taz had described the wooden beds they'd built down there for them. Just like the ones in the boat cabin, he'd said. But you had to have money to go down the trains didn't you? She thrust her hands deeper into the coat pockets and met only fluff.

There were lights and flashes in the skies now. Stumbling down the stone staircase, Addie started to race along the tow-path. Ahead of her the water in the canal suddenly sprang up in a fountain as something hit it. There was a clatter and a sizzling hiss, and an eerie red glow illuminated the base of the railway bridge by the path.

'Incendiaries,' she told herself. She paused by the glowing tube, spluttering in the dirt, and gave it a kick towards the canal. The tube rolled into a dip and tumbled back towards her. Well, what did it matter? There was nothing here to burn anyway.

She hurried on. The noise above was becoming deafening. More plane engines mingled with the reverberating crack-crack of the ack-ack guns. There was the sound of things breaking beyond the walls of the canal but no explosions, thank heavens. It was just incendiaries they were dropping at the moment, rather than bombs.

She looked upwards into the skies just in time to see a 'bread-basket' burst apart above the bridge, releasing its cargo. Incendiaries showered down, some hitting the road above her, others bouncing off the parapets into the canal and sending up more chutes of water.

Addie hesitated. It was the first major raid she'd ever been caught up in. She was tempted to stay under the bridge, curling up like a frightened animal in the intense shadow that provided an illusion of safety. But an even deeper instinct drove her to try and reach the boat.

Taking a deep breath and letting it out slowly to steady her racing heart, she sprinted out in a lull in the noise. There wasn't much farther to go. Just round that bend and she'd be on Cutter's Wharf. She could hear that dog of Joshua's barking frantically. Across on the other bank she could see the glitter of flames reflected in glass. One of the incendiaries had crashed through a house roof and started a fire in the upper rooms.

She flew round the corner and through the gap that led on to the wharf. The outlines of the sheds and outhouses were easy to make out, illuminated by the dozens of incendiaries scattered across the cobbles and roofs, fizzling out their red-hot presence in spiteful spitting pockets. Another bread-basket must have exploded over the yard. Maybe two or three, there were so many of the things.

A flicker of light from the butty caught her eye. It seemed to be coming from the cabin. For a moment her heart leapt. Perhaps Taz was back. He'd come round the street way and beaten her to it.

Then the redness strengthened and grew, and she understood. The *Crock of Gold* was on fire.

Chapter 22

The copper couldn't have secured the doors properly. The incendiary had bounced and crashed over the stern, its force knocking the doors wide enough for it to roll inside. Only the fact that the butty was largely unused as living space saved it from serious damage: with no bedclothes or curtaining, the flames had been denied a quick source of fuel. Instead they'd blistered and scorched the brightly painted designs and eaten into the wood that was starting to crack and spit warningly.

Addie grabbed the bucket from *Rainbow*'s engine room and raced back to the stone steps. She had to stop the flames reaching the cargo areas. Both boats were loaded to the gunwales with inflammable materials. If the blaze got through the thick tarpaulins, they'd never get them out before the boats burnt clean through.

Crouching, she scooped up a pail of water and tried to stand. Her boots skidded on the snow-slippery tread and she nearly pitched into the canal. Half the water slopped out of the pail. Dipping again she staggered back, scrambled on board *Crock of Gold* and sloshed the water indiscriminately around. A wisp of smoke rose from behind one of the cupboards as the fire caught on its contents.

She twisted the wooden batten that held the door in place. It swung out, releasing a thick acrid cloud that caught in her throat. Choking, she pulled the smouldering books on to the floor and stamped on them.

'Get out of there, girl!' Pete Cutter roared at her. She heard boots scrambling on the deck. 'Get out of there before you pass out!' His fingers locked on her arm and she was dragged into the air.

'The boat! I got to . . .' Frustrated, she twisted, trying to get her teeth into his fingers.

'Pack that in . . . Joshua, grab that bucket and start slinging water in there. I'll be back in a minute.'

Showing a surprising presence of mind, Joshua looped the short towing strap round the bucket handle and used it to raise water from the canal. Reassured he knew what he was doing, Addie ran back to the motor, got the big water can and added its contents to the general mess streaming down the butty cabin's walls.

Pete reappeared with a shovel which he used to manoeuvre the incendiary into the bucket and tip it into the canal.

'Ta, mister,' Addie panted, temporarily forgetting she wasn't supposed to be speaking to any of the Cutters.

'Let's get the rest out, Joshua.'

There were dozens of glowing points dotted over the yard. None seemed to have found any kindling: the wet surfaces and stacked materials were mostly brick and clay. The cement, lime and timber had been stored under-cover in the sheds, which looked to be relatively intact. Under Pete's direction, they pulled apart rotting sandbags, dumped the contents over the incandescent metal and used a boat-hook to dislodge those that had landed on shed roofs.

Finally, Pete called a halt. 'Reckon we got them all. Let's take a look at that boat of yours now it's cooled down a mite.'

The *Crock of Gold*'s floor was puddled with water and floating books; its cupboards had blackened scorch-marks among the roses and waterfalls; the cabins ceiling dripped dirty water in a monotonous pit-pat.

Pete peered over her shoulder. 'Not too bad. If you need to replace a bit of timber, we'll fix you up – no charge.'

'Guilty conscience, mister?'

'Don't start that again, girl. What my sister-in-law chooses to do isn't down to me . . . I didn't get a chance to ask you – what happened up the police station?'

Briefly Addie told him, finishing with another stream of oaths directed partly at Ursula and partly at the Cutters in general. 'Just cause Taz dared to go out with yer precious

212

niece. There's plenty of girls along the canal be glad to walk out with my brother.'

'I daresay, girl. But Ursula always did have grand ideas. Although in this case . . .'

'In this case *what*?' Addie demanded, ready to defend her brother to the death.

'In this case I reckon she's got a point, don't you? Iris hasn't been brought up to this kind of life.'

It was exactly what Addie had said herself. But loyalty to Taz made her mumble, 'Dunno. Up to Taz, ain't it? I gotta get the *Crock* scrubbed out.'

'Leave it until morning. Come sleep up the flat tonight if you like. We've a fire.'

'So's half the town, mister,' Addie pointed out as the sound of fire-engine bells racketed past in the street. 'I'm stopping with me boats.'

'Fair enough. I'm stepping along to Kate . . . Mrs Cutter's place. See if her and young Pansy are all right. I'll leave Josh here to watch the yard. Any problems, you give him a holler.'

Muttering that she didn't think she'd ever be that desperate, Addie climbed back on the butty and rescued the floating books. She didn't much care whether they fell to pieces or not herself, since she could barely read, but Taz could, and he set a lot of store on it.

She stacked the wet books, intending to take them back to the *Rainbow* and put them in a low oven to dry. The few bits of crockery were undamaged. It was lucky she kept most of their food in the *Rainbow* . . . Then she remembered. Her new clothes!

The flimsy underwear was wetly transparent. The dresses looked to be OK, although she thought she could detect smoke clinging to the fabric.

'Bloody Germans!' Grabbing one of the books, she hurled it out of the door in the direction of the now empty sky.

Joshua was hovering on the wharf. He caught it, slapping his hands flatly together like a seal. With a grin he threw it back.

'I ain't playing bloody catch, you daft lump!'

213

'What you doing then?'

'Sorting out me clothes.'

'They're all wet.'

'Sharp as a nail, ain't yer, Joshua? 'Ere, take these.' She passed the bundle into Joshua's arms, scooped up the books and climbed back out herself, securing the doors. Pete Cutter was right. It was best to leave the scrubbing out until daylight when she could see what she was doing.

Joshua pushed his way into the *Rainbow*'s cabin after her as she groped around relighting the paraffin lamp. 'Pretty.'

'Yeah, we've a regular little palace in here, Josh. Get off the coal box, will yer? I gotta put some in the stove.'

'Joshua will do it.' Relinquishing her clothes, Joshua set about coaxing a blaze from the grate while Addie ran a string across the cabin and flicked her underwear over it.

'Pretty . . .'

The sooty finger Joshua extended towards the peach fabric was sharply slapped down. 'Don' do that! Didn' your mum teach yer not to touch a girl's . . . a girl's *unmentionables*?'

'Those ain't unmentions, Addie. Them's knickers. And Joshua don't remember his mum saying nothing about knickers.'

'Well *I'm* saying. Understand?'

Joshua nodded obediently. 'Not touch knickers.'

'Good. Now 'op it. I'm gonna go to bed.'

'Joshua could stay. Sleep on boat too.'

'No you can't. Yer boots would be 'anging out the door. Go on – go home and see to that dog. It's barking its flamin' head off.'

She stepped closer and pushed against his chest. Joshua captured her hands in one of his and ran the other down her hair. 'Pretty hair. Like horses.'

'For gawd's sake . . . go 'ome!' Addie tried to twist her hands free, but Joshua's large fingers were crushing them close. His palm continued to rub down her wet hair. He drew a strand out and kissed it.

'Will you stow it? Gerroff me!'

Because of his height, Joshua was bent over her, his short, hot breaths blowing on her forehead. The washing line blocked a lot of light from the solitary lamp, leaving dark patches of shade across his features, but she could see the gleam in his lavender eyes. A flutter of panic jumped into her throat. She hadn't had much experience of boys, but instinct told her what Joshua wanted. She tried to stay calm. 'Let go, Josh, yer hurtin' me 'ands.'

It did the trick. He released her immediately. Addie backed away, feeling the cold wetness of the underwear chilling the back of her neck. 'Now go on. Go 'ome, Josh. Or I'll have to tell yer dad yer been making a nuisance of yourself.'

'Not a nuisance. Joshua likes you.'

He stood there blocking the only way out of the cabin – bulky, muscular, and not understanding his own feelings. Instinct told Addie it was best to stay calm. If she started screaming and shouting, it might provoke that temper of his that the yard men had talked about. She didn't know whether he'd use violence against a girl or not; but she had a fair idea of where any physical tussle would lead.

Outside, the dog's barking became more frantic. It was joined by a rhythmic crashing of metal on wood as Kitchener lashed out at his stable door.

''E sounds scared. Best go see to him, Josh.'

'Not scared. Dog jumped in stable. Horse doesn't like dog. Joshua will let him go.'

To her relief he hauled his big frame out of the cabin, the gunwale dipping sharply under his weight as he jumped back on to the wharf. It wasn't possible to lock the cabin doors from inside, but as soon as he'd gone, Addie dragged the boat-hook in. With an iron cooking pot held in one hand and the wooden shaft in the other, she curled on her brother's bed and lay waiting for the dawn.

The smells of drying paper and clothes, burning coal and paraffin, filled the small space. Her eyes started to droop in the fuggy atmosphere. She struggled to stay awake. The next thing she knew someone was shaking her roughly.

'Wake up, kid.'

'Taz!' She fought blearily from sleep, swinging her legs off the bed and discovering she was still holding on to the handles of the saucepan and boat hook. Last night's

215

encounter with Josh seemed ridiculous now in the damp grey dawn light. 'Guarding the boats,' she muttered, thrusting her weapons away.

'Paratroopers wouldn't have known what hit 'em, kid.'

She examined her brother in the wintry light from the open doors. He needed a shave and his clothes were crumpled, but then so were hers. She'd lain down fully dressed; his bed would be damp from the wetness. She'd dry off the blankets in the engine room soon as they got under way. Her mind was already whirling as she snatched the dried underwear from the line and banged the oven shut on the brown, curled pages of the books. Her main thought was to get out of here as soon as possible. Back on the canals, where it was safe and no one would try to take Taz away.

'Start up the engine, Taz. There's bread and cheese we can 'ave for breakfast. I'll get a brew on soon as we're under way . . . only the *Crock*'s 'ad an hit. It ain't too bad . . . we can get it painted.'

'Hey! Whoa back there . . .' With two fingers in his mouth, Taz filled the cabin with a shrill whistle. Somewhere in the yard the Cutters' dog answered with a series of throaty barks.

'What?'

'We can't go anywhere, kid. Leastways, I can't. They gave me bail, but only if I live ashore.'

'But where'll yer go?'

'I'm stopping up the old lady's place. She came up the police station this morning.' A grin lit up his strained face. 'You should have heard her tearing into them. I'm on bail providing I stay with her. Permanent address, see. I just come by to pick up some of my stuff and see you were OK.'

'The *Crock*—'

'I've had a look. Nothing a decent carpenter can't fix.' He'd been pulling out things as he spoke: his grandfather's old shaving mug and strop razor; a threadbare towel, clean underwear and his other shirt, the jacket he'd worn to take Iris up to Selfridges. 'The old lady's in the yard flat keeping warm. Said to come up for a bite of breakfast.'

'No, ta. I don't want nothing off those bleedin' Cutters.'

216

'Watch the language, kid. And remember it's one of those Cutters who's helping me out. Now get going.'

Grumbling and scuffing her boots over the cobbles, Addie allowed herself to be shepherded across the yard. There was little evidence of the previous night's raid apart from sleet-melted piles of sand where they'd put out the incendiaries, and the part-charred remains of the house across the canal that had taken a direct hit. The brick store flat was full of the smell of bacon and fried bread. Invited to sit herself down, Addie allowed herself another scowl before diving hungrily into the plate set before her.

Nana Cutter poured tea into thick blue and white striped mugs. It was a good strong brew, far better than anything you could squeeze out of the ration. 'Has your brother told you how we're fixed, dear?'

Addie nodded, her mouth full.

'She's grateful for yer help, ma'am. We both are.'

Addie nodded her agreement again, conscious of the grease now dribbling down her chin. She didn't want Taz staying on shore, but at least the old girl had got him out of the lock-up. She masticated the streaky, trying to clear her mouth and gasp out a thank you. While she was still swallowing, the flat door opened and Kate Cutter walked in. Even Addie, who was wrapped up in her own problems, couldn't miss the warmth of the smile that lit up Pete's face as he wished her a good morning.

'Morning.' Kate kissed him lightly on his cheek and then bent over the table and dropped a similar greeting on her mother-in-law's cheek.

Invited to pull up a chair and take a bite of breakfast, she shook her head. 'I've had mine. Thanks to Maury.'

'Yes. We ought to say something I suppose.' Nana hooked up another glistening rasher. 'It's plainly black-market. But if we hand it in to the police it'll get no further than their canteen or some inspector's larder.'

Kate took off her coat. 'Eat with a clear conscience. I'm certain sure we'll not see much more after Easter. I think Maury's softening us up for an engagement on Pansy's sixteenth.'

Joshua had been mopping the grease from his plate with a chunk of bread, apparently oblivious to anything else. He looked up suddenly and said, 'Her birthday too. Seventeen. Have party.'

'What's the boy talking about?' Nana asked her son.

'Me.' Addie raised a dripping mouth from her tea mug. 'It's me birthday too. Same as Pansy's. She's invited us to her party. Don't suppose I'll go now. Her being a bleedin' Cut . . .' Abruptly Addie remembered whose food she was eating.

'It's all right.' Kate squeezed her shoulder. 'My sister-in-law is—'

'A bitch.' Nana finished for her.

'Mother!' Pete glared.

'I speak as I find.'

Kate went to a cupboard and took out a cup and saucer with the familiarity of someone who's done it many times before. 'I came to see if I can help. What's your cargo?'

Taz answered her. '*Rainbow*'s got coal. *Crock*'s carrying rags for the paper mill. I ain't too worried about that, but they're both subbed from the Canal Carrying company. If the factory has to shut down the boilers because it ain't got the coal . . .'

'They'll dock your money . . . and like as not you'll not get the order again,' Kate helped herself to tea.

'I was thinking . . .' Taz cast a sly glance under his dark lashes. 'I've only to sleep at your place, ma'am. If I was to take the boats down—'

'There's a policeman outside the yard gates,' Kate said.

'That'll be down to that whippersnapper of a plain-clothes man I had words with. You cast off, young man, and that flattie will be in here faster than you can say "darbies".' Nana's black eyes twinkled. 'That's handcuffs, to those who don't know.'

'Mother, you're enjoying this!'

'It ain't funny,' Addie said indignantly. 'If word gets out that Taz can't work we won't get no cargoes and then we won't have no money.'

'Tell them he's sick. Laid up for a few days,' Kate said.

'And I'll help you take the cargoes down. If you run the motor, I can take the butty. Can you?'

'Yeah. Course I can. I been steering since I was eight. Ta for offering, but it ain't no job for a landie.'

'This landie was born on a boat, my girl. Born and bred up to them.'

This was plainly news to Pete. 'But you said . . . I mean, Bernard always said your people had a shop. Birmingham way, he said.'

'No. They were boaters. Worked the Severn up to Stourport mostly. I ran barefoot – and bare-bottomed sometimes in the summer – and tramped the tow-path in my dad's old boots stuffed with newspaper in the winter. When I was thirteen they died within six months of each other. My brother and sister-in-law took on the boats, but they made it clear there was no bed for me. So they sent me to an aunt who'd married off the water and kept a shop in Islington. She was kind enough, in her way. Taught me to speak ladylike . . . well, ladylike enough to pass in the shop. And then, when I was seventeen, a photographer stopped me in Regent's Park and told me I was the most beautiful girl he'd ever seen and he just had to have my picture. And the rest you know. The Birmingham story was my idea. I thought Bernie's family would never accept me if they knew I was a boater's brat.'

She'd been sitting at a slight angle to the oilskin-covered table, her eyes fixed on her tea. Now she looked her lover full in the face. There was an unmistakable challenge in her eyes: *Now you know . . . Take me as I am or not at all.*

Pete reached over and took her hand. 'You're the prettiest brat I've ever laid eyes on. I'll take you on, soon as you like.' He looked at his mother. 'Did you know about this?'

'Told me years ago. Fred and Ursula don't know. Let's keep it like that for now, eh? We can tell them later. Be a nice surprise for madam.' The relish in her voice was unmistakable. Those days of having Ursula living under her roof had exacerbated the dislike between the two women into outright hatred.

219

Kate included both Taz and Addie in her quiet, 'I trust you both.'

'Don't worry, miss. We'll keep our mouths shut. Won't we, kid?'

Addie nodded mutely. Kate's story was still jangling around in her brain. Her own brother had thrown her off the boats. Was that what was going to happen to her when Taz wed? It wasn't like she even had an auntie to take her in.

Kate's soft voice penetrated her worries.

'I'll need to borrow trousers, Pete. And a jacket for dirty work . . .'

'I'm not sure.' Pete looked towards Taz. 'I'd offer myself or Joshua, but we've lorries coming in for loading. Making a start on the blitz damage first thing tomorrow. You think they can handle a pair by themselves?'

'Well, I dunno . . .'

'Don't talk over our heads, thank you.' Kate's eyes flashed. 'We can manage very well.' Her expression softened slightly. 'We're only going to the docks. If we get into trouble we can tie up and get a bus back here for help.'

'That's true enough. There's plenty of wharves down that stretch. You just . . .' Taz broke off as the yard dog began to bark frantically.

Joshua stood immediately. 'Dog's worried, Dad. Something bad's happening.'

'It'll be a cat. Or that bloo . . . erm, I mean the horse teasing him again.'

'No.' Joshua was adamant. 'Something very bad. Outside, Dad.'

'Let's take a look then, son.' Shrugging on his jacket, Pete went out with Joshua lumbering behind, the dog responding to an angry shout to hold its noise.

Addie caught her brother's eye. 'The boats . . .'

They saw it as soon as they stepped on to the top of the outside staircase: a thin wisp of smoke twisting into the cold air where no smoke had been before.

'It's a shed, I reckon,' Taz said, unable to keep the relief out of his voice. He clattered down the wooden staircase with Addie on his heels. The dog was circling in excited but silent bursts of energy. It sped away as they approached, stopped, looked back to see if they were following, and led them to one of the smaller store huts.

Pete was balanced with his heels half off the wharf edge, rocking backwards to get a clearer view of the roof. 'One of the beggars has gone through. Didn't spot it in the dark. Must have been smouldering in the rafters for hours.' As he spoke, the jagged gap in the roof belched a larger blacker cloud of smoke. A neighbouring tile exploded with a crack and slithered to the cobbles.

'Shall I tell Mrs Kate to phone the fire brigade, mister?'

'No. We can manage. Joshua, go fetch the ladder from the stables. I'll get the hose.'

They both ran back, leaving the Dixons hovering, wanting to help but left with nothing to do. Finally Taz said, 'I'll take a look inside. See if it's burnt through.'

The shed door was bolted and padlocked, the window too small to climb through and filthy from years of coal and cement dust. Taz rattled the padlock.

'Here. Let me.'

Kate was carrying the large metal ring of keys that normally hung from a nail in her office. They tried the most likely ones in the rusting padlock, but none fitted. 'We hardly use this shed,' Kate said struggling to turn yet another key in the stubborn lock. 'But I thought I had spares for everywhere. We'd better wait for Pete.' She finished on a squeal of fright as another tile shattered in the heat and blew out in a shower of sparks.

Taz took the key from her and twisted harder. The pressure snapped off the corroded securing ring on the door. He pushed his way inside. Sacks of sand were stacked over the back half of the room, while assorted rusting building tools were piled into a corner by the door.

'Good Lord!' Kate exclaimed. 'I didn't even know this was in here.' She pushed her fingers into one of the sacks. 'It's set solid.'

Taz was walking backwards scanning the wooden ceiling. 'Don't see no scorching. It's up there . . . back of the shed,

221

I reckon.' Setting a boot on the lowest sand sack he started to scramble upwards.

'What the hell are you doing? Get out of there!' Pete dropped the hose that was slung over his shoulder and crossed the shed with quick strides to haul Taz off the sacks.

Kate protested. 'Pete . . . we were just checking. It could have burnt inside—'

'It still could. It's not safe. Now you get outside. You too, son. I don't want you getting a faceful of incendiary. I've seen men burnt – it's not a pretty sight.'

'It looks pretty solid up there to me, mister. I was just gonna see—'

'Out!'

He plainly wasn't going to argue. They trooped meekly out and watched as Joshua was sent up the ladder once more. This time he had the thick, wriggling length of the hose clamped under his arm, sending a jet of water into the hole. After thirty minutes the smoke had stopped and Pete took his son's place. Clambering on to the roof, he levered more tiles off until he could fit inside the space and retrieve the spent incendiary. 'Rafters are nearly gone through in one place. Best keep everyone out until we can get it fixed.'

'Let's just get the sand out, Pete. We can use it . . .' Kate put one hand on the dangling metal lock.

'I said no!' Pete hauled her away. 'Now I don't want anyone in there until I can get it fixed. In fact, I'll make sure of it. Joshua, come here boy . . .'

With Joshua's assistance, Pete nailed planks across the door and windows, fetched a pot of whitewash and scrawled 'Keep Out – Danger' in large letters across the makeshift barriers. 'There. Now let's be finding those clothes for you, Kate. If you've still a mind to go boating?'

'I have.'

'What about Pansy?'

'I telephoned Iris from the office. She's going round to explain. And Nana will look in.'

'You don't want me to?'

'Best not, Pete. Not until we're certain sure she's accepted things as they are.'

'Fair enough. Come on . . . What the devil's this?'

'This' was Iris – but Iris as they'd never seen her before. She was dressed in one of her brother's suits. The trouser bottoms were tucked into a pair of his socks and her feet were encased in the wellington boots she used for gardening.

'I've come to help with the boats.' She looked directly at Taz. 'I'm sorry. I'm so sorry. I didn't know mother was going to . . .' Her mouth twisted, holding back the tears.

'Hey, don't . . . please, Iris.' Taz groped in his pockets and took out an oily rag that might once have been a handkerchief.

'Here.' Pete offered his own.

Iris put her hands in her pockets, the overlong sleeves bunching in concertinas at the movement. 'No thanks, Uncle Peter. I'm quite all right. If you just tell me what wants doing, Taz, I'll do it.'

'Don't be daft Iris . . . Er, I mean, it's good of you to offer, but it's no job for a lady.'

'I thought Aunt Kate was going to do it.'

'Yeah . . . she is, but she's . . .' Taz's eyes appealed for help.

'What he means,' Kate said, 'is that I've done this before. You're not used to . . . to manual work.'

Iris's lips tightened with an expression none of them had seen before. 'I'm as good as anyone else. There's women in all the services now . . . a lot of them are younger than me. And if they can do it, I'm . . . I'm *damn* certain I can manage to sail a boat down a little bit of canal! I *can* do it, Aunt Kate. I'm not completely useless.'

'Iris, it ain't just the boat. There's the locks and the unloading . . .' Taz's attempts to explain were interrupted by his sister.

'Well I think it's a bleedin' brilliant idea. We can manage it easy with three pairs of hands. I'll show her the ropes, Taz.'

Addie seized Iris's elbow and marched towards the *Rainbow*. Her head was dipped, letting her tangled hair fall over her face so that it hid the flash of malice that lit up her eyes.

Chapter 23

'Jump! Jump!'

Iris set one foot on the boat's side and gathered herself. The tow-path seemed impossibly far away.

'Go on! Quick . . .' Addie thumped her in the back. Her arms windmilled. The strip of water between the *Rainbow* and the canalside widened . . . and then narrowed just as she was convinced she was going to pitch head-first into it.

She stumbled on to the bank, collapsing to her knees and dropping the windlass handle. There was a hoot of laughter above her head. On all fours she looked up and saw a couple of men, arms leaning on the wall parapet, grinning down at her.

'Don't pay no mind to the gongoozlers,' Addie shouted. 'Just make the lock ready.'

Pushing herself to her feet, Iris retrieved the metal handle and trotted along the path, trying to beat the boats to the lock. She'd been appointed lock-wheeler for the trip.

'That means yer gotta open the lock gates,' Addie had explained. 'I don't suppose you know how to, but you're no use for anything else.'

Iris had bitten her tongue, determined not to be provoked. Addie seemed to have thought better of her first enthusiasm for taking Iris on as ship's mate. She wished she could be on the second boat with her Aunt Kate, but Addie had insisted she ride in the *Rainbow* so she could run ahead as they approached the locks.

In between negotiating the locks, Addie had fired a stream of information at Iris: the stretch of canal between two locks was called a 'pound'; the long towing rope was a 'snubber',

225

the shorter one was a 'strap'; the cargo space was divided into four sections: stern end, stern middle, back of the mast and fore end; getting caught on the mud was being 'stemmed up' . . . Iris's head had started to spin. Facts were going in one ear and flinging themselves out of the other in desperation.

Rainbow was overtaking her. She tried to trot faster, her ankles turning over in the wellington boots. They were no use for this work. Neither was the old suit of her brother's that she'd borrowed from his wardrobe. The long sleeves kept catching on the lock winding handle and the trouser-legs came out of the boots and tripped her up. She'd have been better off wearing a skirt and socks, but she hadn't known. She didn't know anything, she thought miserably, struggling to run. Her father had said as much this morning, when Nana had come round to the house to tell them about Taz.

'Arrested?' Iris had repeated blankly. 'But he can't be . . . I mean, *why*?'

'Stolen a necklace, according to your precious mother. She didn't tell you?'

'No. She never said a thing.' Iris's hands had moved automatically, setting out the china on her mother's early morning tea-tray. 'There must be some mistake. She can't have . . .'

'Took it when he came up here to see you the other night, according to madam.'

'I don't believe it!' Iris's eyes flashed. Ignoring the boiling kettle, she'd sprung up the stairs and marched straight into her parents' room without knocking.

'Iris, darling,' Ursula dabbed at a stain of peppermint cordial that had jerked from its spoon on to her nightdress. 'You made me jump. I feel quite dreadful again, I'm afraid. I don't think I'm going to be able to get up today.'

For once the sight of her mother leaning weakly back against her pillows had failed to frighten her. 'You did it on purpose,' she'd said hotly. 'Made up this stupid story just because Taz took me out a few times.'

'Iris, please don't shout like that. My head . . .'

'What's going on?' Her father had come from the bathroom, a towel round his shoulders and the shaving lather still thick on his chin.

'Mother's been lying. Accusing Taz of theft.'

'Taz? Who's Taz? What's he supposed to have stolen?'

'For heaven's sake, Fred,' Ursula said faintly. 'The young man from the boats. The one your daughter is going out with.'

'A boater? With Iris?' Seizing her shoulders he'd demanded to know what Taz had done to her.

'Nothing! We walked around the shops and went to the pictures. Let me go, Father, you're hurting.' She'd tried to force his fingers open.

'What else? What else did he do to you? If he's touched you, so help me I'll . . .'

'He hasn't! Daddy, you're hurting me . . .' His twisted face under the layer of soap had frightened her. She'd never seen him like this before, not even when he'd been so furious with Ernest for going out with that Rosetti girl.

Nana came in with the tea-tray Iris had abandoned. Dumping it on Ursula's knees, she'd seized her oldest son's ear, twisting hard. 'Let her go, Fred. Now. Do you hear me, boy? You're not too old to be walloped yourself.'

'Ow! Mother, don't! Have you gone mad?'

As soon as her father's grip had slackened, Iris had twisted free and retreated across the room until she felt the hard edge of the dressing table on the backs of her thighs. She'd known, if she looked in the mirror, the scar would be standing proud against her flushed complexion.

Fred jerked out of his mother's restraining pinch. 'I want to know what this man's done to her!'

'What most young men have done to young girls since time began, I should imagine, Fred. Even you and Madam Iceberg over there – once.'

'Did you know about this, Mother?'

'Well of course she did, Fred.' Ursula levered herself up on her elbows. There was a film of sweat over her greying skin. 'She did it on purpose . . . encouraged that lout to pester Iris to spite me. He was here the other evening, threatening me. I didn't tell you; I was afraid of what you might do. Now perhaps you'll take some notice of me and put the old witch in a home.'

'I'd like to see you try. And you're a fine one to be talking about spite. Having an innocent man thrown in jail to keep him away from your daughter . . .'

'He is *not* innocent! My amber necklace, the one that belonged to my mother, has gone. Look in the jewellery box if you don't believe me. It might not suit you to believe it, but it is true none the less, and he deserves to be in prison . . . Oh, Iris, get me some more cordial . . .' Ursula had lain back with a groan, her pulse fluttering wildly in the soft flesh under her chin.

'I'll do it.' Fred's larger fingers fumbled on the small bottle stopper.

His mother raised her eyebrows. 'Well, I'll not stay. I just came to tell Iris, in case she heard from anyone else. And to tell her not to worry. They've let him out on bail while they look for more evidence. He can't take his boats down the canal, mind, so he'll lose out on his money – but I don't suppose that will sit too heavily on your conscience. I'd be sure you've got that necklace tucked away somewhere safe, mind. It wouldn't do for a councillor's wife to be had up for wasting police time, would it? I'll let myself out.' She'd gone before Ursula could get enough breath to argue.

Iris had been left in a small pool of silence with her parents. She looked between them – her mother sickly, her father self-righteous. 'I'll start the breakfasts.'

Her father had followed her down to the kitchen. She'd deliberately not turned round. He'd watched her slicing the bread for toast.

'Iris, you won't see that man again.'

It wasn't even a question, it was a flat statement. He took it for granted she'd do as he said.

'Why shouldn't I? I'm grown up. I don't need your permission to do . . . anything any more.' She'd kept her head down, the hair hiding her face.

His hand had shot out, locking round her wrist. 'You'll do as I say, young lady! There's only one thing a man like that's going to want from you . . . if he hasn't already had it—'

'He hasn't!' She'd tried to release herself but this time there

228

was no Nana to help. 'Let go, Daddy. You're wrong about Taz! He's kind . . . and funny . . . and he likes me—'

'For Christ's sake!' Fred had released her hand and seized her chin, turning it roughly to force her to look into the saucepan lid he was holding up. Their distorted, pop-eyed reflections stared back at her. 'Look at yourself. There's only one thing a man's going to want from you, Iris.'

It was the first time she had realised he found her face repulsive. The knowledge had shown in her eyes, and she'd seen him understanding what he'd said.

'I'm sorry, Iris. I didn't mean to be cruel. You're my daughter. It's my job to protect you. You don't know anything about the world . . . And men . . . well, there's women you marry and women you don't.'

'And you should know, father.' She'd been almost calm as she knocked his grip away. It was as if her emotions had been dipped in ice. 'Excuse me, I have to get on with mother's breakfast tray if she's not getting up.'

'Iris, dear, I didn't . . .'

She'd brushed past him, walking into the larder with her head held high, and a lump in her throat that had hurt so much she felt as if she'd never be able to swallow again.

Her Aunt Kate had rung while she was washing up after a silent breakfast, to ask her to take the message round to Pansy. It wasn't until she'd delivered it and was walking back that the idea of helping out with the boats had started to form in her mind. She'd changed into Ernest's suit, collected her boots from the scullery and walked brazenly out of the house and up the road. Neither of her parents had seen her and she'd left no note.

'The bottom gates . . . close them first! 'Ow many more times you need telling?' Addie's impatient yell jerked Iris back to the present and the cold, grimy tow-path. Embarrassment made her clumsy. She dropped the windlass she'd been trying to fit into the top lock gates. It clanged noisily and bounced towards the canal edge. Addie's loud curse drew a red flush to her ears and earned her another cat-call from the watchers. She managed to stamp her foot down to prevent the handle from falling into the water. But the boats were already up on her and the lock hadn't been made ready. Despite the engine noise, she could hear Addie's exasperated sigh as she throttled *Rainbow* back, allowing the butty to glide alongside.

Kate jumped out and ran along to join her. 'I'm sorry,' Iris whispered. 'I thought . . . It looks so easy when you watch from the bridge. I should have stayed at home. I'm useless . . .'

'Everything's easy when you can do it. Put your weight on this, I'll go across.'

Iris flung herself against the balance beam that swung the lock gate shut. The toes of her boots scrabbled for a hold as she gritted her teeth and heaved the gate closed, forming a barrier across the canal. Panting in triumph, Iris turned towards the upper gates.

'Paddles!' Addie bawled. 'Check the bleedin' paddles!'

Unnerved, Iris spun round and nearly lost her footing. Addie had already explained twice, in a tone of deepest long-suffering, that the gates had paddles under the water, and if they weren't closed, any water coming in from the top of the lock was just going to flow straight out of the bottom again.

'It's all right,' Kate shouted across. 'They're down. Let's get the top set.'

She came back across the gates again, her arms outstretched like a tightrope walker. Together they fitted the windlass and turned, drawing up the upper paddle. Water gushed into the lock.

Iris pushed her hands into her jacket pockets. The palms were blistered, the skin raw from the unaccustomed manual work and the tingling cold of the air and the metal. Her shoulders and neck were aching from the effort of heaving the gates and her nose dripped constantly. She was miserable from the physical pains, and wretched from the realisation that she wasn't capable of doing anything of use apart from keeping house.

The water climbed to the level of the upper pound. Fitting her shoulders against the thick iron bar, Iris dug in her heels and pushed. On the central island, she could see her Aunt doing the same. After an initial resistance, the gates swung out. Kate promptly raced to the lower pair, wobbled over the tops, scrambled back up the tow-path and back on to the butty to help Addie guide the pair into the lock.

Once both boats were safely inside, she had to repeat the process, shutting the upper gates, drawing the paddles on the bottom to let the water out and allow the boats to sink down, and finally dragging the gates open so they could chug out again.

In between her lock duties, Iris huddled on the coal box just inside the *Rainbow*'s cabin, trying to keep out of Addie's way as she steered.

''Ere we go.' Addie swung the tiller over and the boat's nose turned sharply.

They left the main body of the canal and turned into a basin surrounded on three sides by soot-encrusted buildings, their windows protected by wire grilles and their chimneys belching smoke. Addie pointed the nose of the boat directly at the far wall and swung effortlessly to glide alongside the wharf.

'Come 'ere,' she ordered Iris. 'And 'old the tiller still . . . still, mind yer. I'm gonna tie up.'

She clamped Iris's freezing hands to the wooden handle and jumped off. Running to the bow of the boat, she looped a rope to the cleat in the dock and then raced back and did the same with the stern mooring. By the time Kate had nudged the *Crock* in behind them, Addie was ready to catch the ropes thrown to her and lash them into place.

'Back in a mo.' Hands thrust into her trouser pockets, Addie strode over to the building that abutted the canal and disappeared inside.

Kate climbed off her own boat and came along to *Rainbow*. 'I think you can let go now, Iris, it's not going anywhere.'

Iris realised she was still gripping the tiller bar as if her life depended on it. Gratefully she released it and eased her shoulder. 'Everything hurts, Aunt Kate. How can she do it all day long? I'm so *useless*.'

Kate stepped on the gunwale and leant her arms on the cabin roof. She extended her own hands, palms upwards to display rising blisters. 'I could do it once. You learn to live the life you've been given . . . or chosen. You'll see, Iris. I'm certain sure you'll surprise yourself.'

'I doubt it. I've never surprised myself yet. Addie despises me, in case you haven't noticed, and I think she's probably very right.' She didn't know she was crying until a tear slid down her cheek.

Kate came to sit by her, sliding an arm round her shoulders to give her a reassuring hug. 'It's not always like this. These lock beams are metal. Mostly they're wood, easier to work. And the pounds between them are mostly longer. I'm not saying it's an easy life, but it's not near as bad as this. She's taken you down one of the worst stretches. Upriver there's country paths, moorhens' eggs to dip for, farms to buy milk, pubs where the boats tie up, wild mushrooms and blackberries to be taken from the fields . . .'

Iris twisted so she could face her Aunt. Until today she'd always thought of her as a Londoner . . . by adoption if not birth. She'd never seemed any different from the hundreds of housewives that shopped in Camden and walked up Hampstead Heath in their best hats on fine Sundays and public holidays.

'You sound like you miss the canals. Do you?'

Kate wrinkled her nose, flicking back wisps of fair hair that were escaping from the rolled scarf and dancing in the stiff breeze skittering over the brown water. 'I did at first. I was so bitter homesick when I first went to my auntie's shop in Islington, I couldn't eat. I used to plot to run away, hide on a boat going up river . . .'

'But you didn't.'

'I knew there wouldn't be any use to it. Boaters breed their own crews. There wouldn't be any room for me, unless I married one of them. So that's what I decided to do. Soon as I was sixteen, I meant to stand on that canal bank and give the eye to any likely looking lad that sailed past.' She squeezed Iris tighter. 'But by the time I *was* sixteen I'd grown used to living ashore – gone soft, some might say. There's a lot to be said for running water and not having to chip your home out of the ice when the canal freezes over . . . Come on, at least the work keeps you warm.'

She stepped on to the wharf as Addie re-emerged from another factory door with an elderly man. They were dragging what appeared to be some kind of barrow between them. Except this 'barrow' just kept on coming, stretching from the factory to the edge of the wharf. Close up they could see it was some kind of jointed metal chute, this end slighter wider than the rest.

'Bring the blocks out, Davvy-boy!'

An even older man obliged, hauling out several large lumps of wood attached to rope handles. Propped under the chute, they gave it a slight incline downwards towards the factory.

'Ain't you got it unsheeted yet?' Addie complained. She was looking directly at Iris, but it was Kate who pointed out mildly that she hadn't told them she was unloading here.

'Well I ain't tied up to look at the scenery, have I? Here, give us a hand with these straps.' She shouted an apology to the men for the delay.

They shrugged and disappeared into the factory, leaving the boat's crew to get on with it.

Iris's fingers bled as she struggled with the tight knots on the lines lashed across the cargo. The heavy tarpaulins dragged on her aching shoulder-blades as they fought to fold them. She could have cried again when she found there was another layer of tarpaulins roped along the sides and over the single row of planks that balanced on three thick beams set down the centre of the boat. Sucking the blood from her nails, she jiggled the first knot.

'Not like that, you're making it tighter!'

Addie pulled and rolled a line with one simple movement. Iris's attempts to copy her ended in a cat's cradle of rope.

'Let me . . .' Kate took it from her. 'Ask the men if they've got a pair of gloves you can borrow.'

'I couldn't . . .'

'Yes, you can. Go on . . .'

Iris discovered that the chute led into a large boiler room. Davvy-boy and his mate were huddled on low stools in front of the glowing coals creating dream pictures inside one of the half-dozen boilers. Both of them were nursing mugs of milkless cocoa in tar-black hands.

233

Iris's request for gloves led to a round of head-scratching and denture sucking, before Davvy shuffled over to a small pile of coal in one corner and started poking around. Finally he emerged with a pair of tattered and partially finger-less gloves.

'There you are, Careaid, these will keep your hands soft and white as the angels intended.'

The coal had to be thrown up from the cargo area and into the mouth of the chute, after which – hopefully – gravity would deliver it into the factory. Davvy leant on his shovel half-way along the chute ready to nudge things along if gravity looked like it was slacking. Unloading the boat was strictly boaters' business as far as the factory hands were concerned.

After the first few spadefuls, Iris found her chest was heaving and her heart was thundering. Her first loads missed the chute altogether, bouncing and rolling over the quay and forcing Davvy to trudge over and scoop them up, until she got into the rhythm of the work.

Sweat started to pour down her back and soak into her armpits. The coal-dust rose in the air all around them, coating their teeth and dissolving in their saliva as they swallowed. As the level in the boat dropped, the throw got harder. Finally Addie called a halt while she restarted the engine and nudged *Rainbow* along a few yards to bring a fuller section of the cargo area under the chute.

'Why don't you change places with Davvy, Iris?' Kate suggested. 'I'm certain sure he wouldn't mind, a strong bloke like him.'

Davvy's face suggested otherwise. He'd got the cushiest job of the unloading and he wasn't keen to let it go. On the other hand, he didn't want them thinking he wasn't as strong as a slip of a lassie . . .

With relief Iris let him haul her on to the wharf and jump down to take her place. Urging the coal lumps along the slippery metal with the back of her shovel was easier, but it gave her more time to notice the pain in her neck and back.

The end of the load wasn't, she discovered, the end of

the work. Once the cargo area was empty, Addie borrowed a couple of stiff brooms and made them sweep down the wood until the coal-dust was gathered into collectible piles in the bottom of the boat. 'Clean dirt, coal,' she remarked, dumping the dust over the side. 'Better than grain. Grain's a right bugger. Gets in everywhere and sprouts. Got bleedin' plants growing up yer floor weeks after yer unloaded.'

Despite her cheery tone, Addie's skinny frame seemed to be as sweat-drenched and short of breath as the other two women's.

The next stop was the paper mill. Unlike the first factory, it abutted on to the main canal channel and, to Iris's relief, when they unsheeted the *Crock*'s cargo area, she discovered the rags weren't loose but bound into large, round rope-lashed bundles which were hauled up to the first floor by a lethal hook attached to a pulley. It was blissfully easy compared with the coal delivery. None the less, by the time they'd finished and got the receipt signed it was already growing dark.

'I can't believe this,' Addie moaned. 'All bleedin' day to go from Camden to Limehouse. It would 'ave been quicker if we'd 'ave been towed by a flamin' donkey. It's what comes from carrying amateurs.'

She spat out the word 'amateurs' in the same tone as others said 'huns'. Neither of the Cutters were in any doubt who she was referring to.

'It's her first trip,' Kate said. 'And we had a bad road, you know that, Addie . . . every lock was against us.'

'Still took hours,' Addie muttered rebelliously. 'Those that ain't bred to the water had better stop off it, if yer ask me. It only causes trouble.'

'Let's get on, shall we?' Kate said evenly. 'If you still want to?'

'Ain't got any choice, 'ave I? Can't leave the boats tied up here. Any'ow, I got to give these receipts in at the office. Otherwise we don' get paid. And Taz will need cash, won't he, on account of lawyers costing money.'

'I never thought . . . if I can help . . . I haven't much money, but I've some jewellery,' Iris said diffidently.

'Best give it to yer mum then, seeing as how she's short of hers. We don' need Cutter charity.'

'But you may need our friendship,' Kate remarked. 'Shall we untie?'

Addie shrugged, kicked a metal fixing ring, and jumped aboard. Iris Cutter may have stuck it longer than she'd expected, but there was still no way she was getting her hands on Taz and robbing Addie of the only home she'd ever known.

Chapter 24

'That's gunfire! I'm certain sure it is.'

'I know.' Despite the fact that the *Crock* was now on a short towing strap that held its nose close to the stern of the *Rainbow*, Iris had to shout across to her aunt. The noise in the Regent's Canal dock was tremendous.

The gunfire spat again. Instinctively she scanned the sky.

'It ain't a raid,' Addie said calmly, steering towards a row of identical narrow boats moored against the dock wall. 'They're testing the guns . . . see?'

She pointed to a small motor launch cutting busily through the choppy dock water. There was a gun mounted on the front and as Iris watched orange sparks spat from it.

Addie swung the *Rainbow* in a complete arc so that she could moor stern first like the twenty other craft lined up in this section.

Iris watched. She'd already learnt better than to offer help and get her head bitten off. Addie leapt down, took her arm in a fierce grip and put her lips close to Iris's ear. 'Listen, don't say nothing to no one about Taz getting arrested. Tell 'em he's sick. Something they lock you up for . . . you know, keep yer away from yer family . . .'

'Isolation,' Iris suggested.

'Yeah. That's it. Tell them he's got a bad fever. I'm off up the office.'

While she was gone, Kate lit the lamp, heated up water on the stove, and they both stripped to the waist and rubbed off the worst of the coal-dust and sweat. A finger and a lot of spit dealt with their teeth-cleaning, and a vigorous combing sorted out their hair.

237

'I should have brought a change of clothes,' Iris said, reluctantly rebuttoning her brother's crumpled shirt.

Kate had opened the doors a crack, bringing a welcome draught of fresh air into the cabin, which had already started to become unbearably hot and smelly with stove heat and paraffin fumes. 'They're sending the barrage up.'

Iris came to peek over her shoulder. The light was dying, leaving the sky streaked the colour of peach marmalade bruised by random puffs of graphite-shaded clouds that stretched south across Greenwich and Blackheath and away to the Kentish Weald. 'Weather's lifting again. It feels like spring isn't far away now.'

'Bombers won't be either – you can be certain sure of that.'

Iris shrugged on her jacket. 'Do you want to go and find an underground station or a shelter?'

'I don't like to leave until Addie gets back. It would feel like we're abandoning her and the poor girl's got enough troubles at the moment. The *Crock of Gold* is in a terrible mess. It's going to take more than a bit of elbow grease and paint to set that right.' Belatedly, Kate recalled Iris's recent encounter with a German bomb. 'I'm sorry. I didn't think . . . If you'd rather find a shelter, we can leave Addie a note.'

'I don't think she could read it. Anyway, it's quite all right. I thought *you* might want to take cover. Since we got hit I've felt much better *not* going down a shelter. You know the people in the house next door were buried? They say they died in the blast, but I keep thinking, what if they were alive, lying there for hours with the earth over their faces?'

Kate touched her fingers to Iris's lips, stilling the tide of words that were spilling out, and assured her that she couldn't bear to sit in a hard shelter right now. 'I'm aching in places I didn't know I had places.'

'So am I. And I'm getting a headache.'

'It's the lamp fumes.' Extinguishing the light, Kate pushed the end doors fully open. They crouched side by side on the coal box, hair hanging loosely over their shoulders, watching the dusk rapidly changing to night.

Sitting low down like this, all they could see above the

tiller were the tall, skeletal frames of the cranes that gradually lost definition and were absorbed into the blackness behind them. The noises started to trail away too as work died down with the light. Fewer lorries and iron-shod boots rang over the cobbles, and the noise from the ships died down to an occasional throttle or the splash of oars.

Iris drew in a lungful of air redolent with diesel, engine oil and river water. 'It's strange . . . I can smell the sea.'

Kate sniffed too and gave her opinion that it was something stuck on the ships' hulls. 'You did well today.'

'Did I? Addie didn't seem to think so. She thinks I'm a hopeless case. She's probably right. What can I do – except cook a bit and dust furniture?'

'What else have you tried to do? You're as good as anyone else, Iris.'

'That's what Nana says. But she doesn't know . . . no one does . . . how I am inside, how *scared* I am all the time.'

'What are you scared of?'

'Everything,' Iris said bitterly. 'Walking out today was probably the bravest thing I've ever done.'

'You mean your parents don't know where you are?'

'Not unless Uncle Pete's told them. I was so angry with Mother because of Taz, and Daddy because . . . because of something he said. I just . . .' She gestured, her hands moving like moths in the darkness. It was hard to put her paralysing lack of self-esteem into words. She felt at that moment that if she could have had Addie Dixon's self-confidence she wouldn't have asked for anything more from life.

Addie herself *could* ask for more – and she did. She wanted another cargo. She'd prowled the dock listening to the dockers talking before going to the small hut that served as the Canal Company's office.

'There's steel being unloaded from that freighter, the men said,' she said eagerly. 'Going up to Birmingham. We can take that. Twenty-three tons in the motor, twenty seven in the butty. You know us, mister. Dixons are reliable. Ain't never let yer down 'ave we?'

The manager of the Canal Carrying Company punched

neat holes through the two receipts Addie had just handed over, filed them with maddening slowness in a lever arch file and returned the same to a shelf. Unlocking a cash box, he counted out her money, twisted a ledger and handed her a pen. 'Sign there. I've enough boats to take the steel myself. A sufficiency of boats, you might say.'

'Oh.' With careful, printed characters, Addie put her name to the receipt book and then suggested they'd take whatever else was going. 'Must be plenty of other cargoes – all them ships in dock?'

'I'll be filling my own boats first. Giving them priority, you might say.'

'We can take anything that's over, mister. I'll come up first thing tomorrow, shall I? Get me orders?'

'I deal with the steerer, not the hand. A matter of etiquette, you might say. Where *is* your brother?'

Addie ground a boot-tip into the polished floorboards and muttered something about Taz being sick. 'But it's OK, mister. I got two hands helping me out. Good workers. We'll deliver on time. And we won't take no money.'

'Such generosity . . . And why would you do that?'

'Thought we could do a trade, mister.' Addie made herself look the man in the eyes. 'The *Crock*'s got burnt. Incendiaries. Thought you could fix it up for us.'

'Well I'm sorry to hear that. But you know I can't do that. The Maintenance Depot only works on our own boats. Now, if your brother were to reconsider our offer – let the company take over your boats . . .'

'Never!'

'We'd fix up both vessels free of charge,' the manager went on as if Addie hadn't spoken. 'And we'd supply your diesel, give you an allowance for provisions . . . and of course there'd be plenty of work, as much as you can handle . . .'

'We can handle it now. Just tell us what you want moving, mister.'

'At the moment, *you*, I'm afraid, Miss Addie. I'm away to a meeting of my Home Guard unit.' He switched the light out as he spoke, settled a bowler hat on his gleaming scalp and held open the door for her.

She had no choice but to step out into the night and the dying activity on the docks. 'How about some diesel, mister? Me tank's nearly empty.'

'I think we could manage that. Usual price. Come back tomorrow . . . And think on my offer. Most of your cargoes come by way of sub-contracts from this company anyway. Might as well make it regular. And from what I hear your brother owes money all over the place; someone will be taking those boats off him soon anyway if things go on this way. If the Ministry of War Transport don't requisition them first. Better to enter the fold voluntarily. Goodnight.'

Temporarily defeated, Addie mooched back to her boats. She'd pictured herself getting a cargo; organising the repair of the *Crock* and generally showing Taz how indispensable she was to his life. And what the hell had the bloke meant about Taz owing money? The Dixons always paid their way.

She kicked out moodily, sparking her metal studs against the cobbles. If Taz had been here she was certain the manager would have given them part of the steel load for Birmingham. It was all those damn Cutters' fault.

'Bugger them . . . bugger them . . . bugger them . . .' she shouted at the first stars. At least there was one advantage to having Taz out of the way – she could swear as much as she liked without being threatened with a soap dinner.

She greeted Kate's query about leaving the boats here or moving them back to Cutter's with a casual shrug. 'Dunno. Might be picking up a cargo down here tomorrow.'

'To where? We weren't planning on a long trip . . . I've my work at the yard, and I'm not sure Iris could manage on her own . . .'

Addie was dead certain she couldn't, even though Iris had proven far better at the job than she'd ever have admitted. Perhaps a longer trip might put her off good and proper. She'd try again for a load in the morning. 'Dunno exactly. But it's too late to move up now anyhow. Can't see yer nose, much less the bows. I ain't moving the boats in the dark.'

'You have before.'

'That was when Taz was steering.' Addie tried to look helpless, even though it went against her normal nature.

'We can double up in here . . . two in the cross-bed, one on the side.'

Kate raised interrogatory eyebrows at her niece and received a nod of agreement. 'That's settled then. I'll need to phone my mother-in-law. I want to check that Pansy's all right. Is there a phone on the dock?'

'Box outside the gates. Can I come? Talk to Taz? I got some coppers . . .' Delving into her tattered trousers again, Addie pulled out two pennies.

There was a queue – mostly merchant seamen. They tagged on to the end in a silent trio. By the time they reached the box, everyone else had melted into the blacked-out streets. Iris let the other two go inside and walked away a few steps, leaning against the dock walls to get a little shelter.

A couple of men left the dock gates, walked past and then paused. One came back to her.

'Pleeese . . . what you cost?'

'I'm sorry?' Iris straightened up, confused.

'What cost?' The man took paper from his pocket and shuffled it. 'I got money . . . plenty good money . . .'

'What do you want to buy?'

'Buy . . . yes!' White teeth flashed in a broad grin. 'You come . . . good price.'

He took her hand and pulled. Iris tried to drag it away.

'You come. It hokay . . . good money.' The man put his arm round her waist and urged her along.

'Wait.' Iris twisted out of his grip. 'Go away! Leave me alone!'

'What matter . . . good money . . . ?'

Notes were waggled in her face. He was pushing her along with short shoves towards the other man, who laughed softly, showing stained teeth. He smelt of strange, spicy scents and musky sweat.

'Let me *go*!'

They were pulling her by both arms now. Looking desperately over her shoulder she saw that the phone box was already lost in the blackness. Taking a deep breath, she screamed frantically, 'Help!'

The unexpected noise made the first man loose his grip,

but the second hung on. She could see the whites of his eyes rolling. Instinctively she clawed at them. He giggled softly again, moving easily out of her way and holding her off.

'Oi!'

There were footsteps running from both directions. Addie arrived first. Without wasting a breath she drew back her boot and lashed at Iris's captor. Steel connected with his kneecap. With a shriek he released Iris and hopped away, spitting curses in a language none of them understood.

'Iris, are you all right?' Kate flung an arm round her niece's shoulder before turning on the other man. 'How dare you! I'll have the police on you . . .'

The man raised helpless shoulders. 'No police. Pleeze have good papers. Have money . . . see? Good money . . .' He waved the cash again.

'Well now, ducks. Aren't you the answer to a maiden's prayer?'

The second set of feet that had come hurrying in response to Iris's frightened screams sauntered out of the dark night. Totally ignoring the three women, she placed long, polished nails over the seaman's fingers and squeezed gently, imprisoning the wad of money inside their joint grip. 'How about buying a lady a drink then, 'andsome?'

White teeth flashed. 'I have money. Good money. I buy.'

'And I sell. I think this 'ere could be a match made in 'eaven.' She slid round, clamping his arm into hers.

'I have friend . . . see? I buy for him too?'

'I like a man who treats his friends. I have a friend too. Let's go introduce your friend to my friend, shall we, 'andsome?' She captured the second man as he hopped past, still groaning softly. With a seaman anchored to each hip, she finally spoke to the three women: 'This is my patch of wall.'

'And you're bleedin' welcome, I'm sure. We ain't tarts. We work the boats.'

'Well, we're all doing our bit for the war effort then, ain't we, ducks? Come on, lover, let's go find that drink.'

The trio swayed into the blackout, the woman's husky tones keeping up a running commentary of teasing encouragement.

'Are you sure you're all right, Iris? He didn't do anything to you?'

'Yes. No. I'm fine really.' Iris took a deep breath, got her voice under control, and asked brightly: 'What now?'

'I think I could do with a drink myself,' Kate said. 'Is that a pub over the road, Addie?'

'Yeah. It's where all the boaters go. Sailors too. But I ain't thirsty. I'm bleedin' starving.'

'Is there any food on the *Rainbow*?'

'Dunno. I ain't been shopping much lately. There's a shop does fish and jellied eels along there, though. Taz took me once.'

In the end they bought cod and chips and ate the greasy packages walking back to the pub. It was called the Volunteer. As Addie had remarked, it was a pub for those who made their living on the water – river or ocean. They made their way over the sand-covered floor and up to the polished counter.

'Yes, love?'

'I . . . er . . .' Kate looked round and spotted two women in trousers sipping some kind of beer. 'We'll have that too.'

The barmaid regarded Addie doubtfully. 'How old are you, son?'

'I ain't yer son!' Angrily, Addie snatched off her cap, letting the rusty hair tumble. 'And I'm seventeen come Saturday. And I don't want no bleedin' beer anyhow – it tastes like dog piss. I'll have a cream soda.'

The bar was packed and thick with the smells of beer, tobacco, bodies and the gas brackets hissing over the bar and around the walls. The only spare seats were at the table by the two women Kate had spotted earlier.

'Do you mind?' She indicated the chairs.

'Not at all . . . please do.' The woman's voice was surprisingly cultured. It didn't suit the crumpled jerkin and trousers tucked into heavy boots.

'Thought you were boaters,' Addie remarked, perching on the edge of a seat.

'We are . . . at least, we're trainees. Della Milbrook – how do you do . . .'

'Haa d'yer do?' Addie shook hands automatically as more

introductions flew around the table. 'What kind of trainees?' she finally asked when everyone seemed to know everyone else.

'Canal boat workers,' the posh one explained. She touched a small blue and white enamel badge on her jacket that announced, 'On National Service'.

'I ain't never heard of that.' Addie stared suspiciously.

'It's new. We're the first batch the Canal Company has taken on.'

'You mean,' Iris said hesitantly, 'that you can do this as your National Service, instead of going into a factory?'

'Absolutely!' Della nodded enthusiastically. 'There's no chance you'd get us making munitions. I couldn't bear to be cooped up inside. Oh, excuse us, there are our friends.'

After the trainees had left, a small pool of silence fell over the table. Iris's eyes were sparkling as she turned over a growing idea in her head. Addie was miserably depressed; she knew exactly what Iris was thinking. And Taz had been adamant on the telephone. She wasn't to mess around with repairs or cargoes – she was to bring the boats back at first light and tie up at Cutter's Wharf.

Kate sipped her glass of beer before saying. 'By the way, Iris. Your father's been to Nana's house looking for you. He and Taz had words . . . a whole dictionary-full, I gather . . .'

'Did Nana tell him where I'd gone?'

'No. Apparently she just said you were safe, and old enough to be away from home on your own.'

'Good,' Iris breathed with more bravado than she actually felt.

The mood of brooding reflection settled over all three women again until the crash of a body descending into one of the vacant chairs and a glass hitting the table jerked them all into the present.

'Evenin' all together.'

'Get lost, Geoghan.'

'That ain't very matey, Addie,' Blackie protested, pulling himself more comfortably up to the table.

'Ain't it? Good. I don't wanna be yer mate.'

245

'Maybe not . . . but what about the other two lovelies? Three f-f-fancy-f-free blokes and three f-fillies. Perfect.'

He was drunk, but not enough to cause him any problems . . . only those he came into contact with. Leaning closer now to focus on their faces through the thick blue smoke that was settling like a camouflage blanket over the bar-room, he fixed on Kate and exclaimed, 'Why, it's Missus Kate, ain't it? What you doing down here? Mr Cutter wiv yer?' He drew back slightly at the thought, mindful that the Cutters were bosses.

'No. We brought the boats down with Addie. Her brother's sick.'

'What's up wiv 'im?'

'Isolation,' Addie said promptly. 'He's got that stuff puts yer in isolation. Ain't that right, miss?'

'The authorities insisted he didn't move from the area,' Iris agreed truthfully.

'Yeah?' Blackie mulled this over while he took a long pull on his pint. He pulled the back of his hand over his thick lips and belched contentedly as Matthus pushed his way to the table and was told to go fetch another pint.

'You gotta fetch yer glass back, Blackie.'

'Go on, then. And get the ladies a drink.'

Kate reached for her own glass before Matthus could pick it up. 'We've not finished these, thanks.'

'I'll buy yer a drink if yer like, Addie.'

'Well I don't like. Push off, Matthus.'

Matthus pushed back to the bar with his brother's empty glass. Blackie winked broadly. ''E's sweet on yer. Told me how you clean up real nice. You could do worse than taking up with our Matt.'

'Yeah. I could go up the zoo, move in the monkey cage.'

'Monkeys . . . I like that.' Blackie chortled and made soft hooting sounds under his breath. He was still chuckling when Matthus returned with his pint and a soldier who swung awkwardly through the jostling customers on his crutch. Blackie drew up another chair. 'Yer remember me brother Rickey? Used to work the boats before he answered 'is country's call to do his duty.'

Addie tilted her chair back on two legs and looked the wounded hero up and down. 'I 'eard he'd been drafted – along with the rest of the idle buggers of Geoghans who couldn't squeeze on yer boats and claim they was reserved workers. Heard he'd shot his own foot off too . . . to get out of that uniform.'

Rickey scowled. 'Well it ain't true. I was shot fair and square, Addie Dixon. Took off half me toes. I got to go up in front of a medical board. The doc reckons I won't ever be normal again . . .'

'Should 'ave told him you weren't to start with.'

'That's a good one, Rickey! She's got a sharp gob on her, ain't she? Reckon you'll have your work cut out taming this one, Matthus.'

Matthus blushed and muttered, 'Aw, go on, Blackie . . .'

Finding a stool free, he dragged it over and squeezed up to the table. Moving over to make room for him caused the curtain of hair that had been hanging down Iris's face to swing back behind her shoulders.

Blackie paused in mid swallow. His eyes widened in shock. ''Ere blimey . . . It's Miss Cutter, ain't it? I never recognised yer. What wiv the bloke's suit and yer cut-up bits being hidden. What you doing here, miss?'

The 'miss' was slightly more respectful than his greeting to Kate. Since Fred Cutter was the eldest, it was generally assumed among the boatmen that Iris's father must be the overall boss at Cutter's Wharf.

'Told yer, didn' she?' Addie snapped. 'Giving us an 'and. There's all sorts of posh folks going boating these days, ain't you heard?' she added bitterly.

'Yeah?' A sly smile spread over Blackie's sweating face. 'Sure it ain't yer brother she's been giving a hand to?'

'No. It ain't.' Addie reached for her drink, knocked it flying and sent a tide of cream soda into Blackie's lap. 'Oops . . . sorry, I'm sure.'

Blackie's alcohol consumption was still in the love-to-all-men stage. Using his brother's forage cap to mop up the damage, despite Rickey's protests, he told Matthus to get his girl another drink.

'I ain't 'is girl . . . and I don't wanna another drink. I'm going 'ome.' Crashing back her seat regardless of those behind her, Addie thrust her way to the door and out into the street.

'Addie, 'ang on!' Matthus hurried out after her.

Addie put up her fists threateningly.

'I don't want to fight, Addie. I only wanted . . . I wanted to tell yer . . .' Matthus took an enormous breath, then gabbled nervously: 'I'dbewillingto'aveyerasmegirlifyerlike.'

'I wouldn't.'

She tried to leave, but Matthus darted in front of her. 'We could get our own boats, Addie. Canal Company's looking for more crews. Got plenty of work wiv the war see? We could take over a pair.'

'You're barmey! They wouldn't give yer a boat – yer a kid.'

'I ain't. Blackie says I'll be eighteen next month.'

'Don't yer know?'

'I ain't exactly sure of the date. Me mum never bothered much with dates and things, 'cept for trip dates . . . but Blackie remembers blossom was out along the banks when I was born. That's next month, ain't it?'

'Suppose so.'

'How old are you, Addie?'

'Seventeen . . . almost.'

'That's old enough. Blackie reckons me mum was fourteen when she 'ad him. And 'er and me dad were already working a pair. What do you say? Can I come call when we're moored up close?'

'I dunno. What about Blackie anyhow? He can't work your pair on 'is own.'

Matthus's face acquired the demeanour of a rabbit that had been caught out on someone else's carrot patch. 'Thing is, Rickey reckons they'll give him 'is cards from the Army, so he'll be coming back on board.'

'So? Taz said when he was a kid, there was so many Geoghans on your pair sometimes, it's a miracle it was never pulled over at the gauging stations for overloading.'

'Yeah. But, see . . . them at the labour exchange said we

only needed two hands on board. That was me and Blackie, on account of him being too old for the Army and me being too young. Only now I'm seventeen . . . that's grown, ain't it?'

Surveying Matthus's skinny frame Addie gave her opinion that it weren't for him. 'So I'm supposed to be your missus so you can stop out of uniform, is that it?'

'Sort of. But it would suit us both, wouldn't it? I mean, yer gotta marry someone, ain't yer? Might as well be me. Haa 'bout it? Will yer walk out?'

'I'll think about it.'

'OK.' He was still blocking her way back to the dock gates. On being told to move he asked, 'Can I kiss yer then – now yer me girl?'

'I ain't – not yet. And if yer try to kiss me I'll bite yer bleedin' nose off. Go on, get lost . . .'

'Yeah, but . . .' Matthus's inclination to argue was squashed by Kate and Iris emerging from the pub. 'You'll think about it then?'

'Yeah, I'll think about it.'

Addie darted around him and started walking briskly towards the dock gates, leaving the other two women to hurry behind her. She didn't want to talk at the moment; she had to get things straight in her head first.

She'd always despised the Geoghans. Not for any particular reason, but simply because they'd always been the lepers of the canal world. On the other hand, there weren't that many single blokes working the boats. And certainly none that had ever shown any interest in her. She hadn't managed to put Iris Cutter off boating . . . If she and Taz were to wed . . . ? Addie shivered, recalling how Mrs Kate's sister-in-law had thrown her off the boats.

At least if she took up with Matthus she'd be able to stay on the canals. He'd always been the runt of the family, bullied by his elder brothers – and his sisters too, she thought, recalling the succession of sly-faced females who'd cooked and washed on Blackie's boats over the years. Blackie had always claimed they were sisters; others had said they were Blackie's wives – and once Addie had heard her grandfather mutter that it was all the same on the Geoghan boats, a remark she'd never really understood.

She could handle Matthus – he'd do as he was told. It didn't occur to her that the rest of his family wouldn't.

Chapter 25

'Will that be all, Mrs O'Day? If there is any other service the bank can offer, we are always at your disposal.'

'Ain't that a handsome offer, Maury? Always at our disposal.'

'Yes, Mum.' Maury bit the inside of his cheek trying not to burst out laughing.

The bank manager stood as his visitors did so, easing their path towards his office door with an oily smile 'My assistant will telephone you at the . . .' He peered at the documents on his new customer. 'At the Golden Cross public house, to let you know when Master O'Day's cheque-book is ready for collection. And we will arrange for him to have sole access to his account, if that's what you wish, Mrs O'Day.'

''Andsome. But don't put yourself to the bother of no phone calls. See . . . Can I trust you? I mean, you ain't one to spread gossip, are yer?'

'I assure you, Mrs O'Day, the bank maintains a policy of the *strictest* confidentiality where our customers' affairs are concerned.'

'Well that's a weight of me mind and no mistake. But we'd prefer it if yer didn't phone the pub. See, the thing is, Mr Griswald, me cousin, has acted handsome taking us in after the bombs hit me 'ouse, but he ain't one to keep a secret. Most of the family don't know about my Maury's little inheritance, and if they found out they'd be pestering us day and night. And that ain't right, is it? I mean, Grandad wanted my little Maury to have that cash. If he'd 'ave wanted anyone else to 'ave it, he'd have put them in his will, wouldn't he?'

'Grandfather? I thought you said your son had been left the money by his great uncle?'

'Both of them,' Maury said promptly. 'Lived together, didn't they? I was their favourite, weren' I, Mum?'

'Apple of their eye. Well, *eyes* I should say – on account of them having the three between 'em.'

Maury intervened. 'Hadn't we better go, Mum? You got an appointment with the doctor, remember? For yer bunions.'

'So I have. What would Mummy do without her little helper? Well, it's ta-ra for now then. And we'll remember yer 'andsome offer to stop at our disposal, won't we, Maury?'

In one smooth movement Mrs O'Day shook the manager's hand with her right, pinched out her glowing cigarette tip with her left, sending a tube of ash to the carpet, and flicked the butt neatly across the office into the waste paper bin.

'Give your old mum an arm then, son.'

Maury duly proffered his sleeve and together they walked slowly into the cold spring sunshine. They kept up the slow shuffling pace until they'd turned the corner and were out of sight of the bank windows.

'Bunions! Yer cheeky sod, Maury!' With a hoot of laughter 'Mrs O'Day' cuffed her offspring with her large, shabby handbag.

'Well I had to say something . . . stop you pulling his leg like that.'

'Weren't he a scream?' Carla laughed. 'Still, better than keeping it under the floorboards at home. If this lot ends up as a bomb crater they've still got to stump up your cash. Seeing as 'ow they're *always at your disposal* . . .' she imitated the manager's obsequious tones.

''Andsome,' Maury cooed.

They both burst into more laughter, hanging on to each other for support, until a couple of WVS workers abandoned their salvage collection cart and came over to ask if the old lady was all right.

'Yes, ta. It's just one of her turns. Come on, Mum, let's go get yer a cup of tea.'

'He's a lovely son . . . a lovely son . . .'

Clinging together, they fled down a series of small alleys

until they arrived at the small café where they'd told Joshua to meet them. Carla disappeared into the toilets while Maury ordered two teas and two currant buns. When she returned, she'd taken off the turban scarf and spectacles, washed off the heavy layer of face-powder, and done her best to brush out the coating of talcum powder that had turned her black hair grey. She hadn't completely succeeded, and as a result it hung in rather ghostly tresses down her unusually pale face.

'Whatcha thinking?' she asked.

'That you look different. Without all that stuff over yer face.'

'Plain as what the pig sits on, yer mean?' Carla said, spreading margarine on her near-currantless bun.

'I never said that.'

'Thought it though,' Carla said with no apparent rancour. 'I know I ain't no movie star. Never have been. Just gotta do the best with what yer got, ain't yer? Smoke?'

He still disliked the taste of tobacco, but it was something all grown blokes did, wasn't it? He reached out to take one. Before he could, however, Carla put a second into her mouth, struck a match against the table and lit both. She drew in several lungfuls of smoke before passing one across.

Maury could taste her mouth on the filter as he tried not to screw up his eyes or cough. Her stockinged toes wriggled up under his trouser turn-up. Maury moved his leg back out of reach. 'Pack it in. Leave off the teasing.'

'Whatever you say, lover. You really going to marry the little flower-girl?'

'Flower . . . ? Oh, Pansy! Yeah, course I am. I'm taking her up the West End dinner-time to pick her ring.'

He'd managed to persuade Pansy – with some difficulty – to tell the bakery that she had a terrible toothache and that she simply had to go up the dentist in her lunch break.

'I could do more for yer, Maury.'

'Eh?' He stared blankly, unsure whether Carla had just proposed to him or not.

'We're all right together, ain't we? And we both want the same things . . . something better than this.' She waved a hand vaguely, taking in the fuggy café with its condensation-covered windows and its small tables that were mostly occupied by the ubiquitous railway workers and repair gangs patching up recent bomb damage. The only other female customer was a thin, unattractive girl dressed in a neat black jacket and skirt, white ankle socks and a grey woollen beret. Since he had his back to her, Maury wasn't even aware she was there.

'Pansy wants something better too. House, cars, fancy clothes . . .'

'Yeah, I expect she does. But she ain't going to help you get them, Maury. She'll wait for you to bring home the bacon . . . and the eggs too, I expect. Oh I know she'll do her bit,' Carla went on before he could spring to Pansy's defence. 'She'll keep the house clean, and press your shirts and look after the kids . . . but she won't find the deals or keep the customers sweet like I do. And when you start going up, Maury, she'll hang back . . .'

Maury opened and shut his mouth. His natural inclination to spring to Pansy's defence was muddled by the niggling knowledge that Carla was right. 'Yer saying you want us to get married, Carla?'

'Why not? It ain't such a bad idea, is it? Most people get hitched to someone in the end. And I reckon you and me could both do a lot worse.'

'I thought you had. What happened to *your* fiancé? The one works up the market?'

'Who? Oh him. You don't want to believe everything you hear. The bloke up the market gives me ten bob a week to say I'm his fiancée. Leastways, he *did*. Last I heard he'd been called up, so I reckon a soldier's farewell's on the cards.'

'Why'd he do that?'

''Cause he likes men better than women, Maury. A *lot* better, if you get my drift.'

'You mean he's a nancy-boy?' It didn't seem possible. The bloke they were talking about was an ex-boxer.

'Don't go all chapel and smite-the-sinner on me, Maury. It suited us both. Ten bob in me purse and no one to know he does his courting down the public lavs.'

254

'What about Eddie Hooper?'

'What about him? They ain't offering double bunks in Wandsworth Prison that I 'eard. But I could help you there. Maybe I could find out who Eddie asked to look after that confession of yours. It don't matter how high you go, Maury – while your signature's on a piece of paper saying you helped thieve from a warehouse and coshed the nightwatchman, Eddie can bring you down any time he wants.'

Maury knew that. He pointed out that he didn't need her stating the bleedin' obvious. 'And you said you'd help out with Eddie weeks ago. Seems to me if he was going to cough up he'd 'ave done it ages ago.'

'No he wouldn't. Longer he stays in there the more he'll be desperate to keep me coming regular. And that's when I'll start playing hard to get. He'll tell me, Maury, in time. And if you and me was hitched . . . well, it would be no more than me wifely duty to confide in me old man, wouldn't it?'

Maury was forced to pull in his chair to allow a couple of railway gangers to push past. Several others were climbing to their feet, the movements releasing smells of grease and soot from their clothes. They were all beyond conscription age, but big muscular blokes none the less. Surely more to Carla's taste than an undersized seventeen-year-old?

'I told you,' she said when he asked why him. 'You're going somewhere.' Carla leant her forearms on the table and captured both his hands. 'Listen, Maury, women between twenty-one and twenty-two have already been told to register for service. It'll be my lot next. There's no way I'm wasting years of my life digging turnips or making machine bits twelve hours a day. And I'm sure as hell not volunteering to stick on a uniform; khaki ain't my colour and blue ain't much better. What I need is a husband needing his loving wife's care and attention. And a kid.'

'A kid!' So far children had only figured in Maury's future as dim and distant – *very* distant – daydreams.

'Why not? Loving mums ain't expected to do war work. We only need the one.'

'Yeah, but . . .' This was all going too fast for Maury. One minute they were business partners, next thing she'd got them married off and a kid in the cradle. He seized on the handiest excuse. 'Me mum – we'll need her permission . . . and I ain't sure she'd go for it.'

Carla leant back from the table and outlined a descriptive curve over her stomach. 'Tell her I'm already. Will you think about it? What I said?'

'Yeah . . . yeah, I'll think about it, Carla.'

'Can't ask more than that then . . .' She smiled over his shoulder as the door bell jangled and a cold draught played over his neck. 'Hello, muscles. Found us all right then? Want a cuppa and a bit to eat? Daft to ask really – when *don't* you?' Slewing round in her chair again, she shouted across to fetch over a cup of tea for Joshua. 'Better fetch as much sugar as you can spare. And a meat roll.'

'Did you do everything I told you?' Maury asked. For the first time, he'd decided to entrust Joshua with a bit of solo debt collecting.

'Joshua did. Joshua went to the food vans and asked for Maury's money. And then Joshua went to the shop and bought tickets for the dance.' He laid them out in a square on the table top. The crudely printed bits of pasteboard looked tiny under his huge fingers.

'You idiot! I told you three tickets. You've gone and bought four. Can't yer count?'

'Joshua *can* count. Joshua's dad taught him. This ticket is Joshua's.' He stabbed a thick forefinger down on the last square.

'You sure about that, muscles? That looks more like yours to me.' Carla tapped another ticket.

With a serious frown Joshua considered the identical cardboard oblong. 'No,' he said finally, the anxiety lines disappearing from his face like rough plaster smoothed by the sweep of an expert's trowel. 'That one is Joshua's.' He picked up the first ticket with exaggerated care and placed it in his inside pocket before falling happily on a roll filled with circles of spicy continental sausage.

'For heaven's sake,' Maury muttered, glaring at his amused business partner. 'What you want to go to a dance for?'

'Joshua's girl is going. Going with you, Maury.'

'Oi, oi, what's this, Maury? Two-timing the flower-girl already?'

'No I ain't. She's a sort of mate of Pansy's. I said I'd take her along too. It's her birthday.'

'Well now you can be a cosy foursome. Can you dance, muscles?'

'Maury's mum is teaching Joshua. One-two-three, one-two-three, one-two-three.'

Reaching over, Maury shuffled his own three tickets together and slipped them in his breast pocket. 'I don't need you no more today, Joshua.'

'You can walk me home, muscles. We can practise yer waltzing.'

Joshua beamed. 'Are you coming to the dance too, Miss Carla?'

'I ain't been invited, muscles.' She slid a sideways look at Maury from beneath her lashes. His stomach muscles tightened. Carla's amusement acquired a veneer of maliciousness. 'It's all right, lover. I'm otherwise spoken for Saturday night. You given muscles his wages for running your errands?'

Two half-crowns exchanged owners. Maury checked out the change he had left. He'd planned to collect Pansy in a taxi. It would impress her. And please her.

Outside he turned south, intending to pick up a cab from the station.

Carla pulled Joshua in the opposite direction. 'Come on, muscles . . . One, two, three – remember?'

Joshua took her in his arms and they progressed up the narrow street in a stiff-limbed waltz. A group of sailors stopped to watch them. One took a mouth organ from his uniform and started playing 'The Last Time I Saw Paris'. Despite her dowdy clothes and lack of make-up, the men's eyes followed Carla. None of them gave a second glance to the pig-tailed blonde in the beret who stepped out of the café a moment later. Clearing her misted spectacles on the bunched ends of her plaits, Sheila Abbott repositioned them on her nose and stared at Maury's departing back with excited eyes.

Who'd have thought it? Pansy Cutter's boyfriend with

another woman. And a pregnant one too, judging by that mime act she'd just witnessed in the café. She couldn't wait to get home tonight and tell her sister Lottie. After all, as Pansy's best friend, she really had a right to know.

Chapter 26

'Iris Athelea Cutter!'

'Yes. Here.' Iris resisted the temptation to shoot a hand in the air. She wasn't answering the register in the first form. Her mouth had gone dry. She pushed her hands together to prevent them shaking. Now that the moment had come, all her terror at the idea of actually leaving the only home she'd ever known was threatening to overwhelm her again.

The labour exchange supervisor indicated that she should go into the small, glass-walled office with the black stencilled legend: 'Miss J.A. Maynard-Potts'. Following Iris in, she took a seat behind the desk and pulled a form in front of her. The skin between her forefinger and middle finger was stained blue from a leaking pen, and a smear had been transferred to her forehead from her habit of continually sweeping back a stray wisp of brown hair that had escaped from the severe sweep of her french plait.

Iris wondered why none of the clerks had mentioned it to her, and decided it was probably because the woman's bite was as intimidating as her bark. Questions fired between her teeth in an accent that had been chiselled into shape by the most expensive ladies' college her parents couldn't afford.

'Date of birth, twenty-sixth December 1919?'

'Yes, that's ri—'

'Unmarried?'

'Yes.'

'And you are not currently employed?'

'No.'

'Are you suffering from ill-health?'

'No, I'm quite fit.'

'But you didn't think to volunteer for war work?' Disapproval radiated from the austere face like heat from an incendiary.

'Well, yes, I did . . . but you see . . .' Iris struggled to justify her apparent work-shyness. But even as the words formulated in her head she could hear how unsatisfactory they sounded. How could she explain her mother's neediness to someone who didn't know her?

The sight of Ursula's beloved daughter – dirty, sweaty and wearing her brother's crumpled clothes when she'd returned from the canal trip – had resulted in most of a bottle of peppermint cordial disappearing down her throat. For once Iris had refused to be intimidated by the faints, sweating and complaints of chest pains. She'd even appeared to be indifferent to her father's blustering threats to 'deal with that bloody boater' if she went near him again. After all, what more could he do to Taz? They'd already managed to deprive him of his livelihood and keep him cooped up on land when he longed to get back to the water. A plain-clothes policeman had come round to take another statement from Ursula about the missing necklace. He could have been the twin of this frosty-faced female, Iris reflected; his whole being had radiated a coldness that mocked his sunny-sounding surname of Spain.

Apparently he hadn't got any further evidence, since Taz was still dividing his time between kicking his heels at Nana's and trying to repair some of the damage to the *Crock of Gold*.

'It seems so unfair,' Iris had said, watching as he ran a plane over a plank of wood, teasing curls of butter-yellow timber before the metal blade. 'How long can they keep you here?'

'As long as it takes, sonny, as long as it takes,' Taz had said, mimicking the police officer's response to the same question. He'd taken the plank from the vice and squinted along its length. Satisfied with his work, he'd selected another and clamped it into position.

'It was good of yer uncle to say I can work in the yard, seeing how things are between me and your dad.'

'Uncle Pete likes you.'

'I'd say it was more Mrs Kate likes me. A bloke will do most anything to please the woman he loves.'

Iris would have liked to ask what he'd do for her, but she was scared to hear the answer. The overwhelming urge to touch his skin, smell it, hold him close whenever she saw him, was still there. But a natural caution had held her back. Addie had told her about all the canal girls who wanted Taz; in fact she'd implied some of them had done more than lust from afar.

Any further chance to talk about the future had been thwarted by the arrival of Addie herself, with a pair of new shoes she'd just bought from the Cable Shoe Shop in Kentish Town. Apparently she was going to a dance with Pansy on their joint birthday. Iris had experienced a pang of envy. She'd never gone through those girl-to-woman rites of passage herself. The scarred face had chained her to her home.

'Her first, ain't it, kid?' Taz had said, rolling down his shirtsleeves and putting on his jacket.

Addie had nodded absently, her attention fixed on the black patent leather shoes she'd taken from the box to admire once more.

Taz had loaded the cut timber planks into his arms. 'Let's be getting home then.' Seeing Iris's surprised look, he'd hastily added, 'Wood's for the old lady. I ain't pinching it.'

'No . . . I didn't imagine you—'

'Dixons always pay their way,' Addie had said predictably. 'We're doing chores – cleaning, putting up shelves . . . We ain't scrounging off yer gran, if that's what yer thinking . . .'

Iris hadn't been. But she'd learnt it was pointless to try and offer friendship to Addie. For some reason the girl was determined to cling to her dislike. It was an attitude she had in common with the labour exchange supervisor.

'I find it incredible, Miss Cutter, that you did not feel it appropriate to offer yourself in *some* capacity to your country.'

Iris felt her temper rising and knew the scar would be growing with it as the silvery lines of the disfigurement separated from the rosy flush of her unmarked skin. Her situation was made all the worse because she was beginning to suspect that the woman's supercilious attitude was partly justified. Perhaps she had accepted her mother's view of things too readily. All those terrible bouts of illness didn't seem to have had any permanent effect on Ursula's health. But Miss Maynard-Potts's unconcealed contempt had the effect of making her dig in and defend her position. 'I did think about it, of course. But my mother suffers from . . .' From what? Dr Siddons had never been able to put a name to her mother's mysterious attacks. 'My mother,' she said firmly, 'suffers from a rare nerve disease. I was needed at home, Miss Potts.'

'*Maynard*-Potts, Miss Cutter.' A suspicious expression flitted over the supercilious features. 'Cutter . . . Why does that name seem familiar?'

Iris explained about the wharf and the building yard. 'You've probably seen our lorries around Camden.'

'No, that's not it. One moment . . .'

The supervisor went into the main office. Through the glass Iris saw her speaking to a female clerk. A file was recovered from the cabinet and passed over. Flipping the cardboard cover, Frosty-face scanned the contents, nodded, and returned to Iris.

'Why are you wasting my time, Miss Cutter?'

'I'm not.' Iris took a deep breath. 'I've done my very best to explain why I haven't volunteered before. And I've come now, haven't I? And if you'd just *listen*, I'll tell you what I want to do for my war service.'

'It would seem that that won't be necessary.' Taking out a typewritten letter, she passed it across the desk. 'Apparently your service is to be deferred since you have a dependent relative.'

Iris scanned the sheet in front of her with disbelief. In it Dr Siddons explained that her mother was 'severely incapacitated and in need of Miss Iris Cutter's constant attendance'. According to their family GP, Ursula's fragile constitution would be 'irreparably damaged without the selfless and devoted nursing of her only daughter'.

'But this isn't true!'

'Indeed? You mean your mother is *not* ill? I understood you to say that was why you had not volunteered.'

'Yes. No. I mean . . . My mother does suffer from intermittent attacks, but she's by no means as ill as this letter implies.'

'Then why does the doctor say that she is?'

Iris saw only too clearly what had happened. Her mother had found some means – a mixture of bribery and flattery, she suspected – to induce Siddons to write this pack of lies. Faced with such back-handedness, Iris's fears retreated before her anger. Damn it all – she *would* go out to work! How dare they try to stop her!

'I don't know. He's mistaken. And just recently . . . well, I've begun to see that my mother could manage without me if she had to. She has my father to look after her. And Doris, of course.'

'Your sister?'

'Our general maid.'

'Oh?' A gleam lit up Miss Maynard-Potts's eyes as she scented fresh blood.

'Doris is a little slow-witted,' Iris said hastily.

'But simple domestic duties are not beyond her, apparently. We currently have several vacancies in works canteens. And the Land Army of course are always in need of strong, healthy young women . . .'

Iris assured her that, when their maid's turn came, she'd go willingly. 'She's a very willing sort of girl. But in the mean time I'd like to work on the canal boats.'

'I beg your pardon?'

The supervisor had never heard of the Canal Company's scheme to take on female trainees. She was inclined to treat it as an excuse by Iris to delay her employment. 'Since you're mobile, I'm directing you to an engineering firm in Aberystwyth. You'll be trained as a lathe operator. Here . . .' Another slip of paper crossed the desk. 'That's your travel warrant. You should make your own way there and report in five days. Accommodation is provided in hostels. One of the clerks will give you the rest of the details.'

'No.'

It was hard to say who was the more surprised by that single syllable, Iris or Miss Maynard-Potts.

'I want to work on the boats.'

'I'm required to direct you to where your services would be of most use. And since you have no previous experience to offer—'

'I do,' Iris interrupted the fluent flow of this diatribe. 'I've worked on the canal boats. I can deal with locks, unload cargo . . .' she improvised rapidly, turning her overnight trip to Limehouse into a voyage Captain Cook might have been proud to undertake.

'I thought you had had no employment previously, Miss Cutter.'

'*Paid* employment.'

'I see. So this work was voluntary?' There was a slight warming in the accusatory tone.

'Yes. And I could provide a reference from the boaters. I'm sure if you contacted the Canal Company or the Ministry of War Transport . . . I could find their telephone numbers for you . . .'

Miss Maynard-Potts resented the inference that she needed any assistance in undertaking this simple task. However, Iris pounced on the implication behind her protest. 'You'll do it then?'

Trapped, the supervisor pretended to give some thought to the matter, and then graciously agreed to defer Iris's placement until she could make enquiries. Iris was handed a slip ordering her to report back again in fourteen days' time.

'It won't work,' Taz said baldly. 'It's hard, grinding work on the boats. Those that aren't brought up to it can't stick it.'

'I stuck it well enough before.' She glared at the back of his neck as he held and measured the shelves in Nana's hall, taking a pencil from behind his ear to nick crosses in the wallpaper.

'An overnight to Limehouse. And fair weather. No ice to chip out from the front of the boats, no rain lashing in your face as you try to get the cargoes sheeted up, no soaked clothes because you've fallen into the cut . . .'

'Yes, all right . . . I can see you think I'm nothing more than a soft greenhouse plant that's only fit for . . . what? A little VAD nursing, perhaps? Nothing too strenuous, of course. Soothing the odd fevered brow, providing the patient doesn't have anything messy or contagious. Or perhaps a little filing? Somewhere in the country, in case those nasty loud bombs upset my obviously delicate nerves! Stop laughing at me!' she finished explosively as Taz's face split into a broader and broader grin.

'Well yer should hear yourself. I didn't mean to upset you, Iris. I think you're a great girl, you know that . . .'

'But soft . . .'

'Well brought up. A lady. There's nothing wrong with that. It's just that it ain't right for regular boating work.'

'The two trainees we saw in the Volunteer were ladies. Ask Addie, if you don't believe me.'

'She told me.' He picked up a drill and started carefully to bore a hole in the centre of his pencilled cross. His shoulder muscles rippled under his shirt. Iris suppressed an urge to run her hand across his back. Standing this close, in the small hall, she could smell his skin. She wanted him to turn round and seize her, pull her hard into him . . . It just wasn't right; she shouldn't feel like this. Girls weren't supposed to. Mixed up with her awakening desires was the suspicion that the reason he didn't want her working on the boats was because she'd find out the truth about all those canal girls.

Tentatively she stretched out. The tips of her fingers had actually reached the downy ends of his nape hair when the front door opened, bringing with it light, fresh air, and Nana and Addie both weighed down with shopping.

'Whew!' Nana dumped her bag with a relieved sigh and flexed her fingers. 'I'll swear those queues will stretch all the way to Golders Green soon. Hello, Iris dear.' She brushed her granddaughter's flushed cheek with cold lips.

Hugs and explanations were exchanged. 'Boats, eh?' Nana said, unbuttoning her winter coat. 'Well, I'd pictured you in one of those smart little Wren's uniforms . . . still, if it's what takes your fancy . . .'

'Taz thinks I'm too soft for the work.'

'Do you indeed, young man?'

'I don't mean no offence, ma'am. It's just that landies ain't used to boats. They think it's all like a holiday. I've seen them bumping and boring the locks, having their picnics on the banks . . . They don't know what it's like working a boat on a day that's so bitter you can't feel your fingers from first light to tying up. Ain't that right, kid?'

For once Addie didn't jump at this chance to confirm Iris's unsuitability for canal work. Her attention seemed firmly fixed inside one of the shopping bags she'd set on the hall table.

'Kid?'

'What?' Her brother's sharper tone jerked her head up. Even Iris read the guilt written across her freckled skin.

'What have you got there, kid?'

'Nothing, Taz.'

'Don't lie then. And hand it over.'

Reluctantly Addie drew out two small articles and dropped them into her brother's outstretched palm: a lipstick case and a round tub of powder. 'All the girls wear it now, Taz.'

'I ain't saying you can't, kid. You're growing up. That's why I bought you the girl's clothes. But where'd you get the money?'

'I . . . er . . .' Addie's grey eyes flicked in Nana's direction.

'Thanks, ma'am, but we're already obliged enough to you. Take them back, kid.'

'She'll do nothing of the sort. Not after the time we spent queuing for them.'

'I'm not taking charity, Taz. I'm gonna take down all 'er curtains and take them up the laundry – wash 'em and mangle them and set 'em up to dry. Iron 'em too. *And* clean the windows underneath 'em.'

'I see. Well, if yer sure, ma'am?'

'If I wasn't, I wouldn't offer. It's a real bargain. Now, if you'll let me through to my own kitchen, I'll see about making the dinner. Will you lend me a pair of hands, Iris?'

Taz stepped back to let them squeeze past. With all three facing the back, none of them noticed Addie quickly slip a larger package from the bottom of her shopping bag and thrust it into one of the pockets of her overcoat before taking her vegetables into the kitchen.

Chapter 27

'I have to go, Mother. It's time I did something for the war effort.'

'No it isn't. Tell her, Fred,' Ursula appealed to the top of her husband's head, which was all that could be seen over his newspaper.

'What? Tell who what? Looks like the Germans are getting the best of it in North Africa. Damn shame.'

'Never mind the war. This is important. Unless you consider North Africa of more concern than your family.'

Fred lowered his paper with a rustle. 'North Africa does concern our family, Urse. We'll not be seeing young Ernest home this summer if they've to push the Germans back again.'

'Oh . . . well, yes, of course. But he'll be all right, won't he?'

She was asking for the impossible. How could anyone know who'd live and who'd die in a war? It was all down to the luck of the draw.

They were seated either side of the fireplace in the sitting room. Fred reached across to pat his wife's knee. 'He's a level-headed lad, Urse. Ernest will stay out of trouble if he can.'

It was what she wanted to hear. Ursula allowed herself to be reassured and turned her attention back to her other child. 'Tell Iris she can't join up. I need her here.'

'Join up?' Leaning on one chair arm, Fred craned round to look at his daughter who was perched on the sofa behind him. 'What's this about, Iris? You're not joining up, are you?'

'I went to the employment exchange. To see about war work.'

'I thought your mother had sorted that out.'

'I did. Dr Siddons promised me, and he's usually so reliable. I'll telephone him . . .'

'I shouldn't bother, Mummy. He wrote to the exchange. I told them it was a pack of lies.'

'It's not lies. I need you, Iris darling. Please . . . you know that. Tell her, Fred. The Wrens and the WAAFs have plenty of young girls. They can't possibly need Iris.'

'I'm not going to join the Navy or the Air Force.'

'Oh Iris, no . . . not a factory.' Ursula's fingers went to her throat, playing along the string of jet beads. 'It's so *common*. How could I tell people you were working in a factory?'

'I'm going on the canal boats.'

'What! No!' The glossy black spheres wound around Ursula's fingers in a frantic zig-zag. 'It's that man! Oh, God, why didn't the police lock him up? He stole my amber necklace. I know he did.' Ursula's breath whistled through her lipsticked mouth in short noisy gasps. The colour fled under her face powder as her pupils grew larger.

'Hey, steady on, Urse.' Fred knelt before his wife, taking her hands and chaffing them.

Iris wordlessly opened her mother's handbag and found the bottle of peppermint cordial. A dose in a clean sherry glass seemed to provide some relief.

'Don't fret yourself, Urse. She's not going.'

'Yes I am. And you can't stop me.' Iris met her father's eyes steadily. Since she was standing and he was still on his knees on the hearthrug, she was looking down on him for once.

'We'll see about that. This blitz repair contract is classified as essential war work. That's why they've released building workers from the services. If I was to say you were needed in the office . . .'

'That's Aunt Kate's job.'

'She needs help.'

'No she doesn't.'

'If I say she does, she does.'

'She won't lie for you.'

270

'Mrs Kate,' Doris announced, walking in on cue.

The three Cutters stopped in mid-argument. None of them had heard the door knocker.

'And Mr Pete,' Doris continued in her adenoidal bray. Stepping to one side, she let the two visitors in.

Pete looked uncertainly at the three frowning faces. 'Not come at a bad time, have we? Thought we'd catch you before you sat down to your dinners.'

Fred rose. 'No, of course not. You're welcome any time. Aren't they, Urse?'

'I suppose so.' Ursula pulled her cardigan closer, even though the fire was now roaring up the chimney.

'Have you eaten?' Iris asked. 'Dinner is nearly ready. Isn't it, Doris?'

Doris confirmed 'that leek thing' was browning up nicely in the oven. 'I set the table, Miss Iris. I'll be off home now. It's me night on the net.'

'On your what?' Pete asked, helping Kate out of her coat.

'Me net, sir. Mum and me do three hours a week 'elping make camouflage nets. They got a frame set up at the church hall down our street. 'Orrible job, it is. Dust chokes yer something terrible and the dye comes off all over yer hands and clothes. But it's like me mum says – you gotta do yer bit, ain't yer? Night, sir – night, missus.'

Doris was oblivious to the look of glittering dislike Ursula shot in her direction. The way Pete's hands had slid possessively down her sister-in-law's arms as he'd helped her with that coat hadn't been lost on Ursula; and now the wretched maid was dropping hints at their lack of patriotism. Everything in her life was going wrong. Why couldn't she have married a man with a backbone?

She'd realised when she was eighteen that marriage was the only way she would escape from serving behind that dreary chemist's counter. But the Great War had started, drawing most of the young men into the mud of Flanders and sending so few back home again. When the Armistice had finally come she'd been twenty-two, unmarried and uncourted. With so many prettier girls around, she'd been aware that to catch *any* man was going to take a deal of cleverness on her part.

So when Frederick Cutter had seemed attracted to her, she'd overcome a natural indifference to male company and exerted herself to flatter his ego and stimulate his protective instincts with a show of helplessness.

Given her lack of experience it had proved surprisingly easy to hook him. But when she'd realised just how violently in love with her he actually was, she'd felt horror rather than pleasure. She didn't want that much devotion; a quiet respect would have suited her far better.

But he was a good catch. He had offered everything she wanted: a house, a family, and a chance to rise up in the world and leave that dusty dispensary, with its stink of castor oil and wintergreen, far behind. She'd seen herself making something of him once he took over the building merchants and wharf, had pictured them sweeping into grand civic functions, Fred in his chain of office and herself in a couture gown: Alderman and Mrs Cutter, the most important couple in the borough. How could she have known that about that stupid will?

But if she had, Ursula admitted to herself, she'd probably have done exactly the same again. The alternative would have been to grow into an old maid, serving out liver pills and jars of malt liver oil. And if her marriage had been a disappointment, her children had been her greatest joy. Thank heavens she'd had twins and completed her family in one act; it had meant she could put an end to all that unpleasant, sweaty, painful fumbling in the marriage bed.

She'd brought Ernest up to expect to take over the business one day, and Iris had taken her father's place as protector and companion to her mother. But now everything was crumbling around her. Iris was going to leave her, and Ernest's inheritance was going to be snatched away by some little bastard that Kate would undoubtedly produce within the year. They weren't even trying to be discreet about the relationship any more. Pete's thumb was caressing two rings on Kate's left hand.

'I see you've decided to be brazen about it.'

'What?' Kate's eyes flew to her sister-in-law and then followed the direction of her spiteful gaze. 'Oh, yes . . .' Gently removing her hand from Pete's grasp, she twisted the double circlets of gold herself – the bottom one slightly worn, the upper gleaming new, with an emerald in the central setting. 'It's not official of course, but we think of ourselves as engaged . . . and as soon as we can find a house for the four of us, well, we'll think of ourselves as married.'

'Married?' Fred looked between his brother and sister-in-law. 'Well that's a turn up for the books, isn't it, Urse?' Slapping his brother on the shoulder, he claimed a kiss from the 'bride'. Iris shyly added her own good wishes. Both looked towards Ursula. She slid her hands into the sleeves of her cardigan and stared into the grate. 'This fire's going down. Put some more coal on, would you, please, darling?'

'We're going into dinner now, Mummy . . . It would be best not to waste—'

'I'm *cold*.'

Fred caught his daughter's eye. 'Put another lump on, Iris. There's plenty in the cellar. Took a few sacks for fixing up the coal merchant's chimney. Incendiary lodged in the flashing, cracked the bricks wide open.'

Iris tonged a nugget on to the glowing ashes, dusted off her hands and went to replace the fire guard.

'Leave that,' Ursula said. 'It takes away some of the heat. I still feel dreadfully cold. This house has never been right since that dreadful bomb incident.'

'I'll not have that, Urse,' Fred said. 'Those windows are snugger than the originals. And you'll not find a better brick and plastering job this side of the river.'

'I tell you I'm *cold* . . .' Ursula's voice rose to a petulant wail. Her expression invited argument, but no one accepted. Thwarted, she resorted to malice again: 'I suppose once you're living in sin we shan't have to pay Kate's wages any more. After all, since her so-called *husband* gets a partner's share of the profits, it doesn't seem entirely fair they should have two bites at the cherry.'

'That's not fair,' Pete protested. 'She's putting in a full day's work, she deserves a decent wage.'

'Why? You don't draw one. Neither does Fred.'

'Now look here, Ursula . . .' Pete stopped as Kate laid a warning hand on his arm.

'We can sort all that out later, Pete. I'm certain sure I wouldn't want to take more than my fair share.'

'Some might say two husbands from the same family *is* more than your fair share.' Ursula accompanied her bitter comment with another violent shiver. Her teeth clacked audibly.

Iris tucked a shawl over her mother's knees. 'I'll lay the fire in the dining room too, Mummy.'

'I'll do that.' Pete followed his niece from the room and, after an uncomfortable pause, Kate said she'd see if she could do anything in the kitchen and slipped out too.

Ursula huddled further into her cardigan. 'I think I'll go up to bed.'

'You can't do that, Urse. It will look odd. I mean, it's a bit of a celebration . . .'

'You're such a fool, Fred,' his wife informed him. 'And weak. How did I come to marry such a weak man?'

'Because I was the best you could get . . . the best of what was left after we'd gone through Ypres and Passchendaele.'

Ursula flashed a startled glance through lowered lashes. She sometimes suspected he knew the truth, but to hear it stated so baldly was disconcerting. But he'd said it without rancour, as if he didn't mind that there had been no love or passion behind her decision to take him. Perhaps he didn't. After all, she'd been accommodating in other ways. And sometimes it had seemed as if the more indifferent she was to him, the keener he'd become on her.

'You promised. You promised me you'd stop this business between Peter and Kate. I might have know you'd do nothing.'

'What did you expect me to do, Urse? They're both adults.'

'That's rather the point, isn't it? Adults. Breeders. She'll have a son. And then Ernest's chances will be finished. Her son will get Cutter's. And the saving fund. You'll leave me and your children destitute.'

'Don't talk rot, Urse! We've a bit put by. Besides, who's to say Pete won't go first? And even if he doesn't, he'd look after you. Same as I'd have looked out for Ellie if he'd died. Same as we did look out for Kate when Bernie went.'

'Do you think I'm going to type invoices on the wharf?'

'There's no need for that. And keep your voice down. They'll hear you.'

'I don't care. I've been a good wife to you, Fred—'

'No you haven't. Not in every way.'

'You're well aware that the intimate act wasn't possible after children's birth . . .'

'So you claim.' He'd been leaning against the mantelpiece, arms folded. Now he pushed himself upright and came closer. Placing a hand on either side of her armchair, he leant down until his face was two inches from hers. 'Maybe it's time we put that to the test.'

Ursula was already sitting right up against the chair back, but none the less she seemed to shrink away from him. 'Don't you dare, Fred! I've told you, Dr Siddons said it could be fatal. If you loved me you wouldn't think of such a thing . . .'

There was a brief moment while they stared into each other's eyes. There was no sound; both were holding their breath. Then the coals collapsed in a shower of sparks. Fred grunted and straightened up again. 'It's lucky for you I do, Urse. Heaven knows why, but I do.'

Ursula let her own breath go. It had been a close thing. She shuddered as another spasm of cold reached inside her. 'I'm going to bed.'

'What about your dinner?'

'I'm not hungry.'

She pulled her way wearily up the stairs. Her legs felt heavy and wobbly at the same time. And she didn't care what Fred said, the house was definitely colder than it had ever been before. Even with her flannel nightdress on and extra blankets piled on the bed, she just didn't seem able to get warm. The peppermint cordial was warming. She took the remainder of the bottle and felt it sliding down her chest and setting up a warm glow in her stomach.

Thoughts whirled around her head. Ernest in danger in Africa, being shot at and wounded – and then coming home to find some little bastard cousin was going to take what was rightly his . . . Iris – her darling Iris – going away with that man. A nasty, smelly boater with his hands all over her daughter. Doing things to her in the dark. The sort of things no respectable girl could enjoy.

Not like Kate. She plainly revelled in all that disgusting intimacy. You only had to see the way she encouraged Pete to paw her. I wouldn't be surprised if she wasn't expecting already, Ursula thought. She could hear a sound, like the tide crashing and receding on the shore; it pounded with the rhythm of her heart.

It was all Kate's fault. She'd encouraged Iris to take those canal boats down to Limehouse, to stay out all night when her mother had been frantic with worry. Everything was Kate's fault. She hated Kate.

Ursula struggled to swallow and found she couldn't. Her throat seemed to be constricted. She strained for breath. Frightened, she reached out and fumbled for the bedside lamp. Her clumsy fingers didn't seem able to find the switch.

Dimly she heard the thud as it hit the floor. Light flooded into the room. Fred was shouting for them to fetch a doctor. That's right, Ursula thought hazily. Get Doctor Siddons. Fat, stupid old Siddons. He hadn't changed. She was sure he'd been just as ancient and corpulent thirty odd years ago, when he'd come puffing into her father's chemist shop, full of his own cleverness and self-importance.

She could rely on Siddons. Siddons would keep her secret.

Chapter 28

'Mummy? Are you awake?'

'Iris.' Ursula turned eagerly to the left, her nose detecting the antiseptic smells that she associated with her last stay in hospital after the Anderson incident.

'Mummy?' Iris leant forward. 'How are you feeling?'

'Much better, darling.' It wasn't strictly true, but she reasoned the better she claimed to feel, the faster they'd let her out of here. 'I want Dr Siddons.'

'Dr Siddons has had a stroke, Mummy. He's in a ward here himself. The poor man's paralysed. Dr Fraser is looking after his patients. Don't you remember?'

'Young man. Freckles.'

'Yes. We called him to the house after you collapsed. He sent for the ambulance. And he tested your medicine.'

'Test . . . ?' Ursula clutched the sheets higher to her chest. They felt starched and coarse. 'How long have I been here?'

'Nearly two days, Mummy. They brought you in on Thursday evening. It's Saturday afternoon.'

Ursula stared at her daughter's face. It wore an expression she'd never seen before. 'They can't have tested the medicine,' she said, grasping at her last hope. 'There wasn't any cordial left. I took the last of it.'

'Aunt Kate remembered you'd left some down the yard. Fortunately the bottle was air-tight.'

Ursula felt the tears welling into her eyes and spilling down her cheeks. 'Interfering bitch.'

'Mother! It's not Aunt Kate's fault. She thought she was helping you.'

'Go away! I don't know why you bothered to come at all.'

The bell for the end of visiting hours clanged noisily down the ward. Visitors streamed out under the watchful eye of the crisply starched nurse holding open the doors. Iris was still seated.

'Aren't you going too?'

'In a moment.' Iris stared down at her mother. Ursula held her eyes defiantly. 'How could you do it, Mummy? It was so *cruel*. All that time I thought you were going to die, and instead you were just *malingering* . . .'

'I am not. I was not.' Ursula gazed at her daughter's set lips and knew that explanations were pointless. Iris was struggling free of the emotional bonds that had tied her to her mother for so many years. 'Oh, go away, Iris! You wouldn't understand.' She twisted away, hunching under the bedclothes. A tiny core of hope inside her silently urged Iris to plead for her forgiveness. To soothe and tuck her in as she always did when her mother was ill. She was still there; Ursula could hear her quick light breathing above her own.

Heavier footsteps came towards the bed. She wriggled over again, assuming it would be Fred. Instead a thick-set female in a white coat was staring impassively down at her.

'Well now, Mrs Cutter, this is a fine thing. Self-inflicted wounds indeed. And in the middle of a war! Have you no sense at all?'

Iris had moved out of the way, but was still hovering. Beyond her Ursula could see the occupant of the next bed, craning forward to get a look at her. 'Draw the curtains, Iris. I don't care to be on display in a public ward.'

The cheap material rattled on its rings as Iris drew it along the metal bar. It didn't quite drown out the resentful whisper: 'Bloody la-di-da! Who's she fink she is?'

'This is Doctor Fishbourne, Mother. She's been treating you.'

'What happened to the other one? The freckled man?'

'Doctor Fraser is your General Practitioner, Mrs Cutter. I'm in charge of Women's Medical – for my sins. You're a very silly woman, if I may say so.'

'Well you mayn't. You're impertinent. I'll report you. You'll be dismissed.'

'You go right ahead, my dear.' Doctor Fishbourne's thick spatula fingers grasped Ursula's wrist and pressed over the pulse. 'I'd be pleased for the chance to take a rest.' She sighed heavily, rippling the faintest suggestion of a moustache across her upper lip. 'In the mean time, I'll reiterate my diagnosis. You're a foolish woman who may have done irreparable damage to her kidneys and liver.' She lowered her voice and bent closer. 'There are women in this ward who will, bar a miracle, never see their children grow up. Think about that next time you're tempted to abuse your body.'

'I want to go home. How dare you speak to me like that!' Ursula felt the familiar thundering in her chest. Her breath was coming in short, sharp gasps. A grey mist swam in front of her eyes. She wanted Iris to put a comforting arm around her shoulders and murmur reassurance, as she'd done since she was old enough to understand how ill Mummy was. But it didn't happen. Both her daughter and the doctor stood shoulder to shoulder, calmly impassive, while she regained control of her breathing.

'Better?'

Of course she wasn't better. She'd never felt so miserable and alone in her life. 'Yes, thank you, doctor. I'd like to go home now, please.'

'Later. We want to do some more tests and see just how much damage you've done.'

'I wish to leave.'

'And believe me, Mrs Cutter, we have no wish to keep you a moment longer than necessary.' Whisking a pen from her top pocket, Dr Fishbourne scribbled a note on Ursula's chart and clipped it back on the bed base. She half-turned to stomp briskly away, and then paused. Stretching out one hand, she took hold of Iris's chin and turned her towards the light.

Iris flinched.

'Hmmm . . . pity it didn't heal as cleanly as it could have.' One finger gently stroked the smoother, leathery lines of the scars. 'But a little foundation and powder covers a multitude of skins, as they say.'

'But I can't . . . I mean, Dr Siddons said make-up would set up an infection.'

279

'Rubbish. It's quite safe unless you've an open cut. But then the same could be said of anywhere else on your skin.'

'Then why did . . . ?' Iris bit off the rest of her sentence as she glimpsed her mother's face. Guilt and fright were easy to read in Ursula's brown eyes. Iris saw only too well what had happened. With the connivance of Dr Siddons, her mother had found another way to keep her tied close to home. It was ironic that, just when she had ceased to worry so desperately about her deformity, she'd been given permission to hide it from all those cruel stares.

The hospital doctor was still talking cheerfully: 'Go out and buy yourself some Max Factor, Miss Cutter. And then come back and tell the rest of us where you found it!'

'Yes. Thank you. I will, doctor.' Iris looked down at Ursula, her face expressionless. 'Daddy had to go down to the blitz site. One of the bricklayers broke his arm. Daddy's filling in until they can get a replacement. He said he'd look in later. Goodbye, Mother. I have to go. I have a date – with Taz Dixon.'

'Iris! Wait, darling!' Ursula's despairing wail echoed down the ward. Iris didn't pause. The junior nurse closed the door on the last of the visitors.

'That yer daughter?'

Ursula turned. Her neighbour had climbed out of bed and was standing by the edge of the curtain. Scrawny legs and arms protruded from an old coat clasped around her by one hand pressed at her breast. The drooping edge of an ancient nightdress formed a ragged border below the coat's hem.

'I'm Marlene. Hot in here, ain't it? It's funny, it can be cold enough to freeze the whatsits off brass monkeys, but I always wake up wet through. Dunno what's wrong with me.'

Ursula could have told her. During those years behind the chemist counter, she'd sold plenty of useless remedies to those desperate to cure the incurable. Marlene had tuberculosis. It was disgraceful putting her in a public ward like this.

Ursula dragged the sheet up over her nose.

'Gonna 'ave a snooze, are yer?'

Ursula mumbled something unintelligible.

'Fink I'll go find the lavs.'

Ursula kept her eyes tightly shut until she was certain she was alone, and then slipped out of bed herself. She wasn't going to stay in this hospital a second longer. The locker was empty.

'Nurse. Nurse! Someone has taken my clothes.'

'You didn't have any, Mrs Cutter. You were admitted in your nightwear. Don't you recall?'

'Yes, but, I mean . . . Surely I am not expected to walk out of here in *them*?'

'You can telephone someone to bring some clothes in for you. There's a public telephone on the next floor. Do you have twopence?'

She didn't. She had nothing but the nightdress she'd been wearing when they lifted her from her bed to the stretcher and bundled her into the ambulance.

'Never mind,' the girl smiled brightly. 'They said your husband's visiting this evening. He can fetch them for you surely?'

It was a sensible suggestion. Ursula climbed back into bed, grateful to get off the cold linoleum.

Another doctor came to see Marlene, after which she was led away by one of the nurses. 'What about me fings?'

The nurse assured her she would empty Marlene's locker and fetch her belongings to her new ward.

'Ta-ra for now then,' she called cheerily to Ursula. 'Seems they gotta put me in another room. It's a lark, ain't it?'

Privately Ursula thought it was more likely to be an isolation ward. And about time too. She wondered if Marlene was one of the terminally ill women Dr Fishbourne had been alluding to. Probably.

Lying quietly, she became aware of a chill creeping through her again. She needed some more cordial. She'd forgotten the bottle she'd left down at the wharf office, perhaps she'd overlooked another bottle too. There might be some in the bathroom cabinet. The smell and taste of peppermint started to fill her mouth, fuelling her craving. She had to have some cordial. Didn't they understand how much she *needed* her medicine? As soon as Fred got here she'd insist he took her home. There must be a dose somewhere. Maybe Siddons had left some mixed up at the surgery . . . They could call there on the way home . . .

'Urse. You awake?'

Ursula sat up with a gasp. She must have dozed. Fred laid a bunch of daffodils on the blanket. 'Got these for you.'

'Thank you.' She touched the thick, waxy blooms and looked sideways at her husband. He was in his work-clothes; a light sprinkle of brick dust was tangled in the hairs on the back of his hands and he smelt of sweat. 'You should have changed before you came.'

'Didn't have time. Only knocked off half an hour ago.'

'How is the job progressing?'

'Going very well. I can still lay a brick faster than any man in that crew.'

They stared at each other in silence. Ursula looked away first.

'Why'd you do it, Urse?'

'I . . . I don't know. It was just . . .' She broke off, knowing that, whatever her explanation, it would sound mean and cheap.

'I had the devil of a job stopping them calling the coppers in.'

'What!' Ursula lifted a startled face.

'Suicide,' her husband said succinctly. 'It's against the law. They wanted to lock you in a side room. Stick a female copper in with you to stop you trying it again. I had to swear it was all an accident. Told them me and Iris both gave you doses. Didn't realise you'd already taken your medicine, etcetera. Don't think they believed me, but they can't prove otherwise, so they gave you the benefit of the doubt. But they still want to know what you're doing drinking paraldehyde. It's not a treatment any of the doctors here know about. Seem to think it might produce the very symptoms you've been complaining about for the past twenty odd years.'

Ursula looked down at the sheet, pleating the starched edge between her fingers. Fred reached over and captured her hands. 'Why'd you do it, Urse? I've never bothered you, have I? Always given you everything you asked for.'

He sounded bewildered and hurt. She almost thought she'd have preferred anger. How could she explain the glorious power that ill-health bestowed? She'd only discovered herself by accident. After the twins' difficult birth she'd needed some way to keep Fred from her bed. Dr Siddons had provided it. He'd had little choice. That carefully hoarded prescription for Lieutenant Paul Pottle had seen to that. How far-sighted it had been to have claimed to have lost it all those years ago when the police came to investigate.

She didn't know what had prompted her to slip it in her shoe like that. Instinct, perhaps. Her father had got into trouble for failing to keep proper records, of course. But he'd died soon afterwards anyway so it scarcely mattered. And that written proof – that Siddons had been responsible for their local war-hero's death by prescribing a dosage of morphine ten times stronger than normal – had been a god-send. She had never thought of it as blackmail; it wasn't as if she ever asked for *money*. Just little favours. Like the dose of paraldehyde in the peppermint cordial.

'No more than two teaspoons in any one day,' Siddons had warned that first time she'd collected it from his surgery. 'It creates the illusion of a heart complaint. Peppermint disguises the smell of the stuff on your breath.'

'Are you certain?'

'Course I am, m'dear. Some of my male patients are not as patriotic as they wished to appear. When conscription was introduced in 1917 . . .'

He hadn't needed to finish the sentence. A medical exemption was just about the only way a young man could escape the inevitable white feather. 'I suggest you don't use it for more than . . . say six months.'

She hadn't intended to at the time. But she'd began to see how much control a fluttering heart and gasping breath could exert. How wonderfully easy it was to take responsibility for nothing and yet have her every whim indulged. The six months had stretched to a year. And then another. She'd known that at some point Fred had started to look elsewhere; but he'd been discreet enough for it to cause her no embarrassment, and being denied his marital rights had actually seemed to increase his devotion rather than diminish it.

'I'm sorry, Fred. I truly am . . .' She ran a hand gently along his jaw-line, feeling the stubble. 'I didn't know. Dr Siddons said I needed it. How could I know there was anything wrong? I trusted him.' Capturing his hand, she drew his fingers down between her breasts. 'Some of his remedies are very old-fashioned. I'm sure he genuinely believed he was helping me.'

It was a gamble. But men were so gullible . . . She saw the doubts fighting across Fred's features, and moved his hand fractionally so that it rested over the nipple of her left breast.

'Bloody idiot,' he growled. 'I'd sue, but they say the poor bloke won't speak or walk again like as not.'

'How sad,' Ursula said, forcing her voice to convey a good deal more sorrow than she really felt. Her overwhelming emotion was pure relief. At least now Siddons would never betray her. She wouldn't be able to use her heart problems to control the family any more of course, but perhaps that wasn't too tragic. Fred had, after all, grown used to letting her have her own way. And her son, she saw with a flash of disinterested clear-sightedness, was weak-willed and could be coerced into doing what she wanted. Iris was the problem. If she went away now, any vestige of influence Ursula had over her would soon disappear.

She edged a little closer to her husband, letting her shoulder press into the hollow of his. 'Fred, I don't want Iris to leave. Ernest's already thousands of miles away; I don't think I could bear it if Iris went too.' Her voice trembled and rose on the final syllable.

'Steady on, old girl.' Fred gave her a comforting squeeze. 'If they call her up, we'll have to let her go. Nothing we can do about it. Got to be seen to be doing our bit. Especially now. Can't expect those who've lost family to vote for a councillor who's kept his own flesh and blood out of the war.'

'Yes . . . I see that. But not the boats, Fred. She could do better than that. Nursing, for instance.' Ursula was resigned to the fact that Iris would work, but she was determined she should remain living at home. A job at the St Pancras or Hampstead Hospital would be a reasonable compromise. 'And everyone admires nurses, Fred. Just picture her campaigning with you in her uniform.'

Fred had to admit it was a powerful image. 'But if she's got these boats in her head—'

'It's not the boats in her head, it's that boy in her knickers . . .'

'Don't say that, Urse. Not about your own daughter. She's been brought up properly. She'd not do that. And I've warned Dixon what will happen if he lays a finger on her.'

As if propriety or threats had ever stopped two people who were determined to have sex. Ursula had no idea whether they had or not yet, but she was quite certain it was inevitable once they were thrown together on the boats. 'But if she could be separated from him for a while, Fred . . . long enough for her to see sense . . .'

'We could send her to your cousin for a couple of weeks, I suppose. She still got that boarding house in Harrogate?'

Ursula dismissed Cousin Rhoda. 'She wouldn't go. But if the Dixon boy were to leave her alone . . . Is it true his boats are moored at Cutter's Wharf?'

'Pete let him.'

'Kate did, you mean.'

'Same thing these days.'

'Quite.'

'There's nothing I can do about that, Urse. I've tried having a word, but Pete's mind is set on having her. But there's no saying they'll have another kid. Pete and Ellie never did after Joshua.'

'Can you blame them? That idiot should have been put in a home at birth. Look at what he did to Iris – disfigured her for life. The only man who's ever going to look at her now is one who's out for what he can get . . . like that boater. I daresay he thinks she has money. Or she'll inherit some. That's why we must do something, Fred. For Iris's sake.'

'Do what? I can't lock her up, Urse.'

'But you could see to it that *he* was. He's still on bail remember?'

285

Fred consulted his watch before answering. 'What of it? I spoke to the police this morning. They're thinking of dropping the whole business, Urse. They've not turned up any evidence that he took your jewellery, see?'

'But you could see to it that they did.' Ursula dropped her voice even further. 'His boats are tied up at the wharf, Fred. I'm sure they didn't search them properly the first time. If the police were to find other pieces of my jewellery hidden on them . . . pieces that I'd forgotten to check on . . .'

'I couldn't do that, Urse. I mean . . . *I* could end up in jail . . .'

'Who would know?' She grasped his wrist tightly and shook it, causing the watch to drop on her blanket. 'And once he's locked away from her . . .'

'Yes . . . yes, I see that, Urse. But if it got out . . .' Fred twisted free and retrieved his watch. He checked the time again.

'For heaven's sake, Fred, why do you keep looking at the time? Have you got something more important to do?'

The half-hunter was returned to her husband's pocket with a brusque. 'Said I'd go round to Pete's place. Sort out the order books and invoices for those damn trustees. End of the financial year again, isn't it?'

'Will Kate be there?'

Despite her obsession with Iris, Ursula couldn't keep her mind from this growing threat to her son's inheritance. Whatever Fred said, there had to be some way of preventing Pete from fathering another son to take over Cutters. The idea that he could find someone else if she disposed of Kate simply didn't enter her head. He'd been alone since Ellie ran off; he would be again if she could just get rid of her slyly insinuating sister-in-law.

But apparently tonight's meeting was for partners only. 'She's on fire watch or something tonight. Said she'd get her head down for a few hours earlier. I'd best be off. Pete's expecting me.'

He leant forward to kiss her forehead in farewell. But she didn't intend to let him wriggle off the hook so simply. Taking hold of both his wrists this time, she hissed furiously, 'Fred!

286

The jewellery. Put it on the boat. It's for Iris. For Iris's sake. Promise me, Fred. Promise you'll do it.'

He hesitated. Then nodded fractionally before walking away.

Chapter 29

By ten o'clock she was beginning to have her doubts. Fred was suggestible, but he needed her behind him to push – albeit subtly – if things were to get done.

If that Dixon man had arranged to meet Iris tonight, then he'd be safely out of the way for a few hours and it was the perfect time to plant evidence on his boat. But did Fred know that? If only she'd thought to ask him to leave some change for the telephone.

She'd forgotten to ask him about fetching her clothes and the cordial too. The taste of peppermint was flooding her mouth again. She needed her medicine. There were empty bottles in the store cupboard at home, perhaps if she swirled them out with a little warm water . . . The craving for the familiar taste hammered inside her head . . .

Raising her head from the pillows, she looked along the darkened ward. A chorus of snores and coughs from the lumpy heaps of blankets indicated that most of her fellow patients were already asleep. At the far end the shaded light at the sister's desk threw a monstrously distorted shadow of the woman's frilled cap on to the wall behind her as she answered a querulous demand for a bedpan on the other side of the ward.

Ursula's eyes fell on Marlene's empty bed. They'd stripped off the linen, but she didn't remember anyone clearing the locker as promised.

Slipping to the cold floor, she cautiously crouched, eased the door open and felt inside. It was impossible to see anything, but her patting hands detected clothes and shoes. Quickly she dragged the untidy bundle into her arms. 'Toilet,' she hissed at the nearest dark shape under the bedclothes. Clasping Marlene's things close to her chest, she hurried through the ward doors.

Bolting herself in a cubicle, Ursula sorted through the clothes. The underwear was well darned and the skirt and blouse had the limpness of items that had been washed and worn for many years past their useful life.

Feeling slightly dizzy Ursula sat down on the wooden toilet seat. Perhaps she should trust Fred to arrange things properly. On the other hand, he'd said the police were thinking of dropping the charges against that Dixon man. If they didn't move against him tonight, the chance might be lost . . .

And she needed her cordial. This time her mouth wasn't flooding with saliva, instead it was drying up . . .

Five minutes later she eased the lavatory door open a fraction and peeped into the corridor. It was still deserted. Stepping out boldly, she headed away from the ward.

Marlene's shoes were a couple of sizes too large. They seemed to be making an uncomfortably loud slapping sound as she descended the twisting staircase to street level. Several nurses and porters passed her as she reached each landing, but no one challenged her. There was no reason of course that she couldn't leave the hospital. It wasn't as if she were a prisoner. But it might be easier to get away without any interference from the medical staff. If they started insisting she needed a doctor's permission to discharge herself, it could all take several hours.

Clutching her coat closer, Ursula scuttled past a porter in his cubbyhole by the entrance doors and hurried away up the road.

After the warmth of the ward, the chill caught her by surprise. Marlene's budget didn't extend to stockings, and the April night air felt like ice water against her bare legs. Curling her toes to try to hold the slipping shoes on, she started up the street with an awkward shuffling movement.

Huddled in her inadequate clothing, she wove between oncoming pedestrians, alert to the glows of red cigarette tips and the pale ovals of faces looming towards her. One wished her a happy Easter.

The spare key was under the loose flagstone in the back garden as usual. She'd been half afraid that Iris had brought that man home, but the house was reassuringly silent as she let herself in. She trod upstairs, noting once again the rawness of new plaster on the ceilings and walls that Pete and Joshua had patched up after the bomb blast. It really was too bad; she must tell Fred to get some paint and wallpaper and make the place look *elegant*.

Crossing to her own dresser she gratefully drew out a pair of thick lisle stockings, secured them with elasticated garters and replaced the cracked and disintegrating shoes with a decent pair of her own. It would be dirty and wet clambering over the boats. She hesitated over the rest of her clothing. The vessels probably had fleas or rats and by the looks of her tuberculotic neighbour her outfits would be used to such company. She'd keep Marlene's clothes on and put a few shillings in the pockets by way of compensation for their use.

Turning her attention to her jewellery box, she touched each piece with a fingertip. A marquisette brooch belonging to her grandmother; a jet one from her other gran with its matching beads. A couple of rings and a bracelet that Fred had bought her over the years. A pair of earrings to celebrate the twins birth. Surely the police would never believe she hadn't noticed any of these things were missing? And what – a small voice whispered in her head – if something should go wrong and that Dixon man sails away with them?

Her fingers touched the smoothness of glass: an old cordial bottle, forgotten until now, with a thin scum of liquid dried in the bottom.

The need for her medicine swept through her nerves, setting them on fire. With shaking hands she pushed the bottle neck under the bathroom tap and ran a little water inside, swirling it around until it turned milky. Setting it to her lips, she gratefully gulped the foul-tasting solution before returning to the search for something to plant on the narrowboat.

In the end she settled on a silver-back man's brush and comb set and a small coalport vase edged with gold leaf.

They were all wedding presents and rarely used; it was quite plausible that their loss from a trunk beneath the stairs shouldn't have been noticed by now. Relocking the house, she replaced the key and turned southwards again.

This time rather than branching left down Great College Street, she continued straight down the High Street. The steps at the Camden Wharves would provide access to the tow-path and from there she could walk round to Cutter's. After that there was just the dog to deal with; but the mongrel knew her and the worse she expected from it was a few barks to keep face. With any luck she'd be dismissed as a stray cat by any listeners.

The bridge with its canal steps was just ahead of her, the solid bulk of its iron girders standing out against the blue-black starry sky. She stepped out faster, eager to get the business over with. She'd been aware of hurrying footsteps behind her for some seconds; now the runner brushed past, nearly knocking her over in her rush.

'Well, really . . .' Ursula regained her balance and glared into the darkness. The scarved and coated figure was already disappearing down the tow-path steps. Ursula squinted harder into the blackness. By now her night sight had become attuned to the blackout and she was able to pick out details. The thick collar of the woman's coat plus the fringed edges of her scarf identified her. It was that slut Kate. Going round to spend the night at Pete's flat, no doubt. So much for her fire duties.

Ursula walked a few steps down the flight wondering whether it was worth going on with her plans. If Kate was on her way to the wharf, then Fred and Pete's meeting would surely break up soon. She didn't want to run into all three of them on the quay and have to answer a lot of awkward questions.

'Pity she doesn't fall in,' Ursula thought viciously. With that heavy coat on – and the water still at its freezing winter temperature – she might have slipped under before anyone could hear her cries for help.

She looked again towards the curve of the canal. Kate was practically out of sight. Ursula touched the hard edges of the grooming set in her pocket. If only she *were* to fall, two problems might be solved in one night: with that boater man shown up as a thief, Iris would stay at home; and with Kate out of the way, Ernest's inheritance would be safe from any little bastard cousin.

Taking a deep breath, Ursula walked quietly down the final few steps and started along the canal path after Kate.

Chapter 30

Kate had spent Saturday afternoon queuing for goods on ration – and even longer queuing for those being sold on a first-come, first-served basis. Normally she hated the time these shopping marathons stole from her life, but today she was glad of the chance to think quietly away from the family – and Pansy in particular.

She was going to have to make up her mind finally on the subject of Pansy's engagement to Maury O'Day. Apparently he intended to ask Kate's permission this evening before formally proposing to Pansy.

'He wants to do it properly,' Pansy had confided with shining eyes. 'You know . . . you can ask him if he loves me and how he intends to support me and all that stuff. Although he does and he can,' she had finished in a gasping rush.

Kate had been forced to bite her tongue rather than blurt out that she suspected the last thing Maury would be honest about was how he intended to support a wife and family. Maury's source of wealth was a mystery; it certainly wasn't all coming from the hot food stalls he claimed a share in. There were rumours, of course, but not even a little surreptitious dealing in black-market sugar and bacon could account for the amount of cash Mr O'Day had been spending recently. She hated the idea of Pansy spending her life tied to a jail-bird. But what if she said 'no' when Maury asked for her permission? There would inevitably be tears and tantrums – and probably accusations that Kate was in no position to start calling the kettle black.

Any attempt at talking about the scene Pansy had witnessed that night in Pete's flat had always led to a hasty change of subject by Pansy. Kate had sympathised – to see her own mother in the throes of passion like that must have been a tremendous shock for poor Pansy, and she couldn't really blame her for the coldness she'd shown towards her Uncle Pete since. But since she'd become surer that her future lay with Maury, Kate had detected a thaw in the ice. She no longer ran and hugged her favourite uncle as she had done since she was child, but at least he got a civil greeting now. And she'd visited the three-bedroomed corner house that Pete was going to rent for them all on the corner of Chaston Street with good grace, even joining in suggestions for curtains and wallpaper.

Kate had guessed at the time that this improved behaviour was mostly based on the fact that Pansy didn't intend to live at home for much longer, but it had been such at relief that she hadn't asked any awkward questions about Pansy's plans.

Now she couldn't avoid it any further, she reflected ruefully, tucking a precious parcel of hard roe into her shopping basket. If she said no to Maury, she and Pete would have to cope with a resentful and angry sixteen-year-old. And it was doubtful if they could stop her seeing Maury anyway. On the other hand, saying yes was tantamount to throwing her daughter to the wolf cubs, if not their full-grown parents.

Still wrestling with the problem, Kate lifted the latch on the Kelly Street house and stepped into the hall – to be greeted by the most appalling smell. It seemed to be a mixture of rotting eggs, decaying fish and drains.

'Mum! Thank heavens. I thought you were never coming back. You gotta help. It's all right, Addie,' Pansy called over her shoulder. 'My mum's here. She'll know what to do.'

'How can she? Nobody can do nuffing . . . I'll have to stop here.'

Addie's voice sounded oddly muffled. Pushing Pansy out of the way, Kate stepped inside her kitchen and discovered why. The canal girl was sitting on a wooden chair by the bath. She was dressed in her vest and knickers with Kate's best towel draped over her, completely hiding her head and shoulders and hanging down to her skinny chest.

'What on earth . . . ? Pansy, what's going on? And what's that terrible smell? Has the gas main gone again?'

A loud wail from under the towel drowned out Pansy's agonised, 'Mum . . .' Pansy jerked her head towards their guest mouthing frantic silent messages and pinching her nose before saying out loud, 'Addie came round so we could get ready for the dance together.'

'That's nice.' Since the table had been latched up over the bath, Kate pushed a pile of twisted wires covered in strips of disintegrating brown paper out of the way and set her basket on another chair. The cardboard carton Addie had hidden in her coat pocket in Nana Cutter's hallway was half-buried beneath the mess. Picking it up, Kate read the hand-printed legend: 'Endora Home Perming Kit – Guarantees a Glorious Head of Curls Every Time'.

Kate looked at the shrouded figure shivering by the open bath. Biting her lip in a desperate attempt not to laugh, she said, 'I'm certain sure it's not that desperate. Let me see.'

Reluctantly, Addie slowly drew the towel down until it lay in a damp heap in her lap. She raised stricken eyes to Kate, her lips trembling. The sight of her face was sufficient to choke off the shriek of laughter that had been threatening to bubble up from Kate's chest to her mouth.

Addie's long ginger-brown mop was twisted into corkscrews that had exploded into a mass of frizz with the texture of cotton-wool, which stood away from her head like a halo in an icon painting.

'I did just what they said on the box. Truly I did, Mum,' Pansy protested.

'Yes. I'm certain sure you did, my lamb.' Kate twisted the carton to read the crudely lettered instructions. 'Bought it up the market, did you, Addie?'

Addie nodded. 'I sold them fancy knickers and slip Taz got for me to the second-hand clothes bloke. He gave me five bob for 'em.'

'Permanent waving lotions usually cost two or three times that.'

'You reckon the bloke was on the fiddle?'

'I should think it's more likely he mixed it up in a bucket in the shed.'

'I'll knock his bleedin' teeth in, the twisting cheater!'

'Well, never mind. I'm certain sure it's no use crying over spilt milk now. Let's see what we can do.'

Telling Pansy to open the window and put more water on the stove, she wrapped Addie in a blanket and hung her sodden vest and knickers on the oven door to dry while she started rinsing.

'There now,' Kate stepped back, panting, to examine her efforts half an hour later. 'One more rinse with a little perfume should do it. Pansy, fetch the bottle of lavender from my room. There's a few drops left in the bottom.'

Pansy did as she was told, but when she returned it wasn't with her mother's eau de cologne but a small unopened bottle of Ashes of Roses perfume. 'It's Iris's birthday present to me. But you can use it.' To show that she was genuinely sorry for her part in Addie's disastrous change of appearance, she tipped half the bottle into the rinsing jug, releasing the scent of roses into the steamy kitchen.

Kate massaged the warm water into Addie's rats tails and then started to pat them gently with the dry towel. As the dampness left them, the strands sprang into rebellious horizontalness.

'Run down to the wharf, Pansy. Ask your Uncle Pete if he has any Brylcreem.'

'But, Mum, Maury will be here soon.'

'Then the faster you run the faster you'll be back. Go on. And hang the fire thingy on the gate as you go. It's nearly time for my street watch.' She passed over a cardboard square with the white printed notice: 'STIRRUP PUMP HERE', and busied herself putting up the blackout while Addie huddled miserably in her seaman's coat.

It was obvious Pansy didn't want to call on her uncle, but she grabbed her coat and rushed out, returning with a tub of hair cream. 'Joshua loaned it me. Uncle Pete was busy in that old storage shed. The bricks have split with the heat, Josh said. Can I go get dressed now, Mum?'

'Be where that incendiary got stuck,' Addie said, obeying Kate's instruction to hold still as Pansy took the stairs two at a time. 'Night them bleedin' Germans burnt out the *Crock of Gold*.

After she'd finished applying the cream, Kate divided the thick tresses into three strands, pulled them back as hard as she dared and wove them into a single braid at the back of Addie's head, securing it with a large tortoiseshell hair clip decorated with a gilt pattern of roses. Handing Addie a hand mirror, she invited her to admire the effect.

'It looks smashin', don' it?' Addie said, doing an odd bobbing dance with bent knees as she tried to admire herself. 'I'll be ever so careful with yer hair clip. Promise. I won' lose it or nothing. Cross me heart and 'ope to die.' She spat on a finger and sketched a cross in the air before her chest.

'You can keep it. As a birthday present.'

'Honestly?' Addie's eyes sparkled. 'Ta ever so much!' Impulsively she flung her arms round Kate and kissed her. 'I wish you were my mum,' she said simply.

'Well, thank you. I'm certain sure that's the best thing anyone has ever said to me.' She returned the boater girl's kiss and smiled. 'You'd better get into your party frock. Where is it?'

The rust-coloured wool was hanging behind the door in Pansy's bedroom, together with the suspender belt and stockings Taz had bought her for Christmas. 'He bought me these shoes for me birthday, see?' Addie said, holding up the high-heels she'd chosen from the Cable Shoe Shop. 'And yer gran give me this . . . but I never expected nothing from her.' She showed them the tiny brown leather handbag with its pocket mirror, comb and pocket handkerchief. 'Dunno if it's gonna be any use on the boats, mind yer.' Addie's casual tone couldn't quite disguise her pleasure in this unexpected gift.

With Kate's help, the belt and stockings were wrestled on around the sewn-up pair of man's pants. 'You should have kept one pair of girl's panties,' Kate said, surveying the bizarre effect.

'I 'ad to give the bloke all of them to get me five bob. Nobody's gonna see 'em. Now me dress.'

Kate lifted it carefully over the girl's head and twitched it into position. 'There.' She stepped back to admire the effect, smoothing down stray prickles of hair that were already springing out around Addie's forehead and cheeks. 'You look lovely. The boys will be falling over themselves to dance with you.'

''Ave to pick themselves up again then, won't they? I dunno how to dance. I'm only gonna watch.'

'Mum . . . I'm ready.'

Busy with Addie's preparations, Kate hadn't been paying much attention as her daughter slipped into her clothes. Now she turned. The conventional compliments died on her lips.

The dress was new – her present to Pansy. She'd been allowed to choose the pale mauve material and pattern herself. The seamstress had cut it close, allowing the soft material to emphasis the swell of Pansy's hips and breasts. Maury had let her keep the flower necklace as well as the engagement ring, and it lay in the hollow of her throat, while the dark wings of her hair were held off her face by combs so that the matching earrings could be seen nestling on her lobes. Her eyes were alight with excitement, her dark red lips were parted to show tiny pearl teeth, and her skin glowed with an inner radiance.

'What's the matter?' Panic started to filter over Pansy's features as her mother stared in silence. 'Do I look horrid?'

'No. You look quite lovely, my lamb.' Kate found her own voice was trembling. Her little girl was gone; overnight it seemed she'd turned into a young woman with a life to live in her own right. Part of Kate's mind wondered forlornly where the years had gone; it seemed like only yesterday she'd wheeled out a plump, big-eyed toddler in her pram over Hampstead Heath, and now . . . Taking a huge breath, she smiled broadly and said firmly, 'Everything a girl should look on her sixteenth birthday.' Drawing Pansy into her arms she hugged her tightly.

The sound of the door knocker released them. 'Oh, Mum, that'll be Maury.'

'I'll get it. You two be getting your coats on.'

It was Maury. But it was also Joshua. His big frame loomed over Maury's shoulder in the twilight. 'Hello, Auntie Kate. Joshua is going to a dance.'

'How nice,' Kate said faintly, trying to grapple with the idea of her lumbering nephew quick-stepping around the dance floor. 'Come in.'

'Can I have a word, Mrs C?'

'In here, Maury.' She indicated the cramped parlour.

'Ta. Stop out here, Josh.'

Joshua would have obediently lurked in the tiny hall if Kate hadn't told him to go through to the kitchen and take one biscuit from the tin.

'Pansy won't be a minute, Maury. Sit down.'

'No ta, Mrs C. Pansy tell you why I wanted a quick word before we go up the dance?'

'Yes, Maury, she did.'

'So how about it? Her and me getting engaged?'

'She's very young, Maury. You both are.'

'Yeah.'

She waited for him to persuade her, but he just stood quite still, staring at her, waiting for her to make the next move. He was wearing his best overcoat and clutched the ubiquitous brown trilby in his hands. His fingers were threading the brim round and round during the entire conversation. It was the only sign of nervousness he betrayed.

'And you'll be called up soon, won't you?'

'I'll make sure Pansy's taken care of, Mrs C. She'll not be short of cash. I got investments.'

Like many before her, Kate found herself unable to ask 'what investments' because she was scared of the answer. Despite the fact that Maury was twenty years younger than her, she had the uncomfortable feeling he was in control of this situation. Which he was, in a way. He'd have Pansy whatever she said; in her heart she knew it. The only choice really was between saying no and cutting herself off from her daughter, or saying yes and acquiescing to a situation which

301

she knew in her heart would cause Pansy endless heartache and disillusion in the future.

And then, unexpectedly, he gave her a way out.

'Thing is, though, Mrs C, I don't want to do nothing against you. So if you say she's too young then that's it. I'll stop seeing her until you say she's old enough to be walking out regular.'

It was a temptation. Postpone the engagement for six months – or a year, say. Give Pansy the chance to go out with other boys. But if he cared enough to do that for Pansy, wasn't there just a faint chance that, whatever else Maury O'Day did in his dubious life, he really would take very good care of her daughter? And wasn't that the best she could hope for, whoever Pansy eventually married?

'No,' she said. 'If you love Pansy, then you have my permission . . . and my blessings, Maury, to try and make her happy. I'll call her down.'

She turned away and missed the slight flicker of consternation that flashed briefly across Maury's newly shaven face.

Pansy came down eagerly. Love, excitement and anticipation mixed in equal quantities on her lovely face. Even Maury was struck dumb for a few seconds, before he managed to croak out, 'Cor, you're a real smasher Pansy. Best-looking girl in the place, I bet.' His black eyes fixed on the second figure who'd appeared on the landing. 'She's coming then?'

'Course she is. Come on, Addie.'

Gripping the banister so tightly that they could see her knuckles turning white, Addie started gingerly to descend.

'Honestly, Addie, you should 'ave practised in yer heels before.'

'I didn't want to get them messed up before the dance.' With the tip of her tongue protruding from her pink-lipsticked mouth, Addie wobbled precariously to the hall. The three watchers expelled a simultaneous breath as she reached the hall mat and grinned triumphantly. 'Cracked the bleeders.'

'Regular Ginger Rogers, ain't yer?' Maury sent a shrill whistle through to the back kitchen. 'Josh, we're off.'

'Oh blimey, Shorty, you ain't brought yer bodyguard, 'ave yer? Think the quickstep might get a bit rough, do yer?'

'Oh don't fight, you two. It's just going to be the most perfect birthday ever.' Pansy twirled in an excess of joy.

'Yeah, well, get yer coat on then and let's go.' Maury removed her coat from the hook and held it out. Pansy's face fell. 'But, Maury, don't you want to . . . Mum didn't say we couldn't, did she?'

'No. But I was going to do it at the dance.'

Pansy slipped her arms into the coat he was spreading across his chest, before saying doubtfully, 'In front of everyone?'

After considering this picture, Pansy decided perhaps it might be quite appealing. A lot of the women from the bakery were going to the dance, and some of her old school mates would surely be there as well. She pictured their faces when they saw the glorious engagement ring. She wasn't a vain or vindictive girl, but a small part of her couldn't help enjoying this picture. She did, however, insist that her mum must see the gold hoop with its lozenge-shaped sapphire flanked by two diamonds.

'It's quite beautiful,' Kate said with genuine admiration. *And very expensive*, a warning voice whispered in her head. For a moment she was tempted to withdraw her permission, but Maury snapped the jeweller's box shut with his forefinger and the sharp sound broke the moment.

Maury bawled to Joshua again, telling him to get a move on. The large young man lumbered from the kitchen, his beaming face well sprinkled with crumbs. His smile became wider when he saw Addie.

'Hello, Joshua's girl. Happy birthday.'

'I ain't yer girl. I ain't nobody's girl.'

'You can be Joshua's girl then.' With a frown he reached for her hair. 'Joshua likes it loose.'

'You keep your hands to yerself. Don' you touch my hair, yer understand?'

Joshua nodded. 'Not touch.' Fixing those disconcerting eyes earnestly on her, he informed her, 'Dog's dead.'

'Yeah? Well I'm sorry to hear that. He was a good dog.'

'Yes. Joshua's dad is going to get him another one.' Scrabbling inside his jacket pocket, Joshua drew out a small envelope and offered it to Addie. 'Card. For your birthday. Joshua bought it himself.'

'Oh? Ta.' Addie drew out the limp white card decorated with a picture of a man on a donkey and gold script writing. Since she couldn't read, she saw nothing odd about being wished a Happy Easter. 'It's very pretty. Ta.'

'For heavens sake, let's get going.'

''Ang on, Shorty, I got to get in me coat.'

'You can't wear that,' Kate protested at the sight of the old boatman's overcoat Addie was shrugging on.

'Why not?' Addie snuggled the oil-and-water-stained navy wool around her.

'Because it looks just awful,' Pansy informed her. 'Honest, Addie, you can't go out in that.'

'I come 'ere in it.'

'Well you're not going out in it. I'm not walking up the road with you in that.'

'Please yerself.'

'Don't fight. Here, take mine.' Kate pushed Addie into her own light beige coat with its Astrakhan collar and flicked a scarf around her head. 'I'll use yours tonight, Addie. Have a lovely time.' Impulsively she dropped a kissed on the girl's pale cheeks, and then turned and embraced her own daughter. 'You look quite lovely, my lamb. And I'm certain sure you deserve all the happiness in the world.'

'Oh Mum . . . I do love you.'

With a fierce hug, Pansy parted from her mother and slipped her arm into Maury's. Kate switched off the hall light and stood at the door watching the four of them make their way towards Kentish Town High Street. After a few tottering steps, Addie grabbed hold of Joshua's arm and leant against him.

At the end of the road, Pansy turned. In the rapidly descending darkness, Kate just about made out her silhouette waving vigorously. Walking the two steps to her own front gate, she waved back.

The four figures disappeared into the night. And suddenly, for no reason at all, a terrible coldness clutched at Kate's heart and twisted.

Chapter 31

The first person they set eyes on when they stepped into the converted piano factory was Eileen O'Day – with the erstwhile milkman Felonious Monk hovering in attendance.

'Mum, what you doing here?'

'Boiling me washing, what else?'

'You never said you was coming.'

'And why should I? When was the last time you were kind enough to tell me *your* plans, young man? Mr Monk requested me company.'

'But Mum, it ain't right. He's been in prison.'

'Least it's behind me, instead of in front like somes I could mention.'

'That's enough, the pair of you. Hello, Pansy. You're looking very pretty tonight.'

'So do you, Mrs O'Day,' Pansy said politely. Remembering her manners, she introduced Addie. 'It's her birthday today too.'

'Many happy returns, love. Do you live local? I've not seen you around before.'

'She's stopping with my grandmother, Mrs O'Day. So's her brother. They're boaters. Off the canals.'

'Really?'

'Yeah . . . wha' of it?' Addie tossed her hair, forgetting it was tied back until the thick ponytail thumped her in the back.

'I'm sure it must be a very interesting life, love. If you want to hang yer coats and hats up, there's cloakrooms down that corridor. Me and Fel will save you places at a table.'

The two cloakrooms had been converted out of former

offices, with coat racks drafted in from the local schools for the purpose. After they'd hung up their outdoor clothes and paid a visit to the attached women's lavatory, Pansy and Addie joined their escorts, who were hovering outside.

'Isn't it lovely?' Pansy breathed. 'Just like a proper dance hall.' She had never actually been to a real dance hall, since her mother had deemed fifteen too young to visit the Palais or Paramount Halls, but she couldn't imagine them to be any better than this.

The long finishing room of the former piano works had been transformed by the combined efforts of council workers, Red Cross, WVS, and the local scouts and guides troops. The big windows that stretched nearly from roof to floor had been boarded over to allow the use of all the lighting. Some of the bulbs had been covered with a gold-coloured transparent paper, which gave the large room a warm, intimate glow, and a large glitter-ball had been hung from the central point of the roof which, even though it didn't revolve, added to the resemblance to a professional dance hall. A temporary stage had been erected at the far end of the room for the musicians, and the local cinema had been persuaded to loan its red velvet drapes and gold tassels for the evening.

The bar was being manned by the prettiest girls from the WVS – an arrangement that ensured that few of their male customers ignored the pointedly placed box marked *'Spitfire Fund – Please place your change in here'*. Other volunteers were seated at stalls backed by decorated screens urging dancers to buy sixpenny stamps towards Savings Certificates; or to buy a raffle ticket (all proceeds to Red Cross Parcels); or guess the weight of the cake (all proceeds go to tank fund).

One volunteer called across to Pansy as they made their way past. 'Would you like to write to a prisoner of war, dear?' She held out a pen and pointed to the filled sheets in front of her. 'Just put your name and address down and something about your hobbies and interests.'

'Well, I don't know . . .' She glanced doubtfully at Maury, who responded as she'd hoped by telling the woman that she was already spoken for.

'Ask skinny here,' he advised, jerking a thumb at Addie, who'd been hanging back.

'I ain't writing to nobody. Me brother wouldn't like it, miss.' Reluctant to admit in this company that she couldn't write anything but her name, Addie put both hands behind her and backed away.

The long floorboards had been scrubbed and polished for two solid days to provide a dance floor. For Addie, unused to high heels it was a booby trap waiting to happen. Her right foot skidded and slithered away behind her. Attempting to regain her balance, she flailed with her arms, her left foot shot forward and she ended up doing the splits. Several spectators laughed out loud, one started to applaud, and others joined in, shouting for an encore.

Addie scowled, and redness infused her face under the dusting of powder. Scrambling to her feet again, she bunched her fists, torn between running from the hall to escape her humiliation and wading into the laughers with fists flying. The local dentists were spared a sudden rush of broken teeth by Eileen, who grasped the girl's arm and pulled her up, saying, 'Never mind, love, half of them have polished the floor with their behinds tonight. You come and sit at our table with us.'

Felonious drained the last dregs of beer from his glass as they approached and banged the pot down. 'I don' care what they say, this war-brew ain't got the yaw the old stuff 'ad.'

'What's yaw?' Maury asked.

'Very kind of yer, son. I'll 'ave another half.'

Maury would have argued if his mother hadn't told him to get beer for all the men and fruit punch for all the women.

'That all there is?' Maury said. 'I wanted a whisky.'

'Then want will have to be your master, young man. There's a war on, in case you haven't noticed. And there's Rose. Best fetch her something too.'

Maury escaped before his mother could start ordering him to buy drinks for every acquaintance in the room.

The punch came in assorted glasses and china cups, each one having a slice of apple floating on the surface of the dark red liquid. 'Got to bring them back if you want refills,' Maury said. 'Next one to get them in had better remember.'

Having established that they'd reached the end of his own generosity for tonight, he dragged another chair over and slipped in next to Pansy just as the band struck up another waltz and the compere announced that it was a Ladies' Excuse-Me.

Eileen set her willow-patterned tea-cup down and stood up. 'Will you, Mr Monk?'

'An 'onour madam, an 'onour . . . if you'll call me Felonious.'

'I'll do nothing of the sort. It's Mr Monk for now. Now, are you partnering me or shall I ask someone else?'

Felonious stood up and formally extended an arm.

Rose eyed Joshua and asked if he danced.

'Maury's mum showed Joshua.'

'Shall we try?'

She led the big man on to the dance floor, pushed his arms into position and inserted herself in them. With a frown of concentration, Joshua launched himself forward chanting, 'One, two, three. One, two, three,' and swaying and dipping they merged into the swirling crowd.

Pansy smiled shyly at her almost-fiancé. Would it be now he'd propose formally?

Maury nodded and winked at her. He took another swallow of beer and rearranged himself one ankle over the other to watch the room.

Disappointed, she said, 'Shall we dance too then, Maury?'

'If you want.'

She'd have preferred him to sound more enthusiastic about the prospect, but making the best of it, she took his hand and trotted on to the floor.

Maury was a good dancer. He was rather inclined to show off with a lot of fancy twirls and turns that she had trouble following on the highly polished floor, but she knew they made a well-balanced pair. 'If they have a spot prize later, Maury, we could win it, don't you think?'

'Bound to, doll.' He swirled her in another spectacular

movement, sending several less confident couples into a crabwise shuffle to avoid them.

Completing her turn, Pansy managed to wriggle closer into his arms. 'Maury . . . when will you do it?'

'It?'

'You know . . . ask me about getting engaged proper.'

'Later, doll. Let's have a dance first, eh?'

A small knot of anxiety ballooned in Pansy's chest. She knew him well enough to sense that he was stalling. Yet he'd asked her mum before they left, hadn't he? So he must still want to marry her. Perhaps it was the crowds. Maybe he'd got cold feet about asking her in front of all these people.

'It's awful hot in here, isn't it?' She fanned a hand in front of her face as the band swept to a triumphant finish before bursting into a fast foxtrot. 'Shall we step outside for a minute?'

'I ain't hot. You go if you like.'

'No . . . I'll be all right.' She glanced over to the table. Addie was perched on the edge of her chair, fingers pleating the skirt across her knees as she watched the floor. 'We oughtn't to leave Addie on her own. Let's go sit down. You could ask her to dance, 'cept she said she can't. But you could teach her, couldn't you?'

'No.'

Pansy was about to argue when she spotted more late-comers entering the hall. 'Oh look, there's Lottie and Sheila.' She waved vigorously at her friend and pointed to their table, mouthing instructions to bring more chairs across.

Once more, Addie had to be introduced.

'You're off the boats then?' Lottie Abbott asked. 'The *canal* boats?'

'Yeah. What of it?'

'Our mum says they have fleas,' her sister Sheila said. 'And lice.'

'Then your mum's got sawdust in her bonce, ain't she?'

'Well there's no need to be offensive, I'm sure. I was just saying.'

Lottie and Sheila gave a synchronised sniff. Their fair plaits had been pinned up around their heads and decorated with bows, and red lipstick had turned their mouths into cupid's bows.

'Is your mum here tonight?' Pansy intervened quickly to prevent an argument between her new friend and her oldest friend.

'No. She's had to stop home and look after the little ones and Gran.' Lottie drew another nasal breath and looked round the floor. 'There's ever so many soldiers and like here, aren't there? I didn't think there would be.'

'You get in for free if you're in uniform. Said so outside,' Maury said.

'I like men in uniform,' Sheila twanged through another gasp. 'I think they look ever so handsome. I 'spect even you'd look handsome in a uniform, Maury.'

'Ta.'

'I wonder if I'll get to dance with one?' Sheila scanned the dancers eagerly. The crowds reflected in both the Abbott sisters' wire-rimmed glasses as they craned forward, trying to locate an unattached uniform.

'There's one, over by the bar. A soldier, see?'

They all looked across to the small group clustered around the counter with its bowls of punch and kegs of beer. Among the civilians was a khaki uniform balancing against a crutch.

'Oh blimey. It's the bleedin' Geoghans.'

'Who?'

'Boaters. Blackie's the oldest and ugliest of the litter and Matt's the runt. Rickey's sort of near Matt's end. 'Spect I can get him to dance with yer if yer want,' Addie informed the Abbotts. 'None of the Geoghans is special particular.'

'No thank you.' Lottie tossed her head. 'Mum wouldn't like us to dance with a boater.'

Seeing the dark look that flickered over Addie's face, and knowing Lottie's talent for tactless remarks, Pansy attempted to act as peacemaker again. She said the first thing that came into her head. 'Guess what, Lottie, Maury's bought me an engagement ring. We went to this really posh jewellers in Regent Street, and I've just been dying to tell everyone at the bakery all week – especially you, you being my absolute best friend. But Maury swore me to secrecy

. . . cross my heart and hope to die . . . until he asked me proper.'

Lottie straightened her bony shoulders. A look flashed between the two sisters. 'I think I have to go powder me nose. Why don't you come too, Pansy?'

'I don't want . . .' Pansy realised Lottie's oddly working jaw didn't mean she'd got something stuck in her teeth. 'Oh, yes . . . well, I might as well, I suppose. Are you coming, Addie?'

'No, ta. I'll stop 'ere.'

As soon as they were safely in the ladies' lavatory, Pansy demanded to know what was the matter.

'Shush!' Bent double, Lottie walked along the row of cubicles checking under the doors, and then returned, thrusting the doors open this time.

Pansy watched this performance with a tapping foot. Lottie might be her best friend but that didn't mean she didn't get on her nerves sometimes.

'If you don't tell me *this instant* what you got me in here for, Lottie Abbott, I'm going straight back into the hall, see if I don't.'

'There's no need to be like that. I was just checking because it's not something you'd want anyone else to hear. And you ought to be grateful for me trouble, Pansy Cutter, because I'm your best friend and it's only you I'm thinking of. In fact I've been thinking of nothing else since Sheila told me. I was so bothered I let loads of cherry tarts go past without any cherries – not that they are cherries now, it's just this horried stiff jam stuff and it sticks up the belt something horrible—'

'Lottie Abbott, if you don't spit it out I'm going to scream!' Pansy balled her fists into her hips and glared.

'Oh, all right. But I want you to know that I don't really want to tell you, but as your best friend I feel it's my *duty* to. Because it would be on my conscience for ever if I let you make yourself dreadful miserable with Maury when I could have spoken out, and—'

'What about Maury?' Pansy interrupted.

'Well . . .' Lottie sniffed loudly and dropped her voice for effect. 'You know Sheila won the prize at technical college for her shorthand typing? Well she went for an interview at the railway offices in Euston – ever such a good job even though she is only fifteen and maybe a bit too young—'

'Lottie, I'm gonna walk right out in a minute . . .'

'Yes, all right . . .' Anxious not to lose her audience, Lottie poured out the story of Sheila's nerve-calming cup of tea in the back-street café prior to her interview, and the scene she'd witnessed between Maury and Carla – including the handholding, kissing, and Carla's mimed suggestion that she was pregnant.

'I don't believe it. I don't believe a word of it. Maury wouldn't . . . not with another girl.'

'She's not a girl. Sheila said she was quite old. Twenty-five at least. If my boyfriend did something like that I'd just never speak to him again. I certainly wouldn't *marry* him.'

'You haven't got a boyfriend, Lottie Abbott. I don't expect you ever will have, you jealous cat.'

'Well, if that's all the thanks I get for stopping you making the biggest, worst mistake of your whole life, Pansy Cutter, I'm not sitting with you any longer. But you'll be sorry, see if you're not . . .' With a flounce that dislodged one of her red hair bows and sent it soaring into a washbasin, Lottie left the lavatories.

Pansy was vaguely aware that the tiled room was waving up and down in an alarming fashion. A grey and white speckled mist was closing over her eyes, reducing her vision to a pin-prick. Clumsily she seized the cold edge of the washbasin and ducked her head over it. The mist gradually receded, until she was staring at the green verdigris-encrusted plughole. Taking a deep breath, she cautiously straightened up again. Her own wide-eyed reflection stared back at her in the fly-blown mirror above the basin.

It wasn't true; it couldn't be. Maury wouldn't do that to her. He loved her. They loved each other. 'No! No! No!' She dared the reflected Pansy to contradict her. 'He wouldn't do that. He loves me . . . me . . .'

The rest of the party had returned to the table by the time she got back – except for Lottie and Sheila, who'd taken themselves off somewhere.

'And good riddance to the spiteful cats,' Pansy decided. She drank several glasses of punch, bought a round of drinks herself with the money her Uncle Pete had given her for her birthday, danced with Maury, Joshua and an able seaman who was on leave visiting his parents in Highgate, and told herself she was having a wonderful time.

The level of noise, laughter and music rose steadily for several hours, interspersed with the regular rumble of rolling stock clattering past on the railway line that ran down one side of the building. Even Addie was coaxed to stand up with Felonious and Joshua a few times and allow herself to be steered over the floor, providing it was a slow tune she could follow. When the compere finally announced, 'The Lambeth Walk – everyone on the floor for this one', a huge cheer roared into the iron rafters of the hall.

'Come on, Addie,' Pansy urged. 'Everyone can do this one.'

Addie gripped the seat of her chair and jutted out her bottom lip. 'I've seen it before. It's too fast. I'll fall on me bum again and make a fool of meself. I ain't dancing.'

'Yes yer are. You're dancing with me . . .'

Matthus Geoghan had swaggered over to their table, and now he grabbed Addie's arm, trying to pull her up. He released her with a yelp as Addie's teeth snapped shut on the back of his hand.

'Leave Joshua's girl alone!'

'She ain't your girl. She's my girl.'

'I ain't anybody's girl!'

'What's up, Matt? This lot giving yer trouble?' The two other Geoghans had finally abandoned the bar as the customers' generosity in compensating Rickey for his 'war wound' had dried up, along with their supply of free half-pints.

'He reckons Addie's *his* girl. You know you said you'd walk out with me, Addie. Said so down the docks.'

'I said I'd think about it, Matthus. I never said definite.'

'She just wants a little persuading, Matt.' Blackie flicked the back of his youngest brother's chest with the back of his fist. 'All our women wanted a bit of persuading. They soon mind yer once you let 'em see who's boss. 'Ere, I'll show you . . .' Blackie dragged Addie up and clamped her to him, his open fingers groping for a handful of bottom. This time Addie's teeth locked on nose rather than fingers.

'You little bitch!'

Addie was thrust away. Joshua tried to hold her but found Matthus was between him and his prize.

'Joshua's girl.'

'No her ain't. You heard her. Hers gonna be my girl.'

The Geoghans were all full of brewers' courage. They faced down Joshua. Matthus attempted to put an arm around his girl. She promptly slapped his face. Blackie grabbed her wrist and twisted hard.

It was all the provocation Joshua needed. With a roar of rage, he lifted a chair and swirled it around his head like a mace.

Rickey hopped back. His crutch slid and slithered with each heavy-footed hop. The customers in the path of his backward progress left it too late to jump out of the way and he crashed backwards; the table fell forward under his weight, scattering glasses, candles and cloth into the sitters' laps.

'Oi, you!' One of the men seized the back of Rickey's jacket and hauled him to his feet.

Charging to his brother's rescue, Blackie fell over his own feet. Someone else threw a punch. More glass and china shattered to the floor. Furniture was overturned. Neighbouring tables started to join in the fighting. Most people seemed to assume Joshua was the troublemaker, since he was still swinging the chair around his head. A sailor dived low, grabbing his legs. His heavy body went down. Others piled on to hold him still.

Roaring angrily, Joshua tried to dislodge them. It left Blackie a clear view of his ribs. He took advantage of it. 'Bastard loonie!' A steel toe-cap connected with Joshua's midriff.

'Oi! Leave him alone, yer bleedin' coward!' Addie jumped on Blackie's back, her fingers clawing for his eyes. Bending forward he spun; Addie lost her grip and went flying across the room. She landed on her seat. This time her skirt flew up around her waist, giving everyone a clear view of Taz's

316

darned underpants. Despite the fighting, there was a loud burst of laughter and applause.

The band had ground unevenly to a halt as they realised something at the far end of the hall was proving a greater attraction than their efforts. Now the racket attracted a saner voice. The Senior ARP Warden pushed through the crowds and angrily demanded to know what was going on.

Several people tried to tell him at once. Struggling to unravel the shouted explanations, he managed to sort out that the Geoghans were at the bottom of the trouble.

'Right, clear off the lot of you! We don't want trouble-makers in here. Go on!'

Blackie's inclination to fight was quashed by the Reserve Police, backed up by a couple of burly soldiers, and all three Geoghans were hustled towards the doors.

Urged past Addie by the firm grip of a corporal on his shirt collar, Matthus muttered rebelliously, 'You are me girl, Addie. Yer know you said you would. I'll see yer later, see if I don't.'

A jerk and a shake pushed him on, but not before Joshua had overheard what was being said. 'She's Joshua's girl.'

'Get lost, loonie!' Matthus jeered as he was hauled out of the hall.

With a roar Joshua started forward, but Eileen grabbed his arm. 'Now don't go starting another fight, love.' She rearranged his dishevelled tie, straightened his jacket and spat on her fingers before she used them to smooth down his untidy hair just as she would have done with any of her own sons. 'Now why don't you come an' help us get this table put back? And then we can have another dance.'

'Joshua wants to be excused.'

'Go on then.' Eileen patted his cheek and left him to make his own way out of the hall.

'Disgusting . . . drunk . . . a disgrace . . .' The fragments of disapproval reached Pansy's table as the tables were righted, glass fragments swept up and the band were encouraged to strike up a waltz. 'They were fighting over that girl. What's her mother thinking of letting her walk out with men like that?'

'She's a boater!' Sheila Abbott's adenoidal bray trumpeted over 'The White Cliffs of Dover'. 'They all are! They don't act like proper Christians, me mum says . . .'

'Oh, boaters . . . Well, can't expect no better, I suppose. I don't know what they're thinking, letting them in here. Did you see her drawers? What a lark!'

Pansy looked at her friend's face, growing pale with misery. She could see Addie was struggling to choke back tears, but before she could think of something comforting to say, Addie rushed out.

'Addie . . . Wait! They never . . . You're a cat, a spiteful cat!' Pansy shouted at Sheila before flying after the boater girl.

She assumed that Addie had gone to the cloakroom, but when she opened the door the room was in pitch darkness. She was about to leave again when the creak of sliding wood caught her ears. At the same time a draught of cool air played over her hot face. Squinting, she found that the solid blackness of one wall had been cracked where the curtains had been twitched open. As she watched, Addie's outline appeared against the slightly lighter background.

'Addie? What are you doing?'

'What's it look like? I'm going home.'

'Don't, please. They didn't mean it . . . laughing at you like that and everything . . .'

'Yes they did. It's like Grandad always said. Boaters and landies are like oil and water.' She thrust the window wider and flung her leg over the sill.

'Addie . . .' Pansy darted across the room.

Addie was leaning over the sill, her upper half in the room, her legs outside. She suddenly squealed and jerked. 'Gettoff! leggo!' Her head and shoulders slid away.

'What's the matter?' Alarmed, Pansy wedged one foot on the hot water pipes that ran round the walls and hauled herself up.

Addie had landed close to the wall so Pansy couldn't see her, only hear her angry voice: 'Will you gettoff, you stupid lump!'

'Joshua has brought you a birthday present. See . . .'

'I don't want . . . Oh, bleedin' hell. You stupid idiot, what have you done? It's all your fault . . .'

'Pansy? You okay?'

Startled because she hadn't heard Maury come in behind her, Pansy lost her grip on the window sill and slid awkwardly to the floor.

Maury clicked the light on. An immediate roar from outside sent Pansy jumping to her feet again to sweep the blackout curtain back into place.

'What's happening? Where's Skinny?'

'She's gone home.' Pansy sat down on the lower edge of the coat rack. She suddenly felt tearful herself. 'Oh, Maury . . . It was going to be such a lovely evening. I've been looking forward to it for ever such a long time. And now it's all spoilt . . .'

'No it ain't, doll.' Maury left his position by the door which he'd been propping open with one foot, and came to sit beside her, putting a comforting arm round her shoulder. Gratefully Pansy leant against him. This was how it was meant to be – just her and Maury together. He made her feel safe and warm. For a while they sat, both lost in their own thoughts, snug in the protecting walls of coats.

'Maury?'

'Yeah?'

'You don't have to marry me. Not if you don't want to.'

'Who says I don't want to?'

Pushing herself deeper into the hollow of his collarbone and not looking at his face, Pansy told him what Sheila Abbott had seen. 'I mean, if this woman's gonna have your baby . . .'

'Having me kid! Don't be daft, doll. As if!'

'Then it's not true?' She still couldn't look him in the face, frightened that she'd see the lies there if she did. Instead she fiddled with his jacket lapel.

'Course it ain't. Carla . . . she's a business partner.'

'Sheila said she was holding your hand.'

'She's a foreigner. They do that sort of thing, doll. Even the blokes kiss each other.'

'Oh? And she's not going to have a baby?'

'How would I know? If she is, it certainly ain't mine.'

'Honestly, Maury?' Pansy squirmed away. She looked directly into his eyes, praying she'd see what she hoped for.

'Honest, doll.'

They sat there for a moment, held in a private world that not even the rising wail of the alert outside could break. Then Pansy smiled shyly. 'Oh, Maury, I do love you.'

'And I love you too, doll.' Slipping off the rack, he knelt on one knee and took her hand. 'Pansy Cutter, will you marry me?'

'Yes . . . Oh yes! Please.'

They were locked in each other's arms, the ring glittering on Pansy's left hand, when several other women arrived to collect their coats before trooping down to the shelter under the factory.

'We'd best go back too, Panse.'

'In a minute. I'm just going to the lav first, Maury.'

'Don't be long, doll.'

'I won't.' She kissed him passionately on the lips, not caring if the others were watching, then hurried to the lavatory and bolted herself in a cubicle.

Once inside, she let go the tears of relief that she'd been holding on to since she'd told him he was free if he wanted to be, clinging to the wonderful fact that Maury really did love her as much as she loved him.

Finally the rumbling note of distant guns mixed with the roar of far-off bombs exploding penetrated her warm daydreams. The planes' engines were getting closer, and the toilets had emptied. She'd better hurry; Maury would be waiting.

The music had stopped, giving way to the stern shouting of the wardens. It was no longer a matter of choice; everyone was being urged towards the door by the stage, which led to the underground shelter.

The crowd was shuffling forward with a lot of good-natured joking. Ahead of her, Pansy could see Rose, Maury and Felonious being swept along in the crush. She nearly lost her footing and grabbed an iron pillar to prevent herself going over.

She glimpsed Maury by the door. He'd turned to look for

her and was straining to see over the shoulders of the taller people surrounding him, his thin frame braced against the irresistible movement that was carrying him away from her. Lifting her hand, she waved and smiled; she thought she'd never been as happy as she was at that moment.

The darkness came so suddenly that for a moment she didn't register what had happened and continued to move forward. Then the world dissolved around her as the breath was sucked from her lungs and something picked her up and flung her through the air.

Chapter 32

She'd decided to go to bed with him tonight. Through lowered lashes, Iris watched the red-gold lights flickering in Taz's brown eyes as the flames from Nana Cutter's dying fire danced over the last of the coals.

Setting her wineglass down on the hearth rug, she leant towards him, slid her arms round his neck and pressed her lips hard on his. After a brief second, he responded.

Twisting free, she pushed him away and calmly reclaimed her wine.

Iris saw the indecision chasing over his face. He didn't know what to do, or what sort of reception to expect if he tried to take this any further. His confusion pleased her. It was the first time in her life that she'd felt in control, and it was a good feeling.

The whole evening had been a success so far. Her anger at discovering that most of Ursula's ill-health had been self-inflicted had given her a confidence she'd never possessed before. With her scarring hidden under a layer of her mother's best cosmetics and her hair swept back in a new style, she'd taken charge of the evening.

With Nana and Ludo out of the way at the theatre and Addie despatched to her first dance, they'd had the flat to themselves. She'd cooked dinner, using rations from home, and washed it down with a bottle of Ludo's damson wine liberated from Nana's larder. Afterwards they'd carried the remains of the bottle into the sitting room and sat on the rug, sipping the deep mulberry liquid by the firelight.

Taz leant his back against the sofa. Whenever he tipped his head back to take a swallow Iris studied the lean line of his tanned skin, from the point of his chin to where it disappeared into his top shirt button. It really was quite irresistible.

Leaning across, she settled her lips into the soft dip under his Adam's apple and kissed him with small darting movements, tasting the sweat mingling with the damson wine on her tongue.

He reached for her eagerly, pulling her closer. His hands slid all over her as his tongue reached inside her mouth, twisting and probing at hers. Abruptly he pushed her away, holding her at arm's length.

'What's the matter?'

'You ever had this much to drink before, Iris?'

'No. I've scarcely ever had anything to drink before – except sweet sherry at Christmas.' Stretching languorously, she wound her arms round his neck again. 'But I'm not drunk, if that's what you're thinking. I know exactly what I'm doing, Taz Dixon.'

Relaxing, she let herself be lowered to the floor until his weight was pushing her down. Taking handfuls of his shirt, she started to drag it out of his belt at the back. With a groan, he thrust himself harder on to her, scrabbling at her clothes, dragging the top of her dress open and unlatching her bra so he could clamp his mouth greedily on her breasts. She let herself ride up on the wonderful, frightening, incredible feelings that were flooding through her.

He broke away from her for a moment to kick off his boots and unlace his belt, hooking off his trousers and underpants in one smooth movement with his thumbs.

He took off her shoes first, then reached up under the tangled mass of dress and slip and undid her stockings with maddening slowness, spreading his fingers wide to encircle her leg and stroking the stockings down her thighs, her calves, her ankles, before slipping them off her toes. It wasn't what she wanted. Raising her buttocks, she wriggled the rest of her clothes off over her feet and sat naked in front of him, her arms outstretched.

'Iris . . .' The sound came from deep inside him, more of a moan than word.

He dived forward again, laying himself over her, skin on skin.

She'd heard that the first time hurt, but nobody had told her how desperately she'd want the pain. Wrapping her legs around him, she clawed at his bottom, urging him to go deeper, thrust harder . . .

They climaxed simultaneously, Taz rose up on his hands, his body arched, his head flung back. She thrust against him, her spine curving and her legs splaying wide as she strove for . . . she didn't know what – until the waves reached a climax and for a moment they were locked together in a private moment of ecstasy and pain.

And then she was falling away from him. Her heart was thudding and her breath came in short gasps. Taz rolled off and lay beside her, his head next to hers on the rug. All sorts of odd images imprinted themselves on her pupils: a cobweb shivering lightly between one corner of the room and the light-shade; the loud tick of the mantelpiece clock; the cat crouched under the sideboard, its amber eyes winking impassively as it looked at their white bodies. I'll remember this moment for ever, she thought to herself. No matter how many other times this happens, I'll remember the cobweb and the cat and the sound of that clock.

'Are you OK?'

She let her head loll to one side so that she could look into his eyes. 'Of course I am.' Did everyone feel like this? she wondered. She wanted him to reach over and gather her up into his arms and hold her for ever.

Propping himself on his elbow, he stared down at her. 'I wasn't too rough?'

He had a bite mark on his shoulder. Not a nibble but an angry red oval, the deep impressions of her teeth clearly visible. It made her feel almost self-satisfied. Tracing the outline with her forefinger she said, 'It seems I might have been.'

He squinted at the blemish. And grinned. 'Well there'll be no mistaking what I've been up to. Lucky it's winter and I can keep me shirt on.'

'Unless you get some fresh ones by summer, of course.'

'Now there's a thought.' He cupped the swell of one of

her breasts, kissing her gently at the same time. There was no heat in his movements this time. It was a lazy enjoyment of their closeness. Snuggling inside the curve of his arm and pillowing her head on his chest, she listened to his heart as her cheek rose and fell with the rhythm of his breathing.

The door knocker brought them both back to reality.

'Bloody *hell*!' Taz rolled off her and sat up. 'Who's that?'

'Don't answer,' Iris said. 'They'll go away.'

'Maybe your gran's forgotten her key.'

'If she has, I doubt Ludo's forgotten his too. Anyway, it's too early for them. What about Addie?'

'It's too early for her too. But if it *is* her we'll soon know; she'll holler until someone takes notice.'

Iris huddled against him, holding her breath and listening. After another onslaught on the door knocker, their visitor moved round to the window and rapped sharply on the panes. With a conspiratorial giggle they slid closer together, holding their breath.

'It's like hiding from the rent man, isn't it?' Iris breathed softly.

'I wouldn't know . . . I've never had to. Wouldn't have thought you would have either.'

'You'd be surprised. When I was little, I can remember us all having to crouch down behind the sofa when he came round. Even Daddy once. It was the month he had no work at all in the yard.'

'But it ain't like that now? I mean, you've got money put by now?'

'Mmm . . . once they started building again – the council, I mean – a few years back. And the war's been good for business; all those street shelters and underground ones too. Millions of bricks.' She twisted to look into his face. 'Does that sound awful? Being pleased we're making a profit from the war?'

'Plenty are.' Easing her away from him, he crawled across to the window. 'I think our caller's gone.' He tweaked a corner of the curtains and knelt up. 'Can't see no one.'

Iris giggled. He hadn't bothered to dress himself, and the

sight of his bare backside was suddenly irresistibly funny. There were long claw marks over both cheeks where her nails had raked him.

He looked back at her. 'What you laughing at?'

'Nothing . . . sorry.' She tried to stop herself and found the giggles were bursting out like bubbles rising in a boiling kettle.

On all fours he came quickly back towards her, grabbing her by the shoulders and wrestling her on to her back. With a mock squeal of fright she wrapped arms and legs around him, ready to start again. He collapsed with her entwined round him like a snake, as the slow, sinister wail of the alert echoed through the world outside.

'Damn . . . Do you want to go down the cellar? It's fixed up with a bed and everything. Your gran showed me and Addie, case we ever had to take shelter.'

'I know.' For the first time, something struck Iris. 'There's only one bed. Do you think she and Ludo . . . ?'

'Maybe.'

'Heavens!' She tried to picture it as Taz nuzzled at her collarbone. Somehow it didn't seem right to climb into Nana's bed – not if she and Ludo were using it for the same purpose. Surely her grandmother couldn't . . . not at their ages!

Taz was attacking her with more enthusiasm, guiding her hands downwards to help him.

'Let's stay here,' she whispered. 'If the raid comes close we can go downstairs then.'

'Whatever you want. God, you're beautiful, Iris.'

Nobody in her entire life had ever called her that before. She loved him at that moment so much that she felt her heart would explode. All the wonderful aching was rising to a crescendo inside her again. She wanted again . . . needed again . . .

'Iris?'

'Yes?'

'Can I ask you something?'

Anything. She'd do anything he wanted. 'What?'

Instead of continuing, he slid away from her slightly.

Impatiently she tried to pull him back, wanting the feel of his body on hers.

He held her off. 'No, listen . . . You remember what I said about the Canal Company wanting to take over my boats?'

'And you didn't want to call anyone else master.' She made another grab for him, but he held her wrists.

'No, listen, Iris. The thing is . . . it looks like I might be gonna lose them anyway.'

'Why?'

'I owe money.'

'To who?'

He shrugged. 'Blokes. Blokes who'll lend to boaters. Not many will, yer see.'

She relaxed her arms, so he let her go. Instead of stretching out to him, she hugged her knees instead. The fire was dying down. She felt suddenly cold. 'How much do you owe them?'

'With interest, about a hundred and twenty quid, I reckon.'

'A hundred and . . . !'

'There were repairs to the motor; it's gone down three times the past year. Needed spare parts. And some weeks we'd not pick up any loads. And there was Addie's clothes and stuff . . . I wanted to do right by her . . .'

'Not to mention "treating" me to a trip up the West End, and the cinema, of course . . .' Her voice sounded high and tight; she could hear it somewhere far away, like it didn't belong to her.

'Yes. And now the *Crock of Gold* needs fixing up after the fire . . .'

Don't say it. Please don't say it, her mind pleaded, while her face stayed calmly expressionless.

'So I was wondering if you could maybe give me a loan. It needn't be the whole amount . . . fifty quid would do, I reckon.'

'Fifty?'

'Yeah. I'd ask the old lady, but she's done enough for us already . . .'

Haven't I? Iris's mind asked. *I've just given you everything, can't you see that?* Out loud she said, 'Are you sure fifty would be all right?'

The relief on his face was almost comical. She might have laughed if she hadn't been howling inside.

'Yes. Fifty would be great. I'll pay you back, I swear. It's just a loan.'

She rubbed the tops of her arms. 'It's getting chilly. I think I would like to go down to the cellar. Can you go switch the light on, and turn back the bed?'

He sprang up eagerly, dragging on his trousers. 'There's a paraffin heater down there. I'll light that too, shall I?'

'Yes.' She forced out a smile. 'That would be cosy. Go on, then . . .' She jerked her head impatiently as he hesitated still. 'I'll just damp the fire down in here.'

As soon as he'd gone she grabbed her clothes, piling them on in a frantic haste. She was shrugging on her coat when he shouted up the internal stairs that he was ready down here.

'Iris . . . did you hear? Hurry up, I'm getting cold.'

She walked over to the top of the cellar stairs. They turned at a right angle, so she couldn't see the bottom. 'I hope,' she shouted, 'you freeze in hell, you rat! It will certainly have to freeze over before I get into bed with you.'

'Iris?' His shadow appeared on the stairwell's plaster. She'd assumed he'd already climbed into bed. Flustered, she spun away and ran for the front door, fumbling with the lock.

'Iris? What are you doing? What's the matter?'

She spun round, her chest heaving and eyes flashing. 'You . . . you're the matter! How long did it take you to find a girl with a bit of money and a disfigurement?' She scrubbed at the powder over her scars, rubbing it off with the backs of her fingers. 'Or was this an added bonus? Were you just hoping for a girl gullible enough to be taken in by your charms? I bet you couldn't believe your luck when you walked into Cutter's office and saw me sitting behind that desk. *And* I told you I was the boss's daughter! I'm surprised you didn't try to seduce me right then and there, over the desk.'

'Iris, you've got it wrong—'

'No. I don't think so. Go and find yourself some other stupid woman who's prepared to pay you to go to bed

329

with them. I'm sure you'll have no trouble. The country's full of lonely servicemen's wives. I'll even provide you with a reference if you like . . .'

'Iris! It's not like that! Come back here, you stupid woman!' He leapt for the door, making a grab for her arm.

Dragging it open, heedless of the blackout, she fled.

'Iris!'

She looked back. He'd come outside. The skin of his chest and bare feet gleamed whitely in the starlight. Not caring who heard, she shouted at him to go away. 'I never want to see you again! Just leave me *alone*!'

She flew down the road, expecting to hear the slap of his bare feet on the pavement behind her. At the junction with the Prince of Wales Road she stopped, panting, and looked back. There was no sign of him.

With a sob she started to half run, half walk home. Ahead of her she could see the lights reflected under the swollen bellies of the barrage balloons and, further away on the horizon, searchlight beams lancing the night. She ran on, not really caring whether she was hit or not. How could she have been so stupid? So *gullible*? Her father had been right: there was only one thing men would want from a girl like her.

A scar-face, a cripple, a freak.

With a gesture of disgust, she scrubbed her hands over her face again, smearing off the remainder of the make-up. Pushing her hand through her hair, she dragged out the new hairstyle, hearing the combs and pins drop into the road as she ran.

The front door was unlocked. Her father must have forgotten to lock it before he went round to the wharf. The shaft of hall-light surprised her.

'Daddy? Are you here?' There was silence, as if the house was holding its breath. 'Doris, is that you?'

She opened the door to the sitting room. At first sight it appeared to be deserted. And then a whimper behind her made her spin round with a gasp of fright.

'Mummy! What are you doing here? Did the hospital discharge you?' She stared in disbelief at her mother. Ursula was hunched on the floor. Her face was grey and her eyes

330

were blood-shot. Hair stood away from her head in an awry disarray, and she was wearing a crumpled and worn coat that Iris had never seen before. She seemed to be clutching an empty medicine bottle.

'I can't find any, Iris. I can't find any . . .' With a small moan, Ursula started to rock back and forward.

'Can't find any what, Mummy?' Despite her anger at her mother's manipulation, the old habits asserted themselves. Dropping down before her, Iris tried to take her hands and massage the cold flesh.

Ursula jerked them away. 'My medicine, you stupid girl! I can't find any more medicine. It's all gone. Telephone the doctor, Iris, tell them I must have some more.'

'You can't, Mummy. The hospital said you mustn't take it. They said it was a miracle you hadn't killed yourself.'

'What do they know?' Ursula bared her teeth. 'I *have* to have it. Do you understand? I have to. Something dreadful has happened.'

'What? Is it Daddy?'

'Daddy?' Ursula stared at her blankly, not seeming to focus.

Impatiently Iris seized her mother's shoulders and shook her. 'Mummy, listen to me! What's happened? Is it Daddy?'

'No. It's not your father.' Ursula stared bleakly into Iris's face. 'I thought it was Kate, Iris. She had Kate's coat on.'

'Who did?'

'What?' Ursula's eyes had become unfocused. She seemed to be looking straight through Iris.

'Mummy!' Placing both her palms flat against her mother's cheeks, Iris forced her to look straight into her face. 'Mummy,' she said in a loud, slow voice, 'tell me what's happened. Who was wearing Aunt Kate's coat? Where is she?'

'The canal. Oh Iris, it's very bad. Very bad indeed.'

Chapter 33

Something was floating in the canal. A circle of white with two smaller circlets bobbing in its wake. The constable stared down from the road bridge, trying to work out whether it was anything worth salvaging. He couldn't quite see what . . . Abruptly the truth hit him.

'Bloody hell!'

It was a body, the face and hands the only visible things against the dark waters.

He looked frantically right and left. The immediate area was deserted and the nearest police phone box was the length of the street away. Dragging out his whistle he blew three sharp blasts while beating out rhythmic tattoo with his night-stick on the kerb. He paused to listen, and then repeated the performance. This time there was an answering note away to the west.

Stripping off his coat and helmet, he stuck them on the bridge parapet as a guide for the support that was coming, then scrambled up on top of it. There was no time to remove his boots. Taking a deep breath he jumped, hitting the water feet first. The cold knocked the breath from him and the shock of the bitter water shooting up his nostrils made him open his mouth and gulp down more of the filthy stuff. God, had it really been that bad when they'd swum in it as kids? It was a wonder they hadn't all ended up in the isolation hospital.

Treading water, he circled, looking for the floater. It must have sunk already. He took a deep breath, ready to duck-dive, knowing he'd never see anything under there but praying he might just get lucky and feel his way to the body.

The body found him. A hand rose out of the water inches from his face. He made a grab for it. The little finger was missing, the flesh still raw where it had been sliced off. Heaving upwards, he forced the body's head to break the surface. God, it felt cold, maybe it was already too late and he was risking his life to save a corpse.

He kicked harder, aware of the drag of his uniform trousers and the water-filled boots. With his chest heaving, he rolled the floater on to its back and got a hand under the chin. Where the devil was that help? It had sounded like he was along the Chalk Farm Road somewhere. How long did it take to run that distance?

He started to head in for the bank. His mouth dipped under for a brief second, making him kick out violently in panic. He couldn't die in a canal in Camden. It would just be too damn stupid.

Thrashing and fighting the water-logged clothing, he touched the rough bricks of the canalside. He wasn't sure he could heave the body out without help, and there was still no shout from the other copper. He looked up towards the bridge, straining for the reassuring outline of a police helmet. The sky to the south was alight with the silver shafts of searchlights. Thunder and lightning rolled over the sky. It sounded like a distant storm, but like all Londoners he was experienced enough now to recognise the barrage of the anti-aircraft guns. The raiders were coming this way after all.

Tipping his head back, he drew breath while he still had some to spare and bawled: 'Help! Police . . . Help!'

The nearer guns were opening up. Regent's Park, by the sound of it. He could hear the heavy beat of the bombers' engines now above his own thundering heart and panting breath. The distant whistle of descending bombs turned into the sharp rumble of explosions as they found a target. Where the hell was the other bloke?

'Help! Somebody help!'

'Where are yer?'

'Here!' Using the last of his strength, he transferred the body to one arm and thrashed the water with the other.

The dim light of a shaded torch darted uncertainly on the water a few feet from the bank, trying to locate him.

'Here! Here!' He smashed the water harder, splashing spray up in all directions.

The wavering circle slipped back, picking out the striped band on his uniform cuff. 'Oi got yer, oi got yer.'

The other constable's pale face loomed above him. Stripping off the tin helmet before it tipped into the canal, he extended a hand. 'Give it here. Oi'll pull yer up.'

Kicking his legs, which were already numb below the knees, he heaved the woman above his head. Her waterlogged skirt closed round his face, preventing him from breathing. Panicking, he jerked her away, causing the second PC to lose his grip on her.

'Steady, there. You'll have me in there with the pair of yer.'

'Sorry.' With a last determined heave, he got his hands round her hips and thrust. She soared upwards and her weight was gone.

He sank back himself and was frightened to feel the waters closing over his mouth. Desperately, he beat the water with downward flailing arms and broke the surface again.

'Oi . . . don't you be drowning yourself now. Get a hold of this.'

He twisted his wrist into the other man's proffered belt gratefully. The leather cut into the skin of his freezing wrist as he was tugged, spitting and cursing, on to the towpath.

Collapsing finally on his hands and knees, he coughed and choked up a stream of filthy water while his rescuer turned the woman on her face and pumped her lungs.

Her body jerked with each movement as she was told to, 'Come on, now, don't you be dying on me now. Not after my mate here has gone to all this trouble to be saving you . . .' The PC's voice was absorbed in an explosion – far louder than before – to the north of them. 'Blimey! They've hit something up Kentish Town or I'm a Dutchman. Come on now, lassie, come on. Would you be taking just one little breath for me now?'

With a groan, the body jerked. A trickle of water spurted from between her white lips.

Crawling across, water still streaming off his uniform, the first constable took up his colleague's torch and played it over the woman. Her long hair was lying like seaweed over her face. Gently, he stroked it away. His fingers came away sticky with blood. 'She's taken a bad knock somewhere.' He moved the sodden mass over her skull until he found the indentation at the back, where the bone had cracked and was leaking blood and fluid in rivulets that flowed over the pale, freckled skin of her face.

The second man craned forward for a better look. 'Blimey, she ain't no more than a kid. Can't be more than thirteen.' He pushed his fingers to the soft flesh under her jaw-line. 'I can't hardly feel a pulse. I reckon she'll be a goner before morning.'

Chapter 34

The all-clear sounded at two o'clock, but it was nearly dawn before her father arrived home.

Iris went to the head of the stairs as soon as she heard the front door opening and the light switch being clicked up and down. Holding a candle aloft, she said, 'The electricity's off. The telephone isn't working either.'

Fred glanced upwards. 'I thought you'd be down a shelter. You weren't here in the raid, were you?'

'We stayed under the stairs.'

'We . . . ?' Even in the dim light cast by the solitary candle, she saw the anger suffusing his face as the implication of her appearing from the direction of the bedroom occurred to him. 'If you've let that boater feller into your bed, you little slut . . .'

Iris regarded him coldly. 'Isn't that rather like the pot calling the kettle black, Daddy?'

'What the devil's that supposed to mean?'

'I think you know very well.' She held his gaze, until in the end he was the one who looked away. Only then did she say, 'And I didn't mean me and Taz. I meant me and Mummy.'

'Your mother? What are you talking about? She's in the St Pancras Hospital.'

'She came home. She's in bed now. I gave her some whisky in milk to make her sleep. I didn't know what else to do. She keeps saying she wants her medicine.'

'Of course she wants the bloody medicine!' Fred came up the stairs two at a time. 'That paraldehyde stuff is addictive, the quack said. She's like a drunk needing another glass to keep the heebie-jeebies at bay. So help me if Siddons ever recovers I'll see the bloke in court. Where is she?'

Tucked under the eiderdown with her soft brown hair spread on the pillow and the lines of her face relaxed by sleep and lit by the kinder glow of candlelight, Ursula looked at least ten years younger than her forty-five years.

Fred soothed a wisp from her forehead and tucked the edge of the covers tighter under her chin. The tenderness in the gesture surprised Iris. How could he have feelings like that for her mother and yet still keep a mistress? Because no matter how hard she tried to fool herself, she could no longer pretend that the redhead in Selfridges was just a clerk in the council or some building material supplier who was susceptible to a little judicious bribery.

Ursula shook her head and moaned softly as a thunderous knocking reverberated off the front door panels.

'Who the devil's that at this hour?'

'It might be someone from the ARP post.' It had happened before when the post's own telephone had been out of action.

'Fred!' Ursula's eyes suddenly sprang open; her fingers locked on her husband's wrist. 'Fred, you won't let them take Ernest's inheritance away, will you?'

'No. Course I won't, old girl. Don't you fret.'

Their visitor slammed a fist against the door again, but Fred couldn't prise his wife's grip off.

'I'll go.' Tilting another candle against the stub on the dresser until it caught, Iris tripped downstairs again.

Her mind was so certain it would be an ARP warden that her lips were already forming an explanation that their telephone was also out of use when she saw who was standing on the step.

'Please . . . don't . . .' Taz's foot slammed into the door, preventing her from closing it.

'Go *away*! Just go away!' She couldn't push him off the step. 'Get out,' she hissed. 'I've told you, I never want to see you again.'

'Iris, you've got it wrong . . . honestly.'

'I know I did. And more fool me. Now get out or I'll scream. My father's here.'

'I just want to know where Mrs Kate lives.'

'Pardon?' Surprise made her relax her pressure on the door. It flew back, letting Taz step inside the hall and close it behind him.

'Addie ain't come home. I thought first off she'd gone down a shelter, but when she never came back after the all-clear I went round that place they had the dance. It's been hit. They were digging casualties out when I got there.'

'Hit?' The candle stub guttered and sunk as the wick curtseyed into a pool of melted wax. 'How bad was it?'

'Fatalities, they reckon. I dunno. I went up the hospital in Hampstead. The blokes digging them out said they'd taken casualties up there. But I couldn't find Addie . . .'

'Iris? What's going on down there?' Fred descended a few stairs until he could see their caller more clearly. 'What the devil's he doing here?'

'The dance hall's been hit, Daddy. He's looking for his sister.'

'What would his sister be doing here?'

'Nothing if she's any sense, mister. Which she has, unlike her brother. I thought maybe she'd gone home with your cousin. She went round there this afternoon so they could get dressed up together. Like as not she's gone back there. Now, where's Mrs Kate live?' He gripped Iris's shoulder.

This time she didn't try to struggle free as the implication of what he'd just said hit her. 'Oh Lord, Daddy. Pansy was going to the dance. She'll be all right, won't she? I mean, Aunt Kate would have rung if . . . except our telephone isn't working. And anyway, it would be quicker to run here than find a box . . .' Iris grabbed her coat from behind the door and left, leaving her father's reproachful voice behind her.

There were faint streaks of lemon in the sky and a dawn freshness in the air, which was mingled with the inevitable railway soot, and something else: a grittier scent of dust and explosive, carried down the hill on the north wind.

'Why didn't you ask Nana for the address?' Iris asked as they hurried towards the High Street.

'She ain't back neither. Nor the old boy from upstairs. Probably took shelter up near the theatre.'

Iris glanced up the road. 'I can't see any fires.'

'I don't think it caught on fire. Loads got out before it came down, went to the shelters underneath. There's a few still down there, sleeping. Not Addie, though. I looked . . .' He was talking rapidly, his words tripping over each other, not like his usual slow, measured speech at all. Iris guessed he was using sound to drive out the pictures of Addie lying crushed under the bricks of the Carlton Road factory.

They dashed over the main road and down Kelly Street. There was no answer to her knock, but when she tried the latch the door swung open on to an unlit passage.

'Auntie Kate? Pansy?'

Taz came inside behind her. 'Addie! You here, kid?'

The house remained stubbornly silent. Swiftly Iris checked the kitchen. The blackout curtains were still drawn. Running lightly upstairs she looked in the two rooms: Pansy's bed was untouched; her aunt's had an indentation in the covers and pillows, as if somebody had lain on top. She felt it and discovered it was cold.

'What now?' Taz said as she came back downstairs. 'Where'd they have gone? The wharf?'

'No. My father's just come from there.' Her eyes fell on something she hadn't noticed before. A fire bucket, stirrup pump and tin helmet shaped like a pudding basin were jumbled behind the front door. 'They're supposed to be kept by whoever's on street-fire duty. She'd not have gone out and just left them. Unless something happened to make her forget . . .'

The same thought struck them both. Suppressing a shiver, Iris turned up her coat collar. 'Come on, let's go down the main ARP control centre. They'll have reports on the casualties.'

The clerk from the Women's Voluntary Service who was co-ordinating the list of casualties was apologetic but couldn't supply any names yet.

'But can't you just tell us if any young girls have been taken . . . well, anywhere?' Iris pleaded.

Using a ruler as a marker, the woman ran down a hand-written list. 'Hampstead General?'

340

'I've been there, miss. She ain't up there.'

'Some were taken to St Pancras, but they're mostly . . .' She was talking to an empty space; Taz and Iris had already fled into the grey light washing over the streets.

They were half running, half trotting along the pavement, a wary foot of space between them.

'You're wrong, yer know, Iris. I love you.'

'Do you?'

'Yeah. You don't believe me, do you?'

'No.'

They were at the doors to the hospital. Pushing inside, Iris buttonholed a porter and asked about casualties from the raid.

'Down the corridor, first right through the swing doors. The others are waiting.'

The walls were tiled and the floors scuffed with the marks of gurneys. She found herself with her head bent, following the parallel lines of wheel marks rather than looking ahead. Her hair fell over her face in two thick curtains. Taz made to loop one side behind her ear. Angrily she slapped his hand down. 'Leave me alone.'

The black lines went under a set of double doors. She followed slavishly, forcing Taz to swing them open rather than let her walk into them.

There were feet ranged on both sides of the corridor, their owners sitting patiently on the benches waiting. She located a pair she recognised before raising her head – and looking straight into her Aunt Kate's stricken eyes.

'Aunt Kate! Is Pansy—'

'They're tidying her up now, before we go and see her.' Tears trembled and brimmed over Kate's blue eyes. She swallowed convulsively and gripped the hand of the girl sitting next to her so hard that Iris could see the knuckles gleaming whitely through her skin.

The girl didn't seem to mind. Tears were trickling down her own face, puddling behind the lenses of her spectacles and gushing around the sides of the frames. Iris vaguely recognised her as someone she'd seen shopping with Pansy. Beyond them Pansy's boyfriend was huddled against a small, dark-haired, middle-aged woman. She was stroking the back of his neck and murmuring into his hair in a way that only a mother could get away with.

'What about Addie?' Taz demanded. 'That's her coat yer wearing. Is me sister here too?'

'Addie?' Kate looked up in surprise. 'No, she's not. I assumed she'd gone home – back to Nana's. I had to take her coat, she's got mine. Maury?'

She had to repeat his name before he looked round.

'What?'

'Addie Dixon? What happened to her?'

'Pushed off, didn't she?' He rested his head on his mother's shoulder, plainly uninterested in the boat girl's fate.

The next second he was dangling by his lapels from Taz's fists. *'Where . . . is . . . my . . . sister?'*

'Let him go! Set him down. Can't you see his leg's hurt?'

Eileen hadn't brought up six sons without knowing how to control them. A fierce twist on Taz's ear had the effect of making him release Maury, who dropped back on the heavily bandaged knee and gasped with pain before collapsing on the chair as his mother answered Taz's question.

'Your sister left before the bomb fell, young man. A good bit before, in fact.'

The girl with Kate took a convulsive sniff and said, 'There was a fight with some drunk boaters wanting to dance with her – and that big man who's soft in the head. She went after they all got thrown out, didn't she, Maury?'

'Yeah. Jumped out the window. I dunno where she is. Ask Joshua. Or that lot of troublemakers from the boats.'

'The Geoghans?' The possibilities of the Geoghans having Addie chased over Taz's face. His fists bunched.

A nurse threaded her way quietly through the waiting rows of relatives. She came to a halt before Kate. With a convulsive swallow, Kate clutched the stained navy coat around her as if she were suddenly very cold. 'Now?'

'If you want to, my dear.' There was a spot of blood on the starched cuff that slipped under Kate's elbow to help her stand.

342

Lottie's request to come too was met by an enquiry as to whether she was a relative.

'I'm her friend. I'm her absolute best friend – aren't I, Mrs Cutter?'

'Relatives only today, they said. Perhaps later . . . Go home now, Lottie,' Kate said. 'It was kind of you to come and fetch me, but your mum will be worried.'

Lottie stood her ground. Her sister Sheila had gone home, so their mum would know she was all right. She wanted to go to Pansy.

'Your mum will be wanting to see with her own eyes you're safe. Believe me, I know she will, Lottie.'

Swiping her sleeve over her nose, Lottie reached down and dragged off the red ribbon that was still clinging to one of her unravelling braids. 'Will yer give Pansy this please, Mrs Cutter? It's all I got. And tell her I'm ever so sorry for those mean things I said. I never meant none of them, honest.'

Maury stood up and squared his shoulders. 'I'm coming.' His black eyes dared the nurse to object.

Before she could, his mother explained that he was Pansy's fiancé. Putting an arm round his shoulders, she added, 'I'll go with you, love.'

Iris was tempted to say she'd go too, but if Pansy was badly hurt then she probably couldn't cope with a large number of visitors anyway. 'Will you give her my love, Auntie Kate?'

'Yes, Iris. I'll do that.'

'And I'll come and see her as soon as she's feeling a little better.'

Kate raised a bleak face but said nothing. A strange look flitted across the features of the staff nurse, who'd stood back while they were collecting themselves together. Iris sensed she'd said something wrong, but it was left to Maury's mother to tell her what.

'Pansy's dead, love. We're going down the mortuary.'

Iris stood there for what seemed like hours, watching them recede down the corridor. Pansy *couldn't* be dead. Pansy was the baby of the family. She was the little cousin who'd clung to her and Ernest's fingers with her chubby fists, toddling between them round and round the wharf.

The rest of the waiting relatives were staring at her. It took her a while to realise why. They were transfixed by her scarring. She'd quite forgotten it. Instinctively she covered it with her hand. Embarrassed at being caught out, the watchers stared at the floor, walls and peeling notices from the Ministry of Information.

Taz touched her arm. 'I'm gonna go down the canal, try and find the Geoghans' boats. They can't have gone far.'

She went with him because there didn't seem anything else to do here. Morning had arrived outside. Hospital staff were already uncovering those doors and windows that were covered with blackout material rather than permanently painted over.

Both of them were lost in their own thoughts as they reached the main lobby. The sudden shout from above jerked them both into the present.

'Mr Dixon! Wait!'

The aggressive stiffening of Taz's frame and face told Iris that he knew the man running down the curving stairs – and he didn't like him.

'What you want? Matron's earrings gone missing?'

'There's no need to take that tone with me. I was about to send an officer to look for you.'

'No need to look for me. Yer know where I live – at me bail address.'

'And you were there last night, were you, Dixon?'

'It's *Mister* Dixon to you, Sergeant Spain. And, yeah, I was. Why?'

'What about your sister?'

'She went up the dance at Carlton Road.'

'With my cousin Pansy and her boyfriend.'

For the first time the police sergeant seemed to notice Iris. He wore wire-rimmed spectacles like Lottie Abbott's; except his were tortoiseshell coloured rather than gold. The uncovered windows behind them reflected in the glass, giving him an almost reptilian stare. 'And you are, miss . . . ?'

'This is Miss Iris Cutter. Daughter of the house where I carried out me daring jewellery raid. And this here is Detective Sergeant Harry Spain, the one your gran thinks is a . . . What did she say? A useless, half-baked whippersnapper.'

344

'There's no need for the lip, Mr Dixon. You keep strange company, Miss Cutter.'

'Do I?' It was on the tip of her tongue to say that it wasn't company she'd be keeping any longer, but the man's cold manner made her disinclined to allow him inside her private troubles.

'Is your cousin here, miss?'

'Yes, she's in the mortuary.'

'Oh? My condolences miss.' The glass orbs swung back towards Taz. 'Perhaps you'd be kind enough to accompany me back upstairs?'

'What for?'

'Because that's where your sister is.'

'Addie? Why didn't you say? Is she OK? Is she hurt?' Taz grabbed the sergeant, spinning him back to face them.

With deliberate slowness the man smoothed out the creases in the jacket of his brown suit before answering. 'She was taken from the canal with severe head injuries shortly before the raid commenced, Mr Dixon. A member of the metropolitan constabulary risked his own life to jump in and rescue her.' He adjusted his tie. It was brown like his suit and waistcoat. Everything about him was in shades of peat, from his thick, slicked-back hair to his highly polished shoes. 'At first it was assumed she had slipped from the tow-path and fallen into the water.'

'Never. Not Addie. She was raised on the canals—'

'But certain indications have appeared,' DS Spain continued as if Taz hadn't interrupted, 'that lead us to believe she may have been attacked and thrown into the canal. Now, if you'd like to follow . . .'

He was talking all the time he led them up to the first floor and through corridors to the small side room where Addie was lying in a single bed. Iris barely heard him. Her mother's voice swirled in her head, beating out a rhythm to each step like a marching band: 'She had Kate's coat on . . . The canal. Oh Iris, it's very bad. Very bad indeed.'

Chapter 35

Addie looked like an insect husk with all life sucked out of it. Bloodless hands, one padded with gauze dressing, lay on top of a white sheet, while a cocoon of bandages swathed her skull, which rested on bleached pillows. Her chest scarcely seemed to lift the thin cotton hospital gown as she took a breath.

'Kid?' Taz stretched out tentatively to take one of his sister's hands in his own. 'What have those bastards done to you?'

'Which particular bastards would they be, Mr Dixon?' Spain asked from the doorway.

'The Geoghans, of course.'

Iris said quietly, 'They're boaters. They were at the dance last night, causing trouble. Ask Maury. My cousin's boyfriend.'

'His full name being . . . ?'

'O'Day. He lives . . . I'm not sure . . .'

'Oh, don't concern yourself, Miss Cutter.' A grim smile flitted over the detective's face. 'Mr O'Day has already come to our attention.'

'What's up with her? How bad is she?' Taz's question was fired at the nurse sitting by his sister's bed.

She started to murmur that the doctor would speak to him, but the police officer butted in to state bluntly, 'Her skull's staved in. There's other things too. Bruises, broken bones. Finger's come off on the left hand. But the head's the bad one. Even if she comes round, they think she might be an imbecile for the rest of her life. Isn't that right, nurse?'

The girl was young and flustered, and became even more

confused as she tried to talk her way out of the situation without denying or confirming the detective's bald statement.

Taz ran gentle fingers over the thick bandaging: 'What have you done to her? She looks wrong. Her head's too small. Kid? Don't die, you hear me? Wake up.'

'We shaved her hair off for the operation. Please, Mr Dixon . . .' With both palms flat against his chest, the nurse tried to move him a safe distance from the bed. 'Adelaide is still coming round from the anaesthetic. She'll look better once it wears off.'

'Addie. Her name is Addie. She'll not answer to Adelaide.'

'Addie. I'll remember.' The nurse's tone was conciliatory.

'Why do you think it wasn't an accident?' Iris asked the detective.

He stepped forward. The nurse watched warily but didn't try to prevent him easing down the neck of Addie's gown a couple of inches. A ring of ugly purple bruises decorated her throat like a necklace tattooed on the flesh. 'Those are finger-marks. Someone tried to throttle her before she went in the water. They didn't come out until she was on the operating table. That's when I was called in – fortunately for you, Mr Dixon.'

'Why? What do you reckon I need that particular piece of luck for?'

Calmly DS Spain rearranged the gown over the bruising. 'She had no identification on her. It could have taken days to establish who she was if I hadn't recognised her from our previous . . . convergence, shall we say?'

'It ain't what I'd call it.'

There was a spare chair in the corner of the room. Taz sat himself by the bed and reclaimed his sister's hand. 'You can get lost now, mister. I don't want you near her no more.'

'I shall need to question her when – or if – she regains consciousness.'

'You stop away from her! This is your fault. If you hadn't kept us here we'd have been away on the water and the Geoghans wouldn't have got near her. I'd have seen to that. But they'll pay. By God, they'll pay . . .'

'Don't do anything stupid, Dixon. Catching whoever did

this is our job. Where can I find these Geoghan characters?'

'Dunno. They tie up along by the Hampstead Road locks sometimes. If they ain't there they'll not have gone far. No further than Paddington if they let go at first light, I reckon.'

'Right. I shall send a policewoman to sit with your sister. Good day for now, Miss Cutter.' The detective sketched a slight bow in Iris's direction. She almost expected him to click his heels.

Once he was gone there was a silence in the ward except for the barely perceptible sound of Addie's breathing.

The nurse stood up. 'I'm going to tell Sister you're here. She'll want to talk to you. Doctor too. I'll leave the door open. You just shout if anything happens. I'll be back before you know I've gone.'

Taz nodded vaguely, his intent gaze fixed on his sister's face.

'Shall I stay?' Iris asked once they were alone.

'No.'

He didn't even bother to look at her. She didn't know whether she was relieved or hurt. What did it matter anyway? Last night already seemed like a year ago.

She went home via the wharf. It occurred to her that someone ought to tell her Uncle Pete about Pansy – and while she was arranging what she'd say in her head it kept out the sound of her mother's voice complaining: *'She had Kate's coat on. The canal. Oh Iris, it's very bad. Very bad indeed.'* She'd been aware of her mother's growing dislike for her sister-in-law ever since she and Uncle Pete had announced that they were going to live together as man and wife, but surely Ursula wouldn't do something so wicked? Despite her manipulating and snobbery, her mother had never been violent. As children she and Ernest had never had any fear of slaps and spankings, which some of their playmates had taken for granted. Normally her mother hated physical punishment. But a small voice inside her head pointed out that her mother wasn't normal at present. Like a drunk needing another glass was how her father had described Ursula's addiction to the peppermint cordial. And drunks didn't behave normally, did they? Perhaps Ursula had pushed the girl into the water. Addie was smaller and lighter than Kate, but that might not have shown in the blackout if she was muffled up in Aunt Kate's big coat. If Ursula had got her hands round her throat and prevented her crying out, there would have been no telltale accent to give away Addie's identity, would there? Not until she was flying backwards into the water – and by then it would be too late.

'The canal. Oh Iris, it's very bad. Very bad indeed.'

Iris tried to push all these dreadful pictures out of her mind. How could she think her own mother was a potential murderess? And if it was true, what could she do about it? The idea of telling that cold, austere detective sent a deep chill through the core of her body. She'd never understood people who shielded violent criminals, while knowing them for what they were. But now she did. No matter what Ursula might have done, she was still her mother. Never in a million years could she start off a chain of events that would result in Ursula being trapped in a cell with the threat of a noose in the future.

'Iris! Is everything all right at home?'

The shouted enquiry breaking into her frightened thoughts was so absurd that it took her a minute to pull herself together and readjust to what was going on in front of her. The gates to the yard were locked, but her Uncle Pete strode briskly across the cobbles, slapping together his hands and sending out little puffs of brick-dust in front of him as she peered through the gap. 'I've been trying to ring your father. I can't get through on the phone. I was just about to step round.'

'It's not working. I expect Daddy doesn't want to leave Mummy on her own.'

Rapidly Iris explained about Ursula's bolt from the hospital and her present disorientation. Unlocking to let her in, Pete asked why the daily girl couldn't sit with her mother.

'It's Easter Sunday, Uncle Pete. Doris has the day off.'

'So it is. It went clean out of my head. It's because there's

350

no church bells to remind you now. I miss a good peal of bells, don't you?'

His voice sounded too loud and too jovial on her ears. How could he talk like this after what had happened last night? But then, he didn't know . . . She took a deep breath. 'Uncle Pete . . .'

'Tell you what, Iris. Step over to the flat a minute. I got Pansy an Easter egg. You could drop it in on your way home. Found a shop up Hampstead still selling them, would you believe? Don't think she's too grown up for eggs now, do you?'

'Uncle Pete, Pansy's *dead*!'

She shouted the words louder than she'd intended in a desperate attempt to stop the rattling flow of his chatter.

'What? What you talking about? Of course she's not dead!'

Rapidly Iris told him about the hit on the dance hall. 'Didn't you hear?'

Pete shook his head, his eyes dazed. 'No. No. I never. I got a few hours' sleep after the all-clear, then went up the flat for a bit of a wash. I've not seen anyone. Where's your Aunt Kate?'

'At St Pancras Hospital. I've just come from there.'

'Why didn't she come for me? I've got to go to her.' He held Iris at arm's length, his grip too tight. 'What about Joshua? Did she say anything about Josh?'

'No. Why?'

'He went to the dance. Bought a ticket himself. He never came home last night. I thought he'd gone down a shelter.'

'Oh?' Iris stared at him. That girlfriend of Pansy's had said something about a big man being in a fight, but it simply hadn't connected that it might be Joshua.

Their eyes held each other. And then Pete stared over her shoulder and she saw the worry dissolve from his face.

'It's about time you showed up.'

Turning round, Iris found Joshua looming behind them.

'Can I have breakfast, Dad?'

'Get yourself something. And then change into your work clothes and tidy up the cement stacks. But don't go near that shed with the cracked walls. It's worse than we thought.

351

I've had to nail it up again. Sleep down a shelter, did you?'

'Might have done.' Joshua's gaze was on the floor. He scuffed the side of a toe, refusing to meet his father's eyes.

Pete smiled and blinked back a few tears of relief. 'What'll I do with you, eh? Stopping out all night on the tiles . . .' He ruffled his son's hair in an affectionate gesture.

Joshua looked up. And revealed three long, angry, swollen scratches on the left side of his face.

'What the devil happened to you?'

'Nothing.' Pushing his father's hand away, Joshua trudged towards the flat.

Chapter 36

It seemed to Kate that her life had suddenly split and was following two pathways. Along the first, Pansy was still alive somewhere. Any minute now she'd come bouncing in from the shops, or the cinema, or a walk over the Heath, with a rosy flush in her cheeks and her hair in unruly wisps from the fresh winds, her eyes sparkling with life and a joy in the future.

But down the second route Pansy was dead, and Kate had to deal with the everyday routine that came with death. The WVS worker at the hospital had been full of routine. Would Kate like her to make the arrangements with the undertakers? She could ask the clergyman to call. Or perhaps she needed help to sort out something for Pansy to wear? Kate knew she was just trying to help but she wanted to scream at her to stop hurrying Pansy into her grave.

Finally she'd heard her name spoken softly and looked up to see Pete standing there in the chilly gloom of the mortuary room. He held out his arms and she flew into them, trying to draw comfort from the strength of his grip, the familiar smell of his skin and gentle formless whispers of reassurance he mumbled into her hair as he rocked her.

'She's gone, Pete. I want her back. Oh Pete, I want her back!'

'I know, love, I know.' He tightened his cuddle. 'There's nothing you can do down here. Let's be getting you home.'

'No! I can't leave her alone.'

'She'll be all right, Kate. The lady here will stay with her, isn't that right?'

The WVS volunteer gave a small, tight smile, because they

both knew she'd leave once all the relatives and formalities from this incident had been sorted out.

With Pete's grip on her shoulders, Kate felt herself being gently but firmly steered away from Pansy and towards the light.

'Just a moment, my dear . . .'

The green-uniformed volunteer hurried after them and proffered a small brown paper bag. 'Her bits and pieces. It's best you keep them for now.'

Kate nodded, pocketing them without interest.

Upstairs she found Maury and his mother still seated in the marbled reception hall. They'd left so that she could spend a few moments alone with Pansy, and she'd assumed they'd gone home.

'We were waiting for the bus,' Eileen O'Day explained. 'Maury can't walk on that leg.'

'I'm OK, Mum. Stop fussing,' Maury braced himself on the slippery wooden bench, taking care to keep the heavily bandaged leg held out at a straight angle as he struggled to his feet. The trouser leg on that side had been slit up to the thigh and the material was flapping loosely. His hands and face were bruised and cut, with the remnants of a nosebleed dried on his upper lip. He wiped the back of his sleeve over it and his mother tutted automatically and handed him a handkerchief.

'For Gawd's sake, leave off, Mum! Let's go! A bus will be along in a minute. And that flaming copper's coming back again.'

Kate looked round. She couldn't see any uniforms. The only person coming towards them was a mournful-looking man in his fifties with a walrus moustache and an expression of deepest long-suffering. He tilted his hat formally to Eileen and offered Maury his condolences again.

'The lady-wife holds that time heals. I trust it will prove so for you.'

'That why yer so keen to see me doing time then, copper?'

'Maury! Ta very much for yer good wishes, Mr Bell. You'll 'ave to excuse Maury; he ain't himself on account of Pansy. This is her mum by the way.'

Once again the sad-looking detective offered his sympathies. 'And to you too, Mr Cutter. She'd be your niece, would she?'

'My brother Bernie's girl. He died a few years ago. I think you met him when you were asking about that business with Ellie's . . . about the man my wife ran off with.'

'Actually, sir, I think I was asking about the takings from the insurance company's safe, which were the gentleman's other travelling companion that Saturday night. I'm afraid I can't call to mind your brother now, but it was a very long time ago.'

'Fifteen years.'

'As you say, sir. Funnily enough I found my notebook only the other night. Twenty-second of March, nineteen twenty-six. My first venture into the hallowed halls of CID, so to speak. I can still call to mind the smell of the kippers the lady wife had got me as a special treat for my breakfast that morning. And the scorching from the brown paper she used to press my suit. Funny the things that stick in the mind, isn't it? I can't call to mind your brother's face, but I recall you'd broken your arm.'

'That Sunday. My son hit me with a metal pole. He was just a kid then. He's nearly twenty-three now.'

'Time flies, doesn't it, sir?'

''Spect it's because we're all having so much fun,' Maury said, using the wall to help him hop around and get an arm round his mother's shoulders. 'Don't suppose you've got a police car handy when we need one?'

'I'm afraid not. WPC Crimmond and I walked down here. She to sit and watch, and me to check on the young lady's progress. A somewhat futile exercise, since the hospital had already informed the good Sergeant Spain that the effects of the anaesthetic would not dissipate for some hours yet. But then the Sergeant does like to—'

'Throw his weight about?' Eileen suggested.

'Demonstrate his firm hand on the tiller of every case. Dear me, isn't it amazing how one slips into the relevant vocabulary for the occasion? I suppose it comes with the other young lady having a boating connection.'

There was no reason why it should have been Addie, but probably by an association of ideas, Kate's mind flew to her. 'Addie! Did she get caught in a blast too? I never thought . . . Oh God. How awful . . . is she very bad?'

'Multiple contusions and a skull fracture,' Ding-Dong Bell intoned mournfully. 'But it wasn't a bomb that did the damage. It would seem the young lady was attacked and thrown into the canal. We understand she was at a dance earlier last evening? With you, Maurice?'

Maury's face twisted in the defensive scowl he often adopted when he felt he was being unjustly accused. 'She scarpered, didn't she? Bunked out of the cloakroom window. Some of them boaters, name of Geoghan, had a fight over her. One of them reckoned she was his girl. Wouldn't be surprised if they'd had a go at her.'

'And it didn't occur to you to go after her, son?'

The detective's gentle reproof deepened the scowl on Maury's mouth. 'Why the hell should I? She ain't *my* girl.'

The words brought a picture of Maury's girl to all their minds. There was a short, uncomfortable silence.

Pete broke it to ask if they were going to question the Geoghans.

'I believe we are. We shall be talking to everyone who might have been along that stretch of canal last night. That would include you, I assume, sir?'

'Yeah. At least, I don't know about being along the canal. I was in the yard. My brother came round to go over the books. We were in the flat until the alert, and then we went downstairs to the brick store. It's solid as a shelter down there. We played cards for a while and then rolled up in blankets on a pile of London Yellows and got a few hours' shut-eye. It's surprising what you can get used to sleeping through.'

'And you heard nothing suspicious outside, sir? Screaming? Shouting?'

'Not a thing.'

'The dog didn't bark? You have a rather vocal specimen, as I recall.'

'Dead. Hopped into the stable and got his ribs kicked in.'

'How unfortunate.' Whether Bell meant for the dog or the police investigation, no one felt inclined to ask.

Kate announced that she was going to see Addie, and was told it was impossible.

'Relatives and police officers only at the moment, ma'am,' Ding-Dong explained. He raised his hat again and formally wished them all a good morning before leaving.

'Let's go too, Mum. There's two buses gone by already while we been wasting time.'

'Maury, wait!'

Kate dug the brown paper bag from her pocket and tipped the contents on to her palm. The engagement ring and earrings twinkled in the midst of the coiled necklace. Miraculously they all seemed practically unscratched. Wordlessly, Kate extended them to Maury.

He hesitated and then delicately removed the earrings and necklace. 'Can you put the ring on 'er when she's . . . yer know . . . ?'

She nodded, closing her fingers over the precious ring that had meant so much to Pansy as Maury limped out, leaning heavily on his mother.

'She's got six children you know,' Kate said. 'I only ever had Pansy, and now she's gone, just like her dad, and there's no one needs me any more.'

'What are you talking about? *I* need you.' Spinning her by the shoulders, Pete shook her. 'I need you. Don't you ever talk such rubbish again, you hear?'

Kate stared. She felt very strange, as if he were receding away from her down a long corridor, growing smaller and smaller with each second.

'Kate! Kate! Can you hear me?'

She managed to say that she felt very cold.

'Come on.' He pushed her inside his own coat, clasping her arms around his waist and holding her fiercely tight. Clamped together like that, they walked back to Kelly Street.

'You go up to bed, I'll get your blackout down and stick the kettle on. Have you got any brandy or whisky?'

Mutely Kate shook her head. Her legs felt like they were full of sand as she pulled herself up the stairs. The door to

Pansy's room was standing open. She didn't want to, but a force seemed to draw her inside. Pansy's day dress had been flung carelessly over the bed. Automatically Kate picked it up and looked for a hanger. There was one swinging behind the door. Addie Dixon's boy's clothes were dangling from it, the flat cap jutting from a pocket. Kate gathered them into her arms too and buried her face in them. They smelt of the two girls: soap, youth and perfume. If she closed her eyes and breathed deeply she could believe they were still here, glowing and laughing with excitement as they prepared for their first grown-up dance.

When Pete brought up her tea five minutes later, that was how he found her, crying her heart into the crumpled bundle of old clothes as she rocked back and forth on the edge of the bed.

'Kate. Love . . .'

She raised wide eyes to his, her face suddenly etched with lines that hadn't been there an hour ago. 'Oh, Pete, love me.'

'I already do, Kate. More than I've ever loved before.'

'More than Ellie?'

'Ellie was . . . a madness. We burnt each other up. The only good thing that came of Ellie was Joshua. I know there's plenty think I'm daft to feel that way about a lad that's not got the wits of a ten-year-old, but he's my boy and I love him.'

'I know.' She took his face between her hands. 'I love him too, because he's part of you, Pete.'

'Ellie hated him for being part of me. The rotten part of me, she thought.'

'Don't talk about Ellie.' Still holding his face, she pushed her mouth on to his and inserted her tongue between his teeth. 'Love me,' she mumbled. 'Here . . .'

Using her own weight, she pulled him back on to her daughter's bed and started biting him fiercely. She needed him. She needed to feel his heart, to hear him breathing, feel him inside her. It was the only way she could be sure she was still alive herself.

The O'Day house was silent when Maury and his mother

wove their unsteady way indoors. Rose Goodwin had collected Sammy and Annie from Mrs Dibble's and taken them around to her own parents' house so that they could enjoy painting Easter eggs with her own unruly foster child. Pat was still on duty at the fire station.

Like Pete, Eileen suggested tea and bed as a cure-all for Maury's misery.

'I'll stick the kettle on. Make you up a hot water bottle. You get up to bed. Oh darn, how'd that cat get in? I hope it ain't been doing its business in here all night . . . Oh no, it's been at the food. Look at that . . .' She displayed an empty dish with a slick of grease over the bottom. 'I had a bit of meat loaf in there. It would have done for dinner with potato over it. And he's had the butter ration too.' Whipping open the back door she grabbed a broom as the tom that had been treating their Anderson shelter as his own for the past few weeks flattened its skull, lashed its tail and prepared for battle.

By the time she'd shooed it into the cold morning, Maury had pulled himself upstairs. When Eileen carried the tea and water bottle up, the door to his bedroom was locked.

'Maury? Can I come in, love?' She waited a moment before adding, 'I do know how you feel. I went through it when your dad died.'

Eileen made to set the tea and bottle on the landing, then changed her mind and called that she'd leave them across the way in Shane and Conn's room.

Setting them on the wood table that held the wash-basin, she soothed the rumpled blankets on Shane's bed and made a mental note to tick Sammy off for using it as a trampoline again – before walking lightly downstairs.

Inside the dark bedroom Maury sat on the bed and heard her go with relief. She didn't know how he felt. No one did. He'd been prepared to give up everything for Pansy: the contacts, the deals, the respect that came with being a big dealer on the black market. He'd put that all in abeyance when he chose to be loyal to Pansy rather than go with Carla. And now life had spat in his face.

Well to hell with fate or God or whoever was having a good

laugh at his expense – from now on he'd take the best deal and everyone else could take their chances. From now on he – Maury O'Day – wasn't going to care for nobody but Maury O'Day.

Chapter 37

The Geoghans were picked up at the Cassiobury Locks in Watford and brought back to London in a police van.

Matthus drew Sergeant Spain. It was a deliberate move on the detective's part. Thin, pale, undersized and with any backbone long ago knocked out of him by Blackie's tender care, Matthus was the weakest link in the chain. His instinct was to pacify by saying whatever the policeman wanted to hear.

Yes, he agreed they'd all gone to the dance. 'We heard blokes talking in the pub, said you could get in for nothing if yer was in a uniform – and Rickey, 'e 'ad a uniform, didn' he? And me and Blackie got badges, ain't we?' He pointed to the blue and white 'On National Service' enamel badge pinned to his shirt.

'Fond of tripping the light fantastic, are you, Matt? Don't mind if I call you Matt, do you?'

His hands clasped together between his legs to stop them trembling, Matt shook his head. The policeman could call him anything he liked – runt, stupid, dolt, useless – he'd answer to them all. The remark about tripping and light fantastic he didn't understand until the Sergeant rephrased it to ask if he liked dancing.

'S'okay.'

'Okay enough for you to want to go to a dance?'

'The men said they had a bar up the dance hall. Blackie thought we'd get drinks on account of Rickey. He's wounded. Been shot. He's a hero. Gets stood drinks all the time. 'Cept he weren't getting stood no more in the pub, on account of someone saying he'd shot himself.'

'And had he?'

''Spect so,' Matthus gasped in a rare burst of honesty. It didn't last. Pressed to tell the copper about Addie Dixon, he firstly denied seeing her there, then got tangled up trying to explain how he *had* seen her – but he never spoke to her.

'Why not? I heard a rumour you were sweet on her.'

Matthus shrugged, pressed his legs together even harder so that his trapped fingers became whiter as the blood supply was cut off.

'Look at me when I'm talking to you.'

Matt raised rabbit eyes, trying to assess what it was the copper wanted to hear next.

'Why didn't you speak to the young woman?'

'Wiv 'er mates, weren't her?'

It was like extracting teeth with blunt pinchers and no gas, but gradually Spain got him to admit that he'd had to have a few drinks before he could pluck up the courage to go over and talk to Addie in front of all them landies – even though she and him were practically spoken for and set to get their own pair.

'Pair of what?'

'Boats of course.' Amazement made Matthus lift his head and look the detective straight in the face for a brief moment. What other pairs were there?

'What did Addie have to say to that then, Matt?'

'Said as how her weren't mine. Said her were still thinking about it. Then that dafty said her was *his* girl.'

'What dafty?'

That Matthus *could* tell him. He'd taken enough cargoes up past Cutter's Wharf to have seen Joshua around the yard.

'So you got into a fight with Councillor Cutter's nephew, did you, Matt?'

''E started it.' And, Matt might have added, he hadn't done any fighting at all. He'd crouched under a table as soon as the first punches were thrown and left all the violence to his brothers. 'They only slung us out cause we was boaters. Never told no one else to leave, they didn't.'

Spain was well aware of the sequence of events at the dance hall, since he'd already taken statements from a dozen respectable citizens who were eager to lay information against boaters in a way they'd never have done had the brawlers been residents of Kentish Town. But he drew the whole story out of Matt anyway, and then asked what had happened when they all got thrown out.

'Went down the pub.'

'Same one as before?'

No, this was a different one. One Blackie had gone in before on account of fancying the barmaid. It had been a long way. They'd had to go over the canal and down towards the big railway stations. An empty truck had given them a lift in the back. The barmaid hadn't been there but the landlord had locked the doors when the alert went and they'd sat in. Even got a few free drinks on account of Rickey.

'What's the name of this place?'

'Dunno. Can't read. It had a picture of a big cross like they 'ave in church outside. Yellow it were.'

The Sergeant made a note and then got to the question he really wanted to know. Had Matt seen Addie Dixon after he'd left the dance hall?

'No.'

'We got witnesses say you did, Matt.'

'I never spoke to her,' Matt said promptly, swallowing the lie.

'What did you do?'

'Watched. Her run away. Her can run good.'

'Run away from you, did she, Matt?'

'No.'

Spain leant closer, bringing his face into line with Matt's. Matthus watched, mesmerised by the light reflecting off the detective's spectacles. 'Which way did she run Matt?'

'Downhill. Her ran down the hill.'

'Towards the canal?'

'Yeah.'

Matthus strained to understand what was wanted of him. It was plain enough that, had the detective suggested Addie Dixon had grown wings and soared off over the roof-tops that night, he'd have agreed that that was exactly what had happened.

363

With a sigh that could have been satisfaction or exasperation, Spain changed direction: 'What about Blackie? He have a fancy for your girl?'

'No.'

'Never tried to take a kiss from her?'

'No.'

The incident on the tow-path a few weeks ago, when he and Blackie had encountered Pansy and Addie on their way to the *Rainbow*, came back to Matthus, sending a flood of pink-tinged guilt up his grey neck. Pansy was a Cutter – one of the boss's lot. If she'd told about Blackie already, the police would be bound to believe her instead of a boater. He'd tried to explain it was the landie girl Blackie had tried to kiss when Addie kicked him – and he hadn't really been trying to *kiss* her, just needed a hand on account of having a few pints. And anyway, she hadn't complained, had she? He trailed off, sensing he'd caused yet more trouble for Blackie.

It was almost a relief to be locked in a cell by himself. As they were shooting the bolts, he thought to ask how Addie was.

'Bad,' Spain said succinctly. 'Very bad indeed. They say she might die.'

The uniformed constable in charge of the cell keys grinned. Behind the detective's back, he twisted his uniform collar, rolled his eyes and lolled his tongue in a grotesque pantomime of hanging. Matthus promptly burst into tears, curled into a ball and rocked to and fro keenly, softly, until he finally dropped asleep from sheer exhaustion.

Spain returned to his office – or rather, the Head of CID's office that he was currently occupying in the absence of Chief Inspector Jack Stamford, who was away on some unspecified course for Scotland Yard. By the time he returned, Spain intended to have this – his first important case since transferring to Kentish Town – tidily solved, with the evidence irrefutable, the prisoner plainly guilty and the reports a model of police procedure. There could be no room for mistakes this time. Not like the one that had ruined his first foray into the detective branch and caused him to be transferred back to uniform. This time, his superiors wouldn't be able to point the finger.

He'd taken statements from as many dancers as could be traced from the bombed hall, while others made door-to-door enquiries along the route from the hall to the canal. It was slow work since the blackout meant that no one had been looking idly out of an uncurtained window as they might have been pre-war, and those who'd been out and about on the streets didn't necessarily live in that area. A physical search had been initiated along the canal banks from the Hampstead Road Locks to Battlebridge Basin. The doctors had given their opinion that the missing finger could have been sliced off by a sharp blade, such as a boat screw, so it was at least possible she'd been dragged part of the way under a vessel and hadn't gone in the water at the point the constable first spotted her floating. The search teams were instructed to look out for any signs of a struggle and anything that might have come off the girl. Her shoes in particular were missing and they couldn't overlook the chance they'd come off where she'd been thrown into the water.

Accordingly the uniforms had quartered the tow-path and frost damaged clumps of weeds, assiduously examining any discarded piece of rubbish. It was one of these who finally managed to turn up something that brought a gleam of triumph to Sergeant Spain's austere face.

'Where *exactly* did you discover it?'

For the third time the searcher pointed to Cutter's Wharf on the map. 'I had my pole alonga-me, sir.' He proudly displayed the long, polished wooden shaft topped with a curled hook of brass that was normally used to latch high windows open and closed. 'Anyhow sir, I ran it alonga the canal sides just under the water. Things catch, see . . .'

And what he'd fished out had caught on a protrubance just below the surface in the strip of water between the wharf and the canal boat.

'Well done. Very well done indeed, constable!'

Iris opened the door to him. Her heart jumped wildly into her throat while her entire stomach turned over at the sight of him. Ever since she'd come back from the hospital she'd wanted to ask Ursula what she'd meant by 'something bad at the canal', but she hadn't dared because she knew she didn't want to hear the answer. And now here was the policeman who was investigating Addie's attack, asking for her mother.

'She . . . she's not well. She discharged herself from the hospital. The doctors say she mustn't have any sudden shocks . . .'

'Who is it, Iris?'

Her grandmother appeared in the hall behind her. Ever since she and Ludo had got back from the West End shelter they'd spent the night in, Nana had been back and forth between Addie and Ursula. Now she and the detective eyed each other – measuring up for strengths and weaknesses. Nana had won their last encounter when she'd managed to get Taz bail, but now it seemed the detective was scenting victory over something.

He kept them in suspense until he was facing Ursula. 'I'd like you to identify something for me, Mrs Cutter. If you'd be so kind.'

He drew the long string of beads from his jacket, like a conjuror drawing scarves from a supposedly empty box.

'My amber! Oh, you dear man, you've found my necklace.' Eagerly Ursula accepted her treasure.

'You're quite certain that is your property, madam?'

Ursula was positive. She showed him the engraved initials in the gold clasp: 'G.U.S. Those are my mother's initials – Gladys Ursula Sudbury. Wherever did you find it?'

Spain outlined the necklace's location – and his theory about how it had got there. 'He plainly dropped it over the side when my men came to search the boats. Probably hadn't expected you to be so vigilant, madam. No doubt he was expecting to be well away before its loss was noticed.'

'Rubbish! There's been plenty through that wharf since then. You can't prove Taz dropped it any more than any other Tom, Dick or Harry.'

The detective turned a look on Nana that was both deferential and smug at the same time. She was, after all,

Councillor Cutter's mother. 'Tom, Dick and Harry weren't in this house prior to the theft. You are quite *certain* the necklace disappeared just before Mr Dixon left the premises, Mrs Cutter?'

'Quite, quite certain.'

'Oh phooey!' Nana snorted. 'Taz wouldn't do anything like that! Tell them, Iris.'

Three sets of dark brown eyes turned in Iris's direction. She dropped her own mauve ones and fiddled with an ornament. 'I don't know . . . I mean, if the officer thinks he did, then perhaps he did.'

Spain's self-assurance became even more noticeable. At last these people were beginning to see things his way.

'You'll arrest him now, will you?' Ursula asked. 'And put him in prison?'

'That's up to the courts madam, not me. But I shall certainly be formally charging Mr Dixon.'

'His sister's in hospital,' Nana protested. 'You can't be taking him away from her now. She might die, for heaven's sake! Haven't you any family of your own, you cold fish?'

Ignoring the insult, Spain pointed out that he was actually aware of Addie's circumstances since he was in charge of the investigation. And he wasn't entirely heartless. After Taz had been formally charged in front of a magistrate, he wouldn't oppose bail providing Mrs Cutter senior was still prepared to provide a permanent address.

'Of course I am!' Nana snapped at the detective, but her accusatory glare was directed at her granddaughter.

As soon as the policeman left, she accosted Iris in the kitchen and asked what she thought she was playing at. 'Why didn't you tell him you were certain Taz was innocent?'

'Because I'm not.'

'What are you talking about, you silly girl? I thought you were in love with the man!'

'No. I think that was your dream, Nana.' Iris lifted her head, pushing her hair back behind her ears so that the scar was cruelly visible. 'I was to have the adventure you never had the courage to take yourself. Well, I've had it. And it's finished. Daddy was right – men will only want one thing

367

from a girl like me. Only it's not even sex. Taz wanted money. Fifty pounds to give a girl like me an adventure. Quite a bargain, really.'

'What on earth are you talking about?'

Iris told her in tight, measured tones. 'So, you see, I really can't say Taz is innocent. He needed money. Maybe he *did* steal Mummy's necklace.'

Chapter 38

Iris had slipped easily into the old routine of sticking by her mother's side. Ursula, she told herself, needed her. Her mother had flatly refused to return to hospital, despite their doctor's strong advice that she should allow them to carry out tests to determine how much internal damage had been caused by her addiction to the paraldehyde-laced peppermint cordial. He'd also warned that Ursula might display symptoms similar to an opium addict.

'She could become irrational: euphoric one hour, depressed the next. Her behaviour may be wildly inappropriate for the occasion.'

'We'll hardly notice the difference then,' Nana had muttered under her breath.

'I can't stay home,' Fred had said bluntly. 'Pete wants to spend time with your Aunt Kate so I've got to get down the site. You'll have to watch her, Iris. Doris can give you a hand. And your gran.'

Iris had nodded. She'd expected nothing else. So Marlene's clothes had been parcelled up and returned, together with a letter of apology and a five-pound note, and Iris had prepared to deal with the invalid.

However, after a brief spell of weeping and incoherent accusations of persecution, Ursula had become remarkably calm. Her only renege to her former addiction had been to insist on locating a sweet-shop that sold extra-strong peppermints and arranging for a four-ounce package to be kept under the counter for her each week. She soon seemed so much better that Iris had felt obliged to agree to leave her in Doris's care and deputise for Kate in the wharf office.

She'd spent the morning laboriously typing up invoices and orders and sorting out the hourly time-cards, and was busily poring over squiggled figures on a lined cardboard sheet for a temporary plasterer when Pansy's boyfriend strolled in without knocking.

'Oh. Thought Mrs C. would be 'ere.'

'She had to go to the funeral parlour to make the arrangements. Pansy's there now if you want to see her.'

Maury drove his hands deeper into his overcoat pockets and shrugged. 'Ain't no point, is there? She's dead. Gawping at her ain't going to bring her back. Anyhow I got work to do. Josh about?'

'I think he's in the stable, mucking out.'

She went to door and shouted. Joshua slouched out from behind Kitchener's makeshift stable and came reluctantly towards them, his head hung and every step suggesting he'd much rather be somewhere else.

'Got a bit of business on. I need yer. Get yer coat.'

Joshua raised doubtful eyes. 'We going to your house, Maury?'

'Dunno. Might do later.'

'See Maury's mum?'

'I expect so. She lives there, don't she?'

'Is she angry with Joshua?'

'Me mum? No. Why?'

Joshua mumbled at his boots that he'd thought perhaps Maury's mum would be cross. Those disconcerting light lavender eyes peeped from under the thick eyebrows. It was the first time Iris had seen her cousin properly since she'd come into the yard, and at the sight of his face she drew a sharp breath and pushed her fingers under his chin, tilting it upwards to the light in an unconscious copy of the way Dr Siddons had always treated her.

'Josh, those cuts are infected.' She examined the parallel scratches on her cousin's cheek with concern. 'Come into the office, I'll get the first-aid box.'

Joshua whimpered and protested as she applied lukewarm water and Lysol. The result was a cleaner face but angrier scars as they reacted to the disinfectant.

'It hurts, Iris.' Joshua tried to touch the burning skin.

'It will wear off in a minute.'

'Can we go now?' Maury decanted himself from the desk where he'd been perched, opened the outside door, and found himself face to face with the ubiquitous DC Ding-Dong Bell.

He raised his hat with his usual old-fashioned courtesy to Iris, but she saw his eyes flicker towards her scars. She no longer bothered to try and hide them with make-up. What was the point? She was ugly – the world might as well get used to it as she had.

Ding-Dong asked if Mr Cutter was present.

'Neither Mr Cutter is here at the moment. May I help? I'm Iris Cutter.'

It was a courtesy call, Ding-Dong explained, producing his warrant card. They intended to search the narrow-boats tied up alongside the wharf but it was nothing to concern Miss Cutter. They'd try to cause as little disturbance as possible to the work in the yard.

'There isn't any. They're all out,' Iris said frankly. 'What are you searching for?'

Apparently Sergeant Spain had decided to undertake a full scale search of the *Rainbow* and *Crock of Gold* for stolen property.

'That's ridiculous! I mean, we'd have noticed if Taz, Mr Dixon, had brought things on to the wharf.'

'As you say miss. But orders – as those who wish to reiterate the obvious so often point out – are orders.' Leaning back out of the door, he waved at someone. Navy-blue uniformed policemen trooped past the office heading for the wharf.

Ding-Dong's sorrowful eyes fixed on Joshua, who was huddled at the back of the room. 'Mr Joshua Cutter would it be?'

'Might be.'

'We've been wanting to take a statement from you. Some-how my colleagues seem to keep missing you. Maybe you'd like to step up the Station later. Tell us about Saturday night?'

'Joshua doesn't want to.'

'There's no need to be scared, Josh. The policemen just want to ask you about the dance and everything. Isn't that right, Mr Bell?'

Ding-Dong agreed that they were simply trying to establish everyone's movements on that night.

'See, they know your father and my father were here. And Maury was at the dance. And Aunt Kate was at home like Mummy and me. Now they just want to ask what you did? Do you see?'

Joshua nodded at the floorboards.

'I'd best go help the rest then, miss.'

As soon as he'd gone, Joshua announced he was going. He practically ran towards the gates, forcing Maury to trot in order to keep up.

Iris found herself drawn down the wharf where half a dozen uniformed men were clambering over the two narrow-boats. It was, as she'd told the detective, a pointless exercise. She would have sworn there was no stolen property on the vessels when she and Aunt Kate had taken them down to the docks. Otherwise surely Taz wouldn't have agreed to the trip and Addie wouldn't have left them alone on board, free to poke and pry wherever they liked.

A constable stuck his head out of *Rainbow*'s cabin doors and whistled. 'What about this, then? Looks a tad expensive for the likes of them.'

He held up a woman's coat with a thick collar of tightly curled Astrakhan lamb's-wool. Iris recognised it instantly. 'That's Aunt Kate's. She loaned it to Addie.'

'When was that, miss?' Ding-Dong asked, taking the coat.

'Saturday.'

'For the dance?'

'Yes. I suppose so. She, Addie Dixon I mean, had an old man's coat; it's not very ladylike and . . .'

'And your aunt very kindly made a loan of this rather smart garment.' Ding-Dong examined the label sewn inside the coat. 'So she'd have worn it when she left the dance hall, no doubt?'

'Yes . . .' Iris had always assumed that Addie had been attacked on the tow-path. Up until that moment it hadn't occurred to her it was a strange place for the boater girl to be if she was living in Nana Cutter's flat off Maitland Park. 'She must have come back to the boat when she ran out!'

'That was what Mr Dixon suggested, miss. A boater, he said, is happiest on the water. And if the poor little girl had been teased at the dance hall . . . I daresay she was in need of a little happiness, wouldn't you?'

'Yes. Yes . . . I would And she wasn't wearing the coat when she was thrown in!'

'A mercy, I'd say, miss.' Ding-Dong weighed the thick wool in one hand. 'If she'd had this on, she'd have gone and sunk like one of the lady wife's suet puddings. Never a light hand with the suet crust the lady wife, I'm afraid.'

Iris couldn't have given a fig for Mrs Bell's culinary skills. A smile lit up her face with such radiance that for a moment she actually looked beautiful. There was absolutely no way Addie could have been mistaken for Kate if she wasn't muffled up in her aunt's big distinctive coat. And her mother had had no reason at all to thrust poor little Addie Dixon into the canal.

Addie was still hovering in her half-life; she breathed, her heart continued to beat and blood flowed around her thin, pale body. But whatever it was that had made her Addie Dixon had gone. Occasionally her eyes flickered open and fixed blankly on the whitewashed ceiling, but there was no recognition in the dilated pupils. Nor any answering pressure when Taz chaffed her cold hands and talked about their trips on the canals, or when Nana sang softly to her, running through all the nursery rhymes she'd sung to her own grandchildren.

The nurses came every fifteen minutes to check on Addie, but a female police officer sat constantly in a corner of the private room. There seemed to be a rota of them from all the surrounding stations. 'In case she makes a dying statement,' one had tactlessly said. 'Or she gets better and talks properly,' she'd hastily added.

But the doctors had already warned Taz that that was unlikely. It was more probable she'd regain the use of her limbs and perhaps some of her intimate physical functions, but she'd never be able to look after herself again.

'You mean she's going to be a dribbling idiot, who has to be watched in case she messes herself?' Taz said bluntly.

'I'd not put it that strongly. But you should prepare yourself for the worst. There are homes for mentally incapable females. I'll make enquiries about a place.'

'No! You ain't locking Addie away nowhere.'

'Is there someone else who can look after her?'

'I'll do it.'

Like most of the hospital staff, the doctor had heard about Taz's appearance before the magistrates. 'I understand you're on bail, Mr Dixon. If the jury should find you guilty at the trial . . .'

'I never did it. I never stole nothing from anyone.'

'None the less, if the jury should choose not to believe you . . .'

'Which they won't, seeing as how it was Mrs La-di-da Cutter who pointed the finger . . .'

'Then you will in all probability go to jail. And when you're released, there is the possibility of the call-up . . .'

'I've a boat. Reserved occupation.'

Except of course by the time he got out he'd not have because the blokes he'd pledged it to would have taken it. And with nowhere to bring Addie home to, she'd have to stop in whatever institution they'd dumped her in while he was drafted into uniform.

The call-up didn't bother him. But he couldn't bear the idea of Addie being locked up in some mental hospital. He had seen one once years ago when he and Grandad had been out looking for rabbits for the pot. A great big building it had been, red brick with a huge drive and walls all around; the women shuffling about inside had had a vacant, slack-eyed, hopeless look and a strange keening sound that came from their mouths. He'd never forgotten that sound; it was as if the women were no longer human but creatures that lived in all his worst nightmares.

There was no way he'd ever let them do that to Addie. Better, a small voice in his head suggested, to put a pillow over her face now and get it over with. At least she'd go quiet and peaceful and not knowing anything about it.

The policewoman had slipped away to the lavatory. It was that tall skinny sergeant on this shift so she'd not be gone long. Unlike the others she never lingered outside to snatch a quick smoke or flirt with a passing doctor if she could, so he had only seconds. Sliding one hand under his sister's neck, he gently eased out the pillow. Addie murmured and groaned, twisting her head restlessly.

'Kid? Kid can you hear me?'

Addie gave another unintelligible murmur, turned away from him and lay still again.

He touched the back of his fingers to her face. She felt flushed. And she looked so young. With her head shaved and bound in all that bandaging, she hardly looked older than the five-year-old who'd refused to cry when their mum died, instead declaring that she'd work the boat now, 'just like a grown-up lady'.

His fist clenched. It was lucky for the Geoghans they were safely under lock and key at the police station because, he swore to himself, as soon as he got the chance, he was going to see to Blackie once and for all.

He half-raised the pillow over Addie's face, alert for any movement that would tell him she understood what he planned to do. The pillow wouldn't go down the final six inches. It was as if invisible hands were holding his own back.

'Is there a problem, Mr Dixon?' He swung round and found the police sergeant watching him.

Someone had given her a cup of tea. She handed it to him while she flicked the bedclothes back over Addie. The girl twisted and moaned softly again.

'Shall I take that as well?' The pillow was twitched from his grasp and slid smoothly back under Addie's bandaged head.

'She looked uncomfortable,' he explained.

'Yes, she does squirm around a lot. Perhaps that's a good sign.'

'That ain't what the doctor reckons.'

'Well, the doctor doesn't know her as well as you. Neither

do I, come to that. But from what I saw of your sister up Agar Street police station, she's a fighter.'

'Yeah. She's that all right, miss . . . I've forgotten your name?' He wasn't even sure he'd ever heard it. All the policewomen and nurses had looked the same to him; only Addie was real.

'McNeill, Mr Dixon. Sarah McNeill.' She retrieved her tea and re-seated herself before suggesting he might get some air?

'If . . . when . . . she wakes up.'

'I'll come and get you. I promise. Go on.' She jerked a head at the door.

He hesitated. 'I'll just walk up as far as the bridge. Over Cutter's Wharf, yer know?'

'I know.'

The twilight surprised him. He hadn't realised it was that late. Without the routine of tying up, unloading, loading and letting go, time had started to lose meaning.

The weather had started to turn pleasantly spring-like at last. It would, he reflected, be easier on the canals soon. The flowers would be out along the banks and there would be a warm sun playing on your back as you glided over the sparkling waters anticipating the next lay-by. He caught himself. There would be no more canal trips. That life was finished – just like Addie's would have been if that police sergeant hadn't come back in.

She'd known what he'd planned to do, he'd seen it in her eyes. Well, so what? They couldn't arrest you for what you were thinking. Which was just as well, really – otherwise he'd already have swung for what he wanted to do to Blackie Geoghan. Would do if he ever got his hands on the bloke.

He wandered on up to the road bridge where he could stare down at the canal and Cutter's Wharf. It wasn't until he was searching amongst the buildings for a glimpse of a woman's dress, or a head of dark curly hair, that he admitted to himself he'd been hoping to see Iris.

But the builder's yard looked deserted apart from a slight ribbon of smoke drifting from the chimney of the office building. His boats were still tethered to the wharf; their decks looked dirty and the brass was already dulled with the patina of railway smuts and brick and plaster dust. In addition the *Crock of Gold* was still scarred with the brown charred streaks from its recent fire. It would have broken Addie's heart to see it; while she'd never cared much for her own appearance, she'd taken great pride in keeping the craft in sparkling condition.

Tears gathered in his eyes and he brushed them away angrily before anyone should notice. He'd never liked this stretch of canal. Few boaters did. The soot-grimed buildings crowding the banks were depressing and the bridges were generally full of kids who took a delight in spitting at the boats as they passed underneath. There was a handful leaning over this one. He watched one nudge his mate with an elbow protruding from a large hole in his jumper sleeve and then gather up a wadge of spittle into his mouth as the prow of a boat slid into view round the far bend that led down to Cutter's Wharf.

'Oi! Want a thick ear, do yer?' Taz charged. The boys jumped down and fled towards the Rest Centre. He turned back to the canal. Both boats were driving along at a rate that was sending the wash against the banks in a series of deep waves. One actually broke over the top of the brick edge and sent a shower of spray across the tow-path. The *Rainbow* and *Crock of Gold* lifted as the two boats bored past them and slammed into the hard edge of the wharf.

'What's the idiot think he's playing at,' Taz muttered to himself. He looked at the steerer – and then looked again. It couldn't be! But it was: Blackie Geoghan. And Rickey was on the butty, using the tiller bar for support instead of his crutch. As he watched Matt stuck his head out of the cabin doors and said something to his brother.

All three of them were out of jail. Released or escaped, Taz didn't care. Addie's attackers were where he could get his hands on them. Spinning round, he raced for the entrance to Cutter's Yard, the quickest route on to the tow-path, where he could cut them off when they had to stop for the next lock gates.

Chapter 39

'Can I have a word, missus?'

Ursula sighed to herself. It was plainly going to be impossible to persuade Doris to call her 'Madam' rather than 'Missus'. Still, she supposed they all had to make sacrifices for the war effort. And apart from having to cope with a dull-witted daily maid, the future was beginning to look rosier than it had done for some time. Iris had given up that awful boater and settled down at home again. She'd also, Ursula noted approvingly, stopped wearing make-up and was now dressing in her most modest clothes.

And then there was dear Ernest. Ursula touched the letter that had arrived with the second post. Written ten days ago, but at least he sounded well. And he'd been made up to a lance corporal. She must talk to Fred and ask if there was something they could do to get Ernest promoted to an officer. A picture of Lieutenant or even Captain Cutter in a silver frame in the drawing room would look very well until the original came safely home to his inheritance.

And she didn't doubt now that the business *would* one day go to Ernest; she'd found a way to ensure that. It had come to her this morning how simple it would be to use what she knew to make sure everything went to her son. It was amazing how, after all the nastiness of the past few months, the sun had started to shine on her again.

Dragging her mind back from a pleasurable day-dream of the world once this awful war had ended, Ursula tried to concentrate on what Doris was saying.

'. . . so the thing is, missus, the lady says it's our duty to volunteer and let a bloke go fight, see?'

'Doris, are you trying to hand in your notice?'

'Suppose so, missus.'

'Don't be ridiculous! You are needed here. And what on earth are you preparing there?'

Doris scooped up a fat lump of the mess of boiled oatmeal, breadcrumbs, onion and herbs, and rolled it. 'Sausages, missus.'

'They look quite disgusting. Where's the meat?'

'Miss Iris said I weren't to use none. It's to be saved for the funeral tea.'

'What funeral?'

'Why, Miss Pansy's, missus.' Doris stopped in her production of the grey, unappetising tubes to stare in surprise.

Ursula flushed slightly. She'd forgotten that the funeral would be held tomorrow. Recently she'd found that time had an odd way of slipping away and twisting on itself. Only this morning she'd been sitting in front of the mirror rolling curlers into her hair one minute, and when she'd next looked at her watch a whole hour had gone by. It was really most strange.

'Very well, Doris. I'm sure the sausages will be quite delicious. When you've finished that, perhaps you would press my black silk. I have to go out. I have an errand to run.'

There were plenty of people around in the High Street, and Ursula walked confidently despite the dying light. Once she reached the steps to the tow-path, however, she experienced the same uneasy shivers of fear that she'd felt that night she'd followed the supposed 'Kate' along the canal's edge. But the thought of Ernest made her screw up her courage and walk delicately down the stone stairs.

She'd chosen this route rather than going to the yard gates because she didn't want to have to shout or rattle them if they were already locked. It might lead to her being noticed and someone could mention that to Fred. Far better to do this thing discreetly.

Those boats were still here, she noted with annoyance as she made her way through the gap and on to the wharf. There really was no need to provide free mooring for those people any more. She'd have to remember to ask Fred to get them moved before that boater man was put in jail for stealing her necklace. She'd never had any doubts at all that he'd been responsible for the theft – even if she hadn't been entirely truthful in her evidence to the police about the time of its disappearance.

Still, that wasn't what she was here for at the moment. She must try to keep her mind on what she was doing and not let it drift as it did so often now. Perhaps a little help . . . ? Fumbling with the clasp on her handbag, she delved to the bottom and took out a small bottle that had once held cod liver oil. Putting it to her lips, she took a draught of the brandy inside and then popped an extra strong mint into her mouth to hide the smell. The resultant explosion of burning sliding down her throat and into her chest was very satisfactory; almost as good as the peppermint cordial had been.

Breathing in deeply to increase the effects of the alcohol, she walked carefully over the uneven yard to the brick store stairs that led up to her brother-in-law's flat.

She'd been half afraid that Joshua would be here too. Not that the dim-witted ox would have understood what she was talking about, but there was always the danger he might repeat something to the family later. However, once more fate was shining on her. Joshua was out.

'Probably hanging around with that O'Day bloke. I don't like it much,' Pete said, taking the newspaper off a chair so that she could sit down. 'But I suppose it's as well the boy's found a friend. God knows he hasn't many. And if anything should happen to me . . . well, I know I can trust you and Fred to look out for him.'

The idea of Joshua in her house with his large hands and staring eyes filled Ursula with horror. You only had to look at poor Iris's face to see what the idiot was capable of; he should have been committed years ago – and *would* have been if she'd had her way. Well, if Pete went first, she certainly wasn't having Joshua living with them, but she supposed they might be obliged to find a suitable institution for him.

But it was the possibility of her own husband dying first that had brought her here, and she forced her wandering mind back to what she wanted to say.

'I know you did it.'

'Did what?' Pete had lit a spill from the fire and was holding it against the popping ring on the top of the cooker. He didn't turn, but she saw the flame shake slightly and knew he understood, even if he chose to pretend otherwise.

'I know it was you who attacked that girl from the boats.'

'Oh?' He adjusted the gas jet and set the kettle on before coming back and sitting by the table.

'I saw you. I . . . I was walking round the tow-path to the yard . . . and I saw you, with that girl.'

She hadn't realised that Addie was the female she'd been following. Despite the darkness, the woman ahead of her had walked with far more assurance along the unlit path bordering the canal, and had drawn well ahead of Ursula. By the time Ursula had reached the entrance to Cutter's Wharf the figure had disappeared among the storage sheds. Any chance of her sister-in-law 'accidentally' falling into the canal had plainly disappeared . . . unless Kate had only popped around for a few minutes and would be leaving soon. Hadn't Fred said he and Pete were working on the books that night? Wasn't it possible that Kate had simply come round to sort out some query and would come out again after a few minutes? It had occurred to Ursula that if she stayed hidden against the deeper shadows under one of the bridges and rushed forward as Kate came past . . .

It had been sheer madness. She could see that now, looking back coolly from today's viewpoint. While she might not have pulled Kate back if she'd slipped on the bank, there was no way she could have ever deliberately *killed* someone. Not even for her precious Ernest's future.

But on that night . . . She'd been shivering in Marlene's badly fitting and worn clothes, trying to make up her mind what to do. In the end she'd slipped quietly into the yard and started across to the flat, intending to listen at the door and work out whether Kate was staying for the evening. But she'd only gone a few paces when she'd seen a female outline tripping lightly from that direction. At first she'd taken it to be Kate and stepped into the shelter of the lime storage shed. But as the girl had come closer she'd realised it couldn't be her sister-in-law. The form was too thin and slight and the hair too long.

Since she'd never seen Addie Dixon she hadn't recognised her, and as the girl was no longer wearing Kate's coat, it hadn't instantly occurred to her that this was the woman she'd just followed into the yard. So, assuming Kate was still in the flat, she'd remained out of sight, waiting for the stranger to go away. The girl had seemed to be heading for the tow-path, until the sound of a door opening had echoed across the yard. From her own position, Ursula hadn't been able to see anyone else, but she'd guessed it had come from the old shed nearest the wharf.

She had seen the girl change direction – but her view of what happened next was blocked by one of the yard trucks.

There had been voices – one male, the other female. And then suddenly a loud scream. The girl had come running across the yard, heading for the wharf. Ursula had heard the creak of wood and slap of water, and guessed she'd jumped on one of the tethered boats.

Then Pete had rushed past. The edge of the shed she was cowering against had obscured her vision, but she'd heard his angry demands to come back and let him explain, followed by the girl's shouted: 'Stay away from me, yer hear? Or I'll do yer, I swear I will.'

Edging forward, Ursula had dared to peek around. The figures were almost invisible against the dark bulk of the buildings on the opposite bank, but the odd glimpse of pale flesh and the flash of Pete's watch had enabled her to make out their struggling. The girl was cursing like a fishwife and then she'd gone quiet, and the loud splash had resounded around the yard.

Still hidden, Ursula had heard Pete cursing softly under his breath. He'd seemed to be running up and down by the bank with some kind of long pole – trying to fish the girl out, she supposed. And then her ears had caught the quiet thrum-thrum of an engine away to the right. She'd lived near the canal long enough to know it was a boat coming up in the dark. So had Pete. He'd thrown the pole back on to the Dixons' boat and run back the way he'd come, disappearing from view behind the lorry again.

Ursula had waited until the moving boats had slid past the wharf and then hurried out to follow them. The shaded light on their prows had been reassuring as she'd made her shaky way back to the steps and hurried home to cower in the living room, until Iris had come in and found her.

The whole incident had seemed so unreal that, by the morning when her husband returned, she'd been convinced it had been some sort of hallucination – even finding the bits and pieces she'd intended to hide on the Dixons' boats still crammed into Marlene's coat pockets hadn't shaken that belief. Until she'd heard about Addie's rescue. Then she'd finally known who Pete's victim was.

'I suppose you wanted sex. Men seem to have no sense when it comes to that sort of thing.'

'Like Fred?'

'I daresay. I'm well aware that my husband is as weak-willed as the rest of you.'

'You regard the need for physical closeness – for loving – as a weakness, do you, Ursula?'

'Loving – no. I love Fred. I love my children. But as for that other business . . . life would be simpler without it.'

'Most people wouldn't agree with you.'

'No doubt. However, I haven't come here to discuss my marriage. I've come to discuss yours – or at least, what passes for marriage in your life.'

'If you mean Kate—'

'Well of course I do.'

'What about her? If you're planning to tell her this rubbish about me forcing myself on a girl that's no older than Pansy . . . well, maybe you should remember you aren't well, Ursula. Been acting a bit crazy since you came off old Siddons' peppermint jallop. Isn't that it?'

'I wasn't planning to tell Kate anything. I shall leave it to the police to do that. And to judge whether I am a competent witness.'

'Unless . . . There *is* an unless, isn't there?'

'Yes.' She'd been addressing her gloves, noting with annoyance that she was wearing one black and one brown. Now she turned her head to look directly at him. 'I want you to give up Kate. And promise not to form any other permanent liaisons. I've no objection to you going with women,' she explained hastily.

'Good of you.'

'But I won't have any bastards in the family. Male bastards.'

'You won't mind a female one then?'

Ursula's lips tightened. She gripped her fingers tightly to stop her hands shaking. 'I won't have another boy in the family. The business must go to Ernest. He deserves it. He's risking his life for his country. It's only fair. Surely you can see that?'

'And if I can't?'

'Then I shall speak to the police. If that girl dies, you'll be hung for murder. In which case Cutter's will all be Fred's anyway, and it will naturally come to Ernest.'

'Does Fred know you've come here to say this to me?'

'No. I told no one I was coming. It can be our secret, providing you agree.'

'Agree to give up Kate? Because I'd say it's sure as eggs is eggs she'll want another child. Not to replace Pansy – because nothing can do that – but as a comfort . . . something to cling on to.'

'There's no reason why she shouldn't have one. But not with you, Pete. If you have a son, you'll want to leave the business to him.' Her mouth was beginning to feel dry again and she realised that she desperately wanted another swallow from the bottle. But she wouldn't take it out in front of Pete. 'Do you agree?'

Pete rubbed his chin. 'I'm not sure, Ursula. It seems to me that if Fred and I were both to swear you'd gone a bit crazy—'

'Fred wouldn't say that. He's a councillor now. He needs me. A crazy wife isn't an asset at election time.'

'A dead one might be.'

'What?' Ursula felt her heart jump into her throat. She stared at her brother-in-law's implacable face. Surely he wasn't serious? But she'd told him that no one knew she was here. And he could only hang for murder once, no matter how many he eventually killed.

Oh God, she needed the brandy.

She'd actually opened the bag when they both heard heavy footsteps crashing up the outside stairs. Joshua! Thank heavens! Surely Pete wouldn't commit murder in front of his son.

Ursula stood shakily, ready to rush out of the door the moment it opened.

It crashed in on its hinges – but it wasn't Joshua who stood panting in the frame. With one eye puffed and closing and blood steaming from his swelling nose, Taz Dixon drew heaving breaths as he struggled to speak: 'They've arrested him.'

'Arrested who?'

'That bastard son of yours! The coppers have arrested him for what he's done to Addie.'

386

Chapter 40

Joshua didn't like the room they'd locked him in. He knew he'd done something bad and he had to be punished, but this place – with its high barred windows and door with big locks – scared him. And he was hungry.

He wanted to go home.

At first it hadn't been too bad. They'd given him tea and talked about things he understood. He couldn't remember exactly when things had started going wrong and they'd got cross with him. He thought it was when they'd asked him about the dance.

'You had a bit of trouble I hear, son?' the policeman with the glasses had said. 'Got into a fight?'

'They said Joshua's girl was their girl. Tried to make her dance with them. They were hurting her.'

'So you decided to rescue her. Very gallant.'

Joshua didn't know what 'gallant' meant, so he'd contented himself with draining his mug, letting the melted sugar in the bottom trickle down his throat.

The policeman who'd brought him here asked him what had happened when the Geoghans had been slung out.

'Joshua helped to pick up the tables and chairs and then he went to the lavatory.'

They'd both looked at notes in a book and nodded to each other. Then the one with the glasses had asked if Joshua had seen Addie Dixon after that.

'Yes. Joshua went outside.'

'You left the hall? You went into the factory yard?'

Now Joshua thought about it, he decided that was when they'd stopped sounding nice and started to get cross with him.

He'd explained that he'd gone out to see if the Geoghans were still hanging around so that he could tell them Addie was his girl and they weren't to go near her any more.

'And did you find them?'

No. He hadn't seen them. They'd already gone. But he'd seen Addie climbing out of a window, so he'd helped her down.

'Then what? Did you try to kiss her?'

'Might have.' He'd only wanted one kiss. Just as a thank you for his present. He still didn't understand why she'd got so upset. He always kissed people thank you when they gave him something.

'So she got angry did she, son?'

Joshua had nodded, his eyes still on the table-top.

'What about other things? Did you do other things that made her angry?'

'No.'

'We can tell if you're not telling us the truth, you know.'

Could they? Did the police have some magic way of knowing if he was lying?

The policeman had taken his chin like his cousin Iris had when she'd bathed his scratches. Only the man had held him much tighter, squeezing the skin so that it pinched and hurt.

'That looks nasty. When did it happen? Saturday night?'

'Might have.' Joshua had jerked back. He was beginning to feel uncomfortable in there and he wanted to go home, but the man had gone back to asking him about Addie.

'What else made Addie angry, Joshua?'

He'd tried to remember the other times: she'd got cross because of the way he was looking at her once. And she'd said he wasn't to touch her knickers – the policeman had been quite interested in that bit, even got him to repeat it a couple of times. And then they'd asked if he followed Addie after she left the dance hall.

'She ran away, said she was going home.'

And what had he done after that?

He didn't want to tell them. The one with the glasses had become more angry then. All the shouting and angry faces

388

had confused Joshua. He'd wanted them to stop; he'd wanted his dinner; he'd wanted to go home.

It seemed that signing the sheets of paper they had put in front of him might get him at least two of those things.

'You can write can't you, son?' the policeman with the glasses had asked.

Joshua had nodded. His dad had taught him his letters after the teachers had given up on him . . .

They'd given him a newspaper and asked him to read out a piece about buying Savings Certificates. He'd stumbled over some of the longer words but they'd seemed quite pleased with him for reading it all the way through. After that they'd handed him a pen and pointed to the line where he was to sign his name. He'd laboriously scratched 'Joshua Samson Cutter' in his best handwriting and put the pen down with a sigh of relief. Surely he could go home now.

But apparently not. They did, however, promise to fetch his dad. That made him feel better. His dad would punish him for being bad, but at least he'd take him away from this horrible place.

Now he fixed his eyes hopefully on the closed grille flap and waited.

'This is rubbish!' Pete flung the signed confession down with disgust.

Detective Sergeant Spain calmly shuffled the sheets together and remarked that he could understand why Mr Cutter might not *wish* to believe his son was capable of such behaviour. But wasn't it time he faced reality?

'What's reality? I've known Joshua since the minute he was born – you've known him for five minutes. So which of us knows him best, do you reckon?'

'Sometimes we don't know our nearest and dearest as well as we believe we do, Mr Cutter. Everyone has several faces: one for home, one for friends, one for work, one for lovers . . . Who you are so often depends on who you are with, don't you find, sir?'

'Whoever Joshua is, he's not a murderer. You've seen him. The boy's not capable of what you're saying here.'

389

Pete appealed to Ding-Dong Bell, since the man had seemed sympathetic when he'd come to the yard to pick him up. The copper had sent Ursula scuttling with murmured explanations about getting back for supper, and held back the blackout curtain for Taz Dixon with a suggestion that he go home and cool down since, by the looks of him, he'd had quite enough excitement for one day.

Wiping away dried blood, Taz had admitted an encounter with the Geoghans, but doubted they wanted to lay a complaint.

'I'm sure you're right, sir. I'd say those gentlemen have seen enough of the inside of a police station for the time being. Now, if you'd get your coat, Mr Cutter, sir? I've a car waiting outside.'

Pete had planned to spend the evening helping Kate prepare for tomorrow's funeral. She'd wanted to go and spend one last hour with Pansy at the chapel of rest.

In the end, Taz had volunteered to go round to tell her what had delayed him. Pete's initial reaction to this offer was relief that Ursula had already left. Bloodied and angry as Taz might have been, he'd seemed preferable to Ursula delivering the news to Kate – with her false sympathy and sly hints of knowing something special about the attack on the boater girl.

And he'd no doubt she would start dropping hints soon. Judging by the scent of alcohol on her breath earlier this evening, the drink would soon loosen her tongue even if she did intend to keep her promise not to blab about what she thought she'd seen at the canal. Mind you, it was quite likely that this smug, self-satisfied copper wouldn't believe her. He was so damned pleased with himself for getting Joshua to sign that confession.

'It's not worth the paper it's typed on,' Pete said now with disgust. 'Anyone can tell the boy's not capable of reading what he signed.'

'On the contrary, sir,' Detective Sergeant Spain answered, even though Pete had addressed the question to Bell. 'He seems to have a very admirable grasp of English. Much better than I should have expected. I hear you taught him. You are to be congratulated. There's many men wouldn't have bothered with a mental defective.'

'Don't call my boy that!'

'But he's not a boy is he, Mr Cutter?' Clasping both hands together on the table, Spain leant forward as if he wanted to draw Pete into an intimate circle that excluded the Detective Constable. 'I'll grant you he has the mind of a child. But he's got the body of a man. With a man's needs . . . if you follow me.'

'You think he tried to rape the Dixon girl?'

'Well, let's just say we think he may have pressed his courting a little too assiduously. I daresay you've noticed the scratches on his face? Did he say where he got them?'

'A fight. He had a scrape with the Geoghans up the dance hall.'

'We know that. But our mistake was in assuming he returned to the celebrations after the Geoghans had left. Well – not a mistake precisely. None of the other dancers mentioned his departure.'

'That's not to say he did anything to the girl. What about the Geoghans?' Pete protested hotly. 'They were the ones started the trouble.'

But fortunately for the Geoghans, they'd hitched that lift in the empty truck a few steps from the dance hall and it had deposited them outside the Golden Cross. The police had not only traced the lorry driver but a dozen witnesses in the pub that night. Faced with that evidence, the police had had to release the brothers just after they'd placed Joshua in a cell.

'You see how it is, sir. Your lad had motive and opportunity. And there's the physical evidence.'

'What evidence?'

'The scratches, sir. The scratches. Looks to me like a woman's nails have done that. The way we see it, he caught the Dixon female up and followed her along the tow-path. Both going in the same direction: him to your flat, her to her boats. Natural thing to do. And then he became . . . shall we say over-enthusiastic in his courting. Perhaps she started screaming and he panicked, tried to stop her noise. Maybe she fell in the canal by accident.'

It was so close to the scene that Ursula had described it was almost like experiencing déja vu.

It was, the Sergeant suggested, strange that Pete and his brother had heard nothing?

'The walls in the brick store are very thick. What are you trying to imply – that my brother and I helped Joshua get rid of her?'

'Not at all, sir. As you say, those stores are of a solid construction. And with a big lad like your son it could have been all over in a few seconds.'

Pete was silent. Spain seemed to assume that his lack of argument meant he was considering the possibility that Joshua had done it.

'It's no fault on you, sir. You've worked miracles with him. But the time has come to consider the future.'

'Meaning what?'

'I gather from my colleague that your . . . the lad's mother isn't living with you any more.'

Pete regarded the stony-faced DC Bell. It struck him as funny, how he'd stuck in the copper's mind all these years when he couldn't for the life of him have pointed out Bell as the bloke who'd come to take a statement about Ellie and Aloysius Barber scarpering with the insurance company's money.

'My wife left fifteen odd years ago. What's that got to do with Joshua?'

'The point I'm making, sir, is that there's no one to look out for the lad once you're gone. Maybe it's best to make arrangements now . . .'

'Arrangements?' Pete stared blankly. What sort of 'arrangements' was he expected to make if Joshua was being charged with attempted murder? The answer came to him as he looked into the two men's solemn – and slightly embarrassed – faces. 'You want me to have him committed to an asylum, is that it? You can't charge him with murder, can you? He's soft in the head. It won't stick.'

Spain answered him: 'That would be up to the court and the doctors to decide, Mr Cutter. However, I have to say he doesn't fit most people's idea of a mental defective. He's

392

capable of keeping himself decent, he can feed himself . . .'
The detective's thumb touched against his long bony fingers.
'He does some work in a labouring capacity, he tells me; he
can read and write. No, sir, I don't think you can count on
the courts finding him unfit to plead.' He realigned the edges
of Joshua's confession, even though the sheets of paper were
already sitting squarely on top of each other. 'I don't want to
see the lad hang, sir. If you were to want to sign the papers
to put him away before he goes up before the magistrates
. . . well, I'm sure we can delay matters for a short while.
It would require two doctors' signatures on the committal
forms, I believe.'

'So it's a choice between seeing the boy up in the dock
and facing a life locked up in prison, or the rope? Or having
him locked up myself?'

DC Bell interrupted to remark that a verdict wasn't assured
until the jury delivers it.

But Pete knew it was. Twelve strangers, seeing Joshua's
eyes glowering over that big, muscular frame, would feel
an instinctive revulsion to someone who was different to
the normal herd. It would be like a pack attacking the kid
in the playground with the sticking-out ears or the cross-
eyes.

'Can I see him?'

Joshua's relief at seeing his father was overwhelming. He
threw himself forward as he had done when he was a little
boy. 'Joshua's sorry, Dad.'

'There's no need, son. I know you didn't do anything
wrong.'

'Yes, Joshua did, Dad.'

'What?'

'Bad things.' Joshua hung his head.

Pete looked at the uniformed policeman, who was hovering
near the open doorway twirling the ring of cell keys. 'Can we
have a minute alone?'

'Against the rules, sir.'

'Can Joshua come home now, Dad?'

'No. Not right now, son.' Pete squeezed his son's shoulder.

'You stop here for now and be a good boy for the policemen, understand? And you remember that your dad loves you for always.'

'Joshua loves you too, Dad.'

'I know.' Twisting to face his son, Pete gathered him into his arms and hugged him fiercely. 'Don't worry, son. You'll be out of here soon.'

He left the station with a curt nod to the two plain-clothes men who were hovering near the front desk. Let them interpret that whichever way they liked, he thought bitterly as he walked swiftly down the road with long strides, scarcely seeing where he was going.

He needed Kate. But when he reached Kelly Street she was out. He went back to the Castle and had a couple of whiskies. When he tried to order a third the landlord shook his head. 'Two per customer, that's my rule. Bottles are nearly gone and I can't say when I'll get another delivery. I can draw you a half of bitter . . .'

'I'm not coming in tomorrow. Give me tomorrow's double on account.'

'Sorry, mate, it doesn't work that way.'

Pete slapped five pounds on the counter. 'How many bottles did you say you had left?'

The white note was twitched across the puddles of alcohol.

Five minutes later, Pete left with a package cradled under his jacket.

Kate opened the door to him this time. Once more he was struck by how much older she seemed to have grown over the past few days. The light had gone from her skin and the lines over her forehead and between her nose and mouth were etched deep and strong. Without speaking she drew him into her arms and rocked him, much like he'd just cuddled Joshua.

'The Dixon bloke found you, then?'

She disentangled herself from him. 'Yes. Oh, Pete, I'm so sorry. But I'm certain sure the police will soon find out it's all a mistake.'

'He's signed a confession.'

'But he can't have done. I mean . . . he didn't do it, did

394

he?' She looked into his face, cupping it between her hands, her blue eyes suddenly full of doubt.

'No. He didn't do it. But you see? You're his aunt, you've known him since he was a little boy, and you aren't sure now.'

'Pete . . . I'm . . .'

He put his fingers against her lips to silence the apology. 'It's all right. I don't blame you. You can't judge the boy by the rules you judge other folk by, because you and I don't know what's going on in his head. And that's how any jury will see it too.'

'What will you do?'

'Don't worry. I've an idea how to make things right.'

They'd been standing in the hall; now she drew him after her into the back kitchen and set the kettle on the gas.

'Forget that.' He put the newspaper-wrapped bottle on the table. 'Do you like whisky? It's funny, I've known you all these years, and there's so much I don't know about you, my love.'

'I like it better than gin or port, but not as much as brandy. Although I've only ever had a few glasses of any of them.'

'Time to make up for lost time, then. Have you got any glasses?'

She only had two tumblers. They were decorated with frosted green patterns. 'Pansy won these on the hoopla at the Hampstead Heath fair. She was so proud of herself.' Kate's mouth twisted as tears poured down her cheeks.

He took the glasses from her. 'Let's sit in the front parlour.'

'There's no fire.'

'I'll lay one.'

He crumpled newspaper and laid sticks of plywood in a criss-cross pattern, piling coal on top and setting a match to it before sitting back on the hearth rug and opening the bottle of Scotch. 'I'm sorry I couldn't come with you to see Pansy.'

'Taz came with me. She looked like Pansy, but not Pansy. They'd put make-up on her. Far more than I'd have allowed her to wear in real life. But that's silly, isn't it? Because this *is* real.'

'Were you all right? With Dixon, I mean?'

'Of course I was. He's a nice young man. And very much in love with Iris.'

'He said that?'

'Not in so many words. But I'm certain sure that's what he meant.' She was sitting opposite him, cradling her knees and resting her chin on them so that the growing flames flickered in her blue eyes. 'They've quarrelled about something and she won't have anything to do with him. It's sad, isn't it? Love can be so hard to find, it seems a pity not to take it when it's offered.'

Pete edged a little closer. He ran the back of his hand down her cheek, feeling the softness of her skin. 'I'm glad you took it.'

'So am I. So very glad.'

He hadn't put the fire-guard around the grate, and the growing blaze was scorching his cheek. It must have been doing the same to Kate's skin, but she gave no sign of noticing.

'You're the best thing that has ever happened to me, Kate. Whatever happens, I want you to know I've never felt as happy as I have in these past few weeks.'

'Neither have I, Pete. Even after Pansy . . . I don't know what I'd have done if you hadn't been here.' She gulped at the amber liquid in the frosted glass.

He drew her in closer, holding her by the shoulders and pushing wisps of hair from her face so that he could kiss her eyelids and down her nose. She turned her face away.

'What's the matter?'

'It's nothing.' Reluctantly she met his eyes again. 'I feel so bad, Pete. I didn't know what a horrid person I was until Pansy was killed.'

'What on earth are you talking about?'

Slipping her arms round his neck, she rested her forehead against his and spoke downwards so that her breath teased the faint hairs along the top of his lip. 'After we went to see Pansy, we went down to the hospital to see Taz's sister. It was so awful, Pete. Pansy had a china doll when she was little; it lost all its hair and the colour rubbed off its face – and that's what Addie looked like. I kept seeing them both in the bedroom upstairs, getting ready for their first grown-up

dance. They were so full of life, Pete. So pretty. And now
. . .' She jerked her head away so that they were eye to eye.
'Do you know how I felt when I looked at Addie lying there
in that bed, Pete?'

He started to tell her it was all right, not to upset herself, but
she interrupted him with a sharp, mirthless laugh. 'I didn't feel
upset. I felt *angry*, Pete. I was just so *angry*. All I could think was,
"How dare she be alive when my Pansy's gone?" So what sort of
woman does that make me? To be angry because a young girl
didn't die? What sort of person, eh, Pete?' She emphasised the
words with flat-palmed slaps against his chest.

He couldn't think what to say to comfort her, so he started
kissing her. Small, gentle kisses at first, that gradually became
hungrier and more demanding as she responded, until they
fell on the rag rug in front of the fire in a tangle of emotions,
needs and limbs.

Afterwards he would have carried her upstairs but she didn't
want to move, so he brought blankets and pillows down and
they lay in each others arms in front of the dying blaze for
the rest of the night.

When he woke the fire was cold ashes. Kate stirred and
woke as he drew his clothes on. 'Pete? What time is it?'

'Early. Go back to sleep for a while, love.' Stooping he
pressed his lips to the warm skin of her cheek. 'I have to
go. There's something I have to do for Joshua. A couple of
people I have to look up.'

She sat up, holding the blanket to her breasts. 'The
funeral . . . You will be there for the funeral? I need you
with me, Pete.'

He ran a finger round the line of her jaw and smiled. 'I'll
always be with you, Kate. Always.'

Stepping outside, he raised his head to the sky over the
rooftops and reflected that Pansy looked like having a good
day for her funeral. The absurdity of this idea struck him a
second later and he laughed out loud.

He was still laughing as he turned right and made his way
to Cutter's Wharf.

Chapter 41

'Wake up, lover.'

Maury grunted and moaned, blearily pushing the crumpled blankets from his face.

Carla was seated on a chair by the bed, one bare leg poking from her robe as she gripped the edge of the mattress with her toes and rocked it. 'Want a cuppa?'

'Yeah. Ta.'

Retying the robe, she sauntered over to the solitary gas ring.

Maury sat up in the bed and watched her. She'd accepted the news about the engagement philosophically, agreed it was rotten luck that his fiancée had been killed the very night he'd done the business with the ring, and taken him into her own bed with no apparent rancour at being rejected as a life partner.

When he asked if there was anything to eat, she shook her head.

''Fraid not. Not up here, anyhow. Terry might have something downstairs. Want me to look?'

'No. Don't bother. They'll have food after the funeral. I'd best get going. Griswald got a razor I can borrow?'

Crossing to the wardrobe, Carla delved in an old tin box in the bottom and pulled out an old cut-throat.

'That his?'

'No. Here.' She threw a stick of shaving soap on to the blankets. Her tone once again implied that he had no right to question what she did and who she did it with.

When he returned to the bedroom, Carla had dressed herself as far as her slip and was busy brushing off his new suit.

'It's a good bit of cloth, this.'

'Belonged to a titled bloke, according to Levy.'

'Everything in Levy's shop belonged to the aristocracy, according to him. It's a wonder there ain't a whole queue of dukes, earls and ladyships round the block every Monday morning.'

'It ain't a pop-shop. And those sort of people don't go flogging their stuff themselves, do they? Mr Levy goes round their places. Buys it from the servants.'

'Well he ain't going to find many of them for much longer. Most of the footmen and butlers have already been drafted I reckon, and the rate things are going, the parlourmaids will be in khaki by Christmas. And the barmaids too – unless they've fixed up a trip down the aisle before time. How about it?'

'What?' Maury stared at her. Had she not understood what he'd said about Pansy?

'Yeah, I know. You were going to marry her. Fair enough. Your choice. But she's dead now, so you've got to look elsewhere. I'm still available, so what about it?'

'Are you barmy? Pansy ain't bloody buried yet, and you're expecting me to take the ring off her finger and stick it on yours?'

'No I ain't, Maury. I expect me own ring. You can afford it.' Calmly she stepped into her skirt. 'I ain't lazy. I'll work as hard as you do and I'll pay me way. But I reckon a girl's entitled to expect her engagement ring to be bought and paid for. Wedding ring too. After that I'll split all the costs with you, fifty-fifty. I know you don't love me. Maybe I don't love you neither. But we can make it, Maury, you and me. And we can make it bloody good. What do you say?'

She was dead right. He didn't love her. He wouldn't never love anyone like he had loved Pansy. But Carla *would* be useful to him; she'd already proved that a dozen times. And he guessed she was right when she said everyone ended up married to someone.

'Shake, partner.'

Carla held him off. 'We got a deal then?'

'Yeah. We got a deal.'

* * *

It gave him a jolt to discover that she intended to come to the funeral with him.

'Why not? I'm your fiancée, aren't I?'

'Yeah, but . . . it might be best if you didn't mention that. More tactful, like. I'll tell me mum after Pansy's . . . you know . . .'

'Whatever you like, lover.' Flicking through the hangers in her wardrobe, Carla took out a long dress the colour of liquid honey and held it against herself. 'What do you think?' Its flimsy bodice was held up by two shoe-strings, and there was a slit up one side of the skirt.

'You ain't going to the funeral in that?'

'Not the thing?'

'No, of course it . . .' Maury broke off as he spotted the twinkle in the green eyes.

'I just wanted to know if you liked it, lover. It's new. Not bad, eh?' She ran one hand over the silky fabric, moulding it to her shape. 'Now this is something a titled lady really would get herself togged up in. Ah, well . . .'

Re-hanging the dress, she selected a dark green suit. Maury was relieved to see the skirt was knee length. Seating herself at the mirror, she spat on her eyebrow pencil and started drawing feathery strokes over her brows.

Maury dressed himself slowly, still unsure whether Carla's presence at the funeral would be tolerated. What would he do if Pansy's family ordered her out?

Go with her, he decided. It was Pansy he'd loved, and Pansy was dead. Who cared what her family thought? Carla was right. They made a good team. They'd do very well out of this war between them. And she was a link to Eddie Hooper and that damn confession . . .

Would it, he asked her, be a good idea if she found out who Eddie had given the letter to before *he* found out about their engagement?

'He reckons they're sending him to another prison. Up north somewhere. I doubt if anyone's gonna bother with eight hours on a train to tell Eddie about our love lives.'

'What about the letter?'

'Don't worry, Maury. We got a few years before Eddie

gets out, and I'll have found it by then. Trust me, lover.'

'I'll have to, won't I? But just remember, Carla. Whatever we get Eddie can take – while he's got that letter.'

'Let's go, shall we?' She pushed him towards the door.

But instead of following him, she paused to take a book from the box at the bottom of the wardrobe. 'Bible,' she explained. 'For the church.'

'*You've* got a bible!'

'Had one since I was a kid. You never know when a good book will come in handy. Go on then, get a move on.'

Maury made his way down the stairs to the pub.

Carla tripped down after him. One scarlet-tipped thumb slid inside the back cover of the leather-covered book and felt its way over the cloth lining. Despite being old, it was solid and scarcely worn. You could barely make out the outline of the sealed envelope Eddie Hooper had asked her to keep for him. Unless you knew where to look, of course.

At least the service at the graveside had been brief. The coffin, plain except for the two brass handles allowed by the Board of Trade, had been lowered to the accompaniment of the minister's solemn 'Earth to earth,' and Lottie Abbott's much noisier hiccuping sobs. Maury had had to swallow a lump in his own throat several times, but thank heavens he hadn't made an exhibition of himself. A bloke – particularly one who was planning to be something around here – couldn't be seen to be blubbering.

'You're breaking my hand, lover.' Carla's protesting hiss in his ear caused him to realise he'd been hanging on to her with a grip so fierce that her fingers had turned white from the lack of blood.

'Sorry.'

''S all right. Where's Muscles? You ain't sent him off on an errand today, have you?'

'No. I haven't seen him. Maybe they told him he couldn't come. Pansy's aunt don't like him in the house, she says . . . said.'

They both stared across at the Cutters, who were ranged

along the other side of the open grave. Fred Cutter was directly opposite Maury, who was surprised by the look of intense annoyance on the man's face, and for a moment thought it was directed at him. Then he realised that Carla was the object of Fred's tight-lipped stare. Maury sensed rather than saw Carla shift her weight to one side so that her right hip was thrust out in a mildly provocative pose, and wished she wouldn't. It was, after all, his Pansy's funeral.

As soon as the business with the dirt was over, he took a firm grip on Carla and practically frog-marched her out of the cemetery. There was a bus idling at the stop in the High Road, and by running for it and leaping aboard they managed to beat even the funeral car back to Bartholomew.

'You sure you wanna come here?' Maury asked as the maid let them in and gabbled that 'Sir-and-madam-thank-you-for-coming-may-I-take-your-coats-a-light-repast-is-being-served-in-the-dining-room'.

'You sure you want me to, you mean?' Carla said without rancour, helping herself to a sandwich from a plate on the dining-room table and wincing as the taste dissolved on her tongue. 'Gawd, this is horrible!'

Doris leant forward in a conspiratorial manner, even though there was only the three of them in the house. 'There's proper ham in the larder. And a bit of cold lamb too, with cold potatoes and vegetables. I'm to serve it out later when this lot's been eaten. But only to them who's important.'

'We're important, aren't we, Maury?' Carla dropped the half-finished sandwich into the brass fire-scuttle sitting on the hearth. 'In fact you don't get much more important than us. Where's the larder?'

'Oh, miss, I couldn't . . .' Doris stared wide-eyed between them. The front door opened again and more guests trooped into the hall.

Maury was relieved to find that his mum had gone home to get dinner for the little kids when they came back from school. Doris and Iris were kept busy dispensing cups of tea while Fred provided thimblefuls of brandy to the men, apologising for the rather watery taste. He was of the opinion that the off-licence manager was on the fiddle and needed to be reported.

With a half-smile Carla wove between the other guests and out into the hall.

'You going?' Maury asked.

'Before I've had me breakfast? Not flaming likely. Come on, let's see where snooty-drawers in there has hidden the decent stuff.'

She sauntered into the back kitchen, not caring who saw her. The window gave a partial view of the blasted hole in next-door's garden. The sight made Maury's stomach turn over. The shock of his near burial under the dance hall, which had seemed to pass him by until now, suddenly overwhelmed him. His legs gave way and he had to grab the edge of the table to stop himself keeling over. The kitchen floor was waving up and down in an alarming way. From a long way away, he heard Carla tell him to stick his head between his knees, then felt the draught of cool air on the back of his neck as she opened the back door slightly.

There was another female voice asking if he was all right. He thought it was that scarred cousin, but he didn't dare straighten up to find out.

'Yeah. He'll be fine. Bit choked up, yer know.'

The mist was clearing slightly, and he managed to raise his head sufficiently to stop the bile flooding into his mouth. Carla and Pansy's cousin were still talking behind his back like he wasn't there.

'Pansy was lucky,' Iris said. 'Having someone who loved her that much.'

'You reckon?'

'Don't you think so?'

'Maybe. Having a bloke too stuck on yer can be a burden as well, though.'

'Can it? I wouldn't know.'

'Ain't you got a bloke?'

'Looking like this? I hardly think so.'

'There's all sorts out there. No saying you might not have what someone's looking for.'

'Oh, I've got that all right. Money.'

Maury cautiously unbent himself and sat upright. He felt a bit better and would have been grateful for a little attention, but Carla and Iris seemed to have forgotten his existence. For a brief flash of time he wished his mum hadn't gone home. At least she'd have given him a bit of sympathy.

'So your bloke wanted cash, did he? Well there's worse things. The rest of the package suit you, did it?'

'I beg your pardon?'

'Looks give you the tingles? He treat you all right? Give you a good laugh?'

'Yes . . . I suppose so.'

'There you are then. Can't have everything, can yer? Better to take the best on offer and sort him out yourself, I reckon.'

Maury was getting fed up with being discussed like this. What did she mean 'sort him out'? This marriage was going to be run by his rules, not hers, whatever she thought.

The heavy-footed maid returned with a tray of dirty cups, which she deposited with a crash near his ear while braying that the missus said to fetch more tea and where was the meat? The teapot was refilled and she slapped out again with the pot in one hand and a platter of cold ham in the other.

Iris took a carving knife from the dresser drawer and disappeared into the larder, saying she'd cut up the lamb.

Maury straightened up a little further and announced that he thought he felt a bit better and maybe he could fancy a little of that brandy. He looked at his new fiancée hopefully.

Pansy would have instantly run to fetch him a glass. Carla continued to pat down her pockets.

'I've forgotten me matches. You got a light?'

He hadn't. He'd left his lighter in his other jacket.

Carla wandered around opening drawers.

'What do you think you're doing?' Fred Cutter glared at her from the door to the hall.

'Looking for a light. Got one?'

'No. I have not. You shouldn't have come here. People notice. Ursula, my wife, has noticed.'

Maury was by now thoroughly fed up with everyone talking as if he didn't exist. 'She came with me. And she's got as much bloody right to be here as anyone else. And who cares if yer flaming wife notices?'

'Don't talk to me like that in my own house, you little whippersnapper. I've a reputation to think about.'

'Oh give it a rest, Fred,' Carla said casually. She'd managed to locate a box of matches by the cooker and applied one to the tip of her cigarette. 'I'm hardly gonna go up to your wife and tell her what a good time we 'ad Saturday night, am I?'

'You *what*!' The last vestiges of shock cleared from Maury's system and were replaced by cold anger. 'You went out with *him*?'

Carla leant against the dresser and calmly blew a stream of blue smoke through her nostrils before asking why she shouldn't. 'You were out with yer fiancée, remember?'

It was true. But it didn't make him feel any better. OK, he'd been out with Pansy. But he'd loved her and he'd intended to marry her. What the hell was Carla doing out with a bloke old enough to be her dad?

'Having a good time. Spent the night together, didn't we, Fred?' She gave him a broad wink before adding. 'Well, the best part of it anyway, thanks to the raid.'

'That's very interesting, miss.'

The addition of a fourth voice to their quarrel made them all swing towards the back door. Detective Sergeant Spain stepped through it, removing his hat and remarking that he had knocked at the front door but didn't seem able to get a reply.

'A funeral party I gather, sir?'

'Yes. I . . . er . . . my niece, Pansy. Saturday night. She was at the dance hall.'

'And you, councillor, according to your statement, were in your brother Peter's flat at Cutter's Wharf?'

'Yes. Well, I . . . er . . .' Fred looked round the kitchen for help that wasn't forthcoming.

His daughter, however, was. Stepping from the larder with the tray of sliced lamb and a dish of cold potatoes, Iris wished the policeman good afternoon.

Fred paled. 'Iris! How long . . . I mean, did you hear?'

'That you took this young woman . . . I'm so sorry, I don't think I know your name . . .'

'Carla Rosetti. Pleased to meet you, I'm sure.'

Iris looked her over and said, 'So you're the infamous Carla Rosetti.'

'Am I? Well, better to be infamous than ignored, don't you think?'

Iris wrinkled her nose in a way that made the scarring on her face ripple, and appeared to consider the question seriously. 'Yes. I suppose it is really.'

'For heaven's sake, Iris, never mind her! I can explain . . .'

'Explain what, Daddy? That you have mistresses? I already knew that. I saw you with one once. In Selfridges. A dyed redhead with dreadful colour sense. I'd have expected you to have more taste than that.'

'Don't you take that uppity tone with me, miss.'

The detective cleared his throat pointedly. 'About your statement, Mr Cutter.'

'Well, what about it? So I wasn't entirely truthful. What does it matter? I didn't have anything to do with attacking that Dixon girl.'

'We know that, sir. But it's still an offence to lie to the police. I shall have to ask you to give a truthful account of your movements that night.'

Carla laughed. 'That should make interesting reading. Want to know every movement, do you?'

The DS ignored her. Instead, he assured Fred that anything he said would be in confidence. 'There's no need for Mrs Cutter to find out about your . . . er . . . dalliances.'

'She knows. At least, I . . . erm . . . The thing is . . .' With a desperate look in his daughter's direction, Fred muttered that he and his wife had an arrangement. 'Thing is . . . my wife had a difficult time with the twins. She's not up to . . . Naturally I don't want to force her into doing something that might cause her pain.'

'You're a real gent, Fred,' Carla said to the kitchen ceiling.

'Anyway, I have a friend. Hilda. She's a widow. We generally meet once a fortnight. Supper in Golders Green, and then . . . er—'

'Yes. I think we all get the picture, Mr Cutter. But this Saturday it was Miss Rosetti's turn, was it? And your brother

407

Mr Peter Cutter was to provide you with an alibi? Why bother, sir? If Mrs Cutter is, as you say, so accommodating?'

It was Carla who answered the detective. With a sharp bark of laughter she said, 'Because there's a big difference between supper with a middle-aged widow in some cheap Golders Green restaurant and spending twenty guineas on an evening dress for a girl half your age so she can flash her legs at the Dorchester. But I suspect it would take another woman to appreciate that.'

She raised an eyebrow in Iris's direction, who merely said that she didn't see why her father had needed an alibi. 'Presumably mother would have assumed you were with Hennaed Hilda.'

'Don't talk about her like that. Hilda is a good person. It's just that . . . She works for one of my suppliers. We occasionally run into her at social functions. Nothing's ever said, of course, but she was visiting her sister at Easter, and . . . er—'

'She might have mentioned the fact to Mrs Cutter,' Spain finished for him. 'Yes, sir, I think we all get the idea. But I would suggest that both you and Mr Peter Cutter come to the station and revise your statements, just to keep things tidy. As a matter of fact, it was your brother I was looking for. I went to the wharf, but the yard is locked up.'

'Out of respect for my niece.'

'Of course. So Mr Peter Cutter will be here?'

'Well no, actually. He *should* have been here, but he's not shown. Kate, the girl's mother, said he had to see a couple of people about Joshua or something. I don't understand it myself. It's not like Pete—'

'A couple of people? That's what he said is it, sir?'

'I suppose so. He never said it to me. I've not seen him. Can't think who'd be more important than his niece's funeral.'

It was DS Spain who enlightened him. His listeners stared at him in various stages of disbelief and shock.

'Joshua attacked Addie?' Iris finally said. 'I don't believe it. He wouldn't.'

'He has signed a confession. But there's no need to worry

408

about the publicity of a trial. I've suggested to the lad's father that a committal would be appropriate, and he's evidently seen sense. No doubt he's seeking the required doctors' signatures now. Just as well – we can't keep the lad at Agar Street for much longer. When you see your brother, sir, perhaps you'd be good enough to inform him – unless proceedings are put in hand by the end of the day to take the lad to an asylum – we shall have to have him transferred to a prison cell. And don't forget that revised statement, will you, councillor? Good day, ladies.' Raising his hat formally, the policeman left just as Doris bustled back in from the other door to tell them that the missus was asking what had happened to the rest of the food.

Iris passed her the dishes without looking at her. 'I don't believe it. Joshua wouldn't . . . would he?'

'Of course he wouldn't.' Carla crushed the dog-end between scarlet nails and flicked it across the room into the scullery sink. 'Muscles may not know his own strength, but he was as taken as a bee with the honey-pot – with *his girl*.'

'Sounds like that was the problem,' Maury remarked. 'He tried to take a bit too much.'

'Rubbish!' Carla turned to Iris. 'Got a cake? And a tin?'

'I . . . I think so. Why?'

Carla grinned, revealing red smears on her white teeth. 'Gonna smuggle a file in to Muscles, ain't we?'

Chapter 42

'Look at me, Muscles.'

Reluctantly Joshua raised his eyes. He'd been really pleased to see his mate Maury and Carla. And slightly less pleased to see his cousin Iris, until she'd presented him with a box full of cold lamb and pickle sandwiches and a slice of sponge cake.

'Joshua doesn't like it here. Joshua's dad said he'd get him out but he hasn't come back, and Joshua has to feed the horse.'

'I expect the horse is big enough to look after himself. But it seems you ain't, Muscles. Now, you going to tell Carla about you and Addie?'

'Joshua's girl,' Joshua mumbled through a mouthful of bread and meat.

'So how come you hit her, Muscles?'

'Never hit her.'

'The police say you did.'

Joshua sent an angry glare towards the only representative of the force in view at present. The uniformed sergeant, whom Carla had sweet-talked into letting them visit Joshua in his cell, shifted uncomfortably by the door and told them to hurry up. With an attractive smile and a cross of her stockings, Carla gained them a few more minutes in the cell.

'What *did* you do to Addie, Muscles?'

Joshua looked like a large schoolboy who'd been caught stealing jam tarts. 'Made her angry.'

'How?'

'Joshua gave her a birthday present.'

'What present?'

Joshua's reply was inaudible.

Leaning forward, Carla put her fingertips under his chin and made him look at her. 'What present, Muscles?'

Joshua shot a desperate look in Iris's direction and said, 'Auntie Ursula has lots. Joshua didn't think she'd mind him having one.'

'One wha . . .' Iris's eyes widened as the answer struck her. 'The necklace! You took Mummy's amber necklace!'

'Got lots.' Joshua pouted. 'Maury bought a necklace for his girl's birthday. Joshua wanted to give his girl one too.' He fixed bewildered eyes on Carla. 'Joshua's girl was angry.'

'Of course she was, you idiot!' Iris said. 'It's your fault her brother was arrested! Don't you understand that?'

'Did you hit her, Muscles?'

Joshua shook his head. No, he hadn't hit her. She'd hit him. She'd been really angry. Then she'd called him stupid and said she was going home. Then she'd run away.

Carla sat herself on the bunk bed next to him. 'What did you do? Did you chase her?'

'Joshua tried to . . .' But he couldn't find her at home. He'd knocked and knocked but she hadn't answered.

'You knocked on the boats?'

'No. She's living with Joshua's grandmother. Joshua knocked at Nana's house.'

Iris drew a sharp breath. 'Somebody did . . . that Saturday. Taz and I were there. We didn't answer the door.'

'Right. So where did yer go after that, Muscles?'

Once again Joshua looked unbearably guilty. This time, however, it was Maury he seemed to be bothered by.

'Well go on,' his mate ordered. 'Answer her.'

'Went to Maury's house. Thought Maury's mum would come back and tell Joshua what to do to stop Joshua's girl being angry with him.'

'Did she?' Carla asked.

Maury informed her that his mum had spent that night in the shelter under the dance hall.

'What about you, Muscles? Where'd you spend the night?'

'Maury's house.'

'What? You went in our house? Without asking?'

412

'Don't shout at him, Maury, it gets him confused. How'd you get in?'

'Mum hardly ever locks the flaming door, that's how!'

'And you were there all night were you, Muscles? By yourself?'

Joshua shook his head. 'Cat was there. Joshua found him on the doorstep. Joshua was going to cuddle him but he didn't like Joshua.' Unconsciously he touched the long scratches on his cheek.

'OK, I think we all get the picture. You slept at Maury's house with a cat that didn't fancy you.'

Joshua nodded at the floor and asked if Maury was sure his mum wasn't cross with Joshua.

'Quite sure. Mind you, she might be when she finds out it was you who ate her meat loaf.'

Joshua looked alarmed, and Carla gave her intended a warning glare – while responding to the uniformed sergeant's demand to get a move on with another smile and flash of her stockings. Sliding an arm as far round Joshua's muscular shoulders as she could manage, she promised to get it all sorted out for him.

'Can Joshua go home now?'

'Soon, I reckon. We just got to go have a word with your dad. Chin up, eh?'

Smacking a red lipstick imprint on his cheek, Carla wiggled out of the cell promising to come back soon.

'What now?' Maury grumbled, falling into step with her and Iris as they made their way back to the High Street.

'Like I said. Find his dad. Or we could go see yer mum,' she remarked to Iris.

'My mother hasn't been well. I think you're quite right. It would be best to tell Uncle Pete everything. He can get Mummy to clear the theft charges against Taz . . . Mr Dixon, and he can tell the police Joshua didn't attack Addie. Do you think they'll believe it? That it *wasn't* Joshua tried to strangle Addie, I mean?'

'Do you?'

'Well . . . yes. Yes I do.' Iris nodded her head firmly. 'I mean, maybe Joshua might have lost his temper and hit

413

someone, but he wouldn't have lied about it. He's not that clever – if you see what I mean.'

'Uncle Pete it is, then. Down the wharf?'

Iris admitted she wasn't exactly sure where to find her uncle if he had really gone to find a doctor to certify that Joshua was incapable. But she supposed that Cutter's Yard was as good a place as any to start looking.

Carla linked arms with the other woman, leaving Maury to take the route nearest the kerb and giving him plenty of opportunity to observe the pair.

The contrast was striking. Carla wasn't anything special really, but you couldn't help noticing the way the blokes' heads turned as she swung confidently down the road. Iris, on the other hand, seemed to be as invisible as the sandbagged lampposts. It wasn't just the drab clothes and scraped-back hair, it was the way she shrank in on herself as if she wasn't even entitled to the paving stone she was occupying.

He made to swing left with the curve of the road but Iris said, 'We'd better go round the tow-path. That horrid policeman said the yard gates were locked up and I don't have a key. Unless we go back to the house and get one.'

None of them was keen on the idea of becoming entangled in the funeral party and long-winded explanations, so they diverted their way down to the canalside entrance at Dingwall's Wharf. The locks were busy. Several boats were unloading across the canal at the oil terminal, while others were waiting for the water level to drop so they could enter the lower gates at Hampstead Road. The spring sunshine bounced off brass fittings that gleamed like gold, firing the pinks, red and greens of the paintings along their cabins' sides and reflecting off straps scrubbed to a whiteness that was almost painful to the eyes.

Iris held back a moment to look down on the vessels, leaving Maury and Carla to walk ahead.

'What we going to all this bother for?' Maury asked. 'How'd you know Joshua never did it?'

'I do. So do you, don't yer?' Carla replied.

'I suppose,' Maury admitted. 'Still don't see why we have to bother.'

414

'Because,' his fiancée informed him, taking his arm, 'you never know when a set of muscles attached to very little noddle is going to be handy. The way I see it, if we keep Muscles sweet, he'll do pretty much what we tell him. And like the copper said, he really ain't responsible for his actions. So if we gets caught . . . well, not much they can do to him, is there?'

From that point of view, Maury could see that maybe getting Joshua out of this mess might be worthwhile.

'Anyhow,' Carla added. 'I'm quite fond of the big ox really.'

They stepped single-file through the gap that led on to Cutter's Wharf. Iris headed for the stairs to the brick store flat. Kitchener, who'd spent a boring morning so far regarding an empty yard without even the dog to tease, greeted her arrival with a shrill whinny and an insistent crash of his shoe against the stable door.

The noise brought no response from inside the flat. Nor did Iris's loud knocking. She tried the handle. 'It's locked,' she called to the other two, who'd stayed at the foot of the flight.

'Must still be out rounding up his tame quacks,' Carla said. 'What do you think? Leave a note, tell him to come up your house before he goes up the police station?'

'I suppose so.' Iris came down the staircase. 'Do you have a piece of paper and a pen?'

None of them did. The best they could muster between them was Carla's lipstick, which she didn't want to use, 'on account of it's getting bleeding hard to find under the counter or over it – 'scuse my French'.

'There's paper in the office,' Maury suggested.

Unfortunately Iris didn't have a key to that either.

'There must be something around here,' Carla said, looking around the cobbled yard. 'Bit of wrapping paper and some chalk or something.'

'Most of the buildings are locked, but I suppose we can look,' Iris agreed.

The first couple of shed doors they tried were, as Iris had predicted, secured.

'What about that one?' Maury suggested. 'The door's open a bit, see?' He indicated the store nearest the wharfside that had been damaged by the incendiary attack a few weeks ago. A spring breeze caught the wooden door and made it swing fractionally on squeaking hinges.

'It's hardly ever used,' Iris said. 'Daddy said it would probably have to be demolished; the walls are cracked from the heat, and . . .' She pushed the door wide as she spoke.

After the spring brightness outside it took a second for their eyes to adjust to the gloom inside. And then Iris screamed.

'Bloody hell!' Maury breathed. He watched Pete Cutter's boots gently swaying backwards and forwards like a clock's pendulum. He didn't want to look any further, but an irresistible force was dragging his gaze upwards. The world was starting to wobble out of focus again.

'Maury! Get a hold, lover. We'd best go call a copper.'

'What for? There ain't much a copper can do for him. Unless you know one who can really walk on water instead of just thinking they can.'

'It ain't him I'm thinking about. It's them.' Carla pointed to the side wall. It had been partially demolished to reveal a cavity between it and the outside wall. Maury stared into the blackness and felt a deep coldness crawl over his body.

Silently and sightlessly the two skeletons grinned back, amused by his horror.

Chapter 43

Letter found at the site known as Cutter's Wharf, and identified as being in the handwriting of Peter John Cutter:

To Whom It May Concern

I have left the door to the storage shed open in the hope that it will be one of the workmen who finds me and my family will be spared the ordeal. If not – and it's you Fred who come looking for me – then I hope you'll forgive me. (I took Kate's set of keys from her handbag so that she'd not be able to open the yard gates. They're in my flat.)

The bodies in the wall are the remains of my wife, Ellie Cutter, and her lover, Aloysius Barber.

Ellie came to the yard the night she left home with Barber. She wanted the petty cash from the office for their train fares. Barber had a briefcase full of fivers he'd stolen from his employers and yet they still intended to take a few pounds from Cutter's.

She wasn't even put out when I walked in on her forcing the desk open. She told me bold as brass that she was going off with Barber and there was nothing I could do about it. I could have coped with that I think, it was only habit and the boy keeping us together by then, but when I asked her what she'd done with Joshua, she said she'd given him a dose of laudanum to keep him quiet and if I had any sense I'd give him a few more and tell the doctors he must have got hold of the bottle and swallowed the lot by accident.

I lashed out. I just couldn't stand to hear her talking about her own son like that. She fell down and hit her head on the old hearth. I knew her neck was broken. You can't mistake the sound. I can hear it now all these years later. I swear to God that I hadn't intended to kill her, it was an accident born of a temper that I'd not learnt to control back then.

I don't know how long I sat there looking at her laying on the floor. It was Barber coming in brought me to my senses. She'd left him at the gate with her suitcase I suppose and he'd come looking to find out what was keeping her.

He didn't see me at first. I was behind the door. It wasn't an accident that time. Just the sight of his smooth shaven face and the stink of the perfumed stuff he put on his hair was enough. I smelt that scent before on her. I'd guessed she was carrying on with someone, but quite honestly I hadn't cared enough until then to find out who he was. I knew I'd killed Ellie; if I was going to be hung for the lamb I thought I might as well butcher the sheep as well.

We kept all sorts of tools in the office then back before Kate took us all in hand. I got him with the four pound hammer. I worked in the yard regularly in those days when we'd not the work or the money to take on casual men and could swing a weight like it was no more than a cane.

I hit him several times. I don't know how many. Until in the end all the anger was gone and then I finally saw what I'd done.

Once the madness was gone I didn't know what to do. All I could see was the drop in front of me. I locked the office and the yard gates and went home. The boy was asleep like she'd said. She'd left me a letter on the mantelpiece telling me she was going off with Barber and not to come looking for her because I'd not find her. That was when it occurred to me it would solve my problems if nobody could find her.

I went back to the yard and carried the pair of them to the storage shed by the wharf while it was still too dark for anyone to see me from the canal. We were refurbishing some of the sheds and that one had had to have a new wall and roof. I built a second wall just inside the first and put Ellie and Barber where you found them. It was a stupid thing to do but at the time I wasn't thinking right. I should have taken them out into Epping Forest and buried them deep well away from Cutter's. As it was I had to kill a few of

418

the local cats over that summer and hide them around the place to account for the smell.

Nobody questioned that Ellie was with Barber. Why should they? I'd her note to show and Barber had stolen from the office safe, plus he owed back rent on his flat in King Street and debts all over Camden. It would have been surprising if they had shown their faces around here again.

I moved myself and Joshua into the flat in the yard so I could keep an eye on the place. Don't ask me why. Perhaps it was a form of penance, living with what I'd done if you can understand that?

But it's surprising what you can get used to. I managed to make sure we didn't use that shed much and after a while I almost started to forget they were in there. Until the air raids started. I put it off as long as possible, but once that incendiary cracked the walls, I knew I'd had my final warning. I had to do what I should have done years before and take them somewhere else.

First I thought of taking them out into the country as I should have done in the first place, but I had nightmares about being stopped by a road-block or being surrounded by the soldiers on an Army exercise or some other such nonsense.

Then we got the contract for the blitz repair work and I saw my chance. It's not like up here where there are just a few houses or a block of flats gone. There's whole streets flattened down there. Row after row of rubble where homes and factories used to be. Those that were too bad to be repaired, were to be completely cleared and the ground levelled. I'd planned to put the remains in a couple of sacks and dump them in a hole. The way I saw it no one's going to ask what a builder was doing shovelling earth. And even if I was unlucky and they were found later – well there'd be nothing to identify them or say they came from here. Anyone could have sneaked out to those dirt heaps and buried them.

I decided to do the work over Easter because the yard would be empty on the Sunday. I locked myself in the shed and used a cold chisel on the wall. It took longer than

I expected. I'd built that wall like I never intended it to come down, which I suppose I didn't. And I was trying to be quiet. I don't know why. Who'd have bothered if the sound of building was coming from a builder's yard? But it's like when you whisper a secret even though there's no one to hear you speak it. I feared something, some avenging fate, would send a busy-body to find me out.

When I'd got it partially down I realised I needed to relieve myself. I know it sounds stupid, but I couldn't do it in front of the pair of them. I opened the door intending to go across the privy in the yard. Addie Dixon was coming from the direction of the brick store.

She was so pleased to see me poor kid. She'd been up to the flat looking for me. She had Ursula's damn amber necklace. Joshua had tried to give it to her for her birthday. He must have taken it when we were round there repairing after the bomb dropped next door, days before Ursula claimed it went missing.

The Dixon girl wanted me to go and tell Ursula her brother hadn't done it and get her to drop the charge. Which of course I said I would. I told her to go wait on the boat and not to worry, I'd get it sorted out. I'd been in the doorway all the time we were talking, and when she moved towards the wharf I stepped back inside thinking I'd got away with it. But I'd not got the door properly shut before she thrust it open. I couldn't catch it in time.

She wanted me to promise Joshua wouldn't go to prison for what he'd done! It's ironic isn't it. If she'd have hated Joshua, as heaven knows she'd have been entitled to, she'd not have put herself in danger.

I'd left the lamp burning. The wick was down but it was enough for her to see what was hidden behind that wall. She started screaming. If only she hadn't screamed. I put my hands round her throat to try and stop the noise.

She fought me off and ran away. She was heading for the boats I think. I managed to get hold of her again and we were struggling on the edge of the wharf. And then she went into the water. She must have knocked herself out on something as she went in. She floated out to the middle of the stretch. I tried to drag her in with the boat-hook but she just kept bobbing out of reach. And then I heard some boats coming up; so I hid.

I'm not proud of that. I could have asked them for help, but I didn't. I panicked like I'd panicked the night Ellie died. After they'd gone past I went out again and looked for the girl, but she'd gone. I thought she'd sunk to the bottom, but I suppose the boats must have dragged her round to the spot where she was found.

I should have finished what I'd set out to do there and then. But I couldn't. I don't know if you can believe this, but I physically couldn't go back into that shed. I hooked the lamp out, nailed the plank back over the door, went back to the flat and listened to the raid.

When I heard the girl had survived I didn't know whether to be glad or terrified. For days I was waiting for the police to come. But when they did it was to find the necklace. (I couldn't find it the next day and I hadn't been able to mention it without admitting I'd seen the Dixon girl.) It must have dropped from my pocket when I was reaching over to fish the girl out. All the time the police were speaking to me and taking statements, I kept thinking they could see the truth, as it was somehow burnt into my skin like they used to brand the mark on villains in the old days.

And then they took Joshua. It had never even occurred to me that he might be suspected. I didn't think anyone would ever be convicted. How could they be when I knew they were innocent? I imagined the police would eventually drop the case for lack of evidence.

It was a naive idea, I can see that. How many innocent men have ended up on the end of the rope I wonder? When that copper offered me the choice of seeing Joshua in the dock or putting the boy away, I knew it was the end for me.

Do you believe in divine retribution? I don't think I ever did. All that religious stuff the vicar used to spout never meant anything to me except a wasted hour on Sunday mornings. But now I think maybe it does exist. If I'd have owned up to Ellie and Barber at the time, I'd like as not have ended up on the gallows. But God gave me time to

421

*love Kate. And that makes what I'm going to do now a
hundred times bitterer than if I'd never tasted what I could
have had and now never shall.*

*Tell Kate I loved her more than I could have ever believed
it possible to love and that I shall always be with her.*

*Tell my mother I'm sorry and I hope that she can
forgive me.*

*And to Fred – the business is all yours now, which should
please Ursula. Look after the boy for me.*

Taz passed the letter back and asked if he was supposed to
feel better.

'I don't expect you to feel anything in particular,' Iris said
in a tight voice. 'I just thought you were entitled to see it.
It's not the original, of course. The police kept that for the
coroner. But they let us make a copy. The rather austere one
is handling the details.'

'Spain.' Taz stood up and stretched his legs, moving restlessly around the small side ward. 'Mr Austere's name is
Spain. Rhymes with pain. He sent the other one, looks like a
walrus, to tell me the necklace business is being dropped.'

'I'm glad.'

'Are yer? Should never have been started in the first place.
The only reason your mum claimed it was me was to keep you
away from me. She should have had the sense to send me a
few quid – after all that's all a bloke like me's interested in
isn't it, Iris?'

'I'm sorry. You have every right to be bitter with mother.
And Uncle Pete, of course. But I don't think you're entitled
to be angry with me.'

'Don't you?'

'No. I don't.' Her face was without make-up again, the
scars starkly visible to anyone who cared to look. She put
her chin up and stared fixedly at him. 'You were attracted
to me because I had money. Or you thought I had.'

'That's not bloody true!' His raised voice penetrated the
private half-world where Addie lay. Restlessly she stirred on
her pillows and murmured. Taz stepped across the short
distance and re-settled the sheets around her, wiping away

422

a dribble of spittle that had trickled from the side of her mouth.

'Where's the policewoman?' Iris asked.

'Gone. No need to watch her now, is there? They know who tried to kill her. The nurses don't come in as much either. They put her on the bedpan and wash her down, and sometimes they stick a tube down her throat and try and feed her, but they don't talk to her any more. They don't think there's any need. No sense wasting time on someone who's never going to get any better than she is now.'

'Is that what they said?'

'Not in so many words. They keep talking about miracles and hoping for the best. But they're moving her soon. Place in the country where they take incurables. So I'm not holding my breath for any damn miracle. So yes, I reckon I am entitled to think anything I damn well like about your mother. If it wasn't for her and her lies, Addie and me would have been on the water and she'd not be lying in this bed today.'

'You can't know that. She'd gone to the dance for her birthday. Wouldn't you have tried to be in Camden for that night anyway?'

Taz circled the room restlessly again before muttering that maybe he would and maybe he wouldn't. 'She's poison, that woman. I don't care if she is your mother, she wants locking up herself. If you've a cupful of sense, you'll get away from her.'

'I shall. I had a letter this morning from the labour exchange telling me to report for another interview. The woman was going to find out about doing my war service on the canal boats.'

His snort of derisive laughter angered her. She'd forced herself to come down here and see him because she'd felt ashamed for what her family had done to him. But as far as she was concerned it didn't give him the right to hold her in such obvious contempt. She said as much, and was roundly told that, since she had such a low opinion of him, he didn't see why he couldn't have the same of her. 'After, all Iris, it only makes a pair with what you think of yourself, doesn't it?'

423

'What do you mean?'

He came close to her, taking her elbow in a firm grip. The familiar smell of his skin and the tanned V in the open neck of his shirt stirred up exciting, unbearable memories of that night at Nana's flat. Half of her wanted to slap his face, while the other desperately wanted to press herself to his chest and hungrily demand kisses.

Part of what she was thinking must have shown in her eyes, because she saw an answering interest in his and forced herself to release his fingers from her arm and step away from him.

'What do you mean?' she repeated.

'You don't think very much of yourself, Iris, if you think all I wanted from you was money. I'll not deny it crossed my mind after that first time we went out, but it turned into far more than that. For me, any rate. I wanted you, Iris. You were beautiful . . .' He captured the hand that was automatically moving to her face. '. . . and sweet and kind and it made me feel good to be with you. And I thought you were my friend. That's why I asked yer for the money. If you'd have asked me for something, something that I had to give, I'd have handed it over, because that's what friends are for. Or they are on the boats. Maybe it's different for you landies.'

'No. It's just that . . .' Once again Iris tried to touch her scars.

Taz kept her hand down. 'If you can't see further than the cuts, Iris, I reckon nobody else ever will.' He let go of her hand and pulled her into his arms. 'I love you, Iris. If you don't want me no more, that's fair I reckon. But don't keep believing it was just the money I saw.'

Iris stared back. She wanted to believe him. She wanted to believe herself loved and desirable. She wanted him.

With a small sigh, she locked her arms round his neck and tasted his mouth.

He responded fiercely. The rest of the world ceased to exist for them both. They needed each other. Nothing – the war, their backgrounds, the uncertainty of what was to come in the future – could change that.

They were brought back to the present by the arrival of a nurse to rub ointment into Addie's bedsores.

Iris drew Taz gently outside into the corridor, where the continual echoing sounds of the hospital mingled with the pervading smells of disinfectant and polish. 'I'm sorry. About the money, I mean. I have a post office savings book—'

'It doesn't matter.' He pulled her towards the shuttered windows, where they could look down on the everyday bustle of buses and pedestrians streaming past the front of the hospital. 'I've sold the boats to the Canal Carrying Company. It will cover my debts and there will be a place for me – if I want one. I can get fixed up with a mate from one of the other boats. There's several with boys big enough to take the tiller and work the locks. Company's coming up to the wharf tomorrow to haul the boats round to Brentford. They'll fix them up there, get the *Crock* repaired, paint the company name on.'

'Taz, I . . .' She stared at him aghast.

With a smile, he traced her scars affectionately with his forefinger. 'Don't look so worried, funny-face. It's not that bad. I needed them for Addie. While I had the boats they'd not call me up and I could look out for her. If I was working for the Canal Company they could have turned me off at any time and Addie could have been left on her own while I was away fighting God knows where. Well, that don't matter any more, does it?' He looked across to the closed door of Addie's room. 'She doesn't know if I'm there or not no more. They'll take care of her at this place she's going, and as for me – if I get fed up being Steerer Dixon I reckon I'll sign for the Navy.'

He clasped her tighter. 'Will you visit Addie for me? The old lady . . . your gran . . . said she would. But if you would too—'

'Of course I will. I'd . . .' She broke off as Addie's door opened again and the nurse came out. Relief flooded the plain face under the frilled cap. 'There you are! I was so afraid you'd gone. Go in, quick.'

Taz shouldered his way past her, striding to his sister's bed. 'What's wrong?'

'Nothing.' The nurse rushed back after him. Leaning her

face close to the bandaged head, she said loudly, 'Addie! Addie, my dear! Your brother is here. Open your eyes for me again, dear.'

The almost translucent lids fluttered and twitched but stayed closed.

Iris crept quietly to his side. 'Did she . . . ?' she breathed at the nurse.

'A moment ago. And it wasn't just a reflex action. There was intelligence there, I'm sure of it. Addie, dear, please look at me again.'

Scorning such a gentle approach, Taz shouted, 'Kid, can you hear me? Open yer eyes and look at us! Do as you're told, you hear?'

This time the flutter was stronger. The lashes flickered for a second, letting them glimpse the grey eyes beneath.

'Addie,' Iris whispered. 'It's me. Guess what? I'm going to work on the boats for my war service.'

'And I've sold the *Rainbow* and the *Crock* to the Canal Company, kid.'

This time the eyelids shuddered like agitated moths and sprang open. Addie's lips, chalky dry from lack of saliva, moved in silent words.

The nurse bent closer. Addie reformed her words, her breath stirring the tiny hairs that had escaped from the starched cap. The nurse straightened up, a pink flush staining her cheeks.

'What did she say?' Iris asked.

'She said . . .' The nurse hesitated, a small smile appearing. '"Bugger me."'

Chapter 44

Maury hesitated before the gate. A flicker of anticipation still sprang into life whenever he saw the Kelly Street house. But now it was always followed by that terrible blackness as he remembered Pansy wouldn't be opening the door to him.

Kate gave him a bleak smile and stood aside to let him into the hall. 'Hello, Maury. How nice to see you.'

'You too, Mrs C. I wasn't sure you'd be here. Thought maybe you'd be down the yard. Yer still working there?'

'Part time.'

She showed him into the best room. The sun teasing through the net curtains cut bars of light across dusty furniture. 'I really don't like being there. Some days I look up and I'm certain sure I can see Pete walking down by the wharf. They've pulled the shed down, you know? Everything was in there: their suitcases, their jewellery, even Aloysius Barber's briefcase and the remains of the money he stole. And then I come back here and hear Pansy upstairs. Sometimes I can't bear to be inside at all. I walk over the heath or sit down by the canal all day.'

With a conscious effort she pulled herself together and asked if he'd had his dinner.

'Yes thanks, Mrs C. At me mum's.'

'I heard you've got a new girlfriend.'

'Well she ain't exactly a girl. I mean, she's older than me, and yer know . . . I'll always feel for Pansy, Mrs C.'

Leaning forward, Kate took his hand. 'It's all right, Maury. I understand. Life goes on, or so they tell me. You're young and you've got a lot of years ahead of you, God willing. Pansy wouldn't have wanted you to be on your own.'

'Yeah. Ta. 'Ow about you? I mean, with Mr Cutter . . . you know . . . dying. You gonna find someone else too?'

To his horror large tears welled over her bottom eyelashes and slid down her cheeks. Maury was no good with crying. He wasn't used to it.

Awkwardly he came to sit on the arm of her chair and put an arm round her. She leant her head on his chest, crying noisily and making a large damp patch on his new waistcoat. 'Don't, Mrs C. It'll be all right. I mean, yer know, it's like you said. Life goes on.' He felt an ache growing in his throat and had to swallow hard to stop himself joining in with her bawling.

Sniffing, Kate fished in her sleeves for a handkerchief she plainly didn't have. Maury gave her his own.

'Thank you.' Kate blew her nose and dried her eyes. 'There, now that's enough of that. I've no tea to offer you, I'm afraid – I've used all my ration. But there's some cocoa. Or I've part of a bottle of whisky. Pete left it behind.'

Relieved that she could speak of Pete Cutter without another burst of crying, Maury said he could manage a whisky, ta very much. 'Thing is, Mrs C, I come round to ask you a favour. See, I haven't got a picture of Pansy, and I was remembering that big box of photos you show'd us once. So maybe . . .'

Kate was more than pleased to let him take what he wanted. Sipping the generous whisky she'd poured for him, he sorted through the record of Pansy's early life that her father had left behind.

'There aren't any of her grown up,' Kate said, fanning out the photographs. 'But I'll tell you what . . .' She disappeared from the room for a moment and returned with a framed picture. 'This was taken the summer she left school.'

She extended the black-and-white print. It was the Pansy he remembered, with her round face, big eyes and soft cloud of dark hair caught back with a ribbon. 'I'm certain sure she'd have wanted you to have it.'

'Ta, Mrs C.' He stored it carefully in his inside pocket and held out a handful of other snaps of Pansy at various ages. 'Can I have these as well?'

'Of course. Although you can't see much of her in this one.'

Kate smiled through a mist of tears at the shot of the Cutters lined up under the fiftieth-anniversary banner, brushing her fingers over the blanketed bundle in the arms of her much younger self.

'I want it 'cause it's a good picture of you, Mrs C. You don't mind, do you?'

'No. Take it with pleasure.'

'Thanks.' He piled the unwanted photos back into the box and said he had to go.

'You will keep in touch, won't you, Maury?'

'Count on it, Mrs C. Expect I'll see you around most weeks.'

'Perhaps. I'm thinking of moving away. The exchange have vacancies for war workers. There's sewing jobs going, making barrage balloons. Or cooking in a hostel for land girls.' She touched his face and then gathered him in and hugged him like his mum did sometimes. 'Goodbye, Maury. And all my love. Here, take this as well. I don't want it.' She pushed the whisky bottle into his pocket.

''Bye then, Mrs C. Good luck, eh?' Disengaging himself, Maury made his way back into Kelly Street. At the junction with the High Street he hesitated. Which way now? The wharf or the house? In the end he opted for Bartholomew Street. It was the right guess.

The maid who answered the door informed him that Mr Cutter was at home. 'So's Missus Cutter. Both of them are in.'

'Who is it, Doris?' Ursula appeared in the passageway leading from the kitchen.

'Miss Pansy's young man, missus. Least he *was*, only now he ain't, seeing as how she's gorn, and—'

'Good evening, Mr O'Day. Don't leave him standing on the doorstep, Doris, you stupid girl. Let him in.'

'He wants to see Mr Cutter.'

'Then go and fetch him!'

Doris sniffed and slapped off in her over-large shoes. Ursula beckoned Maury inside. She placed her lips close to his ear and whispered: 'How much do you want for the whisky, Mr O'Day?'

429

'What?' He'd forgotten the bottle was there, protruding from his side pocket. Extracting it, he turned it sideways, sending the golden liquid sloshing from base to top. It looked to be about a quarter full.

Ursula snatched it from his hand. 'Wait here.' She was gone before he could recover himself sufficiently to grab it back, disappearing up the stairs in a rapid trot.

Fred Cutter strolled from the back of the house, rolling down his sleeves and brushing dirt off his hands. 'Getting the back garden sorted out. What can I do for you, young Maury?'

'Mr O'Day.'

'Beg pardon?'

'I ain't young Maury. I prefer Mr O'Day.'

'Do you now?' Fred looked like he was about to say something short and sharp on that subject, but he was forestalled by Ursula's return.

'Here you are. Will that be sufficient?' Ursula tendered two pound notes. 'Mr O'Day is collecting for a charity, Fred.'

'Yeah. Firemens' widows and orphans. Me brother's in the brigade. Very generous ta, Mrs Cutter.' He put the notes in his wallet and managed to drop her a slight wink.

'Please feel free to come again any time. We like to give to local charities.'

'I'll remember that, Mrs Cutter. I'm sure there's other charities be pleased of your contribution.'

Satisfied that he and Ursula had come to a mutually agreeable business arrangement, Maury turned his attention to her husband and asked if he could have a few minutes.

Once the living room door was safely shut, he came straight to the point. Taking the photograph he'd just collected from Kate, he held it up, being careful to keep it out of Fred's reach. 'Recognise this?'

'Of course I do. What about it?'

Maury tapped the banner behind the group. 'Eighteenth of March, 1926. Coupla days before Joshua's mum hopped it with the insurance man. And ended up bricked up in that wall.'

A dark red flush suffused Fred's face. 'Do you think

I need reminding? I've just buried my brother, for heaven's sake.'

'I know that.' Maury sat down without being asked and stretched out his legs. 'Have a seat, Mr Cutter. Yer giving me neck-ache up there.'

When Fred sat without protest, Maury knew the man had already guessed what was coming next.

'Thing is, see, your brother told the copper he'd broken his arm on the Sunday. Only he never, see?' He tapped Pete's plastered limb. 'It was already broke on that Saturday. Now, I can see how he might have swung an 'ammer one-handed if he was mad enough. Might even have managed to drag a couple of bodies from the office. But I don't rightly see him mixing up the mortar and laying a wall on his own. Not with him having to put up trestles to reach up to the roof and everything. Now you're an experienced bricklayer, Mr Cutter? What do you reckon? Could you do that?'

'What are you implying?'

'Come on, Mr Cutter. Yer know what I'm saying. Someone gave him a hand that night. And who'd he turn to? Workmen? I don't think so. Better keep it in the family. Ask his brother Fred to step round. Maybe he asked Pansy's dad too – but he's beyond bothering now. Like Pete. There's just you to face the music.'

Fred Cutter was sitting very still. The only sign of movement was the fractional twitch of his nostril hair as he breathed. 'You can't prove it,' he hissed.

'No I can't. All I can do is take this picture up the police station and give it to the copper who's still got his notebook on that weekend. Course he won't be able to prove nothing neither. But you know how these rumours get around, don't you? Councillor Fred Cutter mixed up in a murder? Well, it ain't what yer voters want to hear, is it?'

Fred glared. 'How much?'

Maury shook his head, replacing the precious print in his pocket. 'I don't want money, Mr Cutter. I want you to sign over half the business to Joshua.'

'You *what*? You're mad! The lad's not all there! Dear God, he's not even half-way there!'

431

'Maybe so. But he ain't been certified or anything has he? He's as sane as you and me in the eyes of the law. And he's over twenty-one ain't he? There's no reason why he can't have his name on a company.'

'But why should you want him to? I mean, I know you've taken the lad under your wing – and I'm grateful. Pete was too. But turning over half of Cutter's . . . that doesn't make sense.'

'It does to me. And it will to you if you don't want me to walk up to Agar Street police station.'

'Now look here—'

'No. You look. Joshua's entitled. He's as much a Cutter as you are. It's not like I'm asking for everything, just what he should have. The other half will still be yours. You can leave it to your own kids. And you can still run the business. Joshua won't interfere. In fact, you don't even have to tell him.'

Fred drummed his fingers on his knees. Maury could see the temptation to tell him to get lost boiling up inside the older man, only to be dampened down by a healthy dose of self-preservation.

What Maury had said was true. There was nothing the police could do after all this time. If Fred decided to brazen it out, this wouldn't work. But he was gambling that Fred Cutter valued his good name. The gossip about Pete had already had a distinct effect on the business, from what he heard. Some people, especially those in official positions, were wary about dealing with a murderer's brother. If it got out that Fred had had a hand in their local scandal it could finish Cutter's. Which wouldn't suit any of them, when building was proving to be so profitable thanks to the Luftwaffe's enthusiastic efforts at demolition.

He saw Fred hesitating, wanting to agree, and jumped in to make up the man's mind for him: 'You've got until the end of the week to show me a paper saying Joshua's a full partner in Cutter's.'

He stood up.

Fred followed his lead and Maury knew he'd won.

Carla was waiting for him in the bar of the Golden Cross.

Sliding two half-pints of bitter across the counter, she waited until the railmen had carried them out of earshot and then murmured, 'How did you get on?'

Maury stuck a thumb up. 'Where is he?'

Carla nodded across to where Joshua was playing shove ha'penny with single-minded concentration. 'Does as he's told, sweet as a lamb. Told you he would, didn't I?' She poured two small whiskies and passed one to Maury. 'Here's to partners.'

Maury clinked rims. 'Partners.'

Epilogue

'Here they come, Nana!'

'I can see that, Joshua. Now watch what you're doing with that chair! We don't want the poor girl going swimming.'

Joshua carefully edged the wheelchair back a few inches from the edge of Camden wharf. Down below them, one of the double lock gates had been left ready by boats going down to Limehouse. Now another pair was approaching upstream. The early summer sunshine bounced off their gleaming brasses and lit the glistening new paintwork as they cut through the gently bobbing water. The lead boat entered the near lock first and the butty slid neatly in beside it. A figure leapt from the butty, ran to the lock mechanism, inserted a handle and started to wind in the open gates.

'That's Iris, Nana. Shall Joshua go and help her?'

'No. Leave her to it. She's doing very well. Don't you think, Addie?'

Addie mumbled something inarticulate. Like her hair, her speech was coming back slowly, but she still had trouble with certain words. Particularly those that involved praising the Canal Carrying Company's newest trainees. Huddled in her old navy coat that she had insisted on keeping, she watched as Iris closed the bottom gates and Kate opened the top paddles. Dressed in matching navy trousers, jumpers and thick leather belts, they moved with professional competence, showing off the results of their month's training.

Leaning casually against the *Rainbow*'s tiller, Taz rose with the water level until he was high enough to call across to his sister without forcing her to crane her neck downwards. 'How are you, kid?'

'Watch this.' Gripping the arms of her chair, Addie wriggled up, angrily telling Joshua to keep his hands to himself when he tried to help her. Taking a deep breath, she threw one leg sidewards and forwards and then the other. With gritted teeth, she managed to walk to the upper gates just as Kate leapt back aboard the *Crock of Gold* ready to hold the tiller steady as Iris wound and kicked the lock open.

'Well done, Addie!' Kate called across. 'You'll be back on board in no time. You should see how the company's redecorated inside. Iris and I have got bookshelves and even a wireless in the *Crock of Gold*!'

Addie muttered something that could have been 'soft bloody landies'.

'That's enough of that language thank you, young lady. How many times have you to be told?' Coming up behind Addie, Nana put her arms on the girl's shoulders, allowing her to lean against her. 'The doctor says she's doing very well. We go to physiotherapy twice a week and she's helping Ludo in the roof garden. How are you, Kate?'

'I'm . . . surviving,' Kate said, recoiling a rope and stowing it neatly. A few weeks working outside on another boat while the Dixon boats were refitted had gilded a light tan over her face and lightened her already fair hair. And the sheer physical effort of loading, unloading, crawling under top-clothes to heave around unbalanced loads, cleaning the engine, keeping the cabins spick and span and working the locks, had created a physical exhaustion that let her achieve hours of dreamless sleep when they tied up at night. The result was that her looks were coming back and several times she'd attracted an admiring wolf-whistle from the tow-paths.

'And Iris?'

'I don't know how I am. I'm too tired to notice, Nana,' Iris called back with a merry wave. Like her aunt she was tanned by the outdoor work and her hair was swept back and tied in the nape of her neck with an old scarf. As a result, the tracery of scars showed silver against her cheek for anyone to see and stare. But it no longer bothered her as much as it had once done. If they were going to visit a pub or cinema in the evening, she'd apply a coating of carefully hoarded make-up, out otherwise she ignored the curious looks. Already the regular boaters had grown used to her, it seemed, and no longer took any notice of the disfigurement. She really felt she was beginning to be accepted as one of the canal people. In a few more weeks perhaps she'd feel comfortable enough to consider Taz's urgings for her to join him permanently in the double bunk on the *Rainbow* rather than making him be content with the occasional night visit.

'How's Mummy and Daddy?' she shouted.

'Your father's well enough. Business is good. Your mother is . . . Well, she's no odder than she ever was, I suppose.'

'Give them my love. I'll try to telephone when we tie up. How are you, Nana?'

'I'm old, my dear. And more used to disappointments. I shall survive, don't you worry about me.'

If Nana's voice shook a little, the crash and bustle of activity from the LMS yards behind the locks hid it from everyone but Addie, who was still leaning back against the older woman as she gathered her breath.

'You sure she ain't too much for you, ma'am?' Taz called, steering into the upper pound.

'She's my salvation, young man!' Nana slipped her arms round her new charge and hugged her gently.

The snubber between the two boats was already paying out. Iris leapt back aboard and waved madly as the *Crock* glided away.

'Can we stay and watch more boats, Nana?' Joshua said eagerly.

'Just these ones coming along perhaps, then we'd best be getting back for our dinner. Fetch that chair over so she can sit down again.'

'No. I'll walk.' Arms held out stiffly for balance, Addie lurched towards her wheelchair. Her effort was greeted by a loud cat-call from the approaching boats.

'Oi, look at the gorilla!'

With Blackie on one tiller and Rickey on the other, the Geoghans bumped into the lower lock while Addie took slow, deliberate paces before sinking with a sigh of relief back into her wheelchair.

'Let's be getting over to the steps now, Joshua. You can lif the chair back up again.' Turning, Nana led the way to th staircase up to road level. A loud clang followed by a furiou roar behind her made her swing back.

Blackie was frantically fishing over the side as his painte water-can bobbed past the stern of the boat. 'Get it, stupid' he yelled at Matthus.

The boy hesitated between lock-wheeling and retrievin the can. Another missile flew through the air and knocke the boat's chimney skew-whiff.

Blackie glared upwards. 'Oi! Cut it out!'

'Not bad for a gorilla, eh?' Addie shouted back, a gri splitting her pale face as her chair was wheeled about. 'Bette watch out, Geoghan! I'll be back before you can say "Draf dodger"!'